CRAGBRIDGE HALL

THE IMPOSSIBLE
RACE

OTHER BOOKS IN THE CRAGBRIDGE HALL SERIES

CRAGBRIDGE HALL

THE IMPOSSIBLE RACE

CHAD MORRIS

ILLUSTRATED BY
BRANDON DORMAN

SHADOW
MOUNTAIN

To Kirtlan.

*One day you'll be a published author
and I'll be thrilled to read your stories.*

Text © 2015 Chad Morris
Illustrations © 2015 Brandon Dorman

Visit us at ShadowMountain.com

This is a work of fiction. Characters and events in this book are products of the author's imagination or are represented fictitiously.

First published in hardbound 2015.
First published in paperbound 2018.

Library of Congress Cataloging-in-Publication Data
Morris, Chad, author.
    The impossible race / Chad Morris.
        pages cm. — (Cragbridge Hall ; book 3)
    Summary: Derick and Abby Cragbridge continue their seventh-grade year at Cragbridge Hall, where they run into competitions, new friends, virtual zombies, and real danger.
    Includes bibliographical references.
    ISBN 978-1-60907-979-6 (hardbound)
    ISBN 978-1-62972-509-3 (paperbound)
    [1. Space and time—Fiction. 2. Boarding schools—Fiction.
3. Schools—Fiction. 4. Twins—Fiction. 5. Brothers and sisters—Fiction.
6. Grandfathers—Fiction.] I. Title. II. Series: Morris, Chad. Cragbridge Hall ; book 3.
    PZ7.M827248Im 2015
    [Fic]—dc23   2014036845

Printed in the United States of America
LSC Communications, Harrisonburg, VA

10   9   8   7   6   5   4   3   2   1

CONTENTS

Contents

THE BACKUP PLAN

With a flick of his finger, the mercenary's gun barrel emerged from his tan sleeve and aligned with his index finger. He pointed it at a woman tied and gagged in the corner of a small, cinder-block house. She shifted on the dirt ground, trying to get comfortable. Beneath her blind-fold, she couldn't see the gun. "*Nao quero esperar mais,*" the mercenary said.

The hostage froze.

A short man with a paunchy stomach and a patchy beard stood up and waved his hands to stop the gunman.

Abby triggered her translator. It's hard to spy when you can't understand what the people are saying. She and her friends had been ready to intervene if the bearded man hadn't stopped the gunman, but as long as they stayed calm, she wanted to see if she could get any valuable information.

Her translator recognized Portuguese and changed it to English through the small speaker in her ear.

"Put that away," the man with the patchy beard commanded.

"I'm tired of waiting," the gunman in the tan shirt replied, sending his barrel back into his sleeve. He opened the door to the small house, and light flooded in. Abby had to blink several times to get used to it. The man peered out at a dirt trail. It didn't look like anyone else lived within miles. "Shouldn't Muns have told us whether to kill her or let her go by now?"

"All I know," a third mercenary said, sitting at a bare table on the other side of the room, his cigarette bouncing in his lips with every word, "is that if you shot her before Muns said you could, you'd find *yourself* a hostage in a small shack somewhere." The man gestured to the house around him. "Probably something like this. And you'd likely be guarded by someone with little patience and an itchy trigger finger just like you."

"It also means we wouldn't get paid," the man with the patchy beard added. "I like getting paid. So if we don't, *I* might volunteer to be the guy with the itchy trigger finger."

The man in the tan shirt glared back at his partners in crime, trying to decide whether or not he believed them.

Abby whispered to Carol, "Part of me can't believe Muns would stoop this low, but part of me isn't surprised." They watched the scene as if they were in the same room, but they stood somewhere else entirely—somewhere on the other side of the world. Abby and Carol were watching from the secret basement of Cragbridge Hall, the most prestigious secondary school in the world. One half of the gym-sized basement was dimly lit with a cold, hard stone floor, but the other side showed the small hut in Brazil. They could watch the mercenaries on the other side of the world because of an invention that stood in the center of the room—the Bridge. Its metal console was mounted to the floor. What looked like silver branches jutted out from it, sprawling up into the ceiling. Entering their special keys and a sphere in the console of the Bridge allowed them to see anything in the past or the present. And whatever they watched filled the other half of the large room. What they were watching was the present. The image was faded like a ghost of what was really happening, but the woman who was gagged and blindfolded was going through the horror now.

"I know," Carol agreed. "The fact that Muns would have these guys kidnap her so he could blackmail her sister is terrible. Muns is so creepy evil. He gives me shivers and goose bumps and the heebie-jeebies all at the same time." She shuddered, her blonde ponytail shaking. "The heebieshivergoosbies," she said. "Or the bumpaheebieshivegoos. They should put both of those words in the dictionary and put Muns's face by them."

Abby might have laughed if she wasn't so upset about what she was seeing. "I say it's time we fix this. We need the other two spheres." To be able to travel into the past, they needed three keys inserted and turned simultaneously in the console on the Bridge. Those three keys were already in place and turned. A mechanical arm had also grasped a special sphere and pulled it inside the Bridge. The sphere allowed them to see the present. But if they wanted to travel into the present—to cross into somewhere else on Earth in that very moment, they needed two more spheres. It was all designed so that no one person could manipulate time by him- or herself. He or she would have to counsel with and use the help of another person. Carol handed Abby two more spheres, and Abby placed them over two of the keys. Robotic arms emerged from the control panel of the Bridge just above the keys and grabbed the spheres.

The Bridge trembled. "We have to hurry," Abby said. "We probably have less than a minute." Using the Bridge to see the present put a lot of pressure on the impressive invention. If used in the present for too long, it would shake itself into shambles.

The image of the hostage changed from being a faded ghost of the faraway scene to vivid and clear. Humidity flooded into the Cragbridge Hall basement, making it feel like there was a pool nearby. The smell of dirt and the stench of the neglected home also wafted in, mixed with the smell of the mercenaries' and the hostage's sweat.

Abby and Carol could now cross from the basement of Cragbridge Hall into Brazil, but it would be nearly impossible for them to help the hostage by themselves. Though they would definitely surprise the mercenaries, two unarmed seventh-grade girls would probably not fare well against several trained men with guns. It was a good thing Abby and Carol were not alone in the basement of Cragbridge Hall.

Two other fantastic inventions of the school were with them.

Abby looked over her shoulder. "That's your cue." In response, a gorilla grunted and an alligator chomped his large jaws. Every bit of the animals, from their fur and scales to their eyes and teeth, looked completely natural, but the two creatures were actually elaborate robots. Abby's twin brother, Derick, controlled the alligator. His real body was wearing a high-tech suit in a booth in the avatar lab of the school. Rafa, the Brazilian avatar prodigy, controlled the gorilla from the same lab.

The robot alligator crawled across the basement of the school and crossed into Brazil.

Abby couldn't suppress a smile as she saw the mercenaries' eyes pop wide and their mouths drop open. For them, it was like gaping jaws and razor teeth had simply appeared out of the cinder-block wall—an eight-foot alligator had come out of nowhere.

The mercenary at the table fell back, crashing to the ground and shouting in horror. The gator lunged and toppled the man in the tan shirt as he was trying to trigger his guns.

Rafa's gorilla bounded in. Within seconds, he had ripped the guns from the wrists of the man with the patchy beard and thrown him across the room on top of the man who had fallen by the table.

The Bridge shook harder.

"Fast!" Abby yelled across the room—and into a different country.

The gator snapped at the man in the tan shirt as he scrambled backward, screaming something about a magic alligator coming out of the wall and not wanting to die.

The gorilla jumped forward several feet, hefted the gagged and blindfolded hostage over its shoulder, and crossed back into the basement of Cragbridge Hall. The gator left off chasing the man in the tan shirt and followed suit, creeping madly across the floor. To the mercenaries, it must have looked like they had disappeared through the wall.

As Abby closed the connection, she heard one man scream, "What just happened?" And if Abby wasn't mistaken, another of the mercenaries—a full-grown man—was crying. The scene in Brazil faded away.

"That's what you get for kidnapping people!" Carol yelled back, a little too late.

Abby approached the hostage. "It's going to be okay." She touched her lightly on the shoulder. "We'll take you back home."

The Bridge stopped shaking and began to settle, calm. The group would have to wait at least three minutes before they could use it again to put a very confused and blindfolded woman back in her own living room. For now, they had to let it rest.

• • •

"You rocked," Carol said and slapped Derick's hand. He was no longer controlling the robot alligator from the avatar lab. He, Carol, and Abby all stood in an empty classroom.

Just one bank of lights illuminated the rows of desks. The blinds on the windows were all closed. They didn't have to worry about the students of Cragbridge Hall looking in—they were all asleep in their dorms. They didn't want any security officers or robots watching. They all had clearance to be at the school in the middle of the night, but didn't want to arouse any unnecessary suspicion. "You're cute as a human," Carol said to Derick, "but I have to admit it's cooler to high-five you when you're an alligator."

"It might have been cooler," Derick said, scratching his head through his dark brown hair. It messed up his hair a little, though it still fell in a trendy tousle. "But it was really awkward for me." He sat down on one of the desks. "Alligators have a different center of balance than us and tiny little arms. They aren't exactly built for high-fiving."

"Awkward, nothing," Carol said, throwing her arms around as she spoke. Abby often wondered if Carol could speak without moving her arms and hands. It was like her mouth and her limbs were connected. "For the rest of my life I will be able to say that I high-fived a robot alligator and a robot gorilla that saved hostages from mercenaries in Brazil." She clenched her fist and cocked her elbow. It was a tough-guy move, and coming from a skinny blonde girl, it looked a little out of place. "How many people can say that?"

"Not many," Abby admitted, her shoulders bouncing as she laughed. She loved having Carol around. When Abby had first arrived at the premier secondary school in the world, Carol had been the only girl willing to be her friend.

She would always love her for that. But Carol's ability to lighten up even the tensest of circumstances was often just what Abby needed. "Don't forget that you have to keep this whole thing a secret."

"I said I'll be *able* to say it," Carol clarified. "I didn't say that I would. I wish that you would have let me jump in through the Bridge at the very end so I could say something like, 'If you ever kidnap innocent people again, you can fully expect ferocious animals to appear out of nowhere and bite your evil backsides.'" She took a few steps backward. "And then I would have stepped back through the Bridge all mysterious and awesome. It would have been the best threatening speech ever!"

"Yeah," Derick responded, "Something tells me after the alligator and gorilla, a thirteen-year-old girl just wouldn't be as scary."

This time, several strands of Abby's sandy blonde hair fell over her face as she tried to choke down her giggles. She pulled them back behind her ear.

"And did you say 'evil backsides'?" Derick asked.

Abby wanted to say something funny to add to the banter, but she couldn't think of anything. It would come to her later, when it was useless. "I'm just glad we got all of the hostages back home," Abby said. "They'll be able to recover as a family."

It had been quite the operation. They had used the Bridge to look into the past and find the moment in time each of the various hostages had been kidnapped. Then they had followed the kidnappers to their hideouts, and then found them in the present. When the moment was right, they had sent the avatars across the Bridge to rescue the hostages. Rafa's mother was perhaps the only one at Cragbridge Hall better at the avatars than Rafa, but she hadn't trusted herself to do it. She was so angry about the situation that she was afraid she might get carried away. Instead, she had synced up with the Brazilian police to convince them to protect the rescued hostages from any future attacks.

"After this, I think we should celebrate our heroic rescues with some milkshakes," Carol proposed. "Maybe they leave the ice cream machine on at night. There's always strawberry, chocolate, and vanilla, but today's bonus flavor was eggnog. And since saving kidnapped people burns a few calories, I think we all deserve one."

"For once, I agree with Carol," Derick said. "But it might not be worth the risk with all the security around."

"Ice cream is *always* worth the risk," Carol replied.

Abby cracked the door and peered out. "Here they come." They had been waiting in this particular classroom for a reason: to interrogate someone.

A few moments later, Rafa's mother entered. She was a few inches taller than Abby and Derick, with olive skin and black hair that hung just above her shoulders. A gorilla was only a step behind, carrying a woman over its shoulder. The woman had dark, curly hair and was bound, gagged, and blindfolded like those they had just rescued. Unlike them, however, she was far from innocent. Just the sight of her made Abby clench her teeth. The gorilla set her down in a chair attached to the floor at the front of the room and pulled off her gag.

"I know where I am," the woman said, her hair falling over her blindfold. "We could have talked while I was in my cell. But instead, you brought me out of the basement and up to the school in the middle of the night." She paused, perhaps waiting for a reaction. She didn't get one. "I'm not sitting in just any chair. I'm sitting on Oscar Cragbridge's invention in an English class in Cragbridge Hall." She turned her head toward where she guessed those who were watching her were standing. "You can see my thoughts as we talk."

She was right. On the screen behind the woman, an image appeared of herself sitting in the Chair. In her imagination, her hair looked frizzier and her skin bruised. She apparently thought she was in worse shape than she truly was. She had been kept in a locked room in the basement but treated well enough. Her imagination showed several menacing figures surrounding her: Rafa's mother, other teachers and administrators at Cragbridge Hall, and the robot gorilla who had originally put her in the basement room.

She was right about the Chair, Rafa's mother, and the gorilla, but she hadn't guessed that kids would be watching instead of adults. Underestimating kids—a typical adult problem.

Usually the Chair was used to study literature. As a student sat in the Chair and read *The Adventures of Huckleberry Finn* or *Lord of the Flies*, everyone else in the room could see what the student imagined. However, the Chair could also be very helpful in an interrogation.

A poignant mix of anger, hatred, and sadness swirled inside of Abby. This woman's treachery had put Abby's grandfather and parents in the medical unit of the school, unconscious—tranquilized—and they could stay that way for weeks more.

Abby glanced over at Derick, who glared at the woman. He was probably thinking some of the very same things.

Rafa's mother exhaled slowly to control her feelings. "You've guessed well," she said. She took another deep breath. "I wouldn't expect any less from you, Katarina. You always were clever." She tapped the side of her head.

Carol, who stood next to Abby, turned on her rings and moved her fingers rapidly. It was like typing on thin air. The rings sensed her movements, translating the movement into text, and then processed her message. After she had double-checked the message on the screens in her contact lenses, she sent it to the other students in the room.

> Wow. She knew she was in the Chair. Bright cookie. I usually love meeting another impressive female intellect. Too bad she's also a crazyface who did what Muns asked her to. You can't exactly use her as an inspiring example of achievements among women when she works for Señor Psychopath who could destroy our world.

"We have rescued your relatives, the ones Muns kidnapped to blackmail you," Rafa's mother explained. "They are safe. Now it's your turn. What was the information you offered?"

They would have rescued Katarina's relatives even if she hadn't offered information. But the more they knew about Muns, the better.

"Why don't I just show you?" Katarina asked. She sat back in the Chair. "When I thought that my victory for Muns was inevitable, I asked him to free the members of my family he had kidnapped." She appeared on the screen, a memory of herself, contacting Muns.

"You'll have your keys by tomorrow morning," she said to him. "You can change the past and more."

Muns looked back at her, his hair slicked back. He wore a light gray suit and sat at a large desk, a chessboard before him. He moved a rook five spaces to threaten a knight. "I'm very pleased to hear it."

In her memory, Katarina swallowed hard. "You can release my family now."

An edge of Muns's mouth curled. He didn't look up from the board. "It would be foolish to give up my advantage. And you know I'm no fool. Play your part to the end and your family will be fine. Focus your anger and anxiety on those who keep their keys from me."

"And if I don't?" Katarina asked. "If I back out now?"

"If you waver from my plan, I'll have to make good on my threats," Muns said calmly. He got up from his desk and walked around it.

"But *I'm* your advantage here," Katarina said. "And

if I don't continue, you'll lose that advantage. Isn't that foolish?"

Muns stood up straighter. "You have fire," he said. "To be frank: For your and your family's sake, you must succeed. It is all on the line for you. There is no turning back." He sat on the edge of his desk. "If you fail, you're right—I will lose my advantage . . . for now. But I'm a businessman. I always prepare for the worst-case scenario. I have a backup plan. If you falter or fail, before the year is out, the Cragbridges will again know what it's like to have treasured hostages threatened with death, and they will give me their keys to save them."

The memory faded and all eyes turned to Katarina, blindfolded in the Chair. "There *is* a chance he was bluffing," she said. "But I think something else is coming."

ARE YOU SURE?

It could be anything," Derick said. Rafa's mother had asked question after question but couldn't draw out any new information. Either Katarina didn't know any more, or she was doing an admirable job of hiding it. After returning Katarina to her cell, they all met back in the English classroom. "We have no way of guessing what Muns's plan may be," Derick yawned. It was nearly one in the morning. Doing all this secret work was catching up with him.

"We just know it's going to be terrible," Carol said. "Heebiegoosehivejeebiebumps." She shuddered.

"And if we don't know what it is," Rafa said, pulling his ponytail of dark hair tighter, "it's impossible to prepare for."

"The good news is that Muns is still unconscious," Derick said, and looked over at Abby.

"Oh yeah!" Carol blurted out. "That's because Abby

here gave him a taste of his own medicine." Carol put a finger to the side of her head. "Or, more accurately, a taste of his own tranquilizers." After Muns had nearly sabotaged everything, Abby had used the Bridge to travel through the present and shoot him with one of his own tranquilizer darts. Hopefully he would be unconscious for as long as Grandpa was.

Abby blushed. She was grateful that Muns was also in a coma. "But if he already has someone inside Cragbridge Hall working for him and a plan is in the works, it's still just as dangerous." There were several slow nods.

"Muns did mention hostages," Rafa's mother said. "Perhaps it would be wise to ask security to be more vigilant."

Everyone agreed and Rafa's mother took on the assignment to contact security. It would be better if the request came from a teacher. ·

"We all know security isn't going to stop Muns, or whoever is working for him," Derick said, tousling his hair, "even though they've increased it a lot lately." After Katarina had used avatars to attack and tranquilize members of the Cragbridge Hall staff, increasing security had been a logical next step. There were many more people wearing the gray security uniform and more thin security robots on their single wheels roaming the campus.

"I think we can prepare at least a little more," Abby said. She opened her mouth to continue, but had to wait for a yawn. "We know Muns wants the keys to control time and he wants the Bridge. That gives us a place to start."

"What's on your mind?" Rafa asked.

"We know," Abby said, "that my grandpa gave keys to control the Bridge to several different people he trusted. Everyone who we knew had them is now unconscious in the medical unit, but there is another group, another Council of the Keys." She pulled her hair into a temporary ponytail. She never liked being the center of attention. "If I had to guess, Mr. Sul leads that group." After the avatar battle, Mr. Sul had helped them clean up the mess and had had security escort the soldiers who had broken into campus to the police. He had been the voice of the school at press conferences and talked to parent after parent, assuring them that the criminals had been taken care of and Cragbridge Hall was still safe. Some students withdrew, but most chose to stay. "We need to ask Mr. Sul to warn the other group to stay as vigilant as possible in protecting their keys."

"I wonder," Derick said, "how much we can trust him and the other teachers we think are in his council. Grandpa put us into separate groups for a reason." Derick moved his hands apart to symbolize the groups. "That way one group doesn't know who's in the other, and if there's a traitor trying to steal keys, only one group is in danger. And the other council can come in for reinforcements." Derick scratched his chin. "It's possible that someone in the other council may be the one planning to sabotage the rest of us. We should keep ourselves separate, just in case."

"I think that's smart," Rafa's mother said.

"My thoughts exactly," Abby said. "And so I think we should form our own Council of the Keys."

Carol squealed. "Oh, I'm so totally in." She bobbed up and down with excitement. "It's like our own secret club. But we should change the name to something a little awesomer, like *The Time Guardians*, or *Carol and the Awesomists*."

"You're the headliner?" Rafa said.

"It's nothing personal; I just have the personality for it," Carol said. "And the face for merchandising." She struck a superhero pose.

"I'm not sure *awesomer* or *awesomist* are words," Derick said.

"Doesn't matter," Carol responded. "They are now. And we should use secret code phrases like," she spoke in a lower voice, trying to impersonate a spy, "'The eagle has landed'; 'The wolf has returned to its pack'; and 'The buffalo just sat on the cowboy's foot, and it's going to be really swollen.'"

"What was that last one supposed to mean?" Derick asked.

"I have no idea," Carol said. "I'm just letting the creative juices flow."

"Making a new Council of the Keys may be a good idea," Rafa said. "But I don't deserve to be in it. I don't have a key." He pointed at Abby and Derick. "In fact, only you two do."

Derick looked at Abby. Rafa was right. They were the only two of the group that had keys.

Abby reached into her pocket and pulled out seven keys. All of them had the same metallic sheen and simple design. "These are the keys I stole back from Muns," Abby explained. "They really belong to my parents, my grandpa, and a few other teachers. But we don't know when they are going to wake up again. I think we should give each of you one of them to keep safe until they wake up."

"I agree," Derick said. "You can guard them. My grandpa already gave Rafa's mom the clues to gain her own key." He looked at her. "You just couldn't complete the challenges at the time. We know he trusted you." Derick picked out one key and handed it to Rafa's mother.

"Are you sure about this?" Rafa's mother asked, raising her eyebrows.

"Yes," Abby said, with a slow but confident nod.

"Completely," Derick added. "If it wasn't for your help, I wouldn't have come out of our last scrape alive."

Abby turned toward the others. "Plus, Carol and Rafa, you have more than proved yourselves. You helped us save our grandpa and our parents, and you helped us discover Katarina's plan. Without you two, Muns would have already won." She gave each of them a key.

Carol squeezed the key in her hand and clenched it close to her chest. "This is like 75 degrees of awesome with a forecast of *awesomer* tomorrow," Carol said, gesturing like she was a weather reporter on a news site, "a haze of awesome through the weekend, and awesome raining down throughout the week!" She opened her hand enough to catch another glimpse of her key. "It's too bad I have to keep it a secret. But it's quite fashionable in kind of an antique sort of way. It would be a very cool necklace, especially if I wore it with my blue dress with the frilly white stuff around the neck."

"Obviously, you have to keep it where others can't see it," Derick reminded. "No one can even know you have it."

"Okay, I'll wear it underneath my blue dress," Carol conceded. "Only I will know how truly fashionable I am."

Rafa pinched his key between his fingers then looked at Abby and Derick with his dark eyes. "*Tem certeza?*" he asked.

"*Certeza,*" Derick responded. "I'm not that far in my Portuguese class, but sometimes it works to just repeat the only thing I understood."

"In this case, it worked," Rafa said, smiling wide. "I asked if you were certain and you responded that you were."

"But what should we do with the other four keys?" Carol asked.

For a moment, Abby pinched the spot where the top of her nose met her forehead. "I think we should hide them where no one else will find them. We can retrieve them when their owners wake up."

"That seems wise," Rafa's mom said. "Where did you have in mind?"

"Anywhere we are certain no one will find them," Abby said. "And because we have access to the Bridge, that opens up endless possibilities."

"Let's get to work," Carol said, rubbing her hands together.

"Hopefully this will serve as our backup plan," Abby said. "Now we just have to figure out Muns's."

THE ASH

Abby swung her samurai sword around, smashing it into a flying gold dragon before it could sink its glittering jaws into her. It exploded into a firework of color. She wanted to think she moved gracefully, like a leaf on the wind, but she knew she was more awkward, like an off-balance ostrich.

"Watch out!"

Abby whirled around to see Carol leap off the curved roof of an ancient Japanese building, wielding her sword and screaming, "Hi-yah-yah-yah-yah-yah!" Her blade clashed into another dragon that was swooping down toward Abby, talons poised to strike. After another explosion of color, Abby was safe.

"Thanks," Abby said.

"Sure thing," Carol answered, gliding down and landing

softly on the ground. "Just put *super samurai* on my list of talents. Maybe squeeze it in between *smokin' hot actress* and *genius*. Oh! And add *virtual dragon killer* too." She twirled her swords elaborately while doing a flying leap that landed her closer to Abby.

Abby and Carol weren't really in ancient Japan. They were wearing high-tech suits and visors that allowed them to experience a virtual world. The visors even made a connection with their minds so they felt what it would be like to swing a sword or glide off a roof. In the virtual booth, they were suspended in harnesses that allowed their real bodies to move in any way possible.

"I love how we can move like gravity only sort of applies to us—just like in the old kung fu movies." Carol looked over her shoulder. "Nice touch, Derick."

"Thanks," Derick said, though neither Abby nor Carol could see him. He wasn't in the virtual ancient Japanese world. From inside another booth, he was observing how well they could navigate this world he had created. "It definitely beats my first shot at this." Over a year ago, Derick had built a program that helped kids train to be samurai. That was before he had started at Cragbridge Hall and had access to the best virtuality equipment in the world. "And hopefully it's a good way to relieve some stress."

"Relieve stress?" Abby blurted out. "You throw me into a world where gold dragons want to bite my face and it's supposed to relax me?"

"Exactly," Derick said.

Abby wasn't relaxed. She hadn't been for a while. It

had been over a month since they had rescued the hostages and formed their own Council of the Keys. Nothing out of the ordinary had happened—yet. But that made it worse. It made Abby more anxious. Muns could strike at any moment and she had no idea how, where, or who.

Abby motioned with her virtual swords in one direction and looked over at virtual Carol. "Let's go find that . . . special thing we're supposed to be looking for."

"Yeah, the mystic letter thing," Carol agreed.

"'The Legendary Scroll of Ninja,'" Derick corrected. "Come on! You've got to roll with the amazing theme here, girls."

"The awesome theme is you asking to hang out with me," Carol said. Technically it was true. He *had* asked her to try out his game. She turned her head and winked.

Abby could imagine Derick squirming even though she couldn't see him. "Samurai don't flirt during their epic missions," Derick countered.

"Well this samurai does," Carol said. "But next time, could you make my *katana* handle pink, and my *gi* a light blue? I like to fight my battles in style. Plus, since you're watching, you might as well see me in all my possible cuteness and . . ." Carol couldn't finish because another dragon circled around the building. Abby thought Derick might have purposely sent this one just to get Carol off the subject.

Abby twisted her sword in a way that sent a gust of wind blowing at the dragon, knocking it off course. Carol threw her blade like a spear. More fireworks.

"I like that wicked wind thing you do," Carol said.

"I learned it by accident in the practice dojo," Abby confessed. "And your javelin thing was cool too."

"Samurai don't stop to compliment each other either," Derick said, his frustration coming out in every word. "You only have three more minutes to conquer the level."

"And what happens if we finish?" Abby asked. "Because it had better be fantastic."

"Yeah, like we get to sit in a virtual bathhouse and get foot massages," Carol guessed.

"Oh, and virtual fudge," Abby added. "Did they have that in ancient Japan?"

"They'd better," Carol said.

Derick groaned.

Abby and Carol moved through Derick's world, trying not to be seen by the guards in the firelight or the mystic dragons that guarded the city. Soon they slipped in through a window of the mansion they hoped held the secret scroll. But after only a few steps inside, ninjas crept out from every corner, and a golden serpent the length of six or seven cars slithered out to meet them.

"Not good. Really not good," Abby murmured. "This is definitely not relaxing."

"There had better be an incredible foot massage," Carol said.

But everything stopped mid-surge, frozen still for a moment. Then the scene flickered, and the giant snake and the ninjas retreated.

"We must have scared them off," Carol said. She then yelled back at where the virtual serpent had been. "That's right, creepy snakey slither demon and your naughty ninja minions. Go home. And don't come back."

"You wish," Derick said. "It's another glitch. You can be done for now. I'd better start fixing it if I'm going to turn it in tonight."

The world faded, and Abby and Carol took off their equipment and stepped out of their booths into the math and engineering classroom. They normally would use the booths to create bridges and buildings and cities, but this was a bit more creative. They cracked open the door to Derick's booth.

"It wasn't exactly my style," Abby said, "but it is an incredible challenge. I really think other students will love it."

"I completely agree," Carol said. "But if your first entry actually got into the Race, wouldn't that break a record or something? There are like hundreds of kids who try, most of them a lot older than us." She stepped away and sat on a desk. "And of those kids, some of them super-care. They submit lots of times. They don't just count on one scenario making it. They have lots of backup plans."

Backup plans. Abby was beginning to hate those words.

"I wonder if a seventh grader has ever actually gotten their challenge into the Race," Carol said, bringing Abby back from her thoughts.

"I don't think seventh graders usually do anything in the Race," Abby said. "Except maybe cheer on all the other people in the older grades. They're older and better at everything."

"Oh, I think we can give them a run for their money,"

Derick said, still working inside his booth. "Hold on. I've got another message." Derick must have received an alert.

"Derick," Abby said. "Don't get too excited about every message. I know you'd rather be invited to be on a team that is part of the Race and actually does the challenges instead of just submitting, but . . ."

Derick rushed out of his booth jumping and pumping his fists. "Yes! Yes! Yes!" he yelled out, over and over. "I got an invite!" He did a few celebratory karate kicks.

"No way," Carol whispered then raised her voice to a shout. "That's amazing!" She did a few karate kicks herself.

"That's great," Abby said, stunned.

"Yeah," Derick agreed, stopping to watch Carol's strange karate moves. "Some ninth grader named Alexa Nigh is putting it together. She heard I was part of the Crash."

Abby hadn't thought of that. Though she and Derick were both young, Derick was the newest member of the Crash, the club of students who were the very best at controlling the robot animal avatars. Obviously, he was good enough to attack mercenaries in Brazil. Since avatar ability might be important in the Race, everyone wanted someone who was good at them. Unlike Derick, Abby could barely squeak by with a passing grade in avatars.

"Of course, it's not official," Derick said, now standing in front of Carol and Abby. "They aren't allowed to form teams until after the announcement, but she says I can count on an invite."

"Congratulations," Carol said, then did a few more jabs

in the air and a kick. "I'm really liking this karate celebration thing."

"Just don't hurt yourself," Abby said, having to duck as Carol got a little out of control. "And don't hurt me either."

Derick looked at both of them, then his smile flattened. "Oh. You never know—you may have invites coming."

Abby hoped she wasn't blushing. "I'm not worried about it." She waved him off. "Besides, I barely made it into the school and I'm scraping by with my grades. I don't expect anyone to invite me to the elite stuff." She didn't expect it, though it would be a nice surprise. She wasn't sure she wanted to do it, but she would still like an invitation.

"Whatever." Carol slapped Abby on the shoulder. "You're forgetting you're—" Her voice became guttural and loud. "—legendary!" Her arms flung up and she did jazz hands. "So what if you've never aced a math test. You've stopped an evil mastermind from stealing our keys and destroying the world, *twice!*" She shot up two fingers. "Of course, I helped quite a bit. Plus, I add a flair that's really important to our success." She looked at Derick. "You did your incredible part, too." She struck a pose. "We. Are. The. Best." She changed to a different superhero-style pose with each of the last four words.

"She's right," Derick admitted. "She's also hyper and over-the-top, but she's right. If it wasn't for you, Abby, Muns would have won."

Abby *had* succeeded. But very few people knew. She wouldn't get an invitation, because they had no idea what she was capable of.

• • •

Derick couldn't stop thinking about his invitation as he rode the elevator up to his floor and down the hall to his room. He flopped on his bed and fumbled to take off his rings and set them on his nightstand. But something was sitting on top of his usual mess of clothes and food wrappers. He sat up in his bed and looked down at a small . . . thing.

It looked like a miniature version of Saturn, but the rings around the little planet blended into the sphere. It was also completely silver. Maybe it was his roommate's. He'd have to ask later.

But what was it? Derick touched the saturn and jolted back in surprise, as the thing somehow launched itself into the air and hovered at eye level. There was no sound of an engine or propeller. He had never seen anything like it. The little saturn projected words into the air.

> Analyzing.
> Derick Cragbridge.
> Lived September 17, 2063 to March 29, 2075.

It must have read his fingerprints, or facial features, or retinas or something because it knew who he was. But what was with the "lived"? Past tense. His birthday was right, but according to the little floating ball, he was going to die in a few weeks.

"Weird prank," Derick mumbled to himself. He approached the saturn, getting nice and close to whatever camera it might have. "If this is some team from the Race trying to invite me, or scare me into not joining up with another team, it's not working. I'm not even sure what your point is." He brushed his hand toward the floating ball, but it dodged it easily.

Wow. Impressive response.

More words.

Cannot authorize a nonliving person.

There is was again: nonliving. Prank, or this thing was really broken.

Seeking special authorization.

Special authorization for what? To give him more pointless messages?

Authorization obtained in records. Message coming.

Apparently, the saturn thought it was an okay idea to relay a message to someone it thought was dead. "You're not the brightest little robot off the assembly machine, are you?"

The saturn projected a face, as bright and realistic as if it were on the best of screens, of a girl with short dark hair and tan skin. "I hope this will work." He could hear her clearly. The saturn was a speaker as well. "Well, of course it works. I've been selfing on this forever. I mean, I hope it will work when I send it back to you." She shook her head. "But if you are seeing this, then it did work. I'll move ahead, hoping for the best."

Derick passed his hand through the image just to be sure there was no screen. Nothing.

The image flickered, then returned.

"Derick, I hope this reaches you at the right time." How did she know his name? He looked at her closely. No, he didn't recognize her. He couldn't remember her from any of his classes. He hadn't passed her in the halls. And how did she get the little saturn into his room? There was definitely some trespassing going on. "From what I've been able to figure out, which isn't much, you and your sister came the closest to stopping Charles Muns."

She knew about Muns. Derick immediately looked around his room to make sure he was alone. That probably meant that she knew about the secret as well. And the keys. But she had said, ". . . came the closest to stopping him." She was wrong. They had stopped him. They stopped him flat, dropped-unconscious-on-his-desk-without-any-keys flat.

"Let me back up," she said. "As crazy as this sounds, I think my history is different from yours. Parts of it anyway." She rubbed her eyes. "Charles Muns changed it. That's probably how he became what he is. He shouldn't be. He's caused this mess that no one should have to live in." She frowned and moved her fingers in the air. She didn't have rings, but perhaps something that worked on a similar principle. Maybe she could actually interact with the screen in the air on her end. "Here, let me show you." The face moved and Derick saw a beautiful set of skyscrapers towering over a city. Rows and rows of homes filled the land beneath. "It doesn't look too bad, I know, but glance this." Derick saw person after person walking the streets. There was something about them that seemed dull. Sullen faces, subtly drooping eyes. It wasn't like they were zombies, just missing something. Just living less.

One of them doubled over. It was a middle-aged man. He groaned, loud and hollow, and pressed his arms against his belly as if he had just been sucker-punched in the gut. He grabbed the person next to him, but could barely whisper. "Help me," he gasped.

In under a minute, a tile in the ground in the weird world opened up. A long cylinder the size of a kitchen table floated out. This world really had the floating thing down. A small, egg-looking device detached itself and hovered over to the man. "No skeletal injury. Safe to move," the machine announced in a professional female voice. It was some sort of floating doctor.

A long board with mechanical arms slid out of the cylinder, carefully loaded the man onto itself, then returned into the cylinder. "You will be arriving at the hospital for medical care in forty-nine seconds," the same female voice explained. Then the cylinder disappeared back into the ground. Apparently there was some sort of underground transportation system for the cylinders.

That was a fast response to a medical emergency.

A man with a long gray coat had paused to watch the whole incident. "I'll bet you my stamps, it's the Ash," he said, and shook his head. "The poor guy will be gone within the hour."

"And more likely than not, no one will remember who he was," a woman added. She sat on the ground, apparently

a beggar. She reached out to the man for money or food. He simply shrugged and kept walking.

The face of the girl sending the message returned. "This is reasonably common. They call it the epidemic of our time; a disease that causes people to fall terribly ill, then disintegrate from the inside out. He'll be dead in an hour—and a pile of ash-like grains by morning. That's where the name comes from. They say that the world's best doctors are close to a cure, but people are definitely scared." For the first time, Derick noticed the girl's clothes as she talked. They overlapped at the cuffs and had a row of silver buttons. Strange style. Another row of buttons lined the trim around her neck.

The message flickered again. Derick wondered if something was wrong with the saturn.

"I know it's all a cover-up," the girl continued. "There is no disease." She rubbed her eyes. "Wow. This is a lot to go over. Here's the short version: Muns and his descendants change the past. They do it whenever someone tries to get in their way, or when someone simply does something they don't like. Eventually those changes catch up to our time. If those changes kept two people from marrying, then their children would never exist. If the changes prevented someone from becoming a doctor who would save others' lives, *those* people would no longer exist. There are really countless scenarios. But when those changes catch up to our time, if someone would no longer exist, they get the Ash." She looked down. "Sometimes, it's like they were never here."

The terror of it struck Derick. If he got the Ash, one moment he could be practicing avatars with Rafa, and within the hour, he could be gone. Or Carol. Or Ab— He didn't want to think about it. And Muns had claimed he only wanted to change tragedies in history. Either that was all a cover story, or he would change over time. He wanted control—control over everything.

"We found the keys to the Bridge that you hid." She opened her mouth to continue, but then caught herself before the sound escaped. She shook her head. "Sorry, I shouldn't tell you names. Someone you know organized us and told us about them, but she is a lot older now." Derick's mind raced. Someone he knew organized a rebellion, and she was a lot older? He didn't know what to think of it. But if they found the hidden keys they had to be extremely dedicated. The Council of the Keys had put them in special protective cases and hid them in jungles, on mountaintops, and even at the bottom of the ocean. Rafa had used a fish avatar for that.

"And with a lot of planning and help," the girl continued, "I snuck into Muns's stronghold and used them in Muns's Bridge. I found out more and recorded this message on the self." That must be the name for the little saturn. "I've risked my life for it. But there was a chance to stop Muns. And it all starts with the Race." The great competition between teams? The fantastic challenge? It had something to do with Muns? "I can't tell you more. I don't want to cause some of the same problems Muns does by messing with the past, but this is a chance I had to take."

She moved closer, her face becoming bigger in the portrayal. "And Derick," she continued, "I sent this message to you because you have to do things differently. The way your history unfolds now, you don't have long." Projected from the saturn, Derick saw his own silhouette, with trees and the Watchman—the tower on top of the main building at Cragbridge Hall—in the background. A flash of light. A scream. His scream. "Unless you change what you would have done and succeed in stopping Muns, his plan will take your life."

Derick felt hollow. The taste in his mouth grew metallic. Death? Gone? Muns wins?

Derick heard footsteps coming from behind the girl, not in his room, but wherever she was filming. "Oh, no." Her lips trembled and she began moving her fingers furiously. He had no idea what she was doing. "They've found me." She swallowed hard. "I hope you get this and it works. I hope you can change it—for your sake and ours."

The message closed and the saturn floated back down to his nightstand.

WHOA.
MIND BLOWN.

W eird, huh?" Derick said, the saturn floating back down into his hand. He looked across the table at the other members of the Council of the Keys. They met in Rafa's mother's office, surrounded by pieces of avatars. Derick pushed a giraffe leg off to one side and sat on the edge of a table. "I've watched it like thirty times now."

The room was silent.

"I don't know where that little floating ball thing came from," Carol said, standing next to a fully formed robot rhinoceros, "but it's really rude. Its whole message was basically, 'Hey, I'm from the future. Do better. The fate of the world is on your shoulders. Oh, and you're going to die.' Its mama robot should have taught it some manners."

Abby felt stunned. Her brother, dead? It had been hard to live in his shadow all of her life, but she would never want him gone. She blinked several times, hoping her emotions weren't obvious to everyone. She was surprised at how strong they were and how quickly they came to the surface.

"And look," Carol said. "It's almost made Abby cry. I mean, *rude*!"

Abby sniffled but tried to change the subject. "But do you really think it's from the future?" She hoped it wasn't. She hoped it was some bizarre tasteless joke. But over the past year she had learned that some pretty crazy things were completely possible.

"I've never seen any technology like this," Rafa's mother said. And she was the world's expert at making robotic animal avatars. "It's impressive. I've done a quick scan, and it's just as unique and advanced on the inside." She wore a pair of sleek goggles and held the saturn in a gloved hand. Apparently she could do some sort of scan with the goggles. "I could study this for months."

"So you're saying it *could* be from the future," Carol summarized.

Rafa's mother shrugged. "There is no way to tell for sure, but it's a possibility."

"From the future," Carol repeated to herself. "That sounds like such a prank." Then her eyes grew wide and her mouth fell open. "That gives me a great idea; let's pick out a few students and send them fake messages from themselves in the future telling them stuff like 'Don't eat the food in the cafeteria today. It's been poisoned.' Or, 'The first five answers on your test today are C, A, B, the number 17, and all of the above.' Or 'Isn't that girl Carol Reese super-cute?

You should pay more attention to her and invite her to be on your team for the Race.'"

"That is a funny idea," Rafa said, forcing a smile. "But I think we have some more serious things to think about." He was pulling on wires inside of a monkey arm and making the fingers flex and relax.

"At least my fake messages from the future would be nicer than Mr. Floaty Doomsday Depression here," Carol sulked, pointing at the saturn.

"Bottom line," Derick said. "Do we need to be worried about the Race?"

Abby could only imagine what her brother might be feeling. Did he want her to say that they didn't have to worry about it, that his life wasn't on the line? That he could just compete in the Race and relax? "Muns is still un-conscious," Abby said, "like our parents and our grandpa. But if this message is right, we are in some definite trouble. The stakes are higher than ever."

"The stakes have always been high," Derick said. "The past and future have always been on the line." Was he downplaying it all? Was he looking for a way to rationalize it away?

"Yeah," Abby admitted, "but if this is right, we have to do better than we would have done. We'll have to succeed where we would have failed." She blinked a few more times. "We have to. You have to."

Everyone was silent for a moment.

"This is really serious," Rafa said, setting down the ro-bot monkey arm he had been fiddling with before. "That

future looks *horrivel*—horrible. That Ash is nasty business."
He paused for a second, tucking a stray strand of dark hair
behind his ear. "I'm not even sure I should bring it up, but
do you think maybe we should beat Muns to it? We could
go into the past and set Muns off course. Maybe we could
sabotage one of his first business ventures, or mess up some
assignments in school, or . . ."

"Punch him in the face," Carol interrupted. "Because I
volunteer to do that."

A laugh burst out of Rafa. "Maybe. Anything that would
keep him from becoming what he is."

Abby shook her head. "No. My grandpa warned us
against that." Abby had to admit that she had thought of
it too, and it was tempting. But she knew better. She knew
the catastrophic consequences it could have. "We shouldn't
try to manipulate the past. It's too dangerous. We deal with
troubles as they come."

"This does sound like an exception," Carol said.

"I know it sounds good," Rafa's mother said. "But I
agree with Abby. I don't think that's what Oscar Cragbridge
would want."

"You're right," Derick agreed. "Plus we may mess something else up. What if knocking Muns off track somehow affects Grandpa and he doesn't complete his inventions, or he
never starts this school, or what if it sends him on a wrong
course and it affects my dad, who never meets my mom, and
then Abby and I never exist. And that's just *my* family. It
could mess up a lot more than that."

"We should at least wait and talk to my grandpa about

it when he wakes up," Abby suggested, hoping to stall everyone before they did something rash.

Everyone eventually agreed, though Carol volunteered one more time to punch Muns in the face if there was ever a need.

"In the meantime," Rafa's mother said, raising her goggles and resting them on the top of her head, "we should warn the administrators about the Race. Have them double-check everything. Maybe even cancel it."

Derick grimaced and Rafa frowned.

Boys. They obviously still wanted to compete in the games.

Carol raised her hand to signal that she was about to talk. "But we can't really just say, 'Hey, we got a message from the future, so you need to cancel your games.'"

"You're right," Rafa's mother agreed. "And the Race is the most popular event all year. I know Mr. Sul was looking forward to it, to draw attention away from our last security threat." She thought for a moment. "I'll say I heard a rumor that something unsafe may happen in the Race. That should both protect our secrets *and* alert security. They're interested in any leads of possible danger."

"And maybe let's tell Mr. Sul as well," Abby suggested. "Even though I'm still not sure how well we can trust him."

Everyone nodded.

"I just wish we could ask the girl from the future," Derick said. "Talk to her. Get some straight answers."

"Maybe we can," Abby said.

The group fell into silence.

Abby continued. "I know we've all been thinking it ever since we learned the last secret. When we put three keys into the Bridge, we can interact with the past. When we add three spheres, we can interact with the present. What's the logical next step?"

"The future," Carol whispered in reverence. "Whoa. Mind blown." She pulled her blonde hair back with her hands then fell back onto a chair.

"That is some serious stuff," Rafa said.

"If I could see the future," Carol said. "I'd check out my wedding day. I bet I have a gorgeous dress. Oh, and I'd want to know who the groom is." She winked at Derick. "I bet it'll either be Derick or that beautiful tan boy in the movie about the girl who fell in love with a troll and started an interspecies war. I think it was a sci-fi Romeo and Juliet. Or maybe Gavin from history class, or the guitarist for The Deskjob Rebellion."

"Something tells me that if the Bridge can be used to see the future, we shouldn't use it to see who you are going to marry," Rafa said.

"Why not?" Carol asked. "That way I wouldn't waste my time flirting with other boys."

"By the way you act," Abby said, "I'm not sure you think flirting is ever a waste of time."

"True," Carol said, her eyes rolling to the side as she thought about it. "But if I knew who I was going to marry, then I could walk straight up to him and tell him that one day he'll fall madly in love with me."

"Now we know for sure that you shouldn't use the

Bridge to see who you marry," Derick said. "Nothing would scare a guy more."

"The problem is that Grandpa is unconscious," Abby said, bringing them back on topic. "He can't answer our questions or give us anything that might lead to the answer." He had given them a locket to discover the secret of the past and a black box that gave them clues to the present.

"True," Derick said. He bit his lip.

"Well, I guess we should focus on stopping whatever crazy thing is supposed to happen during the Race," Carol said.

"*Concordo*," Rafa agreed. "And if we are invited, I believe we should even participate in it. That may give us a better perspective of what is happening."

If they were invited. Abby didn't like that *if*.

"If the Race is dangerous, I'm not sure I want you to participate," Rafa's mother confessed.

Rafa pulled another stray stand of dark hair behind his ear that had fallen out of his ponytail. "But if you and other adults are watching the competition really closely, we need people on the inside," he argued. "The more eyes, the more we might be able to catch on to what Muns may have planned."

"I'll think about it," Rafa's mother said. She didn't seem in any hurry to let her son do anything that might be remotely dangerous.

"We still don't know what we're looking for," Abby pointed out. "It could be that unless we can see into the future, we'll never know if we've stopped that terrible future from happening."

Abby looked over at her brother, who looked away.

• • •

"5:32. That's a whole two minutes late," the nurse said. She stood in the white, sterilized lobby, a hall containing several doors stretching away behind her. "I was beginning to wonder if you were going to come."

"I had a meeting," Abby explained.

"I'm teasing you." The nurse laughed and gave Abby a hug. She was really touchy-feely like that. Abby didn't mind though. She was grateful to have someone so loving taking care of those in the med unit. "They're waiting for you." The nurse gestured toward the hall behind her.

"Any changes?" Abby asked, moving toward the hall. She could always hope.

"Nope. Sorry. They're still waiting for just the right moment."

"I hope it's soon," Abby said as she passed the nurse. She walked down the hall, passing two rooms she had been in before—rooms that held other teachers she knew. She visited them at times, but it was the last door on the right she opened most often. She always had to steel herself for what she was about to see. Abby took a deep breath and stepped in.

There were three beds in the room. Not just any kind of bed, but beds that rotated. They were designed to move those who were in them, to keep them from getting bedsores and to help them heal.

Abby looked at both her parents and her grandfather. All of them were hooked up to tubes that kept them hydrated and nourished while their bodies were comatose. They had been unconscious since Katarina had attacked them with tranquilizers.

"Hey, everyone," Abby said, hoping they could hear her. "I'm back." She walked over and held her mother's hand. The nurse kept her hair combed and her clothes cleaned, but there was no life, no laugh, nothing. "I miss you." She glanced at her dad, who was usually so quick to tease and fast to flash a smile; now he lay dull and motionless. Her grandpa, whose mustache and beard made him look like a safari hunter ready for an adventure, looked cold and nearly fake—like a mannequin someone had made to remember the great inventor. "All three of you." She swallowed a few times. "I really hope you'll wake up soon, because . . ." She looked around to make sure she had closed the door and the nurse was nowhere around to overhear. She spoke softer. She told them all about Derick's saturn and the message. Then she waited. She was hoping for one of them to twitch, to raise a finger, anything. Maybe if they knew they were needed it could bring them back to consciousness. She sat in silence for several minutes.

"I mean, the nurse says you'll be fine." Abby brushed away a tear. "It's just a matter of time. But if we don't stop Muns, then Derick . . ." Her voice trailed off. She couldn't think about it for too long. Plus, if the message was right and who knows how many people would be stricken with the Ash, Derick wasn't the only one in danger. Who knew if any of the Cragbridges would survive?

Abby stood up and paced for a moment, then stopped in front of her grandfather. "I wish you were awake to help. To help me know what to do." Still no movement. No sign.

She kissed her grandfather's forehead. "I wish I could ask you whether or not the Bridge could show us the future." She smiled to keep from crying. "Of course, you'd just dodge my question and tell me I had to earn the answer." She looked at him—so pale and, for one of the few times in his life, not wearing his blazer. He wore it all the time. Abby used to think it was because he was an eccentric inventor, but had discovered that the blazer was where he kept a sphere he needed with him constantly, a sphere that could allow him to see the present, anywhere in the world. She wondered where he kept his key that allowed him to interact with the past. Wait. A sphere. A key. If the Bridge could show the future, it would probably come with something physical that Grandpa would carry with him all the time.

Abby walked over to the closet in the medical unit wall and opened its doors. She began to thumb through the clothing Grandpa had been wearing when he was tranquilized. It had all been stored here. Abby felt the blazer, covering every inch. She had no idea where something might be hidden. Of course the sphere wasn't there; Abby had kept it to make sure it was safe. She repeated the same drill with the trousers in the drawer and his shoes. She even brought them over to Grandpa and pressed his fingers along every surface. She knew he had built shoes, belts, and other clothes with fingerprint-activated secret compartments.

Nothing.

She examined her grandfather's rings. Had they been programmed to do something? She looked back at the man on the bed. Maybe he kept something in what little hair he had—or in his beard. That didn't seem likely. It would be something very precious and keeping something there seemed easy for someone else to notice or discover.

Nothing.

She couldn't think of anything else until, as she was closing the closet doors, she noticed something leaning in the corner of the room. Something that wouldn't fit in the drawer. Grandpa's cane.

THE CANE

The cane had an ornate handle but a simple wooden shaft. Abby tapped on it every few inches all the way down to the rubber end. She was listening for a hollow compartment somewhere. It sounded firm.

She inspected it closely, looking for breaks in the grain that might signal that it had been pieced together and held something inside. The body appeared to be crafted from a single piece of oak. At least that was Abby's best guess. She wasn't exactly a wood expert.

No clues. At all. But if there was something else physical to control the Bridge, this had to be it. Didn't it? She couldn't think of anything else that her grandfather always carried with him.

She grabbed the handle and tried to twist it. It wouldn't give. She gripped the shaft with one hand and the handle

with the other and pulled. Surprisingly, the cane lengthened. Not by much, but the handle slid back a few inches,
exposing a metal band around the wood. Abby touched the
metal. When she pulled back, she could see her fingerprint
on the band. Then the band shifted into the handle, revealing a small screen beneath it. Words scrolled across it:

> Bring this key, not to my 89 Liberty Street, but
> something closer to Foote Avenue and Kiowa
> Street.

It was a message from her grandfather. Abby's pulse
quickened just knowing she was on the right trail. But she
had no idea what the message meant. That was nothing
new. Her grandpa always made her work for her answers.

• • •

The four friends passed a pair of teachers griping about
the tardy policy. Derick, Abby, Carol, and Rafa slowed
their pace so the teachers would be out of sight as they approached the door.

"Why are we here again?" Carol asked.

"The clue was a reference to different laboratories of
Nikola Tesla," Abby explained.

"That is a crazy name," Carol said. "I love it."

"It took me a little while to figure it out," Abby admitted. "Tesla was an inventor, and Liberty Street and Foote
Avenue were places he had laboratories. The message
meant that we shouldn't go to his first laboratory, but to
one he worked in after he was more established and had

financial backing. So if we compare that to Grandpa, this would be a laboratory he had after he was established."

Abby raised her hand and could feel it being scanned, but the light didn't turn green. The door was still locked.

"He said to bring the key," Rafa reminded. "It looks like we need it."

"The message said, 'Bring *this* key,'" Derick corrected. "And it was on the cane, so do you think he means the cane is also some sort of key?"

"Probably," Abby said. She pulled out the cane from her backpack. It had been too long to fit in entirely, so the rubber bottom stuck out, but she would have felt weirder holding a cane as she walked the halls. Abby lifted the cane to the lock. She couldn't exactly thread it into a keyhole. She was hoping that just bringing it close to the lock would do something.

Nothing happened.

Again, Abby pulled on the cane and exposed the metal band beneath. She touched it, and the cane vibrated. She saw numbers automatically appear on the security lock near the door, and the door popped open.

They quickly stepped inside and closed the door. The walls were filled with bookshelves, screens with blueprints, several locked cabinets, and a few booths. One portion of the room held a Chair, a metal plate on its back bent up, wires flaring out from beneath. Another part of the office had controls to the Bridge. A machine that Abby didn't recognize stood in a corner. It looked like a small table with a console, a round container on the side, and a large, thick safe-like compartment beneath.

"We use machines like this in metal shop," Rafa said, looking at the same mechanism. "It's used for the small stuff." Abby hadn't thought about it before, but that made sense. Grandpa used lockets and keys and black boxes to teach about his secrets. Someone had to make them, and Grandpa couldn't trust just anyone with the secret messages they contained. So he made them himself. It was a wonder her grandpa found time for it all.

A large desk stood in the middle of the lab with a chaotic mess of machinery scattered across its top.

An image of Grandpa appeared, this one full-size. As always, he wore his loafers, casual khaki pants, a button-up shirt, and his blue blazer. He rubbed his bald head, then smoothed his fluffy white mustache. "Welcome to my office." He spread his arms wide, his cane hanging on his wrist. "Have a seat." The image of Grandpa motioned toward the plush chair behind his desk.

Abby's heart swelled and hurt at the same time. She was listening to her grandfather again, but she knew his real body lay in the medical unit, still unconscious.

"Go ahead, Abby," Derick said, nodding toward the chair. "You're the one who started figuring all this out."

"What a gentleman," Carol gushed.

As soon as Abby sat, screens lowered from the ceiling. They covered the bookshelves and cases and drawings. It was like theater in the round.

"Unless I'm wrong," the image of Grandpa said, "you

have come here wondering if the Bridge can show you even more than you have yet discovered." He smiled, wrinkles bunching up at the corners of his mouth.

"I admit to having another secret or two. By the data related to your fingerprint, you already know the Bridge can show the past and present. Perhaps you wonder if it can also show the future." His white eyebrows raised. "Before we answer that question, I believe you have to consider other questions. For example, if it *can* show you the future, should you look?" He pointed toward Abby in the seat with his cane.

Abby sat there a moment, thinking about the question. Under normal conditions she wasn't sure about the answer. In this case, it seemed more important. Her brother's life depended on it. In fact, hundreds, thousands, or even millions of lives that would get the Ash also depended on it.

"We live in a world where we cannot naturally see the future. I believe that has many benefits." The image of Grandpa paced the laboratory. "For example, there are some things about Nikola Tesla that I have always admired." A slender, mustached man in a suit appeared on the screens. "He is the inventor that changed and improved motors, radio, and the channeling of electricity." The image on the screens changed to show the inventor sitting in a chair while a large coil three times his size shot bolts of electricity in every direction. It was like a concentrated lightning storm.

"Tesla idolized Thomas Edison," Grandpa continued, "but the two became bitter enemies. Tesla fought for his idea of providing electricity through alternating current. Edison fought back, claiming direct current was better." Screens showed Edison speaking about the dangers of his opponent's electricity and even threatening to show what it would do to animals. "But alternating current was the stronger idea and eventually won out."

Abby hadn't really heard of Tesla before her grandfather's first clue. If Tesla's idea was better than Edison's, why wasn't he more famous? "Tesla even had the idea of providing free electricity." An image appeared of a large tower under construction. "And his work was well under way until the businessman who was supposed to be financing his work pulled the plug and ruined Tesla's reputation."

"And this," Grandpa said, pointing at the screen. It showed an old man lying on a bed in a seedy hotel room, his skin taut around his cheekbones and his eyes sunken. He looked like he hadn't eaten well in weeks. "This is how Nikola Tesla died. Penniless, unknown, and all alone. The man had over five thousand patents in his name and changed the world forever, but this was his end—forgotten in a hotel room."

Grandpa looked toward Abby in the desk chair. "If he had known this is how it would end, would he have made our world better? If he could have foreseen the heartache, the breakdowns, would he have worked as hard?" The image of Grandpa took a few guarded steps. "And what about me? Would I have invented the Bridge if I could do it all again?" He looked ahead very seriously then exhaled.

That was a good question. If he had known it would

lead to him and his son and daughter-in-law lying uncon-scious for weeks, would he have done it? If he had known it could possibly lead to his grandson's death, and Muns in control, would he have gone through with it? Abby wasn't sure.

Grandpa placed his hand on his chest. "I believe we need to do our very best. We have a responsibility to think about the consequences of our actions, but not to overly worry about the future." He pointed his cane at Abby. "You need to think very seriously about whether or not you should see the future, if in fact, the Bridge can do that. Seeing the opposition we would face in the future may be a great burden. Perhaps even a pitfall."

The top of Grandpa's desk shifted back and another flat surface rose to the top. On it lay what looked like over a hundred items. One looked like a tangled mess of wire, an-other like a metal star, another like a silver bowl. There was a great variety in their shapes, but each was small enough to fit in the palm of Abby's hand. "If you would like to pursue this question further," Grandpa said, "perhaps one of these objects will help. You will need to make a choice without knowing the future, without knowing the consequence of picking that object."

"Wow," Carol said. "Those are kind of amazing, but I have no idea how they will help us answer the question."

"I guess we just pick one and see what it does," Derick suggested.

"I'll take the star," Carol said, "for obvious reasons." She walked over and snatched it from the table. Immediately she shook and fell to the ground, dropping the star back on the desk.

Abby rushed out of her seat. "What happened?"

Derick reached Carol first. "Don't touch the star," he blurted out, as Rafa bent down to grab it. "I think it just shocked her."

"Is she going to be okay?" Abby asked.

Derick put his cheek to Carol's face. "She's still breathing." He checked her pulse for nearly half a minute. "And she's calming down." Derick continued to check her breathing every twenty seconds or so, just to be sure.

Carol's eyes gradually opened. She looked at Derick, who happened to have his head tilted down toward her. She closed her eyes again.

"Are you okay?" Abby asked her friend.

"Shhhh," Carol said. "Some powerful magic sent me into a deep sleep, like Sleeping Beauty, and I can only be awakened by my true love's kiss."

Derick stood up, his concern wiped from his face. "Well, it looks like we're going to have to figure all of this out without Carol."

"Oh, come on!" Carol said, sitting up. "That was a magical setup! When are we ever going to have that situation again?"

"Magical?" Derick questioned. "You were shocked unconscious and I was making sure you weren't dead."

"Ahhhh," Carol said, fixing her blonde hair, which was a bit frizzy at the edges. "I knew you cared."

"Why would Grandpa shock you?" Abby asked. She

looked around the room until she found a pair of thick gloves on a work table next to a branch to the Bridge. She slid one glove on and timidly pushed the star. Little sparks arced out of it.

"Toss me that other glove," Derick said. Once protected, he picked up the ball of wire. He held it for several seconds, but then the glove began to freeze. He dropped it back down on the desk. "It's seeping out liquid nitrogen or something, because it's freezing instantly."

"So apparently we're supposed to learn to never touch anything," Carol said.

"There are too many objects to really know yet," Abby said. She pushed a bowl gingerly. Nothing. Then she held it up off the desk. Several coins slid from a secret compartment near its top into the bottom of the bowl.

"You have made several choices," Grandpa's voice said. He had appeared again and gazed in the direction of the desk. "Making choices without knowing the results—or in other words, knowing the future—can be difficult. Perhaps it is somewhat like choosing these items. Each choice has a consequence. Some choices hurt, and some reward. Those coins," he pointed where the bowl had been, "are rare and worth a good deal of money. I went back in time and stole them from Thomas Jefferson." He winked. "I'm kidding, but they *are* rare."

Carol scooped them out of the bowl and lifted one to the light to inspect it.

"You'd think you'd be a little more careful after the last thing shocked you and sent you to the floor," Derick said.

Grandpa was still talking. "Can you imagine how life would be if we knew the results to every choice before we made it? It is possible that we would spare ourselves every difficulty and only find rewards. But what would that lead us to be? I've already taught you that going through difficulty makes us stronger. Facing tragedies and trials is when ordinary people rise up and become heroes."

Grandpa paced in front of his desk. "If one of your choices causes pain and sorrow, you learn and grow. You become stronger and don't look back."

He cleared his throat. "You must make the best choices you know how, not fearing what will come. Study your choices, use your mind, and follow your heart and your instincts. But once you've made a choice," he pointed his cane at the objects, "make the most of it."

And then he was gone.

"I totally knew he was going to end all cryptically," Carol said. "And we would have no idea what to do next."

"I guess he's a bit predictable that way," Abby said. "But we need to see the future. We need to know if what we are doing is on track to stop Muns or not."

"Yeah," Derick said. "I think he taught some good stuff there, but I can't just choose not to die."

THE
ANNOUNCEMENT

The marble hall, the gentlemen in doublets, the ladies in elaborate gowns, and the small orchestra all faded away. Several hundred students at Cragbridge Hall clapped and awaited the next number. Tonight the dance committee was putting the Bridge to very creative use. Abby's favorites had been dancing to Miles Davis playing jazz on his trumpet, watching and hearing a group of Ghanaians chant and dance together, and seeing the Beatles play at Shea Stadium.

Three-dimensional images of Polynesian men twirling torches appeared in the gym. The flames spun into what looked like full circles and the crowd gasped and cheered. A drumbeat pounded in the background and the students began to move to the rhythm.

Carol flung her hair and bounced up and down. "Best

dance everrrrrrrr!" she yelled over the music then threw her hands in the air and let out a scream of sheer delight. Guitar and bass entered into the song and the fire spinners whirled, threw, and caught their burning torches.

Abby was very glad she had used extra deodorant—not that girls sweat or anything. She bounced and shook next to Carol and a few other girls. They could only sit and think about her grandfather's message for so long. They needed a break, and the school always had a dance to announce the Race. Of course, knowing the announcement was coming made Abby nervous. Was Muns about to do something? Rafa's mother had been assured that security had it all under control.

Soon the fire twirlers faded and another scene came into view. It was a band on a beach. "Let's slow things down a bit," the long-haired singer called into his microphone, the guitarist beginning to pick out a melody.

Oh, no. A slow song. Abby had no idea who the band was, or the name of the song, but she knew it was a ballad.

"Um . . . do you want to dance?" It was a boy's voice, coming from somewhere behind her. Abby's heart beat faster. The music had only been playing for a few seconds. She didn't know whether to be scared that she was actually about to slow-dance with a boy or relieved that a boy had asked. At least she wasn't going to have to worry about awkwardly standing against the wall, watching all of her friends have a good time.

She turned around to see a boy with dark hair wearing a bright orange button-up shirt. And of course he had blue

eyes. But he wasn't looking at her. He was looking at a brunette standing next to Abby.

"Sure," the brunette answered and followed him a few
steps away from the group.

"I'm so excited to awkwardly waddle with a boy," Carol
said and began peering into the crowd. "Oh, no." She
palmed her forehead. "Looks like some girl snatched up
Derick before he could get to me." Abby found Derick in
the sea of dancing students, swaying side to side with a girl
with curly black hair and a red dress. Abby knew it was possible that Derick kind of liked the girl. She also knew it was
possible that in near-panic he had asked whatever girl was
closest to him to prevent Carol from snagging him.

"Um." Another boy had approached, a little shorter
than the last, this one with an olive complexion.

"Did you come over here to ask me to dance?" Carol
asked. "My answer is definitely yes! Let's boogie!" Abby
wasn't sure if the boy had intended to ask Carol or not, but
caught up in the whirlwind of her excitement, he strolled
out onto the dance floor with her. Carol looked back at
Abby over the boy's shoulder and mouthed the words
"Awkwardly waddling," and gave a thumbs-up.

Again a boy approached the group, and again he chose
someone other than Abby. Then another. Soon Abby was
the only one left. She didn't know whether to stand there
and hope someone would come, or pretend she needed a
drink or to go to the bathroom. She looked around. With
no boy prospects in sight, she started toward the door.

And then she saw Jacqueline, her former roommate who

had kicked her out of their room when she found out her grandfather had helped get Abby into the school. Jacqueline was dancing with a boy who looked a year or so older, maybe fourteen or fifteen. Jacqueline's eyes met Abby's and she led the boy toward her former roommate. "Hey, Abby," Jacqueline said, her black hair sleek and perfect, her smile beaming with teeth whiter than natural.

"Hey, Jacqueline," Abby responded.

Jacqueline looked around. "Why aren't you dancing?"

She wanted Abby to say it. Abby wished she could think of something clever to say, something that would send Jacqueline right back out on the dance floor, but she couldn't think of anything. She shrugged. "I didn't get invited." She forced herself to look directly at Jacqueline and not let her eyes fall toward the floor. She hoped she didn't look embarrassed.

"Huh," Jacqueline said, feigning surprise. "Better luck next time." She sounded nice enough, but the boy was listening. She turned with the boy to go back out to the dance floor, but when he was a couple of steps ahead of her and out of earshot, Jacqueline turned back. "The boys are smart here, Abby. They can tell what you are. I wouldn't expect any invites anytime soon." She flipped her hair and rejoined the boy.

Why did she have to do that? Abby felt bad enough, but now she didn't know whether to clench her teeth in anger, or her eyes to keep them from crying. She stepped out into the hall and didn't come back in until she heard the music start to fade.

Please, no more slow dances for a while.

The band on the beach faded, but nothing immediately replaced it. Abby and Carol found each other next to the refreshment table. The crowd started to grow restless.

An announcer's voice finally broke the silence. "Here to announce this year's competition are two of your student body officers, Sarah Ani and Landon Beane."

The crowd cheered as Sarah walked out onto the stage. She was several years older than Abby and wearing the blue blazer of Cragbridge Hall with a class officer patch beside her lapel. She had short, dark, hair and wore a super-cute peach skirt. Abby wanted one just like it. "Are you ready for the announcement?" Sarah asked, her voice amplified by a small microphone sticker she wore on her cheek. She cupped her hand to her ear. The crowd answered with a burst of noise. She seemed very confident in front of the audience.

Landon came running out onto the stage, raising his hands in the air to get the crowd to scream louder. It definitely worked. He wore a similar blazer and had blond, spiky hair.

Then image after image flashed on screens throughout the room. A falcon flying through the sky. A boy hooked up to an avatar suit. Someone climbing a mountain in the Arctic. A robot moving vertically up a wall. A group of students running from a furious giant in someone's virtual world. Someone riding a horse beside an army of Roman soldiers. "These are images of the Race from years past,"

Landon explained. "But who is ready for this year's challenge?" Again the crowd erupted.

"It is time," Sarah took over, "to introduce *this . . . year's . . . Race!*" She pronounced each of the last words with great power and enthusiasm.

Abby twisted her hair into a ponytail. Everyone else seemed thrilled, but Abby's heart pounded for a different reason. Was Muns's plan about to start? Was he about to strike and take hostages? She surveyed the raucous crowd, looking for anything unusual. She saw several security guards and robots at their posts. That brought a little comfort.

"Around the world," Landon whirled his finger, "there are celebrations in March: Heroes Day in Paraguay, independence days in Morocco, South Korea, Ghana, Tunisia, Cyprus, and Greece, St. Patrick's Day—there's even the NCAA basketball tournament. But no celebration, no challenge is a match for what happens here at Cragbridge Hall!"

More cheers, then a chant, "Race. Race. Race. Race. Race." It sounded primitive and tribal, but thrilling.

"For those of you in your first year here at Cragbridge Hall," Sarah explained, "the Race is a challenge in March every year. It is completely voluntary. If you want to compete, you can make your team as small or as large as you would like, though no team over twelve players or under four has ever won." Images of former winning teams flashed on the screens as the girl spoke. "Each team competes in four challenges, each requiring you to use your intelligence and the great inventions here at Cragbridge Hall to succeed." Scenes of students in high-tech suits, controlling robot animals appeared and disappeared. Then students searching through Bridge events, seeing history in 3-D. Next were students making their own virtual worlds and storing them on spheres. Plus a few things Abby had never seen before. There must be some inventions she didn't know about yet. "At the end of each round, half of the teams are eliminated. By the last event, a small number of teams compete for the championship."

"One of the best parts is that all four of the challenges are provided by you," Landon said, and paused for the yells of the crowd. "Students and groups of students have been working all year and have submitted their challenges. It makes for an amazing variety and a great time!" Landon paced back and forth on the front of the stage. "A committee of students and teachers pick the events—and then we see how you do. If you are the best, you get this!"

A student rushed to the stage and handed Sarah a trophy. It was immediately cast on the screens showing its black obsidian base with a collection of silver figurines on top: a boy thinking, a girl running, a lion roaring, and a humanoid robot reaching forward in an action pose. Each figure represented different possible elements of the challenge. "Each member of the winning team gets a trophy," Sarah explained. "Plus, winning looks great on a résumé. It shows your skill, intelligence, ingenuity, and willingness to work on a team. Team registrations begin tomorrow, the moment the last class ends," Sarah continued. "Be sure to gather your friends, your enemies, the kid who looks at you cross-eyed, whoever you think might have a chance of winning."

"And," Landon said, "there is always a secret prize that

goes along with winning the Race. One year, it was a weekend field trip through the city. Another year, it was three days off of school. And one year, there was actually permission to get an A in the class of your choice." The crowd especially cheered at the last reward. Another student brought him a small metal box. "This box is irreversibly programmed so that it cannot be opened except by the fingerprints of the team that wins. Every challenge is logged through our program and there are ways for us to verify each member of the team during each event." Landon shrugged. "Basically, there is no way to cheat." Wow. They took their prize very seriously. Of course if it was possible that winning the Race might help their grades, some students would do anything.

But it was what Landon said next that left Abby reeling: "And I can give you one hint about the secret prize." Sarah looked over at him in surprise. Perhaps she didn't know the hint. "This year, inside the box is a key." A picture of a simple metal key filled the screen. Abby stared at the image in disbelief. She looked at the design on the top of the keys and the series of notches along the bottom. There was no denying it. This wasn't just any key, but the same kind Abby kept in the secret compartment of her belt—a key that allowed her to interact with the past. "When the winning team presses their fingertips to the box, as it unlocks, it will automatically send them a message with a full explanation of the awards and opportunities your key will open."

"Trust me," Landon finished. "This will be better, more monumental, than any secret prize ever."

Abby swallowed hard.

DECISION

W ell, there it is," Derick said. "That had Muns written all over it."

Abby agreed, walking beside her brother and Carol. It felt great to be out of the hot and stuffy gym, but only on the outside. Abby's insides were scrambling.

"I guess there's a chance," Carol said, "that it's a completely different key and it just happens to look exactly like the most important keys in existence that protect one of the most powerful secrets ever." Derick and Abby looked at Carol incredulously. "You're right," Carol admitted. "It was completed, stamped, and signed by Dr. Doomsface himself."

"*Oi pessoal*," Rafa called out from behind them. "Wait up." He jogged to catch up, his dark ponytail bouncing on his shoulders. He hadn't been with them at the dance. He was a year older than them, after all, and had other groups of friends. "I bet I can guess what you're talking about."

Everyone nodded.

Abby looked around—the hallway was filled with other students walking. "Let's step into a study room." They followed her into a small room outside of the commons and closed the door behind them.

"Do you think they really have a key they are going to give away?" Rafa asked. No one sat on the chairs around the table.

"I don't know," Derick said. "But I guess we have to treat it like they do."

"How did Muns get a key?" Carol asked.

"I wish we knew," Abby said. "Does everyone here have theirs?"

Everyone nodded. They had all double-checked. "I sent a message to my mom too," Rafa said. "She has hers. She's checking with Mr. Sul about those on the other council."

"Good," Abby said. "We'll also have to double-check where we hid the others, but I can't imagine he had a way to find them." She blew out a breath of frustration. "But if we can find who got that key, we find someone on Muns's side."

"That's assuming someone didn't just give it to him," Derick said.

Whether someone working for Muns stole the key, or someone voluntarily gave it to Muns, Abby didn't like it.

"Back to the Race," Rafa said. "If the winners only get one key, they can't really change time, right?"

"True, but they also learn the secret," Derick said. "And that's a big deal."

"Wait, let me think this through," Carol said, lifting her hands.

"Um," Derick said. "You don't usually pause to think. You just talk."

"I didn't say I was going to think in my head," Carol clarified. "I think out loud: Only the team who wins the contest gets a key and learns the secret, right? Maybe they wouldn't even believe it. I mean, the idea that your grandpa discovered time travel and keeps the giant machine in a secret basement below the school *is* kind of crazy."

"It is," Derick agreed, and sat down in one of the chairs. Rafa followed his lead. "But it's also true. And chances are that they will at least be curious and check it out. Then we've got a group of students that we don't know if we can trust with a lot of power. And," he said, raising a finger, "nothing is going to stop them from sharing the secret with others."

"Not everyone is as good at keeping secrets as we are," Abby said, playing with the back of the seat in front of her.

"I'm really proud of myself for that, by the way," Carol added. "I love to talk, and this is a juicy secret, but I haven't told a soul." She shook her head.

"If word gets out," Abby said, "it could bring even bigger trouble."

"The more people that know," Derick said, "the more likely it is that some will side with Muns. Or there may be someone else like Muns who would do anything to control it."

Abby could only imagine what life would be like if that were the case. No thanks. This was stressful enough.

"Plus," Rafa said, "if the secret really did get out, the government could investigate. And they would probably come in and take everything. And who knows how they would use it. If someone was corrupt, we could be looking at world domination."

"I guess the main point is," Abby said, tucking the chair in front of her all the way under the table, "that if the secret gets out, someone is going to realize that the Bridge is the greatest weapon ever invented. If someone gets in your way, you could use it to go into the past and put them on a different course or even eliminate them. Or you could use it to enter the present. You can go anywhere, no limits. You can spy and find out anything, from government secrets to vault combinations. Of course you wouldn't need those because you could use the Bridge to go straight inside the safe, take the money, and come out again."

"We used it to rescue people," Derick added, "but others could assassinate, or kidnap, or fight wars. Really, they could do almost whatever they want."

"To sum up," Carol said, "if the secret gets out, we get a bunch of awful, nasty, icky, no-goodness." She grimaced and shook her hands.

"This has to be part of Muns's backup plan," Derick suggested. "Maybe if he gets the secret out to the winners, then he can bribe them to do what he wants." He ran his fingers through his dark hair.

"Or he can be a meanie-bucket and kidnap their family members and make them do it," Carol added.

"And whoever wins will be some of the most talented people at a school for the most talented people. The best of the best," Abby said.

Rafa cleared his throat. "If that is Muns's plan, then someone on the Race committee has to be working for him undercover, *certo*? Right? How else would they get a key in that box?"

"Yeah," Derick agreed. "We can get a list of them easily enough. I think it's the two students who announced it, a handful of teachers, and then the students whose challenges were picked. They can't participate because it would give them an unfair advantage."

"I've got it," Carol said, looking at the screens in her contact lenses. "Straight off the school site. I'm sending it to you now. Let's go all private eye and check into every one of them for anything suspicious. I'll take all the boys close to my age," she volunteered.

"Surprise," Derick said flatly. "I never would have seen that coming."

"If they're evil, I don't want anything to do with them," Carol defended herself. "That's a personal rule, 'Don't flirt with evil people.' But if they're not, well then, there might be some possibilities." She wiggled her eyebrows up and down.

"Maybe we should divide them up equally and try to

find out more about them," Abby said. "I just wish Grandpa and Mom and Dad were awake. They'd know how to handle all this."

"I do too," Derick said, and rubbed his eyes. "But they aren't, so we have to do our best. We could ask Mr. Sul about it too. He's an administrator."

"I'll have my mom contact him about that too," Rafa said. "He's probably worried about the same thing we are. He's probably already looking into it."

"I hope," Abby said. "But in the meantime, let's look into the list of people." They agreed and divided up the list. "And we'll continue working on Grandpa's challenges to see if the Bridge can be used to see the future. If we're able to know what's coming, that could make all the difference in the world." Abby looked at her brother, thoughts of what the girl from the future had said flooding her mind. Thoughts of her brother's death.

"And one more thing," Derick said, not meeting his sister's gaze. "There is a way we can control this situation." He exhaled slowly. "We could control who learns the secret by making our own team and winning the competition."

"Oh, yeah!" Carol said, pumping her fists and jumping up and down. "Let's do this!"

"That could be exactly what Muns wants," Abby said. "This is probably all a trap to get us to do just that."

"But even if it's a trap," Derick said, "I don't think we have a choice. We have to try to protect the secret."

"I think he's right," Rafa said. "I don't think sitting back and watching will do anyone any good. We have to actively try to stop this."

"But just the four of us couldn't win," Abby said. "There's no way." They would be going up against the brightest and most talented students in Cragbridge Hall.

"You're right," Derick said. "But I happen to know a group of really talented students who have been asking for some answers for a long time, and they may even deserve to know the secret."

Rafa nodded.

"The Crash," Abby said.

STOOP

Derick gazed out over Cragbridge Hall from the top of a three-story building. It was still a few minutes before twilight. Perfect. He moved to the edge and stepped off.

Falling only for a moment, Derick spread his four-foot wingspan and let it fill with air. His beak cut through the wind and his body glided through it, his wings moving with the currents. Usually, this was where he came for his peace, his time. He didn't visit his parents or his grandfather often like Abby did. He didn't like to see them helpless and pale. He soared over the school, letting the wind, the sheer joy of flying, calm him. This. This could quiet his mind. Even if students made noise below, it felt like they were a world away.

Derick knew he could only fly so far; the airspace was monitored. To have real security for the school, they couldn't have people able to simply skydive in. They also couldn't have avatar birds flying out. Sophisticated software tracked the robot birds' speed and altitude constantly; if their flight path neared the edge of campus, they received an instant warning. And if they continued, the avatar would shut down and drop from the sky before it could leave the walls. Because the school had realistic-looking animal robots, they had to protect them. If they didn't, there were many groups willing to exploit their possible uses.

The current shifted and Derick struggled to correct. His peregrine falcon dipped and bobbed for a moment before regaining full control. He was definitely still learning, but he loved to practice.

"Good recovery, *rapaz*," Rafa complimented. Derick saw another falcon tip smoothly to one side and arc through the air toward him. It had a white underbelly with dark spots. With its wings open, it looked like it had brown stripes on the underside of its wings and tailfeathers. The top of its body was dark. His Brazilian friend was in another avatar suit controlling another peregrine falcon. Derick could hear his voice because their real bodies were only feet away from each other. "You're improving fast."

"Thanks," Derick said. "I'm nothing like you yet, but I'm trying." No student was as good as Rafa. He grew up working with the avatars. They weaved back and forth on the currents, Rafa giving an occasional tip.

Derick knew the science of it. That was all part of the learning process. Because of the shape of the wing, more air pressure pushed up against the bottom of the wing than on the top. That's what gave him lift. And it was why engineers modeled airplane wings after birds' wings. Same principle. But Derick didn't think about the science as he flew. It was more about the feeling.

Out of nowhere two more falcons swooped down beside Derick and Rafa. Then another flew in a full loop while a final falcon dove through it. It took spectacular timing and grace, but they were all part of the Crash, the club of students that was the very best at avatars. They were used to doing the amazing.

"Y'all started early," one of the falcons said in a Southern drawl.

"Hey, Malcolm," Derick said. "I was just getting in some extra practice."

"Good," a Latina responded. Maria. It had taken some practice, but now Derick could recognize everyone by voice. Of course, the robot animals themselves didn't talk. He could hear the students' voices because they had joined him and Rafa in the same room in the lab in their high-tech suits, harnessed to fly. "I think today's the day," Maria said.

"The day for what?" Derick asked.

"You'll see," another falcon said, flying in next to them. It was Piper. "Let's go to the tower." Piper flew out, leading the group.

"Okay," Derick submitted. "But Rafa and I have something important to ask all of you."

"Oh, really?" Malcolm answered, pulling out ahead of Derick and just to the side of Piper. "That's really funny, because we've been asking you important questions for over a month now. And you're always stalling." They flew toward the center of the school.

"Yeah," Nia, another member of the Crash, agreed. "When are you going to tell us exactly what went on back in the lab?"

"Um," Derick stalled.

"You know," Piper said. "The day a bunch of soldiers invaded campus and an avatar bull tried to kill you. And somehow your grandfather, your parents, and four teachers ended up in comas. I'd think you'd remember something like that; I know I have a tough time trying to forget."

When things had looked the bleakest, Derick had called the Crash in to help and they had saved his life. Derick and Rafa had told them how Rafa's mother was a key inventor of the avatars and that others had been after her. That part was true, but they hadn't mentioned anything about the Bridge and the secret behind it. The Crash suspected Derick hadn't told the whole story.

"Ever since then, there's a lot more security around this place," Piper said. "Like the tower." Usually the Watchman was the highest point of the school—a tower rising from the top of the commons building. But over the past month, security had built a steel tower and installed equipment meant to protect and control electronic transmissions and to strengthen their monitoring of the airspace. Each falcon landed on a beam near the top. It took Derick three tries; he kept missing and overcorrecting. Finally, he stood with his talons curled around the top of a beam nearly six stories in the air.

"And like that guy," Malcolm pointed a talon at a security officer standing on the corner of the roof of the building, looking down at the commons below. He was only one of many. A security bot rolled on its one wheel along the wall near the guard.

"Have you finished the challenges I gave you?" Derick asked.

"Some of them," Nia said. "I studied George Washington for several hours yesterday, but I don't see what he has to do with anything."

"The challenge is about having the same kind of character as great people in history before I can tell you the secret," Derick said. "Plus, the secret's not completely mine to tell. When my grandfather wakes up, he'll know how to handle this. I'm just trying to get you ready."

The falcons all looked at each other. "The same answer," Malcolm said. "My mama would tell me to find friends who don't keep secrets from me."

"Actually, what I'm going to ask of you may help answer some of those questions," Derick said.

"It doesn't sound like you're going to tell us anything," Maria said. "Let's do this first." The Crash practiced as a club a few times a week. They had taught Derick well and he was having a lot of fun, but he noticed they were giving him harder and harder challenges. Perhaps that was their way of getting back at him for not answering their questions.

One of the falcons turned its piercing eyes toward Derick. "Would you like to know one of the coolest things about peregrine falcons?" Nia asked.

"Right now, I'm just thrilled to be in one and able to fly," Derick said.

"Well, I'm not sure all of what you were doing was flying," Piper said. "Some of it was flopping, and a little of it was falling."

"Falcons can fly up to sixty miles per hour," Malcolm explained, "but that's not in a stoop."

"What's a stoop?" Derick asked.

"A stoop is when a falcon dives for its prey," Piper explained.

"And then they can go up to 200 miles per hour," Maria said, then whistled. "That's fast! Shall we give it a shot?"

"200 miles an hour? Is that safe?" Derick asked.

"It's not about being safe," Malcolm answered. "It's about hunting, getting food. It's about being focused and not holding yourself back at all. It's about really *being* a peregrine falcon."

"So amazing," Derick said. He could only imagine what it would be like to dive at that speed.

"And for you, it's about keeping a secret from us," Maria added, a bit of a kick to her voice.

"I would try to defend you," Rafa said, "but I think you can stoop."

"Just dive and don't hold back," Malcolm instructed in his Southern drawl. And then he leaped off the tower and dove. Two others joined him.

Derick stared in awe as they rocketed toward the ground. Every fraction of a second they increased in speed. They fell faster and faster. At the last moment, they pulled up just above the ground, then glided up into the sky. It looked easy and graceful, but Derick knew it would be terrifying.

Then Rafa and Piper stooped together. Again, the same reckless speed and again, they tilted their wings and ran parallel to the ground at the last second. Both birds glided in wide arcs until they had turned around and looked up at him.

Derick looked down. This was crazy. It was awesome and amazing, but also crazy. Then the chanting started. "Stoop. Stoop. Stoop. Stoop."

So much for flying being a way he could relax and find peace.

Derick wasn't one to back away from a challenge, nor was he one that was easily scared, but his mouth was definitely dry. "All right, Hayabusa," Derick whispered to his robot falcon. He liked to name his avatars. *Hayabusa* was the Japanese word for peregrine falcon, but also the name of a motorcycle that had been the fastest in its time. The second fastest had been named "Blackbird." The company had named their bike "Hayabusa" because falcons hunt blackbirds. "Let's give this a shot." He leaned forward and dove.

He had jumped off high dives before. He had jumped off cliffs into lakes. He had felt the tug of gravity, but this was different. This was embracing it, letting it drive you toward the ground with all it had.

"Don't try to get too close to the ground on your first go," Nia said. "If you don't pull up in time, you're going to destroy the falcon avatar and be in serious trouble with Rafa's mom." Rafa's mother not only invented the avatars, but was in charge of the avatar department at Cragbridge Hall and had to fix them when they were damaged.

The wind ripped across his face, but with a beak and an aerodynamic head, it didn't feel the same; he sliced through it. He was made for this, or more accurately, the robot falcon was. He tucked his feet in and felt himself careening toward the ground. Derick tried to let out an excited scream, but he lost most of the air from his lungs a few feet into the dive.

"Yeah! He's doing it!" Malcolm screamed. "You're invincible. *In-vinc-i-ble!*"

Derick fell faster.

"Okay, now!" Rafa called out. "Open up your wings and plane out, but be ready, because it's going to be fast."

Derick could do this. He kept his dive.

"Derick," Rafa said.

"Now, Derick," Piper commanded.

The ground grew closer, larger. It was only seconds away.

Just a little more . . .

Now!

Derick opened his wings and felt the wind catch them. It jolted him more than he had expected. He'd thought it would be like brakes, slowing him down; instead, it just redirected him, still traveling at full speed. He veered left and then right, trying at speed to figure out how to dodge the Hall, the main building on campus. Right, right was the right direction. He wheeled and began to climb, skimming an exterior wall and feeling his speed taper off just enough to regain control. It's one thing to dive at great speed; it's another thing entirely to try to navigate. He turned in a large curve, still gliding, gradually slowing down, then rose toward the others who were perched on top of the building. Of course, when Derick tried to land, he toppled over, frantically catching the beam below him with one talon and scrambling to remain upright.

"The kid can stoop," Maria said. "But the flying after was a little crazy—and he can't land."

Derick was glad robot falcons couldn't show a red face.

"Hey, I remember that you couldn't turn right for a while, only left," Malcom said, pointing at another falcon with one of his wings.

"That's not true," Maria countered.

"I know," Malcolm said. "But I thought it would be funny." He let out a rumbling chuckle, his deep voice laughing at his own joke. "And it was."

"All right," Nia said, her dark-tipped beak pointing at Derick, "You impressed me enough. What did you want to ask?"

"Let's talk face to face," Derick said.

The group flew their birds into an opening in the roof of the avatar lab building, turned them in to be logged and stored with the other avatars, and then they unhooked their harnesses and gathered in an avatar lab classroom. It was designed for instruction, surrounded with harness stalls and large screens at the front where those in the room could watch what the animal avatars were doing.

Derick looked at his friends. Malcolm was the largest of the bunch, standing at least four inches taller than Rafa. He was also sixteen and had black skin, broad shoulders, and short dreadlocks hanging down onto his forehead. He had played a lot of football in Oklahoma and looked it.

Maria was shorter, seventeen, with long black hair she wore almost to her waist. Her face was round and she had big brown eyes. She wore a dress, which seemed a bit formal, but it was her usual attire.

Piper and Nia both were about average height, but Piper had red hair and wore a bright blue T-shirt. Nia had blonde hair and wore a black warm-up suit that had flames on the sleeves and legs. Piper was sixteen and Nia fifteen.

"Okay," Derick said. "I'm sorry I haven't been able to tell you much, but you need to understand that Rafa and I know something that—" he chose his words carefully, "is powerful, but potentially dangerous. And it can only be shared with those that can be trusted."

"Um," Nia said, "I think the fact that we saved your life tells you that we can be trusted."

"Yes," Derick said, "I trust you."

"*Eu tambem*. So do I," Rafa added. "But we need you to be patient."

"Yeah, that's easy for you to say," Maria piped in, pointing at Rafa. "You know just as much as Derick." She shifted, cocking one hip.

"Finding out a secret," Rafa said, "can be quite a burden."

"And like I've told you over and over," Derick said, "it's my grandfather's secret, so under normal circumstances, he should decide who knows and when."

"And your point is?" Piper asked.

"We think someone else may have found out the secret," Rafa explained.

"And that's bad?" Malcolm guessed.

"Real bad," Derick confirmed. "We think it may be what they're offering as the grand prize to the Race winners."

"Interesting," Maria said, stroking her chin. "The key has something to do with it." She paced in the avatar lab, pointing her toes with each step. "Well, one of us is bound to find out what it is. We've all been recruited by some of the best teams. Chances are that one of our teams will win and we'll find out the secret."

"That's the thing," Derick said, rubbing his chin. "If it were up to me, I'd be fine with you guys finding out, but not necessarily members of other teams. This really is a big deal, and we have to know that we can trust those who find out the secret."

"So, what are y'all asking us to do?" Malcolm asked.

Derick looked at Rafa.

"What if we formed our own team?" Rafa proposed. "All of the Crash together. Then, if we win, you could learn the secret and we could prevent anyone else from finding out about it."

The members of the Crash exchanged looks. "It's not a bad idea," Piper said, shaking her head, her red hair bouncing. "But we'd need more than just us to win the Race. I mean, obviously, we'd have avatars covered, but there's a lot more we would need."

"We'd all probably be pretty good at physical events,"

Malcolm said. He lifted his arms and flexed. "Maybe you're not as good as me, but I think we could hold our own."

"Oh, yeah?" Nia said, and flexed in the exact same position. "I'm pretty sure our muscles are about the same size."

Piper snickered. Then it spread to the whole group.

"That's right," Nia said, confidently hanging on to her joke.

"Oh, yeah?" Malcolm said. "Can you do this?" He walked over and lifted a large wooden desk off the ground, then past his waist, and finally over his head. He slowly put it back in front of Nia.

"Maybe," Nia said. "Maybe not. But can you do this?" She glanced over her shoulder to make sure nothing was in the way, then did three back handsprings in a row. Her warm-up suit swished as she moved. Obviously, she had trained as a gymnast.

"You can always try this, Malcolm," Maria said. She took three graceful steps and then began spinning on one foot, over and over, like a ballerina on stage.

"Show-offs," Piper said. "I don't have an ice rink to join the 'look at me' party." She had been a figure skater back home.

"Anyway," Malcolm said, "even if you're not as buff and good-looking as I am, everyone here is pretty good with the physical stuff. So that would be in our favor. I'm also one of the top in my class at geography. It's one of the reasons I got into this place. I've traveled a lot, climbed mountains, rappelled down slot canyons, camped in deserts . . . My parents really like that stuff. I'm also decent in math, but nothing too impressive."

"I've got math down," Nia said. "Plus I'm buff and better looking than Malcolm." She flexed again and stuck out her tongue at Malcolm. "And I'm good at physics and astronomy."

"I can dance," Maria said, which was rather obvious after her demonstration. "I'm fluent in Spanish, and I'm good at both Spanish and English literature. And I'm not bad at biology."

"Wow, look at all you people good at other stuff," Piper said. "Are we listing all our strengths now? Is this some sort of contest?"

"No," Rafa said. "But I think it's a good idea to see what we're good at. It will give us an idea if we could win."

"Well, then," Piper said, "I've played the guitar for the last six years, but I really doubt they are going to have a classical guitar showdown, so chalk that up as useless."

"You never know," Rafa said.

"What I'm probably best at outside of avatars is robotics," Piper said. "I mean, that's obviously related to the avatars, but I can help build and program robots to do simple tasks." She looked at Rafa and then Derick. "But I'm not good enough to be our expert. We need someone really good if we want to win. Robotics are really popular for challenges. I think we need Jess Maughn."

"I've heard that Jess is the best," Malcolm said.

"Hey, that rhymed," Piper said. "Malcolm, are you and Nia going to have a poetry showdown now?"

"Very funny," Malcolm said.

"I'd do it for money," Nia rhymed, a smile crossing her face. "And buy a bunny and live where it's sunny."

Maria gave Nia a friendly slap on the arm to get her to be quiet.

"Don't try to stop me, honey," Nia continued.

"If we decide to do this," Piper said, "I could invite Jess. Because I'm showing some promise, she's helped me out on a few projects."

Everyone looked at Derick. "First off," Derick answered, "before we worry about anyone else—are you guys in? Will you be part of a team with me?"

"That may depend on whether or not we get the other important people we need," Malcolm said.

"And do we really need Jess before we can win?" Derick asked.

"Definitely," Piper said.

"Plus, we still need someone who is good at using the Bridge," Nia pointed out.

"Actually," Rafa said, "I think we may have that covered."

Derick cleared his throat. "Um. Well. There are two more people that already know the secret," he said. "My twin sister, Abby, and her friend Carol."

"No offense," Malcolm said, "but they're seventh graders. I doubt they know enough to really help us."

"I know," Derick said, "but they are really good with the Bridge. They've practiced more than most." He looked over at Rafa and they shared a knowing look. There was no way he was going to tell them all that Abby and Carol had done.

"But what may be their better asset is that they're good at challenges, at figuring out clues and puzzles. I think they're a natural fit for the team." Maybe he was overselling them, but he was hoping the Crash would go for it.

"Maybe," Maria said, "but we would also need a virtuality expert."

"I'm not bad," Derick said.

"It's true," Rafa said. "He made a virtual samurai world that's impressive." He mocked a few sword swipes.

"And Abby and Carol aren't bad either," he said.

"I'm sure that's true," Piper said. "But if we really want to win, we need the very best. And the very best is Anjum. If we don't have him on our team, I'm not sure we can beat him."

Malcolm nodded. He obviously knew who Piper was talking about. "He won last year, didn't he?"

"Yep," said Piper. "I was on his team. He's the best at virtuality, but he's also a team leader. Really intense, but a good leader. He'll bring out the best in all of us if we'll listen to him."

Again, Derick checked with Rafa, who nodded. "Okay," Derick said, "if we can get Jess and Anjum on our team, will you join up?"

They all looked at each other, then Malcolm nodded. "If you can get those two, I'm in."

"Me too," Maria said.

The others also agreed.

"Great," Derick said. "Any ideas how we can persuade Anjum and Jess?"

BETTER THAN BRILLIANCE

Abby tried to stay far back enough from Landon Beane that he wouldn't know she was following him, but close enough that she wouldn't lose him. She had investigated teachers she suspected of wrongdoing before, but to be following someone a few years older than her felt weird.

He moved down the hall saying hello to many of the students on the way, giving high fives and even hugs. He was definitely a people person. But two halls down, he stepped into a teacher's office and closed the door behind him.

Why was a student body officer visiting a teacher after hours? For homework troubles? Or for something more devious?

Abby casually walked by and read the plaque outside the office: Mr. Silverton, Computer Science.

"Sure, you get to follow the handsome student body officer while I get the bald computer science teacher. No fair."

Abby turned to see Carol leaning against a wall.

"So Mr. Silverton is on our list too?" Abby asked.

"Yep," Carol said. "He's on the Race committee. The question is, 'Is this official Race business? Or are they up to something evil?'" Carol said, changing her voice to sound like a conspiratorial narrator on a webseries.

"I wish there was a way we could tell," Abby said.

"We could just knock and ask," Carol suggested.

They waited for several more minutes. Finally, Landon exited. The lines in his brow were deep. What had he and Mr. Silverton talked about?

"Hey, Jessica!" Landon called out, his expression quickly brightening. It was as though all his worry vanished. He walked a few more steps, then looked directly at Abby and Carol. "Hey, girls," he said, and continued on down the hall.

"Did he know we were following him?" Abby whispered.

"Um, I didn't get to follow him," Carol corrected. "I was stuck with baldy, remember?"

Abby gestured for Carol to lower her voice. Landon was probably well out of earshot, but they should still be careful. "Yeah," Abby said, "but we can't follow him now. He'll either know we're spying on him or he'll think we're silly stalker girls."

"Though I'm still game for following him around, I think you've got a point," Carol said. Realizing their cover may have been blown, Abby and Carol returned to Grandpa Cragbridge's lab.

Abby walked around the edge of the large room and paused to look at a visor charger. "Hopefully, we'll be better at figuring this out than we were with Landon and Mr. Silverton."

"Landon might not have really even known we were following him," Carol said. "Maybe he just saw two very attractive thirteen-year-old girls and wanted to say hi."

"First off," Abby said, "that's kind of gross. He's got to be at least seventeen. We are way too young for him. Secondly, I don't think he's just naturally going to pay attention to us."

"Whatever," Carol said, waving Abby off. How was she so confident? Abby didn't think there was any way Landon was just being friendly. He knew.

"So, back to finding out about the Bridge and the future," Abby said, looking back toward the large desk in the center of the lab. "The last thing Grandpa said was something about making the most of our choices."

"Maybe he just wants us to not bother him anymore and go have awesome lives," Carol suggested.

"We can't do that," Abby said, blinking several times. "Unless that crazy message from the future is wrong, my brother is going to . . ." Tears welled up in Abby's eyes. "Derick's going to die in a week. I have to figure out how to stop this."

"Don't cry, because then I'll cry," Carol said, waving her hands in front of her eyes, trying to dry the forming tears.

The two sniffled for a few moments and took deep breaths. It was better if they didn't think about it and focused on what they could do.

"Okay." Abby wiped her eyes. "Let's keep going." She looked around the office at bits of her grandfather's inventions. "Maybe we should think about why he wants us in his lab. That might be important."

"Good point," Carol said.

The two girls began to wander the room, looking at the inventions and parts and charts for any clue as to what they should do next. Abby looked at a virtual booth. Her grandpa hadn't invented that, but had added the connection between the visors, the mind, and the booth so it was possible to be immersed in a virtual world. She thought of Derick's samurai world. *No. No thinking about Derick right now.* Abby moved on to the metalworking machine in the corner. She didn't think her grandpa had invented it either, but he used it to make the lockets, and boxes, and even some of the secret compartments. He truly knew how to do many things.

She walked to another booth, a booth she knew was connected to the real Bridge in the basement. "It's interesting that my grandpa made so many great inventions, but they've gotten us into all this trouble."

"Yeah," Carol agreed. She was looking at a large chart on the wall covered with equations.

Something about standing in her grandfather's office made Abby feel wrong about what she had said. That may not be how he would look at it at all. "Or maybe they haven't," she said. "Maybe this *is* all going to turn out for the best. Maybe our trial is going to make us stronger."

"You totally sound like your grandpa right now," Carol said.

Abby laughed. "I do sound like him, don't I?" She walked back toward the large desk in the center of the room. As she did, the cane she carried in her pack flashed a few numbers and the desk once again revealed the metal objects. Abby looked at her friend, then back down at the objects. Her eyes fell on the star and the bowl and then the other metal items. She didn't want to touch any of them without a pair of gloves. "Wait. So these were the choices my grandpa gave us, right?"

"Yeah."

Abby looked back at the invention that made lockets and other metal items. "We are supposed to 'make the most' of them. Maybe that's not metaphorical. Maybe we're really supposed to make something good out of them."

"What? Oh!" Carol said as she looked in the corner at the metal shop machine. "That just might be it."

They both walked over to the machine. Abby synced into its console. "I haven't done anything like this before," she admitted.

"Me neither," Carol said. "Metal shop is an elective and I definitely elected not to do it."

"It looks like there are various settings," Abby said, "depending on how much work you want to do by hand and how much by machine. We can even craft our own molds and make other metal objects."

"Could we melt down one of the objects from your grandpa's desk to do it?"

"Let's give it a shot," Abby said. She began to fiddle with the settings she'd found through her rings. She could design three-dimensionally. Using her rings, she formed a sphere in the design matrix, then stretched it, thinned it, made it thicker. Each hand motion did something different.

"Is this going to take a while?" Carol asked.

"I'm not sure," Abby said, still manipulating the program. "I've never done this before."

"Okay," Carol said. "I'm going to go visit the metal shop to see if I can make a pattern there, save it, and bring it back here. Maybe I can ask the teacher some questions if I need to."

"Sounds great," Abby said. "Sync up if you need anything."

Within moments, Abby was alone in her grandfather's lab. She was trying to make something worthwhile, trying to learn about the power of the future in the same room where the greatest inventor who ever lived had worked on some of his most amazing inventions. She thought back over her time with her grandfather. He got her into this school. Though she didn't have the grades for it, he said she had heart, that she faced her fears and didn't quit trying. He said that was a trait that some of the most talented people in the world could look up to. He believed in her. He said she had something to offer.

Heart.

Abby paced for a moment. Maybe that's what she would

make—a heart. Maybe she could decide that no matter what the future held, she could face it. She could keep trying. That felt right, like something Grandpa would want.

Abby went to work. She programmed as best she could, pulling the shape into the form she envisioned. She didn't make it precise or symmetrical. That would be too perfect for her. She selected a simple predesigned chain to make it into a necklace.

Once she had it all designed, she clicked the button for the machine to make it. The machine synced to her rings and a message appeared.

> **Warming up.**
> **Insert desired metal into the holding area.**

A drawer in the thick, safe-like container beneath the console opened.

Abby looked back at the objects on Grandpa's desk. At first she grabbed the bowl; it was the shape that had rewarded her. But that wasn't how her life had been. She'd had to work for what she achieved. She'd been through pain. She'd faced the difficult. She put on a glove and grabbed the star. It vibrated in her hands as it tried to shock her. That was more like her life so far—one shock after another.

She dropped the object into the holding area, hoping the heart wouldn't come out with the ability to shock. It slowly closed.

> **Ready?**

No. She wasn't. Her life had been like that shocking star.

She returned to her design and added a star to the front of her heart, long and short rays of light reaching out from it in all directions. Like a small firework. It didn't look half bad.

She approved her design, and the machine began to do its work. It heated up and began to move and shake.

Grandpa appeared, walking toward the corner of his office that held the metal shop machine. "Very good. Because we can't see the future, no one makes perfect choices all the time. In fact, even if we could see the future, I doubt we could make perfect choices. But after we make a choice, make the most of it. Learn from it. Choose to take the difficult and make something worthwhile out of it."

He took a few more steps, his cane in hand. "Another lesson of the future is that trying once is rarely good enough. You must keep at it. It is a game of diligence. Being steady is better than genius. Trying invincibly day after day is better than small moments of brilliance."

Abby liked that. It felt true. Of course she probably liked it more because she could try; she could press forward. And she didn't feel like she'd had too many moments of brilliance.

Grandpa looked back at the objects. "Remember, try over and over again. You have some work to do."

Oh, no. That was probably literal. In true Grandpa style, she'd have to prove she could try, over and over again. She had to make object after object into something worthwhile.

And she still didn't have her answer.

ANJUM

I f we hadn't decided to make our own team, someone would have fixed their awesome detector," Carol
said, "and figured out that we are off the scale." She did a
short celebration dance, including a heel click at the end.
"Someone would have invited us to be on their team."

"I'm not sure heel clicks have ever been a sign of awesome," Abby said.

"Oh, yeah they are," Carol said, and did a few more.

"I'm still nervous about Muns," Abby admitted. "And I
wish we knew why Landon and Mr. Silverton met up."

"Me too," Carol said. "I also wish we had finished
changing those objects."

Abby did too, but right now, they had to convince
Anjum he wanted to be on their team for the Race. They
both walked to the booths where they could be part of the

virtual meeting. Anjum had set it up and chosen the virtual location. Everyone invited to be on the team was going to meet together.

Abby put on her visor and suit and entered the code with her rings. As soon as the virtual world appeared, she gasped in surprise. Her feet were off the ground. She was hanging in the air, completely weightless.

It was disorienting at first, but she saw several other students floating inside the large room. The girls' hair stood out like large tufts of cotton candy. Maria's hair was especially crazy; her long dark locks that normally rested on her back nearly down to her waist were now floating straight up at least a foot and a half above her head. It looked like she was standing on a huge fan. Piper's red hair looked like a big red shrub on the top of her head. Malcolm's dreadlocks spiked outward in every direction. Even Rafa's ponytail stood up in the back.

Abby waved to everyone. Of course she knew her brother and Rafa. She had also met the members of the Crash and remembered their names, though it took a moment with Nia. Just next to her, though, was someone she didn't know—a rather tall girl with a thin nose and blonde hair.

"Hi, I'm Abby," she introduced herself and offered her hand.

The girl nearly whispered back, "Jess," and smiled a big uncomfortable smile. She didn't shake Abby's hand. Abby always felt shy, but Jess was another level of timid.

Abby felt her own hair floating wild while she surveyed

her surroundings. Her mouth dropped open. One large wall was nothing but window, and Abby stared out at a huge planet, an endless expanse of stars surrounding it. She recognized the planet, but it took several seconds to completely grasp the wonder of it. She was floating in a zero-gravity room on a space station orbiting Jupiter. Bands of varying colored gases stretched across the world, with a swirling red spot toward the bottom. Abby stared, transfixed by the spectacular scene. She thought she could pick out moons moving in orbit.

"So incredible!" Carol said. "Seriously, I don't know what to say, except: *beautiful* and *crazy* and *awesome* and . . . who transported me into *space*? I'm not complaining. It's ridiculously amazing. I'm just wondering what's going on." She spoke as fast as ever.

"Hello, girls," a boy's voice said. He had a thick Indian accent. Abby turned to see a boy with dark skin and black hair. He pushed off a wall and slowly floated toward them. "I'm Anjum. Welcome to my version of outer space."

"You *built* this?" Abby asked, steadying herself with a handhold.

"Yes," he said with a nod. "I'm decent at putting together virtual environments. It is, of course, based on real Space Agency footage. If you count, you'll find all sixty-four of Jupiter's moons." He gestured out the large window.

"Well I give you an A," Carol said. "A+++ . . . and some extra credit . . . and some cookies. But I guess here they'd have to be virtual cookies and they wouldn't be nearly as

cool. Except—if they were virtual, you could taste them, but not actually gain the calories. Oh, that would be genius."

"Thanks," Anjum said, letting out a high-pitched laugh, which was a bit shrill and grating on the ears. "But I don't think a grade from *you* will help me much—or your virtual cookies. No offense." He laughed again.

"So is this the team?" Carol asked. Abby had no idea how Carol could walk into a room of strangers—or, in this case, float into a virtual room—and act as if everyone was her best friend. "All right, let's get to winning the Race."

"Let's not jump to any conclusions," Anjum said. "I assumed you were here to ask me to be on your team."

"I thought we weren't jumping to conclusions," Carol said, pointing at Anjum and winking.

Anjum laughed. "Very good. Very quick. I apologize. *Is* that what you are here for?" He spoke fast, but not as fast as Carol. Few people did.

"No," Carol said. "We're putting together a dance party and we were wondering if you have any interest in dressing up as Elvis or a disco king. Oh, or maybe doing a riverdance."

"Sorry about her," Abby said. She could see concern on the others' faces. They were worried that Carol was spoiling everything, and frankly, Abby was too. "We *are* asking you to be on our team."

"Yes," Derick said, pushing off the wall toward Anjum. He overshot a little and Anjum had to move across a rail to keep Derick from colliding into him.

"That's interesting," Anjum said. "And much more

99

tempting than the dance party." He smiled at Carol. "I don't dance."

"What? Who doesn't—" Abby cupped her hand over Carol's mouth before she could finish.

Anjum kept talking. "I have been busy assembling my own team. Of course, Rafa and Jess, you know this." Rafa and Jess both nodded, though Jess's was so subtle you could barely see it. Obviously he had invited them. "And to be frank," Anjum continued, "I believe my team will win again, so you don't have much chance of persuading me."

"Before you decline," Rafa said, "you should know that the team we are proposing is my first priority. And if the Crash is all on one team, we will likely beat you in any avatar events."

Anjum nodded. "Yes, you would." He tapped his finger on his cheek. "That's a really strange move. It's like you're shooting the moon. It would obviously give you an overwhelming advantage in a few events, but you would lack strength in others." He looked at the team. "I understand why Derick would be on the team. He's in the Crash. But why these two?" He pointed at Abby and Carol. "Why invite two unproven seventh graders? Won't they just get in the way?" He tilted his head a little toward the girls, but not enough to throw his floating body off-balance. "No offense. I'm just speaking frankly."

Derick looked like he was going to say something, but Rafa spoke first. "We like to work together." He had definitely taken the lead in the discussion. That was probably smart since Anjum had tried to recruit him; he might have some extra influence. "And you'd be surprised what those girls are capable of."

"No—really," Anjum said. "I did my research before we met, and they don't have much to offer. Again, no offense."

"Oh, yeah?" Carol said. "Well, you're not very nice and probably don't have much to offer on the dance floor." She broke out into a few moves, which she had to modify since she was floating. No offense." She giggled. "I kind of like this. It's like we can say whatever we want and then just put 'no offense' on the end of it."

Anjum smiled. "She does have spunk." He gazed at the rest of the team. "If by chance, I were to accept, you need to know that *I* run the team. *I* make the decisions. Like all good leaders, I do welcome your thoughts, and in fact, will rely upon them—but I'm in charge." He watched them carefully for reactions.

"We thought you'd say that," Rafa said. "And yes, we're prepared to let you lead."

Anjum nodded. He didn't say anything for nearly a minute.

"Well, I guess we'd better get going and let you think about it," Carol said. "But the correct answer is *yes!*"

When Anjum didn't respond, everyone started waving good-bye. It would only take a flick of a finger to get out of the virtual meeting.

Anjum raised his hand. "Here is where I stand. If Jess and the Crash are in, I am tempted. However, I'm still not sure about the seventh-grade girls. I have a few names I'd suggest to replace them."

"No offense." Carol said the phrase before Anjum could. "We know."

"No," Derick said. "They're on the team."

Anjum thought some more. "Jess?"

Jess smiled wider than the situation called for and she mumbled, "I'm in if you are. But if not, I'll probably walk." That was the most they'd heard her say.

Anjum nodded. "There is a stipulation to the Race," Anjum said. "And that is that if a team chooses, they can release up to three players of a team and replace them during the games. Of course, their replacements can't be from any other team." He unconsciously moved himself up and down in the zero gravity. "The rule exists to save a team when members get sick or have emergencies, but I know the rules well. I know the loopholes. I'll join your team, but if Abby and Carol mess up significantly even once, or if they hold us back, they're off the team."

Abby took a deep breath.

"Wow," Carol said. "No pressure."

"No offense," Anjum added.

SUSPECTS

Right on!" Carol said, once again standing in Rafa's mother's office. "I'm ready to win the key, protect the secret, get that awesome trophy, and flash a killer smile when I'm standing on the podium." She waved and beamed, then pretended to be handed a trophy. She took a bow, and when she came up, she had tears in her eyes. She *was* a decent actress.

"I'm still nervous about messing up," Abby confessed, sitting next to an array of robot fingers. "Because if Anjum replaces us, someone else gets the key and finds out the secret. Or what if we're on the team and we don't win? Then an entirely different team finds out the secret." Derick hoped his sister could relax and do well. She had done it before.

"Let's not worry about that now," Rafa's mother said,

sitting on a tall work chair near a lab table. "You'll do fine. That's assuming I don't sense it's too dangerous and pull you from the contest." She looked at each of them intently, then sighed. "In the meantime, we were all assigned to look into those on the committee," she said, changing the subject. "What did you find?"

"I haven't had a lot of time," Carol said. "And I'm still disappointed that you assigned me to the bald guy and a girl. Abby and I found that Landon and Mr. Silverton were meeting together. We really didn't find out any more than that. I think Landon might have realized we were following him. Sarah, the girl who announces the Race, doesn't seem that into it, really. I mean, she volunteered to emcee, but she's never played on a team and didn't submit any of the challenges."

"I looked into Mrs. Flink," Rafa said. "She's a biology teacher and seems to be pretty wrapped up in her work. I haven't found anything suspicious yet, but she's been very busy. I remember that she was there when we first met Mr. Sul. I think she may have a key." Derick used his rings to find Mrs. Flink's picture on the faculty page. He recognized her bushy red hair. He had seen her that day too.

"I looked into a few of mine," Rafa's mother said. "Oh, excuse me." She typed on her rings. "I just got a video message from Mr. Sul." She looked at them. "I asked him to investigate the key being offered as the prize in the Race. I see no harm in watching this all together. We need all our minds on this. I'll put it on the screen." With a few more movements of her fingers, Mr. Sul's introductory message appeared.

> Please watch the attached video message. And forgive the fact that you have to go through several layers of security to open it.

Rafa's mother did have to go through several layers of security. Not only did she need to put in several passwords, but she had to have her rings authenticated and scanned for viruses. The message must be important.

Finally, Mr. Sul appeared on the video screen. He was an Asian man with dark hair that hung just below his ears. "Hello, I apologize for all my precautions, but you'll understand why in a moment." He clasped his hands together. "We have some serious concerns. Those concerns have led me to make some difficult decisions. You see, when Jefferson and Hailey Cragbridge were left unconscious, my Council of the Keys became quite small." Just hearing his parents' names made Derick tense. He knew that they had been members of the other council. Grandpa had probably put them there so he was sure he had people he could trust in both councils. Now they were unconscious. He hoped Mr. Sul was trustworthy.

"The information I'm about to show you," Mr. Sul continued, "makes me wonder if a few members of my council should be considered suspects. Normally I would work hard to keep the other members anonymous, but under the circumstances, if they are somehow involved, I want you to be prepared to help us."

Mr. Sul took a deep breath. "Two of the members of my council also serve on the Race committee. They immediately launched their own investigation and, of course, I had many questions of my own. I apologize for the delay, but it took us a while to gather all of our information. I share this video hoping that it may help us prevent a tragedy."

Derick noticed he was clenching his fists nervously. The next video opened. He saw two people sitting at a table looking back at Mr. Sul: Mrs. Flink and Mr. Silverton. Mrs. Flink spoke first, "As a committee, we decided on a prize and cleared it through the administrators, but it had nothing to do with a key."

Mr. Silverton, the computer science teacher, nodded his bald head. "So we were as surprised as you with Landon Beane's announcement about the prize. I've met with him several times about it." That might have been what Carol and Abby saw. "You see, I made a secure channel for the committee to send messages back and forth to one another. Students have been known to try to hack in to get advance information about the Race. It is not uncommon for us to send several messages back and forth, as we have many decisions and necessary adjustments to make for such a large event."

Mrs. Flink's head of red hair bobbed in agreement.

"Landon knew about the box the winners would open that would tell them about their prize," Mr. Silverton continued, "but he received a message through our channel just before he went on stage telling him to announce that a key would be inside, and that the box would read the winners' fingerprints and send them a message about the key and what it unlocked. The message also included a picture of the key." Mr. Silverton palmed his beard. "Landon assumed the message was from the committee. I asked him for the file he received and he gladly sent it. I'll show you what I've found."

Mr. Silverton flicked his fingers, lighting a screen behind him with a three-dimensional mass of numbers that formed dense pathways. He hefted his thick body out of his chair and pointed at the screen. "This is a visual representation of the code I had set up for our secure messaging system. It is a way I organize my thoughts." He used his fingers to navigate along a pathway. "This," he said, pointing at a picture of a small virtual envelope, "is the message Landon received. It had the entire committee listed as the sender, a protocol we normally use to communicate with students or teachers about the Race. But because it was sent through the committee's channel, it is most likely that it came from someone on the committee." He gestured toward the screen. "Now, if we follow its path back to its origination, we should be able to find out who sent it. But we encounter some very interesting problems." Mr. Silverton triggered the view to follow a trail through his virtual map. "Here," he said, "it splits forty-two ways, all leading in unpredictable directions. This is a complicated piece of code which makes it very difficult to discover the original source."

"Which was done on purpose, obviously," Mr. Sul said. "We're dealing with someone who didn't want us to find them."

"Agreed," Mr. Silverton said. He waved his hand across the screen. "I was able to eliminate thirty-eight of the paths as well-made distractions." Multiple pathways disappeared.

"That leaves us with four other paths," Mr. Silverton said. "And this one loops back on itself, so that's a dead end. Or, I guess more precisely, it is an infinite loop that never goes anywhere new." Apparently his love for specifics would not let him leave with an inaccurate statement. "These last three are our most viable options."

"Who is capable of doing this kind of work?" Mrs. Flink asked.

Mr. Silverton sighed. "That's the real question right there. They must have quite the talent. This goes far beyond the average person's skills."

Mrs. Flink nodded.

He returned to the screen. "Here's one of the three promising rerouted paths." He moved his hand to show a different pathway. "It leads to an unlikely suspect—Mrs. Flink."

"*What?*" Mrs. Flink burst out. "I'd have no idea how to do that."

Mr. Silverton nodded. "I know." He looked back at Mr. Sul. "As you well know, Mrs. Flink is a biology teacher and has no special background in computer science. Either this is a talent she has hidden very well or she had help or this is just a smoke-screen."

"You'd better believe it's the third one," Mrs. Flink said. "I didn't do it."

"Thank you, Mrs. Flink," Mr. Sul said. "But you will

understand our caution. Sometimes it is the least likely person that actually is the culprit."

Mr. Silverton nodded. "The second option, in my opinion, is mind-bending." He followed a path through several walls. "Each of these walls represent code that's trying to keep us from tracking this trail further. Though, for me, they were somewhat easy to pass through."

"Were they not well-made?" Mr. Sul asked.

"Oh, very well-made," Mr. Silverton said. "I didn't say there were easy to crack. I said they were easy for me. Under most circumstances, it would probably take a whole team thousands of hours to get through them."

"And you're that skilled?" Mrs. Flink asked.

"No," Mr. Silverton said. "They're mine. I set these code walls up every time I open a communication channel. To be completely honest, one of the three viable options leads straight back to me." He palmed his beard again. "It looks like I'm a suspect." Mr. Silverton and Mrs. Flink shared an awkward look.

"I appreciate your honesty," Mr. Sul replied.

"But I didn't do it," Mr. Silverton said. Derick thought his complete honesty could help rule him out. But then, if he was this good at cracking codes, couldn't he have hidden any evidence that might lead back to himself? "And if I didn't do it, that means someone hacked in and, not only used extremely complicated procedures, but they made it look like it was me." In frustration, he let out a short burst of air, ruffling his mustache. "This is an extreme level of competency."

"Well beyond me," Mrs. Flink emphasized.

"And the third?" Mr. Sul asked.

Mr. Silverton pulled his hands back and the view of the pathways retracted. "Here's the final possibility," he said. He showed the message again, and then followed its path through several twists and turns. Abruptly, it simply dissolved into nothing.

"That one's different," Mr. Sul pointed out.

"It's quite a technical move," Mr. Silverton explained. "A self-destructing pathway. Once the message finds its destination, it begins to disintegrate its own trail."

Mrs. Flink threw up her hands and made a noise that made it clear how confused she was.

"And what do you think about this one?" Mr. Sul asked.

"Well, there are a few ways it can be done, but the most likely is that it was actually initiated by the person or persons who received the message. If they know what they're doing, they can disintegrate the pathway," Mr. Silverton said.

"Landon?" Mr. Sul asked. "He would have had to have sent the message to himself to make it look like it came from someone else."

Mr. Silverton nodded. "He'd have to be more talented than he lets on in class, but yes," Mr. Silverton said. "From what we know right now, Mrs. Flink, myself, and Landon Beane are the best suspects."

Mr. Sul stood. "Thank you. But that only tells us who could have sent the message. What about the key inside the box?"

Mr. Silverton cracked his thick knuckles. "We mentioned that as a committee we had no plan to put a key inside." Mr. Silverton flicked his fingers and a semi-transparent image of the box appeared. "I had the box scanned, and sure enough, a key is inside. Also based on the scan, it's the real deal." He looked at Mr. Sul solemnly.

"And it can't be opened?" Mr. Sul asked.

"Once the box was closed, the code went into effect," Mr. Silverton said. "Only the winners can open it. And though I created it, even I can't change it. Maybe I did too good of a job." He wiped some sweat from his bald head.

"How did it get in there?" Mr. Sul asked.

"I wrote the code," Mr. Silverton said, "but I didn't fill the box. That was Mrs. Flink's job."

Mrs. Flink looked back at Mr. Silverton and nodded. "It was," she admitted. "We intended to put a small screen in the box that explained the prize." She used her fingers to show the size of the screen. "I received a message telling me that it was ready but that Mr. Silverton had retrieved it and put it in the box." She rubbed her temples through her red hair. "We were very busy and I appreciated the help. When I saw the box next it was closed and locked. I didn't think anything of it."

Mr. Silverton shook his head. "I never sent that message, nor did I fill the box. After we heard Landon's announcement, Mrs. Flink forwarded that message to me. I analyzed it, and again, to be honest, it has three possible pathways it might have come from: Me, Landon Beane again—or Mrs. Flink could have sent it to herself. The same suspects might have sent the message to Mrs. Flink."

"This is all part of some complex plan," Mr. Sul said. "But why put the key in the box? Why offer the secret?"

The other two shook their heads.

"Of course," Mr. Sul said, "it's possible either one of you is behind it and wouldn't tell me if you did know." He shook his head. "But I don't like it. Perhaps I should cancel the Race. It would be difficult to rationalize to the other administrators and to explain to the students, but if it's what's best, I'll do it."

"Perhaps that would be best," Mrs. Flink said.

Mr. Silverton raised a finger. "I'm not sure you can. That's the last thing. When our suspect put the key in the box, they also altered its programming. It would have taken great skill, but it was still possible before the box was closed. From what I can tell, they added the feature that will send the information to the winners about the secrets the key unlocks."

"Yes," Mr. Sul said, "we know that."

"But," Mr. Silverton said, "they added a sort of timer. As near as I can tell, if the box isn't opened by the end of the last scheduled day of the Race, then that information will be sent to every student in Cragbridge Hall." He cracked another knuckle. "We have to assume it's a message about Oscar Cragbridge's secret."

The scene of the three teachers sitting at the table changed to an image of only Mr. Sul. "As you can tell, we're in a difficult situation. After much thought, I decided to get school security involved also. I told them that some-one had meddled with the prize without telling them the significance of the key. Because Mr. Silverton is a suspect, I couldn't completely trust his information. I needed some-one else qualified to investigate the strange messages." Mr. Sul paused a moment, gathering his thoughts. "Because they don't understand what's at stake, security thinks it's an elaborate prank or a feud between members of the Race committee. But they aren't amused—and they are looking at it seriously."

Mr. Sul took a step closer in the recording. "You men-tioned that some of the students, including your son and the Cragbridge twins, were forming a team to try to win back the key. You wondered if competing was dangerous. I am having school security monitor it all, but I'm afraid that our only hope for keeping this secret safe is their team winning the Race."

THE BIG OPENING

Abby and Carol stepped out of the Hall and approached a crowd that surrounded an outdoor stage. The stage, flanked by two large screens, stood on the grass between a shrub sculpture of Abraham Lincoln and another of a man dunking a basketball; Abby wasn't sure who it was. A small stream ran through the grounds on the far side of the stage. The sun was on its way down. Reds, blues, and violets made a beautiful background.

Abby took a deep breath. She was extra-anxious after watching the video from Mr. Sul the day before. She looked around for any sign of her team.

"All right, everyone," Anjum said in a group chat through their rings. Everyone was linked to the call, but could only be heard if they selected talk mode using their own rings. That way they didn't hear everyone all at once.

"Let's meet together on the far right of the stage, by the bush trimmed to look like General Washington."

This was the opening ceremony. It wasn't a big deal, just introductions and a clue as to how to prepare for their first event in the Race.

"Are you coming to watch all the excitement?" someone asked.

Abby turned to see a girl with long dark hair, dressed in a navy jumper and red shoes. Jacqueline. "Nah, I'm actually on a team," Abby responded to her former roommate.

"Really?" Jacqueline said. "Why would anyone want you?" Her cadence was happy and bright, but her words were biting.

"I'm definitely not the star, but I'm going to try to help out," Abby said honestly. If it were an event instead of just introductions, she would be a nervous wreck. "And . . . cue the next insult." She pointed back at Jacqueline.

"It turns out . . . what?"

"You're pretty predictable," Abby said. "It's like you feel you move higher in life if you can somehow push me lower."

Jacqueline glared back with a nuh-uh face. A boy ran over and grabbed her hand. It was the same boy from the dance. "It's getting started. Come on, Jackie." She smiled and ran off with him.

"Oh, holding hands," Carol said. "Looks like little miss prissy has a boyfriend who got her onto a team."

"She is way too young to date," Abby said, remembering what her parents had taught her.

"I know," Carol said. "Like my mom says, 'Up to fifteen,

it's doesn't hurt to flirt. From sixteen on, you don't have to wait to date. But until college or after, it's too scary to marry.'"

Abby smiled. Carol definitely believed that it didn't hurt to flirt.

"I just had an absolutely terrible thought," Abby said.

"What?"

"What if Jacqueline learned the secret?" She spoke quietly to avoid listening ears. "She hates me. She hates that my grandfather got me into Cragbridge Hall. She would probably post the secret all over the school, all over the web. She'd call the news within five minutes."

"Yeah, especially because she'd get to show off her pretty face and her cute clothes," Carol said. "By the way, did you notice those red shoes she was wearing? Seriously cute."

"Yeah, I totally noticed them," Abby admitted.

"She's such a wolf in sheep's clothing," Carol said. "Really cute sheep's clothing."

"Yeah," Abby agreed.

"Except I'm not exactly sure how that phrase works," Carol said. "First off, sheep don't even have clothing, so I'm assuming we're talking about wool coats. So how does a wolf get a wool coat? It's not like it shears sheep. And it can't sew; it doesn't even have thumbs. And it can't order clothes online. I really think we're giving wolves a lot more credit than they deserve with that phrase."

Carol had a point, Abby thought, though it wasn't very useful.

"What's worse," Abby said, "is that if Jacqueline got the

key and if Muns or someone who works for him contacted her, she might do whatever he wanted just to get ahead. And she might get others on her side too."

Carol looked back. "That's an awful thought." She shuddered.

Abby and Carol found Derick, Rafa, Jess, and Malcolm by the George Washington shrub. A few minutes later Maria, Nia, and Piper showed up.

"Looks like you're all together," Anjum said through messaging. "Remember that we hooked up our rings and you gave me permission to track you. You can shut that off at any time, but it will be really helpful during our challenges. This will serve as a good trial run." He cleared his throat. "And you should all know that I'm not going to be there. Sorry. I have a thing about crowds. In fact, I usually prefer not to interact with people face-to-face at all. It's one of the reasons I'm so good at virtuality. But I'll be watching the school's feed and will be with you through your rings."

Abby never would have guessed Anjum was anxious about crowds from their first meeting. Maybe they all had secrets.

"Welcome, everyone!" Sarah, the student body officer, walked out onto the stage, Landon right behind her. They weren't wearing their blazers. It was too hot for that. They wore matching navy blue T-shirts with the words *Cragbridge Hall* in big white letters, and the question *Are you ready to Race?* beneath it. "Registration is closed. We have all our teams!"

Landon waited for the crowd to end their cheers and

whistles before continuing. "There are fifty-two teams competing this year. Take a look." He motioned toward the large screens along the sides of the stage. With the sun down, their light burst out of the darkness. The word *Revolution* scrolled across the screen with the image of a young man beneath it. Not bad for a team name. The teams had been encouraged to name themselves after something to do with history, literature, science—something education-based. A creative name would earn a small amount of points, but it would only make a difference if the final score was extremely close. An image of each person on the Revolution team flashed on the screen.

The next team name appeared on the screen—the Argonauts. The name came from a group of mythical Greek heroes who went on a search for the Golden Fleece. Abby had really liked a lot of what she knew about that story. As Abby watched to see the members of the team, Jacqueline's face crossed the screen. Maybe Abby didn't like the Argonauts as much anymore. They saw the Fellowship of the Race, Infantry 312, and about twenty others before it was their turn—the Spartans. Anjum had chosen the name. Derick wanted the 20th Maine after the soldiers who defended Little Round Top in the Civil War, but it wasn't catchy enough. The Spartans were famous for being some of the fiercest warriors in history.

Abby's face came on-screen. They must have pulled it from her original Cragbridge Hall application. She looked nervous, and a year younger. So much had happened since that photo was taken. She had found that she could contribute. She belonged at this school. She had saved her grandpa and her parents, and had protected the keys over time. But her stomach still filled with waves.

Carol's picture was next. She looked a little younger and wore a large toothy grin. It looked like a glossy pic of an actress. It probably was. "We look gooooooood," Carol said, elbowing Abby. "Seriously, they might want to just give us the trophy right now."

"I'm not sure looking good has anything to do with winning," Abby said.

"Well, if it does, we're off to a good start," Carol said.

After all the teams had been introduced, Landon spoke again, outdoor lighting clicking on to illuminate him. "Remember that after every event, half of the teams will be eliminated. We start with fifty-two teams. So after the first round of competition, only twenty-six will remain. After the second round, there will be thirteen, and after the third, we'll narrow it down to six. Those six teams will then compete in the final round for the championship."

Abby swallowed hard. They would have to make each cut, always at least in the top half of the competition. Otherwise, they'd be eliminated, and someone else would find out the secret.

"The highest score," Landon continued, "wins the trophy and will earn . . . the . . . prize." He said the last words very awkwardly, like he wasn't sure what to say after the trouble from the last announcement.

Sarah jumped in. "And now the clue that will tell you how to prepare for the first event in the Race. The clue is . . ." She paused dramatically, and held it an uncomfortably long amount of time. Several more sets of outdoor lighting turned on. "That there is no clue. This challenge is a bit different. As a committee, we decided to start off this year bigger and better than before. No preparation. So ready or not, here it is!"

No preparation? The Race was beginning right now?

"Team, this is crazy," Anjum said in a group chat. "But I like it."

"True to the name of the Race," Sarah said, "this challenge will require your speed, knowledge, and skill with many of the inventions in this school. You are on the lookout for squares like this." Sarah raised an object above her head. It also appeared on the screen for everyone to get a better look. It was barely larger than her palm, was mostly transparent, but had a navy blue border.

"I want you to move," Anjum commanded. "Don't worry about the instructions; I'll patch you in. Derick and Rafa, go to the avatar lab. Get there fast. Jess and Piper, to the robotics shop." Before Anjum could move on to the next order, the first four students were already on their way. The crowd seemed too excited to even notice them moving in the dark—except for Jacqueline. Abby saw her watching them. She started speaking with the boy she had been holding hands with earlier and pointed in their direction.

"As soon as anyone touches one of the squares," Sarah continued to explain to the whole crowd from the stage, "it will read your fingerprint, give points to your team, and give you the next clue."

"Malcolm, to the geography wing," Anjum directed. "I'm in a virtual booth. Nia, you stay here. It may be where we get the first clue. Abby and Carol, to a Bridge lab." Abby thought he sounded a bit more commanding as he mentioned their names.

As Abby and Carol began running to the closest Bridge lab, Abby saw several members of Jacqueline's team get up and leave, jogging in different directions. They were copying their strategy.

"Each team will have a different route of clues." Abby heard Landon's voice explaining the challenge as she ran toward the Hall, the building where the Bridge labs were kept. "Some challenges are the same, some are different, and some come in a different order, but each journey has been determined fair by the committee. Follow the clue you gain from one square to find the next, and then the next. Each team will need to find seven squares. As soon as you have all seven, you have completed the challenge. The fastest team wins."

Abby and Carol entered the doors of the building. Anjum was a genius. When they found their first square, they would already have their team scattered across the campus at different inventions. Even if the next clue didn't lead to an invention they were at, they would have someone closer to where they needed to be than the other teams who were all gathered in the same place.

"Please turn on all the outdoor lights," Landon said over the earpieces connected to Abby's rings. She was jogging down the hall toward the Bridge lab. She had seen the campus lit up at night; it was like a football stadium during a night game. "There are squares in the branches of each tree surrounding this stage. Now, find one and BEGIN!"

"Nia, go!" Anjum commanded.

"I'm on it," they all heard Nia say. She must have left her rings on, because they also heard her steps and her heavy breath and her feet as she ran. She sounded fast. Not a surprise for a member of the Crash.

"Everyone else to your positions as quickly as possible," Anjum said. "Many of you aren't there yet. Unless the clues really surprise me, this should pay off."

They all heard rustling. "Dang tree. It had to be tall," Nia's voice came across the call.

"Don't even pretend that's hard, Nia," Malcolm said. "You climb trees several times a day."

"Yeah," Nia answered, "but as a monkey. It's . . ." she panted, "a bit more difficult as a human. Ouch! And it's scratchy. I see it. Almost there." After a few more seconds— "Got it. Come on, come on . . . It's analyzing my fingerprint. Come on . . . This thing is slow."

"Judging from what I can see from the broadcast, Nia, you were the fastest up a tree. Good work," Anjum said.

"Okay, here we go," Nia answered. "The clue is a list of words: *Think, Epic, Divine, Poem, Gates, Statue, Comedy*."

"Unless someone has already guessed this clue," Anjum said, "Derick and Rafa, use your rings to search all the words together. Malcolm and Maria search whichever words sound most unique to you together. Nia and Jess, no rings, just think how these could all work together. Piper, you take *divine*. It stands out to me. Search it with the others."

"Maybe I should take *divine* too," Carol said. "It fits me."

"Abby and Carol, search whatever you want," Anjum said.

Was he letting them do whatever they wanted because they naturally came at the end of the list, or was it because he didn't trust them to take an assignment? Abby decided that it was best not to think about it and get to work.

They went through combination after combination.

"Epic poem," Carol called out. "It sounds like something fitting for Cragbridge Hall. And I've got a list of them: *Paradise Lost, The Epic of Gilgamesh, The Divine Comedy, The Iliad.*"

"*Divine Comedy*," Anjum said. "Those words are also in our list of clues. That's the right track, Carol."

She did it. The challenge had only been going for less than a minute and Carol had already proved she had a place on the team.

Relief, followed by jealousy.

"Wait. Wait. Wait," Malcolm's voice came over Abby's earpiece. "What's the *Divine Comedy* about? All I remember is that I was disappointed that it wasn't funny."

"Oh, I know that one," Piper said. "It's some guy's journey through the kingdoms of the dead."

"A story?" Maria said. "What are we supposed to do with a story? Read it aloud in the Chair?"

"We could study its history on the Bridge," Abby suggested.

"Not yet," Anjum responded. "What about the other words? Is there a statue in the poem? Gates? And what about the word *think*?"

"There are gates. Dante stops to think there," Jess threw in, her voice quiet but firm. "At least that's what my search says."

"*The Thinker*!" Malcolm called out. "It's a famous statue by Rodin, but some people think it's supposed to be Dante thinking at the gates of h-e-double toothpicks. Sorry . . . I promised my mama that when I went away to school I wouldn't swear or drink or smoke."

"It's different when it's part of an epic poem," Maria said.

"Not for me," Malcolm said. "Or my mama."

"Isn't there a copy of *The Thinker* somewhere on campus?" Derick asked.

"Just outside the math hall," Anjum said.

"And going into math is kind of like the gates of h-e-double hockey sticks," Carol said. "Someone was really thinking on that one."

Abby heard giggling across the wire.

"Malcolm is closest," Anjum said. "Run to the statue! Run! Run! Run!"

OSCARS AND
ANCIENT ARGENTINA

I f I had to guess," Anjum said, "we're in the lead, but let's not act like it. Read the next clue as soon as you've got it, Malcolm."

Malcolm's Southern drawl came over the message, winded from the run. "All right, here it is: *Treasure chest, Filter, Not yourself, Maiden's hair.*"

"You know what to do," Anjum said. "Call out whatever may be a good guess."

"Maybe it's me," Carol said. "I've got great hair, and I'm a maiden."

"I asked for *good* guesses," Anjum quipped back.

"Wow," Carol said. "Don't get grumpy. It's bad for team morale." Derick bit the inside of his cheek. He had insisted Carol be on the team and she was popping off whatever came to mind. Maybe it was how she dealt with the pressure. At least she had helped on the first clue.

"Maiden's hair" sounded unique and kind of weird. Derick typed it into his rings then skimmed over the first entries. "Wait," he said. "Maiden's hair is also a name for a saltwater plant you can put in aquariums."

"That's it," Anjum said. "Filter, treasure chest. They fit."

"And we have the largest aquarium in the zoo portion of the school," Rafa said.

"You can only go in as avatars," Anjum added.

"We're on it," Rafa called back. He and Derick already had their high-tech suits on and had hooked up to harnesses to be ready.

"Uh," Derick said, not keying his rings so everyone else could hear. This was just for Rafa. "I've never done fish before."

"Just follow my lead," Rafa instructed. "You'll do fine." Derick would do better than fine with most of the avatars, but the fish were the only group he hadn't done. And Anjum could have picked any of the other members of the Crash, but he had picked Derick. Time for a crash course.

Crash course. Derick chuckled to himself. *Dumb.*

"There are two giant aquariums, but one is freshwater," Rafa instructed. "I think it has to be in the saltwater tank. Choose an oscar. I think they're easiest. Don't worry which color."

Oscar? That was a kind of fish? It didn't sound like it. More like the first name that popped into a kid's head when he brought the fish home from the pet store. Of course, it was also Derick's grandpa's name. Derick quickly searched through the fish and picked the first oscar he saw. It had a bright orange body with black splotches.

"The machine has to find your avatar and drop it in the water," Rafa said. "What you want to do is flex your muscles on one side of your body while you let the other side relax. Then switch. That will move your caudal fin back and forth—that's the fin at the very back. You use your other fins to steer."

Derick tried to think of the movements, flex one side and relax the other.

"I'm in the aquarium," Rafa said. "You'll be here soon. For me, it helps to just imagine I'm a fish and do what comes naturally."

Yeah, but he had done all of these avatars for years. Derick synced to the fish avatar just as a mechanical arm dropped it into the water. "Whoa!" It was like suddenly being on a roller coaster as it careened downward. Derick took in a quick breath before he hit the water. He tried to stabilize himself with his fins on the side. It worked a little, but felt flimsy. He tried to kick too, but quickly figured out he currently didn't have legs, and his fins definitely didn't move like legs.

What had Rafa said? Flex one side while relaxing the other. Derick tried and flipped himself entirely over to the left. He relaxed the right side and flexed the left, but overcorrected. He was now laying on his right side as he went through the water.

Derick held his breath for nearly half a minute before he realized he didn't have to. His real body wasn't in the water.

"I'm checking the treasure chest," Rafa gave an update. Derick saw his friend's fish darting at the treasure chest like a torpedo. "Start into the maiden's hair."

Derick couldn't quite bring himself upright, but managed to swim down into the plants that looked like green tufts of hair. He weaved around one, but couldn't see anything out of the ordinary. A large flat fish darted right in front of him. It seemed startled. Maybe it hadn't seen sideways swimming avatar fish before. Derick moved to the next plant, and then the next. He was on his fourth one when he saw it—something white in the middle of the plant. He circled his front fins, trying to hold himself in place to get a good look. It definitely didn't seem like it belonged there. He tried to grab it with his mouth, but ended up just bumping it with his fish face. It probably would have been better if a different member of the Crash were here.

His bump was enough to turn the white piece of plastic. "Something's here," Derick said. "It says 'Room three. Four across. Two back.'"

"Good job, Derick," Rafa said.

"Of course," Anjum said. "They had to put the actual square somewhere else. When you're a fish you can't exactly put your thumb to one and be identified."

"My best guess is that it refers to the classrooms next to the avatar lab," Rafa said. That made sense. They were the closest rooms and where students learned all about the different species of animals and how to become like them with the help of the avatars.

Derick concentrated away from his robot fish and back on his real body. He pressed the back of his neck to sever the connection between him and the fish. Abandoned, his fish avatar would simply float to the surface. That might also freak out the fish who had seen him swimming sideways.

Derick unharnessed himself as fast as he could and darted into the hall. Room one. He ran farther down, passing room two. When he entered room three, Rafa was already there, looking underneath a chair.

"Got it," Rafa said. "It's reading my fingerprint."

"Good job, you two," Anjum said. "Everyone else get ready."

• • •

Abby waited. She hated waiting. Her grandfather's secret was at stake and she was doing absolutely nothing. Nia and Malcolm had run to the first clues. Derick and Rafa had swum through the aquarium. And she was just waiting by the Bridge listening to Carol comment about everything—from how cool Malcolm's deep voice sounded to how Derick would probably make a very cute fish.

And she waited as Nia had to play the next seven notes of Beethoven's *Ninth Symphony* from where the clue had stopped playing. She grabbed a guitar, looked up the piece, followed along, and eventually plucked out the notes. Turns out her guitar hobby was useful after all.

And Abby waited as Maria and Jess dissected a virtual

frog in the Biology lab to find the next clue. The clue was written on the frog's liver. So gross. Abby was glad she didn't have to do that one.

"It says the next challenge is for five members of the team," Maria said. "And the key words are: '*Virtual plains, Millions of years ago, The sixth sphere, Five species.*'"

"It's at the virtual booths," Anjum said. "I'm already there. Malcolm and Maria, you're the closest. Come help me. Then Derick and Rafa and Carol and Abby, each of you send one of your pair and leave the other just in case we need you for the next challenge."

Carol turned to Abby. "I really want to go super bad, but you're faster."

Abby took off. She sprinted down the hall toward the physics and math rooms where they had labs of virtual booths. She was better at running distance than speed, but she was fast enough. With every step she hoped she wasn't about to mess this up. Anjum was giving her a chance and she didn't want to be kicked off the team. And she definitely didn't want anyone else finding out the secret.

"The clue had to be about the sixth sphere in the holding bins," Anjum said. "Whatever virtual world that sphere holds, we're going in." There were several sounds of rustling as Anjum moved. "I've got it. Everyone sync in with my world as soon as you can."

Malcolm and Maria said they were nearly in the room.

"I'm stepping into the world now." Only a moment passed before Anjum whistled. "Impressive! Whoever made this is good."

It had impressed Anjum, the student who had made a virtual space station orbiting Jupiter.

"Whoa!" Malcolm said. He must have made it into the virtual world as well.

"Quit gawking, boys, and figure out what we are supposed to do," Maria scolded. Abby liked her sass.

Abby raced past another line of lockers, seeing students from other teams running in different directions. She was only a hall away.

"We have to find the key words," Anjum said. "And I would guess they have to do with the list you can access at the upper right-hand corner of your vision. There are five species listed there." *Five species.* That was one of the clues. "Quickly look at all of them and keep your eyes peeled. I'll go north. Malcolm, east. Maria, south. Rafa, west. And Abby," he paused. She didn't like that pause. "Pick a direction."

She was a leftover. Abby didn't know what she was about to face, but it still felt like she wasn't a high priority.

"Just some friendly advice," Malcolm said. "Don't get stomped or eaten. I'm pretty sure that will kick you out of the world. Oh, and you can also select a huge virtual tranquilizer gun. I'd recommend it. I doubt these things are *all* vegetarians."

What was going on? And what kind of species were in this virtual world? Abby raced into the room just in time to see Rafa step into a booth. She went into the next, put on her suit, hooked herself up to the suspension equipment, and synced up to the world Anjum was in.

In an instant, she felt a warm humid mist and smelled a mix of ocean and leaves. She gazed at a stretching landscape of mountains and trees with a green-water coastline within a mile or two. Then she saw it. A bird. No. Not a bird. It flew closer and closer. It didn't have feathers, but a long snout and clawed feet. And it was the size of a car.

Abby jumped behind a tree as the flying beast flapped past. She didn't know whether to be impressed or terrified. She was in a land of dinosaurs!

Abby selected a tranquilizer gun and it appeared in her hand. She picked the smallest one, a thin rifle. She didn't want to use it, but if she had to, she hoped her aim would be true.

Abby loaded up the list of species in the right-hand side of her vision and scrolled through it. Apparently, these were the kinds of dinosaurs they were supposed to find, all from the Cretaceous Epoch in Argentina. She didn't see that coming. When she thought of Argentina she thought of soccer, the Iguazu Falls, and that song about not crying for Argentina. She didn't think of dinosaurs.

Some of the beasts on the list were smaller, like the Alvarezsaurus. The pictographic beside it showed that it was about six-and-a-half feet long and ran fast. It had a tuft of feathers slicked back on the top of its head and more on its tail. Others were huge, like the Giganotosaurus— Tyrannosaurus Rex's larger cousin. Abby hoped she didn't see one of those.

Abby walked through the brush, gripping her rifle. She

couldn't help feeling like she was in a movie or a video game.

"I found a Microsaurops," Anjum updated. He was the virtuality master and apparently the fastest of the team. "All you have to do is sneak up close enough to read the words on it. This one had them on its side. As I doubt these dinosaurs draw on one another, I can only imagine they are the key words. The words I found were *Great Wall* and *globes*. We have to find them on each of the species. We only have four more sets of words to go."

"Good to know," Maria said. "I'm trying to work around to what I think is an Unenlagia. I have no idea if I'm saying that right. Anyway, I thought I saw something behind its neck. I'm going in for a better look."

The others were tracking something. Abby had only seen the flying dinosaur and, thankfully, that one wasn't on the list. She could only imagine how hard it would be to track down something that could fly.

Abby pushed through trees for several minutes before they opened up to a large plain with little mounds scattered across the ground. Abby crept closer. Each lump curved in at the top and cradled a handful of eggs. This was some sort of nesting ground. And it was calm and empty.

For about ten seconds.

Abby felt the tremors in the ground first. It was like thunder coming up from the dirt and shaking her legs. Then the largest living thing Abby had ever seen stepped out of the trees.

Her mouth dropped open in complete awe.

Its head peered forward four or five stories above her, its long neck reaching forever back to the rest of its body. It moved slowly, its heavy form thudding against the plain as it walked toward a group of towering trees. It pulled huge groups of leaves from the treetops, crunching down on its meal. Then it moved to another thicket. After it took a few more steps, Abby got a better idea of its entire size. It was about as long as the inside of a gym, including the bleachers on the ends. It seemed like a moving building.

Abby checked her list. *Argentinosaurus*. It was named after the place its bones had been discovered and was about 115 feet long and could weigh over 100 tons. It was one of the largest dinosaurs ever discovered. This had to be it.

But she couldn't see any key words. Of course, if they were on the other side, she wouldn't have seen them. Abby snuck out of the brush and crossed underneath the Argentinosaurus's huge tail, which it carried several feet above the ground. She just hoped it didn't come down on top of her. It had to weigh several tons. Even in a virtual world, that wouldn't feel good.

"*Everest*, *Chichen Itza*, and *Petra*," Maria said over their earpieces. "It's really weird to see words painted on a dinosaur. It doesn't quite fit the whole theme."

"This sounds like we're up for a geography challenge next," Anjum announced. "Malcolm, unless you are tracking a dinosaur right now, I want you to leave and go back to the geography lab. It sounds like we may need you there. I'm moving your way."

"Just give me a minute," Malcolm said. "These things are scary beasties, but I'm getting closer."

"I think I've spotted the Alvarezsaurus," Rafa added.

"I'm checking out an Argentinosaurus right now," Abby said. She was glad that she had something to say, that she hadn't failed yet. She couldn't take her eyes off the huge creature. Though it was massive and awkward, there was also a grace to it. Its long neck moved smoothly as it walked, its tail swaying slightly with each step.

Abby darted forward, trying to get a good view of its other side. It wasn't as easy as she thought it would be. The dinosaur moved slowly, but its steps were a lot larger than hers. She had some catching up to do. Thankfully, it found another tree with leaves it liked and craned its neck to pull them off. Abby got close enough to pick out the letters *g-r-a*. There had to be more. She just needed a few more steps.

With a whoosh, the forest broke open and a rush of teeth and growling crashed out. Then two more. Three giganotosauruses. Abby recognized the bigger cousins of the T. rex from her list. Not her favorite realization. Somewhere in Abby's mind she knew they stood several stories tall and were longer than school buses, but at the moment, all she could think was that she had to get out of there. She screamed as one knocked into the side of the Argentinosaurus and then bit into its flank. It clamped its jaws a few times, moving its teeth back and forth like a saw to scrape and tear the hide.

The huge plant-eater roared in pain.

One of the other Giganotosauruses raced around the tail

and bounded toward Abby, showing its ruler-length teeth. Apparently, it had heard her scream and thought she might be an easier meal.

Abby screamed again. In the back of her mind, she thought she heard other members of the team shouting. Were they sharing key words? Were they coming to help her? Her mind was not clear enough to hear what they were saying.

She sprinted away, fumbling with her rifle, but the predator caught up in a matter of a few steps. Abby pointed her gun behind her and shot. She peered back, hoping to see it wobbling with a tranquilizer dart in its front. It was only feet away, running as fast as ever. She pointed her rifle again as the beast leaned forward and opened its jaws wide. Abby was sure it could swallow her whole.

A huge tail clobbered into the Giganotosaurus, catching it in the jaw and side. The meat-eater flew backward and toppled over. The Argentinosaurus was fighting back.

Abby didn't stop running, but now had a clear view of the key words on the dinosaur—*Grand Canyon, Taj Mahal.*

"Grand Canyon and the Taj Mahal," she repeated to the others.

Another roar. More pounding feat. Another predator. And the Argentinosaurus was busy with the third one. Abby fired twice behind her as she ran, the second dart sticking into the beast's thick hide just under its head. But it didn't slow down. This was it for Abby. She wouldn't turn around again. She wouldn't look into that horrifying mouth. And if Anjum thought this was making a significant mistake, she was off the team.

A whistle cut through the air. The steps behind her became uneven, slower. Then slower. Then a thud. Abby looked over her shoulder to see the beast crashed on the ground.

"Got it," Anjum said through Abby's earpiece, but she also saw him. He stood just outside of some trees, waving his hands and a large tranquilizer gun; it looked more like a bazooka than a rifle. "Sorry it took me a little bit, Abby."

"Amazing," Malcolm said. "I've been tracking them this whole challenge, but Anjum came out of nowhere. And those guys are hard to keep up with."

"Malcolm, get going," Anjum commanded. "Abby, the Giganotosaurus closest to you had key words on its back—our last ones. Read them to me."

Abby had to crawl onto the virtual beast to read the words—*four players*. She hadn't messed up her part. At least, not yet. But the next challenge was going to be another group event.

LESS THAN A
SECOND

Derick rushed through the halls, a huge smile on his face. The Race was fantastic. The challenge. The adrenaline. He loved it. Well, except for the fact that he had let Rafa go to the last challenge. He had no idea it would be a dinosaur world. Now he was running to the geography room. He doubted this would be as cool.

A memory seeped into his thoughts. The girl from the future. Muns. The Race. And his death. He didn't want to die. But it didn't seem like it was going to happen. This was just a bunch of kids doing spectacular challenges. There didn't seem to be anything sinister about it at all. Derick cleared his mind. Right now, he had to protect the secret. They had to win.

"Second-to-last event in this round," Anjum said. "We can't slow down now." At the end of the last event, they had found a square in the room with the virtual booths, which Rafa had touched to log their time. The square had repeated the key words.

Derick ran into a geography room where Piper and Jess both sat in desks with globes in front of them. Anjum continued his instruction, "Malcolm's on his way, but we need to find all the places we have key words for from the dinosaur challenge."

Derick sat down in front of a globe. It seemed alive. Clouds moved on top of it as it rotated slowly on its axis. It was a spherical screen.

"Derick, you take Mt. Everest," Anjum directed.

Derick had used the globes before. He knew he could guide it with the touch of a finger. He was about to spin it to the right country, but where was Everest? He knew it was the tallest mountain in the world, but he didn't know where he could find it on the globe.

Malcolm burst in and sat down, sweat pouring down the side of his head and passing by his huge smile. "Any questions?" he asked. "I know my geography."

"Everest," Derick burst out.

"Almost the northeast corner of Nepal in the Himalayas," Malcolm rattled off.

Derick looked at the globe. Now he had to remember where Nepal was. By China. He used his fingers to spin the globe by China. Then he zoomed in by pressing his fingers against the globe and spreading them apart. He zoomed down past the clouds; the land grew larger and more detailed. He zoomed in closer and closer. But nothing was labeled. That made sense. The real Earth wouldn't be labeled. The landscape gained more and more detail.

He logged into his rings and looked it up. There it was, between India and China. He moved closer and closer until he could see snow-capped mountains, and dark spots of rock and crevasses.

"Got the Taj Mahal and the Grand Canyon," Malcolm said. He was fast. "Key words were *feet* and *Dogood*. Weird."

There were several peaks. Derick turned the view to show him a profile view of the mountain range, looking for the tallest. It was huge though, so he checked his rings to help quicken his search.

"The key word from Petra was *the*," Piper said. "I'm not sure how much that helps."

Derick zoomed in on the top of the legendary mountain. He saw piles of oxygen bottles and tents left there by those who had conquered the mountain. Talk about littering. And he found a key word stamped into the snow in large letters: *bridge*.

● ● ●

Abby watched as the sixteen-year-old boy left a letter underneath the mat. It was the shop where *The New England Courant* was printed. But it wasn't just any dark-haired teenager; it was a young Benjamin Franklin.

"This can't be it," Abby said. "How could they have left a clue or a square here?"

"Just stick with it," Anjum said. "The clues were: '*bridge, at, of, Dogood, the, real, Mrs. Silence, the, feet, the, past*.'"

"And Mrs. Silence Dogood was Benjamin Franklin," Abby said. "He couldn't get published when he was sixteen, so he wrote letters pretending to be older. It totally worked."

"And he pretended to be a woman," Carol said. "That's a little wah-wah-weird. And it says here that men wrote in and offered to marry her." Carol was reading information through her rings. "I mean, 'she' was really a teenage boy, but they thought she was an older lady. So awkward."

"But how is that the last clue?" Abby asked. She was trying not to panic. The first round of the Race ended at this challenge. And of course it had to use the Bridge. And of course, she couldn't figure it out.

"I think we may still have the lead," Anjum said. "Everyone think."

"The pattern that makes the most sense," Abby said, "is 'At the feet of the real Mrs. Silence Dogood.' But we still have *bridge, the,* and *past* left. It has to be at Benjamin Franklin's feet, but where in the past?"

"Don't worry, sis," Derick said over their communication channel. "You've got this, but I'm coming your way, just in case it helps."

She didn't want to waste the brainpower to respond. There were thousands of entries logged into the Bridge about Benjamin Franklin. Narrowing it down to the period of time when he had pretended to be Mrs. Silence Dogood helped, but that was still a ton of ground to cover. Franklin had sent in letters every two weeks, fifteen times. That was hours of footage. They didn't have hours. It was almost like she had it completely wrong.

Maybe she shouldn't be standing at the Bridge at all. She wished she could rewind time and go back to when they all had stood at the outside stage and have someone else take her place on the team.

"Wait," Abby said. "That's it. What if I shouldn't be standing here? What if I'm at the wrong bridge?"

"All of the Bridge booths show the same episodes in history," Anjum said.

"No," Abby responded. "What if the clues aren't referring to the past and the Bridge, but are telling us to go past a bridge? Isn't there a small stream that runs through part of the Cragbridge Hall grounds?"

"Yes," Piper said.

"And isn't there a bridge over it?" Abby said.

"Yeah," Piper confirmed.

"And don't we have a shrub that is shaped like Benjamin Franklin out there?" Abby asked.

"Genius, Abby," Anjum said and let out another high-pitched laugh.

She didn't stop to feel the compliment, but opened the door of the Bridge booth and bolted. "I'm on my way. Is there anyone else closer?"

"Malcolm is coming out of the geography rooms now, but that's about the same distance. Everyone run to that hedge," Anjum yelled. "Go! Go! Go!"

"Good luck beating Abby at a run," Carol said.

Abby raced out of the building and across campus. Under the bright outdoor lights, she saw other students consulting with each other, or whizzing back and forth looking for clues. Were any of them up to any foul play? Were any of them ahead of them and going to win the round?

She ran up the path and saw a small wooden bridge over the stream in the distance. And there was Benjamin Franklin's shrub. There were few people you could make a shrub of and have it be recognizable, but Benjamin Franklin was one. His bald head, long hair, and portly figure were easy to see even if they were only branches and green.

Abby slowed her sprint and dropped at Franklin's feet. Sure enough, a square leaned against one leg. She put her finger to it and moments later she was identified. Words streamed across the small device.

> You have completed your challenges. First team
> to bring their last square to the stage wins.

"I've got it," Abby said. "And I have to bring it back to the stage."

"Run, Abby. *Run!*" Anjum nearly screamed in her ear.

She did. But as she took her first steps, the world went dark. All of the outdoor lighting, all of the lights within the school, everything. Dark.

Abby slowed, not wanting to collide with anything or anyone.

This wasn't good. It could be a freak power outage, but what were the chances? She hoped everyone who had a key was on their guard. Someone working for Muns might be trying to steal keys.

It was probably best for Abby to keep moving. She did, her eyes getting more accustomed to the moonlight. She changed her course around the silhouettes of a tree and a few shrubs, just in case Muns had someone following her. Her heart pounded. She might be ambushed any second.

"You okay, Abby?" Derick asked.

"Yeah," she responded in a whisper, trying not to draw attention to herself. "What's going on?"

"I don't know," Derick admitted. "An electricity failure, I guess. But it's big. And strange for a school with so many generators."

Then everything came back on at once. It was like someone had flipped the switch back on. All in all, the lights had only been off for a few minutes.

Abby looked around. No threats, just students talking on their rings or racing in different directions. She bolted toward the stage.

"Hurry, Abby," Anjum prodded.

"I'm coming up on the stage," Abby said, but just as the words left her lips, she saw a boy sprinting ahead of her. He was darting toward the stage. She turned on all she had, pounding her legs, willing them to go faster.

The boy was a few steps ahead.

Abby forced herself to gain speed.

The stage was only feet away.

With a final push, Abby lengthened her steps and reached out with her square to Landon, just as the boy did the same with Sarah.

Landon grabbed Abby's square and quickly slid it into a small machine. Abby saw Sarah doing the same next to him. "Oh! Nailbiter!" Landon said, watching a screen. After a few seconds he spoke again. "So close. You got second place."

They must have lost by less than a second.

"Wow! That was close," the boy from the other team said. "Good try."

Abby tried to smile back at the boy. He was being a good sport about it. Of course she recognized him. He was the boy who had been holding Jacqueline's hand. Jacqueline's team had just won the first round.

IN THE DARK

You have finished the first challenge," Landon announced. The large screens flashed image after image from all the teams in the challenge. They must have had cameras everywhere. Abby even caught a glimpse of herself running to the feet of the Benjamin Franklin shrub.

"You made it into the highlight video!" Carol squealed, and slapped Abby on the arm. "Lucky licorice sticks!"

Abby thought her run looked funny. And she didn't really like licorice, especially black licorice. It tasted like medicine. So it probably wasn't very lucky.

"In first place," Sarah announced, "the Argonauts!" The screens showed footage of Jacqueline's team. She had been in a music challenge. Abby knew that she designed her own clothes, but hadn't known she was musical. The rest of the team seemed expert enough to bring them into the lead.

"And in second place," Landon announced, "the Spartans!" There was more footage of their team. Derick's fish avatar swimming sideways made a lot of people laugh. Anjum tranquilizing a Giganotosaurus brought cheers. Thankfully, they only showed a glimpse of Abby running scared from the giant beasts.

The announcers went on to list the top ten teams. "The other sixteen teams who made the cut are listed here." The screen filled with team names. Tension filled the crowd as each team looked to see if they would continue or had been cut. Some teams celebrated; others dropped their heads. Abby's team hadn't won, but at least they were still in the competition.

"Let's give a round of applause for all our teams," Landon said, and led the clapping.

"And now your clue for the next round," Sarah said. The words *Greek mythology* scrolled across the screens.

The crowd murmured with excitement.

It seemed like a broad topic. There could be a lot of different challenges around Greek mythology.

Abby received a message. She moved her fingers to check it, hoping it was a response from Rafa's mother or Mr. Sul about the mysterious power outage. Abby had sent questions to both of them as soon as she had finished her part of the event.

The message wasn't from either of them.

It was a message from Muns himself.

• • •

Abby, Carol, Rafa, and Derick moved through the halls quickly. They had all received the message and they only had a few minutes before curfew, when the security bots would start sending kids to their dorms. They opened up the secret passageway and made their way toward the basement.

"Has anyone opened the message yet?" Rafa asked.

"I'm still putting it through another filter," Derick answered.

"I haven't even tried," Abby said. "I just have to know if he's back." The thought made her heart heavy. If Muns was awake, she knew he would want revenge. And he wouldn't hold anything back.

Derick was still making sure the message was safe when the group opened the huge door to the room with the original Bridge. What looked like a large metal tree stood in the center of the room, its branches shooting up into the ceiling. They retrieved their keys from their secret hiding spots and put them in the console. Abby added her sphere and began to search through the present.

She could look anywhere. She could visit any place in the world in that very moment. But she wanted to see her old enemy.

Abby moved the perspective of the Bridge through Charles Muns's mansion. She first peered into his office, but he wasn't there behind the large ornate desk. At least he wasn't plotting in his comfortable chair.

Abby went from room to room, surveying the rooms

with elaborate rugs and artifacts in glass cases, but there was no sign of Muns. Finally, Abby found him in a room down the hall, his body on a bed, hooked up to several tubes and machines. It was the first time she had seen his hair flopped all over and not neatly slicked back.

"Whew!" Carol breathed out in relief. "It doesn't look like he's awake. Not at all. And I hope he stays down."

"Me too," Rafa said. "But then, who sent the message?"

"Whoever it is has access to Muns's messaging system," Abby said.

"I've got the message ready," Derick said. "I'll let you sync to me, so you can see it without going through all the filters yourself."

> Abby, Carol, Rafa, and Derick,
>   As Charles Muns is indisposed at the moment, I'm sending a message on his behalf.
>   I admire your attempts to form a team and protect the secret. Since you once had to go through challenges to obtain the secret and a key, it is only fair that you should have to pass some more to protect them.

The style was Muns's. When he sought revenge, he always had to make it fit the offense he thought had been committed. Abby's grandpa had once argued against Muns that if time travel were real, they should not use it go back in time and prevent tragedies. He specifically mentioned the *Titanic*. So Muns had threatened him by kidnapping Abby's parents and placing them back in time on the *Titanic*. Muns had then held Grandpa hostage in the same auditorium where they had debated. And because Derick and Rafa had used avatars to stop Muns's plan, he used an avatar to seek revenge. Then he placed Grandpa on the *Hindenburg*, the late–1930s dirigible, which had also been called the *Titanic* of the sky. Muns's revenge plans always fit. The question was, who was sending messages for him?

> However, it looks as though you will have to do better if you want to succeed.

Whoever was Muns's spokesman had been watching them. He knew about their second-place finish.

> There will always be those who do what Muns asks, and one of them was with you in the halls tonight.

It was obvious that someone within Cragbridge Hall was working for Muns, but reading the words still made Abby's throat stiff and her stomach anxious. There had been hundreds of students and teachers in the halls. As far as she knew, it could be anyone. Maybe it was Mr. Silverton, Mrs. Flink, or Landon. No—Landon hadn't been in the halls. He had been on stage the whole time. Or it might be someone else. Abby thought of Katarina. Sometimes Muns bribed or threatened people into loyalty.

> And they took something.

Rafa said he would send a message to his mother and Mr. Sul immediately to notify them. This wasn't good.

The Bridge rattled under the pressure of showing the

present. As Abby looked back at Muns on his bed, someone walked into the room. Likely a nurse, she checked several tubes and watched the readings on the machines.

Tremors ran through the Bridge. Abby moved to take the sphere and the keys from the console, but decided to watch for another moment.

"Hello, Mr. Muns," the nurse said. "I believe you can probably hear me now. Perhaps some of our treatments have helped."

It made sense that a rich guy like Muns would have the best care available.

The Bridge rattled again.

The nurse spoke. "All the signs seem to point to the fact that you are going to wake up within a week or so, maybe sooner."

Abby turned the keys.

This was not good at all.

• • •

"What happened when the power went out?" Derick asked. He was back in his room, talking in the bathroom with the fan on so his roommate couldn't hear. The Cragbridge twins' Council of the Keys couldn't meet in person because it was past curfew and it would arouse unnecessary suspicion for them to be up and about.

"Did anyone get attacked? Are their keys missing? Did someone steal something?" Carol rattled out her questions one after the other. "The anticipation is killing me. I mean, not literally. If I had to die, going because of anticipation just sounds wimpy. I'd rather die while skydiving into a volcano to save some hot guy from aliens or something."

Derick wished this wasn't just a chat on their rings; he would love to elbow Carol right now.

"Nothing has been reported missing," Mr. Sul said. "I have met with my council and all of them have their keys." Mr. Sul had agreed to answer their questions directly.

Derick exhaled. Thankfully, they didn't have a stalker in the darkness ready to attack. "All the keys we know of are safe too."

"I've instructed all teachers to check their equipment," Mr. Sul said. "But nothing has come up missing yet. After the keys, our biggest concern are the avatars."

"They're all there," Rafa's mom said. "I quadruple-checked. I also supervised the lab during the Race. Everything is in order. I have lists of everyone who used them. And I change all my security codes at random times during the day. There is no one else who could use them or take them without me knowing about it."

"That's good to know," Mr. Sul said, "and very wise. I just don't know what else they would want to steal. In the same building are geography globes, copies of the Chair, the Bridge, chemistry labs, and virtual booths, but so far, nothing has been reported missing. Plus, the copies of the Bridge in the labs are not the original Bridge; their controls can't let others go into the past."

"But we can't be too careful with Muns," Derick said. "Something did happen during the Race. Or so Muns's message claimed."

"Oh, I assure you, we will take every precaution," Mr. Sul promised. "I will continue to double-check with all the teachers. I will double security shifts, and perhaps add more during the next round of the Race."

"And," Mr. Sul continued, "in the spirit of transparency, I should also show you the footage from our council's meeting about the power outage. It just ended." He typed quickly on his rings, sending the message.

Derick opened the message and selected the video. He saw Mr. Sul, Mr. Silverton, Mrs. Flink, and two new figures, both in gray security uniforms. One was a woman, probably in her early forties, her dark hair cut just above the shoulder. The other was a younger guy, probably in his late twenties. He had blond hair and a trim beard, the kind male models wear to try to look more manly.

Mr. Silverton cleared his throat. "Chief Shar," he addressed the female officer, "your officer was quite helpful in the investigation." Apparently the female was in charge—probably the head of security.

"He is our expert on such matters," Chief Shar said, nodding at the officer with the blond beard. "Because you yourself are a suspect, I thought it would be necessary to get a second opinion."

Once again Silverton showed a computer pathway. "Essentially someone hacked into our system and turned off all the power. The trail is a tangled mess." His screen showed pathways that interweaved.

"Though we cannot be sure of all the pathways this may

have come from, our three suspects remain in the mix: my-self, Mrs. Flink, and Landon Beane," Mr. Silverton said.

"That's correct," the young security officer with the blond beard said. "And . . ."

"And," Mr. Silverton said, "you, Mr. Sul." He paused. "You just became a suspect. One of the paths shows that you could have caused the outage."

The security officer nodded.

"That's impossible," Mr. Sul defended. "I was patrolling the halls. Plus, I wouldn't know the first thing about hack-ing into our power system."

"That's good information to know," the officer said, "but you're still a suspect."

The video ended.

"I assure you that I am up to no foul play," Mr. Sul testi-fied. "I've even sent this same video to my Council of the Keys."

Great. Muns was waking up, Derick's parents and his grandpa were still in a coma, and almost everyone they thought they could trust was a suspect.

ONE-INCH SPIES

"You did well," Anjum told the Spartans. He stood at a beautiful virtual redwood podium in front of a screen. Behind the screen were steps to a large domed building. And above him, several towering streetlights illuminated the scene. They were bright enough that Abby could see the transparent ceiling over the whole city. The large thick bubble protected them from the rock above. It was another of Anjum's worlds, this one a city under the crust of the earth.

It was hard for Abby to concentrate. She had been thinking about the blackout the entire school day. They had to figure out what was stolen and who had done it. She had also thought a lot about Muns. She had stopped to visit her parents and her grandpa, but the nurse said there was still no sign of them coming to.

"But we came in second," Anjum continued. "And second is not good enough. Doing well is not good enough." He stepped out from behind his podium. "Derick." Anjum pointed at Abby's twin, who sat on one of the plush couches in the city square. At first they had struck Abby as odd— nice furniture in the city square. But if the whole city was underground, nice furniture could be kept outside of houses. It wouldn't get rained on. Everything was under shelter. "You obviously need to improve your fish skills. When I heard you were a member of the Crash I mistakenly assumed you could use all the avatars."

Derick raised his eyebrows, then bowed his head.

Anjum went from person to person pointing out their weaknesses. "And Abby, you need to figure out the clues sooner, and run faster. You slowed when the darkness hit. If you'd done either of those, it could have meant first place for us."

"Wait a second," Carol said, standing from her blue velvet couch. "I think we rocked it, and Abby was a big part of that."

"We came in second," Anjum said, pounding his fist on the podium. "No one ever 'rocks' second place. Not good enough."

"Yeah, we already know we didn't win," Carol said. "So encourage us. Tell us we did a good job. Say stuff like, 'You were better than my expectations. I'm so glad to have you on our team. Oh, and you looked so pretty while you did all sorts of challenges. You almost won!'"

"I told you that you did well," Anjum said. "But we need to do better."

"But let us be happy for a moment," Maria said. She was braiding one of her exceptionally long strands of black hair as she listened. "We did really, *really* well."

"No," Anjum said. "I don't want you happy right now. I want you happy on the day of the final challenge. After that's over, I want you to be the happiest people in the whole school. Happy because you rose to the occasion. Happy because you truly met and conquered the challenge."

"But we—" Nia started.

"No. Stop right there," Anjum interrupted. "A good leader settles for nothing but the best. You are only as good as your last decision, your last effort. We were second place. So let's not waste time thinking about our 'almosts.' Let's look forward and look at what we can be."

"Wow, intense," Carol whispered.

Anjum smiled. "Thank you."

Abby would have never wanted a leader like this under normal circumstances, but he seemed perfect for their situation. The secret was at stake. Second place wouldn't protect it. Only a win would work.

"I think Anjum's right," Malcolm said. He nodded at their team leader. "And I'm going to call you *Coach* from now on."

"Call me whatever you want as long as we are winning," Anjum said. "Now, the clue was '*Greek mythology.*' There could be several different challenges that would fit the theme."

"Maybe we'll have to go into a virtual world and do something like the labors of Hercules," Nia suggested.

"Or try to kill Medusa without being turned to stone," Maria said.

"Put me in, Coach," Carol said. "I'll take care of Miss Snakehair."

"It may not be virtual at all. We may need to use the Bridge to study the culture where the myths come from," Rafa suggested.

The idea of a whole challenge where Abby would have to spearhead the Bridge made her stomach turn. She hadn't been invited to the team for her skills. And she felt that. She was one bad decision from being kicked off the team. She wished she felt wanted, felt included, but there wasn't much she could do.

While the group continued to brainstorm, a message popped up on Abby's rings. It wasn't from Mr. Sul or Muns. It said it was from 'The Messenger.' That was cryptic. She ran it through several file checks and opened it on a safe server online just to be careful.

There was no video, no picture, no attachment. Just words:

> Abby and Derick,
>
> I'm sorry for reaching you anonymously, but I cannot tell you who I am for reasons you may understand. I cannot share this information with all of my council, for it may implicate at least one of them.

Before he was tranquilized, Oscar Cragbridge
assured me that I could trust you with any important information I found. In fact, of all those with
keys, he said he trusts you the most. I believe
something was stolen last night. I received a message from someone speaking for Muns that said as
much. This was disturbing to me, for it solidifies
the fact that he knows I have a key.

I was monitoring the halls during the Race
when the power went out. I tried to calm the
screaming students down—it was rather pitch
black inside a school without lights—but as I did,
someone carrying something bumped me. I could
feel a container of some sort against my arm.
Then I heard a door open and close. I could have
been mistaken, but I believe this was Mr. Silverton's classroom door. I don't want to involve
security at this point just in case it pertains to
secrets they should not know. Perhaps if we all
pursue this further, we can find out the truth.

The Messenger

P.S. I hope your team wins. Your grandfather
would be proud of your efforts and ingenuity.

Abby thought through the message as best she could.
It was probably from someone on another Council of the
Keys, and he or she believed Mr. Silverton may have stolen
something. Of course, she also didn't know that she could
trust the anonymous messenger.

"Abby," Anjum said. "You haven't said anything. Are
you focused?"

"Sorry," Abby said.

"Don't be sorry. Be better," Anjum said, "or you're off
the team."

• • •

Walking down the hall had never been such a thrill ride. Only an inch tall, Derick clutched the laces of Carol's shoe. Rafa rode on the imitation leather face. Each step Carol took felt like an amusement park ride, her foot rising high and moving forward with a rush of momentum.

Carol moved to the side of the hall, and pretended to tie her shoe. "All right, guys, you're just a door away," she whispered. "I can't believe I'm talking to spiders. And I can't believe I'm hoping they think I'm cute." She shook her head. "All right, I'm going to help Abby out in Grandpa's lab. Well, not my grandpa's, but yours." She pointed at a spider. "Or yours. I can't really tell which one of you is Derick. Sorry. You're equally hairy and creepy."

Derick wished he could also be in his grandfather's lab. If the Bridge could show the future, it might save his life. It might save the whole world from the Ash. But for now, he and Rafa had to investigate. He tried to wave at Carol with a spider leg to signal which was him. He wasn't sure it worked.

The spider avatars were a secret. Derick hadn't even known they existed until they discovered that Katarina had used one to spy on them a few months ago. Rafa's mother had made them recently. There were only two.

And this was the perfect opportunity. The teachers had all been called to a meeting, probably to report the inventory they'd taken to see if anything had been stolen or to report if anyone had seen anything suspicious. Rafa's mother agreed this would be a good time to look into Mr. Silverton's room.

It was Carol's idea to give them a ride and it was a good one—much easier than trying to weave their way through the halls as spider avatars and not have any students hanging around after school notice them, or maybe squash them. When using such new and delicate avatars, getting squashed would be a very bad thing.

Rafa jumped down off Carol's shoe. Derick tried to follow, but slid off her toe, caught a leg on the sole of her shoe, and flopped onto his back. His legs wriggled as he tried to get himself upright again.

"Oh, so that one's Derick," Carol said. She put her finger to his legs so that he could grip it and flip back over. Derick blushed. Thankfully, his robot spider couldn't. "Good luck," she whispered. "Message me if you want a ride back. Or if you want to chat. Or if you want to meet up for lunch tomorrow. Whatever."

The two spiders crept along the hallway where the wall met the floor. Derick followed Rafa, but it was extremely awkward with eight legs. He had to think about each leg, and the others sometimes felt like they were in the way. There was a rhythm to it, though, and once he got going, it got easier.

They eventually scrambled under the door to Mr. Silverton's room.

"Looks empty," Derick said, "but it's hard to tell when you can only see from the floor."

Rafa scurried up the wall.

"So amazing," Derick said.

"Give it a shot," Rafa said. "Your avatar has the same gripping hairs that real spider legs have. And that is a huge deal. My mom is a genius."

Derick took his first step up the wall and was surprised how easily he stuck. As he took several more steps, he realized that grip was not the only thing that felt different. It was surreal to feel gravity tug at him as he climbed so easily. And it was strange to spend so much time climbing a wall that he'd normally think was an average height. By the time he was to the level of the light switch, it felt like he was several stories in the air. It was a good thing he wasn't afraid of heights.

Derick gazed out at the room. There were plenty of desks and screens, but no people. A large oak desk stood in the corner for the teacher, and behind it, an office door.

"It looks like there's only one place to hide anything in this room," Derick said.

"Let's go," Rafa said, and moved up the wall and across the ceiling.

Derick followed suit, though he took his time moving from the wall to the ceiling. A slipup there could send him all the way to the ground. "It's funny that I don't like spiders as a human," Derick said, "but *being* a spider is so amazing!" It felt like the blood rushed to his head a little, but Derick knew that his real body was still suspended right side up in a harness in the avatar lab.

They crawled down the wall on the other side and under the door to the office.

FLAMES

It was the first time I've ever been okay with spiders on my shoe," Carol said. "Normally, I'd probably do a crazy freak-out dance." She threw her arms in the air, stamped her feet, and pretended to scream. "But that would be terrible if I stomped one of Rafa's mom's best avatars. Bad move."

"Well, it was a good idea," Abby said, looking down at the display of the metal shop machine. She was shaping another object inside her grandfather's lab. "I meant carrying the spiders to the room. Not the stomp-on-expensive-robots part." She paused to watch the metal form into a sun, then drop into water and sizzle and steam. "I hope we're getting closer," she said. "I've made so many of these, I don't know what to do." She lifted up her heart necklace, then looked down at a collection of orbs, bracelets, and rings. After they were remade into something else, none of them shocked or froze as they had before.

"I know," Carol said. "I wonder if there's like a certain design he wants us to make. I've made some killer ones, but I just don't get why we have to keep going."

"Diligence and patience," Abby repeated, starting another design. She decided to make another version of her first necklace. She liked it, but she had learned a lot in making design after design. She made another heart, this one slimmer and a little smaller. She thought it would look better that way. And she placed the star on the front of the heart, but a little off-center. She made her own chain, with links that were more oval than round. Then she used a glove to find another object that tried to shock her. It wasn't a surprise anymore. She was ready for it. She put the object in the machine and began the process. Several minutes later, steam rose off her new heartstone. She let it cool in the pile of other creations she had finished.

She started in on a crescent moon.

Clank.

Carol must have finished another creation.

Clank. Clank. Clank.

"Um, Abby, you should see this," Carol said.

Abby looked over at her creations resting on a table. One object was moving, pushing the others out of the way.

"It's like it's alive," Carol said. "And it's separating itself from the others."

It moved one direction, then another, creating a circle clear of anything else metal. Then it stopped in the middle.

The new heartstone.

"This is just a crazy guess, but I think we're supposed to pay attention to that one," Carol said.

Abby picked it up with a glove first, just to be sure. When she tried it with her fingers, there was a small vibration, but no shock. It must have identified Abby somehow, because her grandpa immediately appeared again. Seeing his wrinkled face was a great relief after so much work.

"You have done very well," Grandpa said, in his usual khakis, button-up shirt, and blazer. "You have made enough objects to prove your determination and patience, which are both great allies when preparing for the future. Please remember that." Abby didn't know how he knew that she had made so many. Perhaps the machine that made them had been tracking it somehow.

The screens lowered throughout the room again. "Yet patience and diligence are not enough." A girl appeared, wearing armor and sitting astride a horse. An army of soldiers marched with her. They started in the corner of the lab and made their way front and center, as if they were marching toward the girls. "This is Joan of Arc," Grandpa said. She looked young, a teenager with dark hair. She was probably the same age as some students in the older grades at Cragbridge Hall.

Scenes flashed one after the other of the teenage girl: Joan before a king, then Joan speaking with military officers, and finally, Joan in full armor marching into war. "She tried to help France in a time of great need," Grandpa explained. "She tried to help free it. She made the siege of

Orléans successful faster than anyone anticipated. And she was in the heat of the fray." Joan charged with other soldiers and was struck by an arrow between her neck and shoulder. Abby cringed. That must have hurt like crazy, but it didn't look fatal. "She has been used as an example of courage throughout history. She was remarkable."

Grandpa's brow furrowed. "Joan was captured." The screens showed her in chains and imprisoned in a few different locations. The last was a tower. "She was feisty and even leaped out of a seventy-foot tower trying to escape." The screens showed Joan falling from her tower and slamming into the moist ground below. A moat had made it softer than most. "She was caught and interrogated several times, then stood trial." Joan stood before a series of men. "Do you know how her story ends?"

Abby wasn't sure.

Grandpa fell silent, letting the action speak for itself.

Guards tied Joan to a pillar, a large pile of sticks prepared beneath. A mocking crowd had gathered, screaming and spitting.

A soldier dropped a torch on the sticks beneath the teenage girl.

Smoke.

Embers.

Crackling.

Flames.

Abby could only imagine how it would feel to be Joan: the crowd jeering, smoke rising to her nostrils, flames licking her feet, then up her ankles. The flames grew higher and higher. Joan clenched her teeth.

Two clergymen held a cross in front of her, and Joan gazed at it fiercely. She cried out in pain, and then again. The flames lapped higher, feeding off the wood. She yelled again.

Thankfully, the screens went black. Abby didn't have to watch anymore. She didn't think she could have.

"After she died," Grandpa said, "her body was burned twice more to reduce it to ashes. Those ashes were thrown in the river."

The screens lit back to life to show rushing blue water with black specks floating on it.

The image of Grandpa sat down and leaned forward on his cane. "When I showed you Nikola Tesla, I asked you if you would work as hard if you knew the future held difficulty and sorrow. You have proven that you can work diligently and patiently. And now I ask a harder question: What if doing what you believe is right requires you to give it all? If Joan of Arc could have seen her future, would she have made the same choices?" Grandpa paused, letting his words sink in. "She was a remarkable young woman and is remembered for great reason. Would she have faltered? I like to think that she wouldn't have, but she did not face that choice." He looked forward, his eyes piercing. "If you would like to gaze into the future, you have to be willing to do what is right, no matter what you see. You cannot back down from a challenge or a difficulty even when it looks as though you may fail. You act. You move deliberately and then let the future happen."

Abby's heartstone vibrated.

"Take your most recent creation to the simulator," Grandpa instructed, and pointed at the door out of his laboratory. "Before I trust you with the power to look into the future, I must know that you will do what is right no matter the cost."

"Oh, no," Carol said. "I hope we don't have to go through what Joan did. I really don't want to feel what it's like to be a human shish kebab."

"Me neither," Abby admitted. "But we need to know. We need to be able to save Derick. We need to save who knows how many people from the Ash. We probably need to save ourselves." She clutched her heartstone in her hand. "I'm going."

• • •

Mr. Silverton's office was messy, filled with different screens, replacement parts for rings and contact lenses, equipment used to fix such small pieces, and a few moving posters for old movies on the wall. They looked divided between epic fantasy and space travel.

Rafa and Derick used their spiders to search through the office for a few minutes. "Unless this picture of a wizard with a blue sword wasn't originally his, I'm not sure he stole anything," Rafa said.

"What about that closet?" Derick asked.

"*Sim*," Rafa agreed in Portuguese. "I think that's our most likely bet."

"But there isn't any room under the door. It's sealed up really well," Derick pointed out. "So what do we do?"

"We do what real spiders do," Rafa said. "Look for any imperfections and push our bodies through."

"Isn't there like a vent or something we could go through?" Derick asked.

"It's a closet, Derick. Most people don't run vents into closets."

"Right," Derick said, feeling stupid.

They found a spot about halfway between the hinges and Rafa was able to squeeze the spider avatar through. Derick followed, seeing a light flicker on inside the closet. Rafa must have walked near a motion sensor. For a moment Derick got stuck and thought about how embarrassing it would be to have lodged an expensive spider robot inside a closet door hinge. There would be no easy way of explaining that. But he wiggled his torso, got two legs through the other side, and pulled his body the rest of the way.

"So far, it's just more supplies," Rafa said, scurrying across the top shelves.

Derick decided to start at the bottom. The ground was dusty around the edges, which made for rough going, as small as he was. But he noticed a spot where the dust had been pushed back, and black marks on the floor like something had been shoved along the ground in a hurry. Derick followed the trails to a large white case. It lay on its belly and had large latches. Derick climbed over them to the top and saw a label:

Chemistry room property. Use only under
teacher supervision.

"Can you think of a reason why Mr. Silverton would
have a large chemistry case?" Derick asked.

"Maybe it's a hobby," Rafa suggested.

"By the looks of this trail through the dust, it was put
here recently," Derick said.

"I guess it depends on what chemicals it holds," Rafa
said. "It could be acid, or something to make poisons or
gases to put people to sleep. Unfortunately, as spiders,
I don't think we can flip those latches."

"Do you think we found our guy?" Derick asked.

"We might have," Rafa said. "But we can't just tell Mr.
Sul. There's a chance he may be in on it."

"Good point," Derick said. "Let's leave an anonymous
tip with security that there is a chemistry case missing and
it's in Mr. Silverton's closet."

"That's not enough for them to search his private
space," Rafa said. "He'll have to give them permission."

"He's already a suspect," Rafa said. "If he doesn't say yes,
he'll move to the top of their list."

Derick closed his eyes and exhaled long. Maybe he had
just caught Muns's undercover agent. Maybe his life was no
longer in danger. Maybe.

THE GALLOWS

Abby stood in front of the simulator, Carol by her side. She wore a suit similar to those used with the avatars and the virtual booths. She would feel what someone in history felt.

Abby knew that she would face a challenge in history. She had done it before. And that was precisely why she faltered now. She knew how much grit it took. She knew the difficulty. But in the challenge she had faced before, the person in history had survived. She wasn't sure that was the case this time. Would she be like Joan of Arc? Would she have to face death?

The idea of dying, even virtually, was terrifying. She didn't know how Derick could handle it.

Derick. He knew what it was like to think death wasn't too far away. If he could face the threat, so could she.

Abby took a deep breath, unlocked the thick metal door, and stepped into the simulator. As she entered, her heartstone vibrated. It was communicating with the simulator somehow.

And then she was in a small shoemaking shop. Shelves full of shoes and the smell of leather filled the room. A middle-aged lady with short curly hair and a work apron was speaking in a language Abby didn't understand. Abby turned on her translator. It sensed Dutch and translated the dialogue.

"You see," the woman said, "you are such brave boys. Good boys. I need your help." Abby obviously was in a boy's place in history. "There are a hundred Jewish babies in an orphanage that will die if we don't save them. Will you help me?"

Someone was going to kill babies? Why? Abby couldn't think of anything much worse. The babies couldn't have done anything wrong. Of course they hadn't done anything right either. They hadn't had a chance yet.

"If we get caught, they may arrest us," one boy said.

Abby nearly jumped. She hadn't realized the other boys stood just behind her. She looked over her shoulder and found several boys, all teenagers.

"And kill us," another added.

Who would arrest and kill those who were trying to save babies?

"That is true," the shoemaker woman said, "but, God willing, you may also save one hundred precious babies, one hundred souls of our Lord." Something about the way the woman spoke carried hope with her words. She honestly believed they could do it.

"But how would we save them?" another boy asked. "Helping Jews escape is a crime, and I don't think the Nazis will miss us smuggling a hundred babies."

Nazis. That was it. Under Hitler the Nazis had systematically killed millions of Jews. And somewhere in Abby's mind, she thought they had occupied several of the countries close to Germany. One of those countries must have spoken Dutch.

The woman smiled. "The Lord has prepared a way," she said and walked behind a desk. She pulled out a tan jacket with large buttons down the middle. A bright red band was wrapped around the left arm, a swastika on it. She also pulled out a matching hat and pants. "You will be wearing these." They were Nazi soldier uniforms.

"How did you get those?" a boy asked.

"You see," the woman said, "it is not only the Jews we help. There have been several Nazi soldiers that have tired of working for Hitler. They do not want to persecute and kill Jews. We have helped them escape to a better life, as we have many Jews. But we asked them to leave their uniforms. We thought they might be useful, and they will be."

Abby's heart grew watching the woman, someone who had helped Nazi soldiers quit their disturbing work and who helped save Jews. She was gathering others to help rescue innocent children. "Will you help?"

Each boy agreed and so did Abby. How could she say

no? This act may lead to her virtual death, but she still said yes. She felt a tingle inside as she said it. It was right.

"Such brave boys. Good boys," the woman said. They felt like such wonderful titles the way she said them.

But Abby didn't feel the tingles when the scene shifted and she walked into the orphanage. The boys simply stated their orders to remove the babies and began to haul them out of the building. Abby could see the fear in the eyes of those who ran the orphanage.

The Nazi uniforms brought hate and terror. Thankfully, no one questioned or stopped them.

The scene changed again and Abby walked up to a nearby farm with an infant nestled into her elbow and against her chest. She was no longer wearing the uniform, but carrying a Jewish baby was dangerous enough. The woman in the shoe shop had instructed her to ask those at the farm to please take on the baby, to care for it. It was their chance to save a soul.

The bushes rustled. Nazi soldiers streamed out, their guns pointed at Abby's heart. Or so she imagined. The rustling was just the breeze in the leaves. With every step, she was sure it was about to happen. But it never did. She arrived at the farm and the good people accepted the child. The scene faded away.

"Very good," her grandfather said, walking through the simulator room.

Relief swept over Abby. She had passed.

"Not every brave choice ends in tragedy," Grandpa explained, the image of his cane clunking against the ground with every step. "In fact, most do not. But we must be prepared if that is the case."

And then he disappeared.

No. Disappearing was bad. That meant there was more.

Another scene engulfed Abby. The first thing she focused on was a man in a long white shirt and vest. "You've each been hand-selected," the man said. "General Washington has asked that I assemble a special group to do reconnaissance. Do you accept?"

Reconnaissance? General Washington? Wait. Abby was in the time of the Revolutionary War and George Washington was putting together a group of spies?

Abby looked around her and saw some young men in uniforms and others in work clothes. They accepted. She did too. She didn't know what else to say.

"Very good," the man said. "You will be my Rangers. I have a mission for one of you. I need someone to sneak into New York and tell us every move the British military makes. You will not be in uniform and you will be behind enemy lines. Some may think this behavior is contrary to the good form of a gentleman, but it is necessary."

No one stirred.

"If you truly desire to be free," the general or lieutenant or whatever he was spoke again, "we need more information about our enemy."

"I'll do it," Abby volunteered. It was her test. She wasn't sure she would have volunteered otherwise.

She received instruction, then changed into average clothes and traveled across the harbor.

The scenes changed rapidly, Abby seeing them more than experiencing them. She moved from place to place. There was a British invasion and a great fire. She wrote information about the British military. Then she was questioned by a British commander who had found the information. She had been discovered.

Abby felt cords around her arms and legs. She looked around. Apparently she had been bound and was lying on a greenhouse floor somewhere. It seemed like an unlikely place to keep a prisoner. Then Abby remembered that armies would simply commandeer people's property during war. A soldier in a British uniform raised her to her feet and marched her across the yard until she saw something that sent fear to the point of sickness through her body—a gallows. They were going to hang her.

They gave her a chance to speak, but she didn't know what to say. She imagined that the person whose place she was in probably said something very memorable.

They prodded her to stand on a stool while they put the noose around her neck. Unless there was some daring rescue coming for America's first spy, she was doomed.

And then they kicked the stool out from under her.

She fell, tensing for what was coming. All her weight instantly fell on her neck. It hurt and wrenched, squeezing away her breath. She gasped for air.

There was no relief, no breath.

She struggled, twisting her body, hoping for a gasp. Her consciousness started to slip away.

The scene faded and her grandfather stood in front of

her. Abby gulped down several breaths of wonderful air. She grabbed her neck, feeling no rope nor wounds. Her feet stood firmly on the floor.

"Nathan Hale was a bright young man," the image of her grandfather said. "He graduated from Yale and wanted to help in America's revolution. When he was asked to be part of the Rangers, perhaps he accepted because he didn't feel he had contributed much. And, factually, his spy mission was a failure. He was discovered and hanged. But he did what he felt was right. In his final words he expressed his regret that he only had one life to give for his country."

Abby had heard of those words.

Grandpa waited solemnly. "We need more people who do what is right, no matter the consequences."

A compartment in the simulator wall opened, shifting out of the thick brick. It was about the size of a shoe. Abby walked over, wondering what had been hidden in the wall.

A visor. Like those used with the avatars or in the virtual worlds.

"You have to see the world the right way," Grandpa explained. "You must be willing to do what is right, no matter the cost. You have proven that you can do that. You are closer to being trusted with the secret of the future."

Abby took the visor and put it on.

Inside the mask, she saw another virtual version of her grandfather. "I have one more fear about you seeing that future: I fear you will believe what you see more than you should."

And then he was gone.

• • •

Derick floated on the currents, looking at the ground below. He veered his falcon left and then dove. It wasn't a stoop but was still fast. He wasn't here for thrills, but to think.

The girl. The future. Ash. Dying. The Race. Mr. Silverton. Mr. Sul. The message from Muns. The Messenger. He didn't have answers for all the questions in his head, but hopefully discovering the container in Mr. Silverton's closet and tipping security had done some good. Hopefully Muns's plan had failed and his life was already saved. They had taken the time to use the Bridge to check on the scheming businessman again, but he was still unconscious.

If Muns's plan wasn't foiled, and Derick was still going to die, he would miss this place. He would miss flying over campus. He would miss school. He would miss his friends and even his sister. When they first came to Cragbridge Hall, he wasn't sure she would be able to make it. But now . . . Well, now he knew differently. Grandpa had seen more than he had. Maybe brothers don't always see what's best in their own sisters.

And now Abby had found the next step in the challenges to see the future. She had messaged him to say that she had tried the virtual booths and the avatar labs with the visor and nothing happened. It was another mystery. He had made a few metal objects trying to catch up to her, but he couldn't do it all. Plus, he was supposed to be studying up on his Greek mythology for the next challenge in the Race.

He would miss his parents. He hadn't spoken to them in . . .

He could feel tears, but couldn't wipe them. His arms controlled his wings and were currently very busy gliding through the sky.

He would miss his grandfather too.

No. He wasn't going to think about death anymore.

Another message came through from Mr. Sul. Derick landed his falcon on top of the tower. Below, he saw the security guards watching as they always did.

He selected the video message.

"This isn't right," Mr. Silverton said. The portly computer science professor sat at his desk in his room, flanked by Mr. Sul and two security officers. "Someone set me up." He stared at the chemistry case that had just been discovered in his closet. Mr. Sul had been informed by security and recorded the scene with his rings. "Check the security footage. I was monitoring the hall when the power went out." He pointed toward the hall outside his room.

"And from your position during the Race," Chief Shar responded, "the power was off long enough for you to steal into the chemistry room and get back here."

Mr. Silverton's mouth opened then closed. Finally, he spoke again. "This was well thought-out. Whoever is responsible for this knew what they were doing. And they want me out of the picture."

Chief Shar looked down as the blond-bearded officer opened up the container. Vials of various substances stood upright in protective foam. "Tell us your plans," Chief Shar said. "What were you going to use the chemicals for?"

"It wasn't me," Mr. Silverton said. "I don't know what I'd do with the chemicals."

"Fine," Chief Shar said. "Stealing is cause for dismissal at this school. Tell us everything or you will be out of Cragbridge Hall and in our station downtown within the hour."

"I don't have anything else to tell you," Mr. Silverton said. "I don't know anything. I've tracked the hacks as best I could and was frank and honest with you about me being a suspect. Now I'm being frank and honest again; I don't know anything."

If he wasn't telling the truth, he was a decent actor.

"It is the administration's decision to make whether he's dismissed or not," Mr. Sul said. "For now, let's hold him in your security cells on campus. I want to be totally sure there isn't more to this."

Chief Shar looked at Mr. Sul for a moment. "Silverton has the know-how to send the mysterious messages and perhaps hack into the electrical system. He stole the chemicals. And now we have him. This is likely the end of the case."

"I hope you're right," Mr. Sul said. "But in the off chance this isn't the end, let's keep him close."

"I'm telling you," Mr. Silverton said, a few beads of sweat on his bald head, "I am a trusted friend of Oscar Cragbridge and I've been set up. Someone deliberately wants me out of the picture."

"You're not in a position to speak anymore," Chief Shar said, pointing for emphasis. "Looks like we found the man behind the mystery."

Derick exhaled long and slow. It made sense. Mr. Silverton could do it all. Derick wondered what the computer science teacher had planned for the rest of the Race. What was he trying to accomplish? Thankfully, they would probably never know.

The scene with the officers and Mr. Silverton faded and left only Mr. Sul. He was no longer in Mr. Silverton's room, but in his own office. "We have other news as well," he said. "Mrs. Flink just reported to me that she discovered that her key is a fake. It does not work in the doors leading to the Bridge. Someone switched it out and her real key is most likely in the box for the Race. Mrs. Flink can't remember using it for over a week, so the timing fits." Mr. Sul grimaced. "Though we can't know for certain, it is logical that Mr. Silverton was the thief. He spent a lot of time with Mrs. Flink and because they are on the same council, he likely knew where she hid her key. Plus, he has the know-how to make a reasonable fake. It is most likely that he stole her key and put it in the box he made. We will continue to investigate, but this stands to reason." The video faded.

Derick took off again, his falcon wings spreading wide. He felt lighter, his robot body bobbing on the currents. Derick could be out of danger. No more reason to worry about the secret, or about dying.

As he glided over the campus again, his relief melted into concern. What if Mr. Silverton had told the truth? What if he *had* been framed? Then not only was someone still free and working for Muns, but they just pulled off a rather elaborate setup to get the computer whiz out of the way.

GOING MYTHICAL

Welcome to the Mold for your second challenge," Sarah announced. The student-body officer with the short, dark hair stood on the same portable stage, but this time in front of a free-standing building about the size of a gym. "This is the biggest 3-D printer in the world. It can make nearly anything out of hard plastic. It even has programs to place rebar foundations, and reinforced plastic to make it structurally sound."

Landon took over, standing beside Sarah on the stage. "After the machine carves the plastic, the shards left over fall to the bottom and are swept away. Then when it's done, the Mold can melt the plastic down and reuse it for the next game." Landon gestured toward the crowd. "You may have been lucky enough to use it after a drafting course to see how the house or building you designed would actually look in real life. You may have used it in design or engineering classes. But today we're going mythical."

Sarah stepped forward. "An ingenious group of students has devised quite the legendary challenge."

"It may have been true that Crete was once a very real power in the ancient world and Athens bowed to them," Landon announced. On the screens beside them, pictures of Earth zoomed in until they showed Crete, an island in the Mediterranean Sea. "It was definitely the case in a particular Greek myth. King Minos, a son of Zeus, reigned there." A king in blue and gold robes and a simple matching crown stood on-screen. "One of Minos's sons sailed to Athens and competed in their version of the Olympics." The screen showed young athletes boxing, wrestling, and racing chariots.

"Wow," Carol said. "I didn't study this one, but I'm surprised we've gone this long in a Greek myth without someone dying, or something really weird happening."

"Jealous of his success, some killed Minos's son," Sarah added.

"There it is," Carol whispered.

"When Minos found out about it," Sarah continued, "he sailed with his great navy to find those who killed his son." Ship after ship crossed the screen, their sails filling as they traveled toward Athens.

A different king came onto the screen. He did not look as strong or as confident. "But when the king of Athens had no way of telling who had actually done the deed," Landon said, "he let King Minos place a punishment on his people.

He was at the mercy of a stronger military power." The screen showed one king bowing to the other. "King Minos decreed that every seventh year, seven of the fairest young men and seven of the most beautiful maidens would sail back to Crete."

"He would probably pick us," Carol said, watching the screen depict the story.

"I don't think we'd want him to," Abby replied.

"And they were sacrificed to a beast in the labyrinth," Sarah stated matter-of-factly. At the word *labyrinth*, the screen went dark.

"On second thought, I think I'd be okay being the eighth most fair in that land," Carol corrected.

Scene after scene of twists and turns inside a huge dark maze appeared on the screen. The walls were over three stories tall. Boulders, holes, and divots were strewn along portions of the path, and stairs raised up and down to lead to a second story of maze or back to the main floor. "This is the challenge students here at Cragbridge Hall made," Landon explained. "The Mold has been turned into the labyrinth!"

The crowd erupted in applause.

"Now to choose who will enter," Landon said. "We only have twenty-four teams left, but only six teams are here. The remaining eighteen teams will also compete in groups of six teams. Only the top three teams of each group will move on. Each of you may have two members of your team enter the maze. Unlike the myth though, we won't base it on who is the fairest. We will let you choose."

"But first," Sarah jumped in, "let's be sure you are

familiar with the rest of the myth. Those who were selected had to enter the maze and face the man-eating monster inside . . ." Her voice rose in excitement. "THE MINOTAUR!" A great beast with a muscular man's frame and a large bull head roared on the screen. Then he brandished his horns. It would only take one good swipe with those to do serious damage.

"He is so creepy," Abby said. "Of course a man-eating anything is creepy."

"That's one thing I never understood about the minotaur," Carol said. "If it's part man and part bull, why does it eat humans? Humans don't eat humans, and bulls are vegetarians. It doesn't make any sense. The ancient Greeks were so inconsistent."

"Don't try to ruin this," Derick said. "It's awesome."

"Maybe when you put the head of one species on another it messes up their appetites," Carol theorized. "If you changed my head, I'd be pretty upset and I'd be willing to bet that my stomach would be too." She inflated her tummy with air and patted it twice. "That has to be it."

"Pick the two people on your team that you think would fare best against the beast," Sarah instructed. "As you choose, it may be helpful to know that there will be chances to gain weapons within the maze."

The team gathered. Anjum took the lead, speaking through their sync. "I'm open to suggestions," he said. "I love a virtual challenge, but for this, my initial leaning is for members of the Crash. You're athletic and can control your bodies well. This seems like it could be physically demanding."

Several of the team agreed.

"Rafa, you lead the Crash; I'll let you pick," Anjum said.

Abby could feel herself breathe deeper. She wasn't even being considered—exactly how she wanted it to be. She would love to stay as far away from anything that eats people as possible—even if it's only a virtual thing. And even if its head was technically supposed to be a vegetarian.

"If everyone else is okay with it," Rafa said, "I'll go." The other members of the team almost instantly nodded. Rafa was probably the best in the school at body control. "And I'll take Maria. She's fast and limber. I think we should stand a shot." Again the team agreed, though Malcolm dropped his head. He looked like he had wanted to be picked.

"Those who have been chosen, please come forward," Sarah said, gesturing toward the stage. Rafa and Maria joined members of other teams in a small group toward the front.

Landon surveyed the cohort. "Fittingly, we have a very good-looking group." He moved his fingers as he counted them. "And we now have twelve competitors. But something isn't quite right. We still don't have our Theseus." He paused and looked over the audience. "The question is, 'who knows the story well enough to find out how we get him?'"

Abby knew the answer, and before she realized what she

was doing, she grabbed Derick's hand and threw it in the air along with hers. "We volunteer," she yelled.

"There it is!" Sarah called out, pointing toward the twins. "Theseus was not selected. He volunteered. We were open to taking two volunteers, and we got them both in one shot."

Abby would have encouraged other members of her team to volunteer instead, but she had been too afraid that someone on another team knew the answer to the riddle.

"Well done, Abby," Anjum said. "We now have four times the chances to win."

A compliment from Anjum went a long way.

"Ask the judges if we can trade Abby for Malcolm in the maze," Anjum said. "No offense, Abby."

She didn't feel complimented anymore, though she hoped the judges agreed with Anjum's idea.

They didn't.

During the wait, the crowd grew restless. Landon raised his hands to calm the group. "I know. I know," he said. "Stop talking and let's get to the challenge."

The crowd cheered.

"We're almost ready," Sarah said. "You want to be like the hero of the myth—Theseus." A pic of a heroic young man wearing only a loincloth popped onto the screen. What did the ancient Greeks have against clothes? "Each of you has your own entrance into the labyrinth, where you have a fair shot at getting to the minotaur first." Sarah gestured toward a row of openings in the wall of the building. Each of the participants stood in front of a separate entrance.

Abby and Derick took the last two. She looked over at her brother. The idea that she would have to go in alone was far from her favorite.

A loud roar came from the middle of the labyrinth, and Abby cringed.

"The walls and boulders have all been made by our submitters, carved out of plastic by the Mold," Landon explained. "But they also did an overlay of a virtual world. That is how you will see all the myth of this challenge." Assigned students approached those stepping into the maze and handed each of them a special visor. "You will see what is real, plus a whole lot more."

A visor. They used visors inside the Mold. Maybe this was where Grandpa wanted her to come with the visor he gave her. Abby would have to come back later. Hopefully Grandpa didn't want her to face a minotaur too.

"In the myth," Sarah said, "Minos's daughter falls in love with Theseus and smuggles in a weapon for him to use. The designers of this challenge have also smuggled in weapons for you, though they have been much more liberal with your choices. They are from various Greek myths. You'll need to find those weapons to survive the challenge."

Get in, find weapons, face the minotaur—that was Abby's goal. Hopefully she could do it quickly and get out.

"But along with the extra weapons, there are also extra dangers. Those who designed this challenge also included extra monsters from Greek mythology. For each monster you conquer, you gain points for your team. But I will warn you, it may take some time and effort to figure out how to destroy them. Other members of your team can watch you on the various screens we have around the maze, or sync up and watch you on their own rings. They can help and advise you if you'd like."

Good. Anjum could do what he did best.

"Also, in the original story," Sarah continued, "Theseus used a ball of twine to leave a trail so he could find his way out. We've done this for you electronically. If you get too frustrated or are in too much pain—or are just tired of being lost—simply select the option to leave the labyrinth on your virtual screen through your rings. You will see a map of the labyrinth and how to return. Of course, the moment you do, you are removed from the competition."

"I think that's it," Sarah said, glancing at Landon for confirmation. He nodded. "Let's get to it."

"Each monster is worth a point and whoever conquers the minotaur receives five points and takes the challenge," Landon added. "Go!"

There was no more time for Abby to think about how much she didn't want to do this. She plunged into the maze.

INSIDE THE
LABYRINTH

Thirty feet in, Abby was surprised by the darkness. Eerie. Of course the fact that monsters could be lurking anywhere didn't help. Every now and then there was a virtual torch, but that was all. She found herself slowing down to stay on her guard, especially while her eyes acclimated to the darkness.

"You're doing awesome, Abby," Carol encouraged. Abby could hear her through her earpieces. "Your crazy run into the darkness was a great start. Their cameras picked it up even with just a little light." Suddenly Abby remembered that everyone could watch her as she moved through the challenge. Of course, she would be one of fourteen they could see, but it still made Abby feel very uncomfortable. It is one thing to step into a terrifying situation, but another to know that everyone can see you cringe and cower at every sound and rustle.

"I'll do my best to help you find that minotaur monster thing," Carol said.

"Thanks," Abby said. "But where's Anjum?"

"He's helping Rafa," Carol said. "And Jess is there to offer suggestions. He assigned Malcolm and Nia to help Maria. Piper is with Derick and I'm with you." It was clear where Anjum expected success. "Don't worry," Carol said. "We'll show them what a couple of seventh-grade girls are really capable of."

"That's kind of what I'm afraid of," Abby admitted.

Abby rounded a corner, then, after walking a few feet, ducked into a hole in the wall and up some stairs. The darkness was thicker now, but her eyes were getting used to it. She could feel the walls and rocks as she moved and even stumbled over them. That was something harnesses in virtual worlds usually prevented.

At the top of the stairs sat a wooden chest, its metal hardware and lock made of a dull gold.

"Open it," Carol said.

"Wait," Abby interrupted. "I'm not sure I should just rush in. Wasn't there a girl in Greek mythology that opened up a box and a bunch of monsters came out?" Abby could picture grotesque creature after grotesque creature streaming out of the wooden chest. "Pandora's box, I think." She thought she had the name right.

Another growl from the minotaur. It rumbled and rolled throughout the walls, but still sounded quite distant.

"Good sound effects on that roar," Carol said. "I give them full points. Oh, and yes. I just checked it out on my rings. Pandora opened up a jar and released all the evils into the world."

"So don't open it," Abby confirmed.

"Uh, weren't you listening? It was a *jar*. The whole box idea was based on a mistranslation. Unless the students building this challenge didn't do their homework, you should be fine."

"Okay." Abby took a deep breath, undid the latch, and creaked the chest open an inch. She extended her arms and stepped to the side, just in case something terrible, furious, and evil came rushing out. When nothing happened, she opened it a bit more. Inside she saw a virtual bow and a quiver of arrows. Symbols that Abby didn't recognize were burned into the leather quiver. She set her rings to translation mode and looked at the words.

It was Greek for *poison arrows*.

"All right! We found some weapons," Carol said, celebrating. "Watch out Mr. Minotaur, we are coming to tan your hide, or brand your backside." She giggled. "Did you notice how I used cow jokes there? I'm pretty sure that's going to be a theme."

"The question is if I can shoot this bow," Abby said, "and actually hit anything."

"Yeah, that is a good question," Carol confirmed.

"Plus, the arrows are poisoned."

"Oh, that is such a crazy mythical thing to do," Carol said. "Careful not to touch them. That sounds like a tragic end to a Greek myth. So it would fit the whole theme, but would be terribly counterproductive."

Abby stepped further into the labyrinth. This time at least, she wasn't helpless.

• • •

"That one is a waste," Derick said, looking down at a wooden barrel filled with some sort of oil. His last two finds were a spear and two metal wristbands that gave him Hercules's super-strength. Both were cooler than a barrel of oil. "What am I even supposed to do with it?" Derick asked. "Throw it at the minotaur? Maybe it will get in his eyes and be really inconvenient. It might give me a second or two while he blinks it out."

"The barrel is big enough that you could hide in there," Piper said. "Or take a bath."

"No thanks," Derick said and slid the top of the barrel back on. He gripped his spear as he turned the corner.

Huge horns.

And they were charging at him.

The minotaur.

Derick barely had time to react, dodging to one side.

No. Not the minotaur. This creature didn't stand on two feet like a man. It was a bull. But it was massive, its bronze hooves pounding into the ground as it charged him.

The bull turned and galloped toward him again. Derick jabbed at it with his spear, but had to jump out of the way. Derick was quick enough that the bull couldn't gore him with its horns, but it shifted its weight and slammed its large body into him.

"Ugh," Derick cried out as he hit the wall. In sheer reaction, he pushed back against the bull. It toppled head over heels several times before lumbering back onto its feet.

Herculean strength. Derick could get used to this.

Derick lifted his spear again and readied himself. This bull was going down. The beast turned and snorted, then opened its mouth—and out came a long burst of flame.

"*What?*" Derick blurted out. "Was its mother a cow and its dad a dragon? What kind of bull can do that?"

"I'm looking it up," Piper responded, "but I don't think your strength is going to do much against that fire."

"What do I do?" Derick asked. The bull circled around again.

"Hang on," Piper said. "I'm finding it."

Faking one way and jumping the other, Derick managed to dodge again, but the flames nearly singed his face as the bull passed. His spear caught on fire and Derick had to discard it onto the labyrinth floor. "There has to be someone who conquered this thing, right?"

"The oil," Piper said. "You have to go back and bathe in the oil. That's how Jason killed it."

"Jason?"

"Yeah, like Jason and the Argonauts. He bathed in some oil that made him invincible to the flames."

"Great," Derick said. "Just one problem. The bull is between me and the barrel."

• • •

A bird rocketed around the corner and Abby fell to the ground as it swooped by. She screamed as the bird shot metallic feathers at her, one barely missing her leg.

"I hate this thing," Abby cried out. "Why did I volunteer for this?"

"Pesky stymphalian bird," Carol said. "I'm not sure I said that right. Why aren't Greek words easier to say?"

"I don't care what it is," Abby said. "It's shooting knifey feather things at me! I want it to leave me alone!" She nocked a poison arrow to the bow and let it fly.

Not even close. Turns out it takes a lot more practice to shoot a soaring bird in the dark than Abby had ever had.

It didn't have room to circle around. The bird had to perch and then change directions. While it slowed to land on a rock, Abby turned and ran. She ran up some stairs, and hid behind the first thing she saw that could block her from view—a box.

"Oh good, you found another box," Carol said. "Open it up."

"I'm more worried about the crazy bird that shoots evil feathers at me," Abby said.

"It may hold something that can help get rid of Mr. Flappy Deathfeathers," Carol said.

Abby heard the beating of wings. She didn't move. It grew louder and closer. She pushed herself as far up against the box as she could.

The stymphalian flew past.

Abby still waited, making sure the bird wasn't just perching to come back again. When she hadn't heard anything for a few more seconds, she got up and lifted the latch on the box. The lid was heavy, but a light flashed and flickered as she finally got it open. She gazed inside.

"*Lightning?* Oh, yeah!" Carol celebrated. "You just got the power from the big guy himself. Grab that stuff and let's go find us a minotaur. We'll light him up from his human feet to his cow face."

Abby smiled. Several bolts flickered inside a long pouch.

"What if this is a trick and it electrocutes me?" Abby asked.

"Just grab it," Carol commanded. "You've got the power of Zeus and you're second-guessing?"

Abby touched it and quickly pulled back. It felt hot, but didn't hurt. She grabbed the entire pouch, and put its lid over the top. Good. You couldn't see the amazing light when it was capped. That might be important when trying to sneak up on the minotaur.

"I know you're trying to be careful," Carol said. "But you've got lightning. You don't have to hide from anything."

"Yeah," Abby said, "but it looks like I've only got four bolts. I'd better make sure to use them wisely."

Flapping.

The caw of a bird.

The stymphalian was back.

"Sounds like an awesome time to use them wisely," Carol said. "Let's fry this chicken."

Abby opened the pouch and grabbed a bolt. The bird

came into view. Knowing she would have to throw it, she waited for a good shot. It came closer and closer.

Abby reared back and threw the lightning. She never felt very confident throwing anything. Derick said she threw like a girl, which was of course accurate, but assumed that girls couldn't throw well. She threw well this time. The lightning struck the bird and a flash filled the corridor of the maze. The bird squawked and a thunderclap echoed off the labyrinth walls.

But when the light and smoke faded, the bird was still there. It was stunned and regrouping, but appeared to be unharmed.

"Why didn't that work?" Abby asked, dumbfounded.

"Yeah, that thing should be charred bird, ready for some ancient Greek dipping sauce."

If lightning didn't get rid of it, nothing would. Abby ran.

She raced down the stairs. But what about the next challenge she faced? What about the minotaur?

Suddenly Abby had an idea. "It's all based on myth," she said.

"Well, duh," Carol said. "It's not like throwing lightning at birds that shoot metal feathers is something that happens every day."

"No," Abby said. "I mean, I think we have to do this based on the myths. The only way to kill the bird is to do it the same way it happened in Greek mythology."

The flapping came closer.

"Because no one killed this kind of bird with lightning in a myth, it doesn't work."

"Oh, that's kind of a cool twist," Carol said.

The wing beats grew louder.

"I'm not a huge fan of it right now," Abby said. "Find me a story when someone killed one of these things before it shoots me with one of its metal feathers."

THE MINOTAUR

Derick sprinted, the bull charging behind him. He could feel the heat of the fire from the bull's breath, but it hadn't reached him.

Yet.

"You see that large rock up ahead?" Piper asked. "Wait until the last second and then jump behind it. The bull should go past and you can double back to the oil."

"That's if . . . I'm not burned . . . to nothing . . . before then," Derick said, panting. He wasn't sure he could run there fast enough, but with a fiery bull on his tail, he had good motivation.

He heard the snorts as the bull gained ground, its large brass hooves churning the dirt.

Almost there. As soon as Derick passed the rock, he jumped to the side. The bull tried to follow, but scraped into the edge of the boulder and bounced off-balance farther down the corridor. It managed to breathe out fire at him as he passed. Derick ducked, the flames barely missing his face.

As Derick got up and doubled back toward the oil, he smelled something burning.

"Um, Derick," Piper said, "your hair is on fire."

He reached his hand up to the top of his head and felt flames.

"Aaaggh!" Derick screamed as he patted it down with his hands and then pulled his shirt over his head to smother the flames.

Piper giggled.

"Sure," Derick said. "Laugh at the guy who just got his hair burned by a giant fire-breathing bull."

"I am," she said.

Normally, Derick didn't worry too much about how he looked, but he wondered what his head looked like now.

"It's not that bad," Piper said. "I mean, you have a bald spot, but it's just virtual."

"Great," Derick said. "Well, I doubt the minotaur will care. In fact, he might appreciate it that I've been a little cooked before he tries to eat me." Derick ran back toward the oil. He knew the angry bull wasn't done with him yet.

"Oh, wait a second," Piper said. "I just got an update. Maria is out. She was turned to stone by a Gorgon. And it sounds like four others have been eliminated too. We are down to nine. Rafa and Abby are both still going strong, though Rafa is closer to the center. In fact, Anjum thinks he's approaching the minotaur."

Derick stepped into the barrel of oil. "Go, Rafa," he said, the oil up to his waist. "Hopefully I can get there soon to help him out." Derick couldn't imagine that the minotaur would be an easy challenge. "And that's awesome that Abby has lasted this long." He sank deeper into the oil.

"Anjum didn't give her much credit at first," Piper said, "but you've got a pretty amazing sister."

Derick would have answered, but he had already taken a big gulp of air and descended all the way into the tub of slimy oil. It felt so wrong, so ineffective. He was taking a bath that got him so much dirtier than he was already. But Piper was right; Abby was amazing. The more he watched her work and try, the more he was impressed with her. He hadn't always been. Perhaps time shows some of people's greatest qualities.

As he came up, he saw the bull.

"All right. Let's see if this oil stuff works." Derick stepped out of the barrel of oil and walked toward the bull. It had begun its charge.

Derick felt much more confident knowing he had the strength of Hercules as well. At least if he survived the fire, he would have a chance to beat the bull.

Derick began to run at the monster. Crazy. He was charging the largest enemy he had ever faced, hoping to survive a blast of fire and defeat it with his super-strength—so many different levels of completely awesome.

The bull let out a stream of fire, longer and larger than any before. Derick actually reached into it, to see if the oil would work. He didn't feel the heat. No burn. Nothing.

Oh, yeah!

Derick slammed into the bull and, with his super-strength, throttled it off to the side. It hit the wall and fell to the ground. In moments, it was back up again, but completely confused.

The two wrestled, smashed, and hit, all within clouds of fire the bull breathed out. In a few moments, the bull lay unconscious on the ground. It's hard to wrestle with Hercules and win.

Derick panted.

"Great job, Derick," Piper praised. "If it wasn't for your singed hair and bald spot . . . and being covered in oil and dirt, that could totally be a movie highlight."

Derick touched his head again. It was still a bit sore. He knew it was a trick. His real hair was still there, but the virtual machine deceived his mind into thinking it wasn't. "That was one of the most amazing things I've ever done," Derick said. "If only my hair were still here to enjoy it with me."

He only took a moment to rest.

"Tell Rafa I'm on my way."

• • •

"Man, I don't like these birds," Carol said. "I guess they were the pets of Ares, the god of war. They eat people—and their little birdy bombs are toxic."

"Really?" Abby said, running away from the flapping.

"Put that at the top of my list of ways that I don't want to kick the bucket," Carol said.

203

"Just tell me how to get rid of it," Abby called out.

"Almost there," Carol said, obviously reading over information. "The poison arrows. That's how Hercules did it. And you've got some!"

"I already tried that," Abby said. "I'm a terrible shot."

"Try again," Carol encouraged. "I'm pretty sure that's the only way to get rid of them."

Abby slowed to a stop. She had a case of lightning bolts, but she was going to have to try to shoot poison arrows. That felt foolish.

She pulled the bow off her shoulder and nocked an arrow, careful not to touch the tip.

The bird came into view. She waited until the stymphalian came close enough that she thought she could actually hit it. The arrow shot straighter than she thought it would, true to its target. But the bird, taking lessons from the lightning bolt, was on guard and dodged to one side.

"Try again," Carol said.

Abby did. She nocked another arrow, pulled back, and released. Again the bird evaded.

After the third time, Abby had to do a little dodging of her own; the metallic feathers whizzed past her. She wanted to run, but by now it was too late. The bird was almost on her. She reached into her quiver and discovered one more arrow. This was it.

She nocked the last arrow and pulled back, but had to elude another feather. As she stepped to one side, the arrow slipped and fell to the ground.

Abby quickly scooped it up and tried to nock it again.

The bird was dangerously close, but it wasn't shooting any more feathers. Abby realized that the bird's beak was made of metal. It opened once and then closed with a clank. It was coming to stab her.

Abby only had a moment.

The bird dove.

Abby felt a sharp sting.

And then she was out.

The bird must have shot another feather at the last moment.

"Oh, dumbfeathers!" Carol groaned. "You're out. And you were doing so well, too." Abby thought she heard Carol kick something. "Looks like you'll have to follow the map out of the labyrinth."

Abby stood up slowly. She hadn't really wanted to be in the labyrinth, but now that she had lost, she felt a tugging at her insides. She saw a map of the labyrinth and followed a dot that led her toward her exit.

"Don't feel bad," Carol consoled. "I think we're down to the last four, but Rafa is out. After a long fight, the minotaur got him. Derick's our last chance."

"Wait a second," Abby said. "How did Rafa try to kill it?"

"With a sword," Carol said. "That's how he dies in the myth."

"That's right, but I studied this one," Abby said. "It's not just any sword; it's Theseus's sword. His father hid it and his sandals under a rock so that when Theseus was old enough to move the rock, he would be strong enough to prove he was his son and face the challenges he needed to. Derick has to find the sword that is hidden under a large rock."

• • •

"I think I might know where it is," Derick said and moved back through the maze. He had dodged the fire-breathing bull beside a boulder. Maybe that was the large rock he was looking for.

After a few minutes and several wrong turns, he found it. Derick used Herculean strength to lift the giant rock. It felt no heavier than a jug of milk. He was sure Theseus had to work harder at it.

Sure enough, a bright sword and some sandals lay on the ground underneath. "Do I have to wear the sandals?" Derick asked.

"I don't think so," Piper answered, "but I'd put them on just to be safe."

"Hardly my footwear of choice when having to fight a legendary beast," Derick said, but he took off his shoes and put on the sandals. He couldn't tell if they were real sandals or if his mind was tricking him, but he couldn't feel the ground beneath his feet.

Another loud roar rang out through the labyrinth.

"Only three left," Piper said.

Just then a girl turned the corner. Another student. She wore a tunic like in ancient Greece. Derick was sure that was only through his visor. She looked at him for a moment and then his sword. The girl lifted a large trident in one hand and smashed it against the ground.

The earth shook and Derick fell against the boulder.

"No offense, kid," she said, "but I need that sword."

"None taken," Derick responded, regaining his balance and picking up the boulder. With his Herculean strength, he hurled it in her direction. It felt like he was tossing a basketball.

The boulder shattered into a million pebbles and fell to the ground. When the dust cleared, the girl in the tunic stood with her trident where the boulder had last been.

Great. Now he had to fight another student who had a trident that could cause earthquakes and shatter giant boulders.

"Poseidon's trident," Piper whispered. "This is going to be a challenge."

The girl reached into a pouch and pulled out some sort of cap.

"If I had to guess," Piper said. "That's Hades' cap. Get out of there."

"Why?" Derick asked.

The moment she put the cap on her head, the girl disappeared. He now had an invisible enemy.

Derick turned and ran. He moved through the maze as fast as he could, racing around corners and up stairs. Three times he felt earthquakes, but the last was more faint than before. He was gaining some distance.

"I think the best thing we can do is try to beat her to the minotaur," Piper advised.

Derick agreed and tried to weave through the maze

toward the roaring, never knowing when he might be struck from behind. It was at least another five minutes spent in the darkness, including backtracking from two dead ends, before Derick stepped into a large dark space. He could hear the deep breathing of the minotaur.

THE FINAL BLOW

You and the girl with the trident are the only ones left," Piper said. "We have a guaranteed second place, but if you really want to get that key and protect that secret, you have to win."

Derick stepped into the darkness, his sword out in front of him. He had seen scenes like this in the movies over and over again, the hero gradually working his way into the dark room until the monster leaped out and surprised him.

But it didn't happen that way at all.

The moment Derick entered the room, the minotaur roared and came storming out of the black. It was much larger than he had anticipated—at least eight feet tall.

The monster was on him before he knew what to do. Derick went with his first reaction and swiped the sword at the beast, but the minotaur hit Derick's arm enough to deflect it. Derick punched with his other hand and caught the beast in the shoulder, smacking it to the side. Hercules was definitely Derick's favorite. The minotaur recovered and charged again, but more cautiously this time. When Derick readied to jab again with the sword, the minotaur grabbed him by the wrist and squeezed. Derick dropped the sword and cringed in pain. The beast grabbed his other wrist and did the same. Derick felt the pressure—but worse, he felt the wristbands snap and fall to the ground. His Herculean strength was gone and his sword lay on the ground.

In desperation, Derick pulled down hard, hoping to slip out of the monster's grip. Because of the oil that still covered his skin, it worked. But the minotaur was in quick pursuit, swiping at him with its horns. That would have been the end for Derick if the earth had not shaken. Both Derick and the minotaur lost their balance and fell to the ground.

The girl was here.

As Derick got to his feet, he saw Theseus's sword raise from the ground and float in the air. It moved quickly toward the minotaur. The girl was about to win.

But the beast sniffed, apparently catching her scent, and turned in time. It lashed out where the arm holding the sword would be. The girl cried out in pain and the minotaur kicked with one of its bulky legs. Derick heard more grunts and then the girl appeared, unconscious against the wall, the Hades cap fallen from her head and her trident beside her.

The minotaur shifted his position and turned. Derick

had no weapons and was facing one of the fiercest beasts in Greek mythology.

"He's between you and the sword," Piper pointed out. "Circle around."

Derick tried, but as he moved one way, the minotaur jumped in that direction. Derick ran the other way, but the minotaur corrected himself enough to block Derick's path to the sword. After a fake and circling more, Derick realized he was coming close to the girl. Her body lay unconscious against the wall, but that was probably a virtual trick. She had lost; the real girl was probably finding her way out of the maze. After a few quick steps, he picked up the trident and slammed it into the ground.

The earth shook and the minotaur fell. Derick put on the cap. He knew the beast could still smell him, but he thought he'd give it a try.

The minotaur hazarded a few moments with his back turned to Derick to pick up the sword. Derick wasn't quick enough to take advantage of the circumstance.

Derick began to circle and picked up any weapon he could find from those who failed before him. He hurled spears and shot arrows. They found their mark, but the minotaur did not fall. It had to be defeated with the sword.

Then Derick picked up a pair of sandals. Unlike his, they had little wings on them.

"Great," Piper said. "From Hermes—but I doubt they can make you actually fly; you're literally moving through a physical maze."

Derick replaced the sandals he was wearing with those

of Hermes. He'd had no idea the challenge would require him to change shoes a few times. But as Derick moved, he felt a difference. He wasn't flying and he wasn't actually moving faster, but the minotaur moved slower. The sandals gave Derick the illusion of great speed. He moved in closer to the minotaur and dodged a swipe with the sword. When it followed up, trying to gore him with its horns, Derick struck one with Poseidon's trident. The horn shattered. The minotaur roared. Then Derick hit the ground with the trident, causing the beast to fall and drop the sword.

With his great speed, Derick raced around the creature, picked up the sword and delivered a final blow.

The minotaur disintegrated into nothing.

"You did it! You did it!" Piper screamed. "We won! We won!"

• • •

"And now to announce the winners," Landon called out, flashing a big smile. He stood on the same stage as before, now under the lights. It had taken all of the afternoon and well into evening for all the heats to finish. The Spartans had won their heat, which guaranteed they would move on, but they still didn't know how well they had scored in the overall competition. "In third place . . ." he said, pausing for effect as always, "the Revolution!" He waved a team up onto the stage. Abby didn't really know any of them and they all looked several years older than her. She had heard that the girl who led them was a certified genius.

"In second place . . ." Sarah announced, waiting longer before divulging any information, "the Argonauts!" Abby watched as the team took the stage and bowed. Jacqueline smiled and waved like she had done it all herself. She gulped up the attention. But she hadn't even entered the maze.

"And in first place . . ." Landon said, priming the crowd. Each winner so far had won their heat. There were two other teams who had won theirs. This could be them. Landon looked over at Sarah. "Do you want to announce it, or should I?"

"Go ahead."

"Are you sure?"

"Announce it already," someone yelled from the crowd, earning some laughs and cheers.

"I'm not sure," Landon joked. "Maybe we should just wait until tomorrow."

"You've played with them enough," Sarah said, slapping him on the shoulder.

"In first place," Landon continued, "the Gladiators!" Another team of older students took the stand.

"That's not fair," Piper complained. "By the time the other heats went they knew it was the labyrinth. Word got around that they had to kill the monsters the same way they were killed in myth. They didn't have to discover it like we did. They racked up more points."

"Rigged," Malcolm said. Obviously the team was frustrated.

"Don't you dare blame your circumstances," Anjum chided in all their ears. "If we want it bad enough, if we try hard enough, no one can take a victory away from us. Any blame outside of ourselves hurts us. It's up to us. Nobody else."

"But . . ." Carol began.

"No," Anjum cut her off. "No excuses. We have to want it more."

It was probably true, but Abby didn't want to hear it. They were a step farther from protecting the secret. She watched as the overall results scrolled on the screen. They were in fourth place for the event, and tied for third overall.

"One more round of applause for our winners!" Sarah called out, and raised her hand to her ear.

They excused the teams to return to their places off stage. Landon calmed the crowd. "We think that you would probably like a clue about the third challenge. Well, we are going to give you more than that. We will give you detailed plans. You're going to need time to prepare."

"You see," Sarah said, "for the third challenge, you will need to build virtual robots that can do a specific task."

Everyone on the team glanced over at Jess. She looked away shyly, but with her lips tilting up in the corners.

"You have three days to prepare," Landon said.

And then the lights went out.

A THIEF IN THE
DARKNESS

To the robotics lab. Now!

It was from the Messenger.

"Abby, Carol, Rafa, let's go, now!" Derick called out and turned on a flashlight extension he had on his rings. He had installed it before he left his room, just in case.

They wove through the crowd in the dark. It was tricky; people were shifting, uneasy without the lights. Eventually they made it out and into the main building. Soon they were jogging through the halls. Derick wanted to run, but couldn't see far enough ahead of him.

He had no idea what he was about to find. The last time the Messenger had led them to discover what Mr. Silverton had stolen. Had someone stolen something from the robotics lab?

"Where are you going?" Malcolm called out, obviously running behind them.

Derick didn't answer.

"I'm coming with you," he said.

"Me too," he heard Nia and Maria call out in unison.

Derick didn't know what to do. He hadn't thought the others would follow, and now his chances of persuading them to leave this alone were probably nil. He also couldn't stop. He had to find out what awaited in the robotics lab.

In the moving light from his rings, Derick caught a glimpse of a figure in a security uniform. He made a split-second decision. "Come with us," he said. "Something's wrong in the robotics lab."

"What?" the security officer asked.

"Something's wrong," Carol repeated. "You're a security person, so come secure it."

The officer ran alongside until they approached the lab. She asked a few more questions, but they didn't know how to respond. Through the window they saw a flicker of light.

"There's someone in there," Rafa said.

"I can't open the door," Carol said, pulling on the handle. She was smart enough to do it quietly so it didn't warn whoever was inside. "It's locked and coded."

"I can't open it either," the security officer said. "I'll call in to get an administrator here."

"I know the code," Jess said. Apparently she had also followed too when all the action hit. "I'm the teacher's aide." She approached the door and pushed in a few numbers on the keypad above it.

The door opened.

"You wait here," the security officer said, triggering a stun gun to come out of her sleeve and align next to her pointer finger. But once she stepped inside, Derick followed. He didn't know what he was about to see, but he wasn't going to miss any clues. Every glimpse could be important.

The small light quickly disappeared.

They had been noticed.

"Stay where you are," the security officer said in a loud and commanding voice.

They heard some shuffling.

They reached the aisle where the light had been. Just then, all the lights in the room flickered back on.

The security officer lowered her stun gun slightly. "Would you mind explaining what you're doing in the robotics lab in the darkness, Mr. Sul?

• • •

"I wasn't stealing them," Mr. Sul said. "I received a message that I should go to the robotics lab immediately, that these robots were going to be stolen." He pointed at an array of robots students had been making that were stored in the lab. They were a mix of humanoids, mechanical arms, and box-like machines. "Someone intended to use them to transport something dangerous without being detected."

"What were they going to move?" Abby asked.

"I don't know," Mr. Sul admitted. The sides of his head glistened with sweat, matting down his black hair beside his ears.

"Show me the message," Chief Shar said, standing tall and serious in her gray security uniform. She had been called in and showed up on the scene a few minutes after they found Mr. Sul.

"Gladly," the administrator responded and moved his fingers, controlling his rings to find the message. "Wait. It isn't here anymore. It's just disappeared."

"Right," Chief Shar said. "Please sync to my assistant and he'll look it over." She gestured toward the guard with the blond beard. Mr. Sul complied.

"You have another situation to worry about, Mr. Sul," Chief Shar said, her voice a little louder and more commanding. She logged onto a screen in the robotics room. "How do you explain this?"

The scene was obviously footage from a security camera.

"This is from the hall outside an electric panel," Chief Shar said.

Mr. Sul appeared in the footage, looked over his shoulder and then unlocked the door with a code.

The footage changed to show the inside of the room.

"We placed extra cameras here after the last incident," Chief Shar said.

Mr. Sul appeared again, opened the box, and then placed a small metal device inside it. He screwed the panel back on, closed it up, and left.

"That . . . I didn't do that," Mr. Sul stammered.

"We just saw you," Chief Shar said, her voice flat. "You may want to try a different defense. I think you and Mr. Silverton were planning something together." Her voice rose as she accused the administrator. "He could shut down the electricity with a clever hack, but after we busted him, then you had to use a device; you don't have the same computer skills he does. Then you came here, intending to steal working robots. Perhaps you would use them to steal the chemicals Mr. Silverton was arrested for. Or perhaps you had other plans."

"No!" Mr. Sul nearly yelled. "I want that footage analyzed. Every pixel." He jabbed his finger toward the screen. "I never did that. I was never there. And I only responded here because of a message I received."

"There's nothing here," the security officer with the blond beard said, shaking his head. "I've been through it all. There is no message today that has anything to do with what he says. No warnings. Nothing even close."

"But that's impossible too," Mr. Sul said, rubbing his temples.

"Messages like that don't disappear without a trace," the security guard said, looking at Chief Shar. "Like Mr. Silverton showed us, they can be encrypted. They can try to throw us off the scent, but they don't just disappear."

"I got a message too," Derick said. "That's how I knew to come here." He didn't know if he should volunteer that information, but it would have to come out eventually. They would need to know why they all came running to the robotics lab and perhaps it would help them determine whether or not Mr. Sul was telling the truth.

After Chief Shar asked for a copy of the message, Derick sent it to the blond-bearded officer. After a few minutes, he reported back. "No, this is different. It's been rerouted several times, but the message was definitely here. Mr. Sul's was not."

"Analyze it," Chief Shar said. "I want to know who it is from."

Blond beard nodded.

Derick hoped he hadn't been foolish. Security might discover another member of the Council of the Keys and whoever it was could receive some unwanted attention.

"I didn't believe Mr. Silverton when *he* said it," Mr. Sul said, "but I have also been framed."

"Then why are you on my security cameras, and why do we have your fingerprints at the scene?" Chief Shar asked, her voice raising almost to a shout.

Mr. Sul cradled his face in his hands. "I don't know." He clenched his eyes closed. "I don't know," he repeated.

JENKINS

Derick stepped into a volcano.

It was another one of Anjum's virtual worlds: a heat-resistant observatory hanging on the inside of the rupturous mountain. The walls, ceiling, and floor were all transparent and showed an unparalleled view of the red and yellow lava rolling and cracking beneath them.

"This place is amazing," Derick complimented, gazing around him.

"Thank you," Anjum said in his Indian accent. He took a few steps along the transparent floor. "Not to be rude, but we don't have time for compliments. We have another challenge to prepare for."

"Okay, I'll be quick." Derick wanted to get back to his grandfather's office anyway. "It's just that you're the person I know that's best at all of this virtual stuff." He motioned toward the lava beneath him. "And I was wondering: Is it possible to make a virtual few minutes of footage look so real that no one can tell it's really virtual?"

"Doesn't this look real to you?" Anjum answered with a question.

"Yes," Derick said. "I mean, it's spectacular. But could you make something realistic and have it be so good that even if experts examined it they couldn't tell that it wasn't real?"

He had been thinking about the footage of Mr. Sul from yesterday and his claims of being innocent.

"That is a very strange question," Anjum said. "Does it have to do with the secret you're keeping?"

Derick didn't expect that. "Maybe," he said honestly. "I'm not sure." He turned away from Anjum and looked out against the inside of the volcano.

"Curious answer. I've overheard other members of the team speaking of your secret. Perhaps we will all find out at the end of the Race."

"Maybe," Derick admitted, turning back to the olive-skinned leader of the Spartans. "Hopefully it's us and not anyone else."

"Yes," Anjum said. "I think we have a shot." He nodded several times and gazed out at the bubbling magma. "The answer to your question is 'maybe.' There are many who are very talented at virtuality, but it would take a whole team of the very best working long hours to pass something off as absolutely real."

It was possible that Muns could have a whole team

working on virtuality, but they would have to hack in and put it into the security camera files. And it would have to be good enough to fool the security expert, the guy with the blond beard. "Thanks," he said. "I was just really curious."

Derick said good-bye and logged out. He was walking toward his grandfather's lab when he received a message from Abby. She wanted to check on Muns.

• • •

Muns lay in bed.

Abby looked at him through the Bridge, her heartbeat rising. His hair still fell in a tousled mess; his body still lay motionless. It was his eyes. They had cracked open. It was only a sliver and only for a moment before they closed again, but they had opened.

"Oh, no no no no no," Carol said, shaking her head. "I'm not a fan. Just go back to sleep, Mr. Muns. Sleep really deep. Maybe dream yourself up a nice new business, or a girlfriend who could calm you down, or some better pajamas." Apparently Muns's solid black scrubs were not good enough sleepwear for Carol's taste. "Even dream of taking over all of time and having all control over everything. But let's just leave it in your dreams and not make it our nightmare."

Abby couldn't agree more.

"Better yet, Muns," Derick said. "Why don't you wake up enough to call off whatever plan is going on and then you can go back to sleep?"

That was wishful thinking. Once he was awake, Muns

would be interested in every detail of whatever plan was going on. That was if he wasn't furious and did something drastic right away. Abby couldn't imagine he would be happy about spending weeks comatose. The only thing she knew for sure was that Muns would want his revenge, his control.

Why couldn't those in the med unit at Cragbridge Hall have their eyes crack open? Abby would love it if any of them showed signs of coming back to life: Ms. Entrese, Coach Horne, Coach Adonavich, Mr. and Mrs. Trinhouse, but especially her parents or her grandfather. Abby had checked with the nurse again before coming to the basement. Though she hadn't noted anything too significant, there were some changes in mental activity and heart rate in Coach Horne. He might be on his way to coming to. He had been a professional weightlifter and was the largest of all who had been tranquilized. Perhaps his strong body was recovering quicker. Abby asked the nurse to let her know the moment there were any more changes in any of them.

"Just relax, Mr. Muns," his nurse said. "I've said it before, but I doubt you remember. It will probably be a few more days before the tranquilizer is fully out of your system and you're completely awake."

"A few days," Abby repeated.

• • •

"Hello, Jess," a small silver robot said in a voice that sounded completely human. It stood its eight-inch body up on the desktop and walked to the nearest edge to greet them. Its metal casing was painted to look like it was wearing a tuxedo. The entire team had walked into the same robotics lab that Mr. Sul had been busted in a day ago—everyone except Anjum. He was on rings sync as always. They passed through the classroom and into a locked room behind, a sort of office for the teacher's assistant.

"Hey, Jenkins," Jess responded. It wasn't a whisper. It was the closest thing to a normal tone that Abby had ever heard from Jess. Perhaps she was a little more confident on her home turf. "I brought my friends today."

"Oh, good," Jenkins said, pressing his small silver hands together. "Would you like me to grill up some chicken wraps and throw on some music?" A beat pumped out of the speakers on his legs and he did a series of impressive twists and turns. He ended with a backflip and his head turning all the way around. His dance seemed a little inconsistent with his otherwise formal demeanor.

Carol clapped. "Oh, I want one! I want a robot just like him." She did her own version of Jenkins's dance. "He has some moves!" She leaned forward to get a closer look at the robot. "I like you, amazing robodude."

"Thank you," Jenkins responded with a slight bow. "And perhaps," he said as he scratched his head with one of his metal fingers, "you missed the simple detail that my name is Jenkins, not 'Robodude.'"

"Sorry," Carol apologized with a giggle. "My blunder." She reached out to give a high five to the robot. He paused a moment, and Jess nodded. Jenkins tapped Carol's hand. She beamed. "I give high fives to the coolest robots." Derick gave Carol a warning glance. Perhaps she was remembering how she high-fived him as an alligator. She couldn't talk about that.

"You *made* Jenkins?" Derick asked, keeping the conversation going and not giving Carol a chance to spoil anything.

"Yes," Jess said, her face reddening in a proud blush. "And I keep upgrading him. I spend the last month of every semester making him a little better than he was."

"So, what does he do?" Carol asked. "Besides awesome dance moves?"

"Um, excuse me young lady," Jenkins said. "I'm right here." He waved. "You can ask me."

Jess looked at her robot on the desktop. "Go ahead and explain, Jenkins."

He bowed slightly. "I do whatever Jess wants me to. I proofread her papers, go through her files and weed out old or corrupt ones, organize her collection of boy-band videos—"

"Oh, I totally have a collection too," Carol interrupted, her eyes dancing. "Do you have the new one from the Electri City?" She broke into song, "The way you walk. The way you laugh. It makes my heart beat twice as fast."

Jess giggled, then looked to the floor.

Jenkins cleared his throat—as if he needed to. "I also clean the lab and do routine maintenance on several of the school's robots, such as the lawn bots."

"Do you want to show them, Jenkins?" Jess asked.

"I'd be delighted." He jumped off the table, landing perfectly stable. He walked over to a group of closets and raised his hand. The door opened. He obviously had the code for it. A cylinder rolled out. It was about three feet wide and seven inches tall. Jenkins cocked his elbow and out came a screwdriver. He removed several screws and a panel, revealing the blades for mowing, the extendable tubes for aerating, and the long blades on the side that trimmed. In a matter of minutes, he had sharpened the blades and oiled the joints, then closed the top. Jenkins slapped his hands together. "And now it's ready to clean the grounds." With a gesture, he sent the mower bot back into the closet.

"Impressive," Maria said, her long dark hair bouncing as she nodded.

"Jess and I are friends," Jenkins said, and gestured toward his creator. "But we aren't like those pairs you hear about where the robot and the human are each other's only friend and that's all they ever talk to. I mean, I sometimes hang out with the duct vacuums—even the welders. I'm a highly social, self-actualized robot."

"You've got a great personality," Maria said, and reached down and shook his hand.

"It's all her fault," Jenkins said, and pointed at Jess. She blushed.

"So you did the building and programming?" Nia asked.

"Yes," Jess said. "He has very versatile movement and can learn new jobs, so it's usually just a matter of teaching him."

"Is he like the security bots at all?" Piper asked.

"In some ways," Jess said. "They learn their routines and protect the grounds or halls. They can stun if things get out of hand. Jenkins doesn't do that. I could get in trouble if I built a robot like that. Jenkins is just helpful."

"Thank you," Jenkins said and bowed.

"Go ahead and show them around," Jess said to her small companion. "I'll just finish up a bit and show you the designs I've finished for the next challenge."

Jenkins nodded and began a tour of the robotics lab. He showed them the different parts and programs, and the collection of bots he did the maintenance for. "And this," Jenkins said, "is the Ping-Pong table. Would anyone care to challenge me?"

Malcolm snickered. "I will." He reached over and picked up a paddle in his large hand.

"Fantastic," Jenkins said, then walked across the room and triggered a door that opened up to some sort of supply closet. "Quad 12, could you bring me my shell?"

A machine that looked like a bench with moving legs walked over to a shelf. The top half of a humanoid robot used its arms to crawl off the shelf and onto the quad. It had a red body and head, but a hole where its face should be. A small black bow tie was painted on its neck to match Jenkins's.

"The quads are used for moving heavy objects," Jenkins explained. "They can go up and down stairs or across uneven terrain. And they can carry up to 500 pounds and run roughly twenty miles per hour. But my shell is just for me. Don't be jealous." He let out a quiet laugh.

The quad brought the robot torso over to the table. Jenkins then pushed a button and the shell's chest opened up. Jenkins stepped inside and rode a small elevator to the head. He sat in the face and took over a set of small controls. "I'm ready for you." He moved his right arm and the torso's larger arm reached and grabbed the paddle from the table.

Just then, Jess walked by. "Oh, no," she said. "I should have warned you about that."

Malcolm served and Jenkins moved the arm so that it bumped the ball in an arc that landed on the other side of the table. Malcolm easily knocked it back. They went back and forth several times.

"Not bad," Malcolm said.

"Are you warmed up?" Jenkins asked.

"Yeah," Malcolm said.

"Serve it up then, challenger," Jenkins said.

Malcolm smiled and knocked the ball harder than he had before. It bounced once and Jenkins struck it back with surprising speed. Malcolm wasn't anywhere close to returning it.

"Oh, you're that kind of robot, huh?" Malcolm said, as if he played Ping-Pong with other robots.

"If you are referring to the kind that can beat you silly, then yes," Jenkins said.

Carol giggled.

They played for another ten minutes. Sometimes, Jenkins would slow up and let Malcolm return a few, but then he would strike the ball with such speed that Malcolm didn't stand a chance.

"Wow, you're good," Malcolm told the bot. "Have you ever thrown a football?"

"No," Jenkins said.

"I'll bring one in tomorrow," Malcolm promised. "And a baseball bat too. I bet you could *smash* a ball."

"I would be happy to play," Jenkins said, nodding at the Southerner.

"I'm ready to show you what I have," Jess said. She waved the group over to the other side of the lab. She lifted up a small robot, about the size of a fist, with a propeller on top. "I know you've been involved in the planning, but this is one of the robots I've designed for the challenge. I built a simple prototype."

"In two days?" Derick asked.

"Yeah," Jess said. "I was able to adapt some previous designs. Everyone has to. Plus, we were required to turn in our designs. We get points for them, and the Race doesn't give us much time. And Anjum and I talked. We thought we should design quickly and use our time practicing. I can make adjustments as needed."

"She is quite amazing," Anjum said in everyone's ears. "But we need amazing."

Jess continued, "We'll use a few of them for the initial stages of the challenge, to get the cameras set up and linked to the elevators. They aren't large enough to carry anything substantial though." She pointed to a screen. "You'll use a virtual cockpit like this one." The screen showed several levers, controls, and dials. "I'll let Anjum decide who drives what."

"I will be interested in any history or talent any of you

have with robots or games similar to these," Anjum added over the sync.

Jess moved over and pulled out what looked like a car about the size of a shoe. "I think for most of the challenge we should use these. I've adapted a previous design and made about four of them. They've got wheels for speed. We shouldn't have any uneven terrain. They also have arms." She flicked her finger and the metal over the wheels extended. They were like two slender steel hands with three long fingers. They rose on thin arms. "They can extend up to six feet, so we should be able to reach anything we need. Also, they have a pair of drills." Jess flicked her finger and two thick drills came out of the front of the car and spun, moving back and forth. "They can create enough of a space for the vehicle itself to get through."

"That's nice. We don't have to worry about doors," Nia said.

Jess blushed.

"And they have these." She flicked a finger and two tiny cannons emerged from the sides of the vehicle. They rotated in every direction. "The details for the challenge said we might need them. So they are there, just in case. I don't really have much you can shoot for practice, other than these nuts and bolts. The virtual ones will shoot tranquilizers."

"Have I ever told you how much I like to shoot things?" Malcolm asked.

"It sounds like you may get your chance to show us," Piper said.

"The cars also have suction tubes on the bottom," Jess explained, "enough they can drive up walls. However, you can't move super fast or the suction isn't enough to keep you attached to the wall."

"You are a genius," Anjum said.

"I'm so glad you know how to do this," Abby said. "The best thing I've ever engineered was my entry in the egg-drop contest."

Everyone looked at her.

"You know, that contest where they give you, like, bags and paper and straws and you have to create something to protect your egg from breaking when it's dropped off the school roof?"

No one immediately answered.

"I remember," Derick said. "And I think I beat you."

"I got second," Abby said. "But that's beside the point. Sorry for interrupting."

"Anjum will assign you your robots, and then you need to practice using the virtual cockpits to control them," Jess explained. "I think their designs are solid, so winning is going to depend on our ability to control them and work together."

They had to win. They had caught Mr. Silverton and Mr. Sul. Now the primary job was to finish the Race, get the key, and protect the secret. That is, if they had caught the right guys, and they both hadn't been set up.

WALLED IN

Abby approached the Mold, the visor from her grandfather in her hand. She had left robot practice early. That hadn't thrilled Anjum, but she had waited for two days to schedule a time in the Mold. The administration had opened it to anyone who wanted to try the minotaur challenge, and it had been completely booked up.

She didn't really know what to do. Abby walked into an outer room attached to the Mold, the control center. Her rings were scanned and her identity checked against her reservation time, then she was admitted. She approached a console with two screens. She could choose one of several preset molds, or create one of her own. In some ways, it was similar to the machine she used to create the array of metal objects.

Her heartstone began to vibrate, somehow communicating with the Mold. Abby heard muffled words and quickly pulled the visor over her head.

"You'll have to forgive me," her grandfather said, inside the visor. It was just him, standing in his usual blazer in front of a completely blank, white background. "Using the Mold is going to require a bit of preparation." Her heartstone continued to vibrate and settings on the display of the Mold began to change. They were moving to Grandpa's presets.

Abby removed her visor to take a look. Through a large window, she could see inside the Mold. First the floor and sides heated up. She could see them turning a dark red. The plastic that had been molded there began to melt.

"While this environment forms," Grandpa said, as Abby hurried to put her visor back on, "I want you to think of your past. What challenges have you overcome?" He waited. This seemed weird. Was this some sort of therapy? Remembering her last year, Abby thought of several difficult experiences.

"Now," Grandpa continued, "think about the challenges you currently face." A series of quick and vivid thoughts jumped to the surface at that prompt.

"How do you hope these challenges will end?" Grandpa asked. That was easy. Abby thought of her successes: stopping Muns, winning the Race, gaining the key, saving the secret, and saving her brother.

"How do you fear these challenges may end?"

That also came quickly to mind, unfortunately.

Abby lifted the visor to peek at the Mold. All of the plastic had melted and covered the floor of the Mold. A large mechanical plow moved across the floor, shoveling the plastic into a large bin at one end.

Thick steel rebar rose out of the floor. Mechanical arms on tracks lowered from the ceiling and twisted and moved the rods into holes in the foundation. She could see them twist in to be secure. Then came whirring and clinking. Hundreds of machines ran across more tracks, releasing plastic and sculpting it around the metal foundations. It was a symphony of creation. They had only been at their work for a few minutes when the metal window coverings lowered. Abby tried several times to sync up to the machine to raise them, but they would not move. Perhaps Grandpa didn't want her to see what she was about to face.

After a long wait, the screens indicated that the environment was ready. Abby had no idea what to expect, but she made sure her visor was on tight and stepped in.

She had moved from a control room to a wide open field. The grass was long and green, a collection of trees reached high with their branches and leaves. The sun brought a warmth, but not a brutal summer heat. Perfect.

"Abby," Grandpa said, walking in the long grass beside her, "you have endless possibilities." He pointed to a beautiful horizon. "Those endless possibilities are your future." He took a few more steps, leaning on his cane. "But the strange part about endless possibilities is that they do not always look beautiful. Sometimes they are disguised."

In an instant, the field was gone and Abby stood in her

home. "At times they look like this," Grandpa said, though she could no longer see him. He wasn't walking beside her anymore. She saw her old living room: the screens on the wall and the couch and lamps in the corner. There was a painting of a beautiful harbor on the wall. A rush of homesickness fell over her. "Look around," Grandpa said. "Feel it. Remember."

Abby reached out and touched the screen. It showed picture after picture of her, her parents, and Derick. Many included Grandpa as well. She took a deep breath. She hoped her parents and her grandpa would be back soon. Back to help her. She didn't want to do this on her own anymore. And Derick. She had to keep him with her.

"This is where you learned a lot about yourself. Where you learned to keep trying." She saw herself in several spots of the room, one after the other. She sat on the couch struggling with math homework; then she came down the stairs and paused to tie her running shoes before leaving through the front door; and then she paced, teared up, and rushed up the stairs after receiving her rejection message from Cragbridge Hall. Of course, her grandpa had switched that.

"But sooner rather than later, it was time to move on," Grandpa's voice explained. The room went gray and a light shone on the doorway. Abby followed it, and as she did, she stepped out of her old living room and into the halls at Cragbridge Hall. "Your endless possibilities looked like this. Do you remember walking the halls on your first day here? Go ahead."

Abby began to walk, taking in the virtual environment

that was so familiar to her. She knew some of the people who passed by, but others were almost as if they weren't complete; their faces were blurred or completely blank. Perhaps Grandpa hadn't finished his work. She couldn't blame him. If she stopped to think of all the work he had done to lead her to the secrets, she wondered how he'd ever have had the time. She knew he had a great work ethic, but he accomplished more than anyone else she knew.

An announcement through the halls indicated it was time for first period. Abby turned from one hall to another to get to her class. She sat in her desk. She could feel the real plastic desk beneath her.

"You faced some difficulties at this time in your past, didn't you?" On the screen at the front of the room, Abby saw glimpses of the trials she went through in her first few months at Cragbridge Hall: Jacqueline kicking her out of her room, her father and her parents being kidnapped, trying to find the secret, and leaping onto the *Titanic* as it sunk. It had been the hardest time of her life up to that point. How had her grandfather put all these images together?

"But life continued," Grandpa said. "And it didn't get any easier."

Another bell rang and Abby got up to leave with the crowd of students. She thought of other challenges she had faced since the *Titanic*: seeing those she loved tranquilized, crossing into the past and onto the flaming *Hindenburg* to save her family.

As she stepped out into the hallway, it changed. There were no longer classrooms on either side, but a dark corridor

in dim torchlight. "And you face challenges now," Grandpa
said.

Flapping.

Abby turned to see a stymphalian bird gliding toward
her through the black. It seemed just as real and mean as
the one that had shot her with a metallic feather a few days
ago in the labyrinth. She ran. With the bird right behind
her, she darted and turned through the maze. She took a
flight of stairs two at a time and then hid around a corner.
The bird couldn't turn that sharply and passed her. Abby
sprinted farther away.

How had Grandpa engineered this? It was so personal;
it included her own experiences. She thought of how the
Mold itself had been formed to be a journey from her home,
through her school, and now into part of the labyrinth.

Abby moved ahead through more twists and turns. She
had no idea where she was supposed to go. She hoped she
wasn't about to face the minotaur. After another corner, the
labyrinth gave way to grass and an open sky. Relief swept
over Abby as she stepped out into the sunshine.

But that same relief disappeared as the ground
rumbled. Abby turned to see two massive creatures—
a Giganotosaurus snapped at an Argentinosaurus. Abby
looked back at the maze, but knew that wasn't where she
was supposed to go. She couldn't go backward to understand
her grandfather's message. Plus, she didn't want to face the
metal-beaked bird again. She saw an opening on the other
side of the dinosaur battle.

She sighed. It was never easy.

Abby raced toward the opening, the fighting dinosaurs biting and swinging their tails at each other in front of her. Abby veered to circle around them, but at one point, the Argentinosaurus backed up quickly and nearly stepped on Abby.

After crossing by the dinosaurs, there was a wall with an opening. Abby walked in only to be greeted with an image of the girl from the future and a man fallen with the Ash. And then the bright light. She heard Derick scream.

She would rather face the bird or the dinosaurs than see that.

"And now, how will it turn out?" Grandpa asked, his voice coming through the visor. "What should you do?"

Three paths opened in front of her. "You must make choices," Grandpa said. "And see what the future brings." She had walked through her past. Now it was all about the future.

Apparently Abby had to try one of the passages. Knowing that her grandfather often would test and try her didn't make the decision easy. She picked the hall on the right.

Abby walked forward and around a corner into a dead end. There a screen portrayed Jacqueline and her team on stage in the school auditorium. "Congratulations on winning the Race," Landon said in his blue blazer. "Please press your fingers to the box." Jacqueline's team did and the box opened. She retrieved the key and held it up in front of a cheering crowd. The message explaining what the key did and how it allowed those who controlled the Bridge to actually time travel would have been automatically sent.

The scene changed and Jacqueline shared the secret online and spoke with the news. Then hundreds of soldiers and government people in suits and uniforms arrived at the Cragbridge Hall gates. They showed badges and forms. They passed security. They dismissed the administration. And the children left. The school was no longer operational. Were they going to use it to experiment, to train soldiers? Abby didn't know.

Was her grandpa saying this would happen? Was she seeing the future now?

Abby didn't want to look anymore. She wanted to pick a different path. She turned to run back the way she had come, but the hall was no longer there. The way she had come had been replaced with a wall and another screen. When—how—had the wall moved?

On the screen, Abby saw Muns in a bed, unconscious. And then his eyelids popped open. He struggled to his feet and left his bed, assistants speaking to him as he tried to leave his room. He grabbed onto the corner of a desk to steady himself. Someone handed him a collection of keys. He got on his rings and began speaking with several people, the government agents and administrators that had taken over the school. Muns was behind it all. He had bribed and worked until his people were in all the right places. And now he was ready to change time. Muns smiled wide. "I will need some assistance at the Bridge."

Abby turned, looking for a way out. A third wall and

screen had blocked her path, pressed against the other two. She was trapped, entirely closed in! She saw a coffin—black, glossy, and cold. Her parents stood by it, awake, tears streaming down their faces. Grandfather stood next to them, his chin quivering. And Abby. She saw herself, clutching her mom's waist and sobbing uncontrollably. The Crash stood behind them. Rafa's hair completely hid his face. Carol was curled in a ball on the ground, and Anjum and Jess looked on from behind.

She didn't need to look in the coffin. Trapped inside the Mold, Abby's breaths became short and her mind foggy. She had to get out of there. She didn't want this future. She couldn't even *stand* to see it, to think about it. She whirled in every direction, but only saw her worst worries portrayed on the screens, her greatest fears coming to life. She was completely walled in. She had nowhere to go.

Abby wanted to scream. Why had she chosen this hall? Why was her grandfather doing this to her?

"This is the future," Grandpa said simply. "And you are trapped in it. There is nothing you can do."

Abby looked at the walls again. How could she have known that her choices would lead to this?

"There is nothing you can do," Grandpa repeated, "unless you choose not to believe it."

Abby had to calm herself and repeat what her grandpa had just said. Choose not to believe it? What did that mean?

Abby looked at the screens and her fears again. How would not believing what she was seeing, denying her own fears, help her? She saw herself sobbing next to the coffin.

How could choosing not to believe that her brother was going to die get her out of this trap? It wouldn't change the fact that she was walled in.

But she had to try.

Abby closed her eyes and willed the walls away. When she opened them, she saw her brother's coffin, the school fallen, and Muns awake and with the keys. Nothing had changed.

It didn't matter what she believed. Her grandfather had trapped her with his crazy experiment. She saw her nightmares, but was also stuck in the Mold. Abby wondered how they would get her out of here. Would they have to cut through the plastic walls? Would she have to explain why she was here?

She saw the images of her failure one more time, and couldn't take it anymore. She ripped the visor from her head, and nearly flung it to the ground. But she stopped, completely taken by surprise. When the visor was away from her eyes, she saw something she didn't expect—open space. No walls. She wasn't boxed in. She looked back behind to see the path she had come down. It was real, but it gave way to a wide open area. Through the visor, she'd seen walls that weren't really there.

Abby stepped beyond where the walls had been.

"Very good," she heard her grandfather's voice from the visor. "You chose to see things differently. The images I showed you were from your own mind," Grandpa explained. "This visor is special. I equipped it with some of the same technology as the Chair. As you answered my questions earlier, I had a program design this challenge based on your memories. And you filled in the images. These were your fears of the future. You can decide to let them box you in, to make you feel helpless, or you can remove them from your view and see your endless possibilities."

Abby put the visor back on. She stared back at the open field, wide trees, a brilliant sun, and her grandfather.

"You see," Grandpa said, walking through the tall grass, "one of my great worries about looking into the future is that you may actually believe what you see. What if your worries are correct? Will you wall yourself in? Will you be helpless?"

Grandpa lifted his cane and hung it around his wrist. "No matter what you see in the future, I refuse to believe that it is certain, that it is set, that it cannot be changed. Perhaps it is showing you what will happen if you continue on the same path you are on, but what if you change that path? What if you improve more from what you would have done? Does it not stand to reason that the future will change too?" Grandpa brushed his hand along the top of the blades of grass.

"Though we cannot change the tragedies of the past, we can work to make our best future. And if you use the Bridge to look into the future and see something that does not look favorable, it is not destined. I do not believe our futures are written in stone."

Abby watched her grandfather fading away in the tall grass. "Now, if you must look into the future, take what I have given you and go to the Bridge in the basement. But remember: the future is not destined. We can always make it better."

THE ANTIDOTE

Abby moved her robot along the edge of the hallway, its large wheels rolling quietly across the tile. She hadn't had time to go to the basement to try to see the future. Anjum had called an emergency meeting and had told them they had to practice during every available hour before and after school. And with security increases, it was near-impossible to sneak into the basement at night. She had also received the good news from the med unit that Coach Horne had opened his eyes for a moment and Coach Adonavich had shown signs of coming to. Though that was great to hear, it was also a reminder that Muns might be fully awake. And Abby couldn't get to the basement to check.

This was no longer robot practice. It was the real event.

Abby glanced at the other windows showing in her

visor. She could see what the other robots on the team could see. She didn't know why she kept checking them. She couldn't tell what was going on anyway. She had to focus on her one part of the challenge. She had to get this right. They needed to do well at this event if they were going to be able to come back and win. Otherwise, Anjum might just kick her off the team and she wouldn't be able to look out for any bigger problems. Or worse, her whole team could be eliminated from the challenge.

It did relieve Abby to know that security was strong. Because they had been instrumental in discovering Mr. Sul in the robotics lab, Chief Shar had a follow-up meeting with them. They had not yet been able to identify who had sent the message to Derick, but they had examined the footage of Mr. Sul and saw no signs of it being a fabrication. Chief Shar wanted to allay any possible fears that anything else would happen. She promised that the situation was all under control, the criminals were in custody, and the Race could proceed as planned. As a precaution, though, they had officers at every major electric panel, and the officer with the blond beard had been working tirelessly setting elaborate firewalls and other blocks so no one could hack into the electrical systems again. He was also personally watching all possible ways of entering those cyber channels. They didn't want any more incidents.

"Another zombie coming your way, Abby," Anjum warned. He had managed to hook up to the building security systems and was playing lookout. Abby could hear him through her earphones. "Then I need you to get to the end of the hallway to make sure Malcolm has backup."

Abby clicked a few virtual buttons and her robot stopped. Hopefully the virtual zombie wouldn't even notice her, but the briefing instructions they had received an hour before the challenge made it clear: these were no pop-culture zombies, no moaning idiots slowly meandering around looking for lunch. They were as intelligent and as nimble as they had been before they were infected. Of course, they did like human brains. They were also fast, and hungry enough to bring the humans to near-extinction.

Abby had to be on her guard. That's why she was there. Well, her virtual robot anyway. Zombies couldn't smell robots. And they were all looking for the antidote to the zombie virus. It was quite a nice setup for the third challenge. Full creativity points to whoever thought of it.

"Is it okay if I think that zombies are super gross?" Carol asked. "I don't even want to get close to virtual ones with my virtual robot. Their skin is so nasty. They really need some good lotion."

Abby smiled as she waited. In their notes for the challenge, they found out that a Dr. Joel Hilton had discovered an antidote to the virus that caused the zombies, but was caught before he could start his work of curing them. The zombies had destroyed him and all of the cure—except for three vials in the doctor's safe. The trouble was getting to the right room.

"Abby, get ready to fire if it notices you," Anjum said.

She rotated a small barrel on the robot and aimed it

at the center of the hall, waiting for the zombie to appear. She really didn't want to pull the trigger. She didn't even like virtual shooting. It would only take a few commands to shoot any threat, but that would be a last resort. Plus, it would cost the team. As part of the scenario, they lost points for shooting any zombies. She liked that. She wouldn't be surprised if a teacher had added that part, but the guide to the challenge had explained that the motive was to leave no trace so that the zombies wouldn't try to retaliate against whatever humans were left.

"I still think it's stupid that we lose points for shooting zombies," Malcolm's voice came through a little too loud. "It should definitely be the other way around."

"That's gross," Carol said, like she had at least seventeen times since the challenge began.

"No, it's not," Malcolm defended. "They're dead. Shooting the undead is like getting dirt dirty. It doesn't really matter. Plus, it's all virtual."

"It's still gross," Carol said. "And violent. Boys are weird."

"I could probably shoot more of them than Malcolm," Nia added.

"You've *got* to be kidding me," Macolm blurted out.

"Focus," Anjum said. "We've got a challenge to win. And we've got to follow the rules."

Abby watched a form appear in the hallway several yards away.

"Remember," Anjum continued, "we can't let the zombies see us, because in this scenario if they know more humans exist, they will resume their tracking. It may lead them to finding the underground human shelter." His voice grew urgent. "Rafa's team, retreat. You've got a group of zombies coming your way. Go back the way you came. Go. Go. Go."

A few seconds later, Rafa called back. "Where to now? We're at the end of the hall. They'll see us soon."

"Veer to your left," Anjum instructed.

"But we need to double back if we're going to make it to the antidote," Rafa said.

"Go left!" Anjum commanded. There were several tense moments of silence. All the while, Abby watched a zombie coming her way.

"I think we're clear," Rafa said.

"Go down the stairs and see if you can make your way north from there," Anjum directed. "But as of now, we're going to have Malcolm's team go for the antidote. I think they are in a better position."

"Or they could just go back and shoot their way through," Malcolm said. You could hear the hope in his voice. "I'll go with them. Maybe the judges would give me style points if I shot with my eyes closed, or with my robot spinning around and—"

"I would totally get more style points than you," Nia bantered back, "especially when I . . ."

"It's not a carnival game," Carol chimed in. "I think you should only get style points if you dressed them in bright-colored tuxedos and fixed their complexion problems. Oh, and if you could teach them to do a dance in unison, that would definitely be worth a bonus."

"Why am I picturing a bad music video right now?" Derick asked.

"Keep focus, people," Anjum said.

"Listen to Anjum," Piper answered.

The zombie was only feet away. It walked normally, dressed in a polo and slacks, but Abby got the best view of his black imitation-leather shoes. Even though the hall was only half-lit at night to conserve energy, Abby thought she could see both emptiness and hunger in the man's face. Whoever had programmed this had done a great job.

The zombie didn't notice Abby's robot.

"You've still got seven minutes until the challenge time for the most points is up," Anjum updated.

"I'm drilling through the wall," Malcolm updated. It was easier than trying to override all the security locks on the doors. Also, it was easier than going through the hallways where the zombies roamed.

"Jess, how are the elevators and the security?"

"Both are fine," she answered. "I've got the security camera on a loop and I'm controlling the elevators."

"Your robots are brilliant," Anjum said. "And I know it's no small feat to run a few at a time. Piper and Nia, get in position to enter the lab with Malcolm."

"We'll be there in a moment," Piper said.

"Scratch that," Anjum said. "Zombies are coming to intercept you. Move to the south corridor. We'll use you to run interference for our escape. Did everyone copy that we will now plan on escaping through the south corridor?"

Voice after voice confirmed the order.

"Abby, you're closest. Get in there to help Malcolm, but don't drive too fast. You've got a zombie coming back and he'll hear your motor. You should have just enough time before he turns the corner."

Abby's heart pounded as she sped her robot toward the hole in the wall.

"Gradually increase your speed," Anjum said. "The farther you get down the hall, the farther away you are from the zombie. But you have to get into the hole before he turns the corner, or you'll give away everything." He paused. "Don't mess up."

"Thanks," Abby said.

"You've got this, Abby," Carol encouraged. "I know driving virtual robots away from zombies may not seem like it's your natural talent, but you've really caught on quickly. Kind of like me and social skills."

"Go a little faster," Anjum said. "He's starting to pick up speed. He may have heard something. Go as fast as you can!"

Abby hit her accelerator.

"You have about three seconds. Two," Anjum counted. "You're not going to make it."

Abby drove her robot into the shadow of a trash can, and hit the brakes.

She waited.

"Quick thinking," Anjum said. "Wait. I'm not sure he's

seen you. But he is walking in your direction. Shoot him if you have to."

"You get all the luck," Malcolm said.

"How far away am I from Abby?" Carol asked.

"You're a floor above her," Anjum said.

"I've got a drill on this roboto," Carol said. "Let's give it a shot."

Abby started hearing sounds above her. The zombie stopped.

"Brilliant, Carol," Anjum said. "Drive a few feet to the south and do it again."

"South? I'm all turned around in here. Tell me forward or backward."

"Um." Anjum was obviously checking his cameras. "Backward."

Abby heard the same sound, now a few feet farther down the hall.

"The zombie is taking the bait and following the sound," Anjum said. "Move, Abby, but slowly so he can't hear you."

Abby crept up the hall, nervous that at any moment Anjum was going to bark out another order. She slid into the other room with Malcolm.

"He's going toward the staircase, Carol," Anjum said. "He's coming to investigate. Now it's your turn to get out of there. Again, good work."

Abby rolled into a room with several tables lined with different kinds of equipment. Charts and boards with written sketches and equations all over them filled the walls.

"This is definitely a lab," Abby said.

"Yep," Malcolm agreed, "but I still can't find any sort of safe."

Abby looked around. There were cabinets; some looked locked. "We could start drilling in those, but that would take us all night. We definitely wouldn't beat the time we need to, and the zombies would probably find us." She rolled her robot to get a better view. "If you were a scientist who just discovered a cure, where would you hide it?"

"It could be anywhere," Malcolm said.

"He'd have to tuck it away. Even if the zombies are intelligent they might not be able to break into it if it was secure enough. What looks the hardest to get into?"

They both chose the cabinet in the corner of the room. Malcolm began to drill again. They broke through the wooden doors and Malcolm rolled inside. There stood a large metal safe.

"Bingo," he said.

"You'd better hurry," Anjum directed. "I think the zombie is tiring of not finding Carol. Abby, get in there and drill with Malcolm."

Abby did. It made her very nervous. She didn't want to accidentally drill into her partner. She moved very slowly. Soon her drill was rolling just beside Malcolm's.

It didn't take long. "We're through," Malcolm said. "But my robot has some sort of short; it has a delayed response."

"It's virtual," Derick said. "How can it break down?"

"But it's based on a real robot," Jess answered. "If you put it under the same amount of pressure that would hurt or break a real robot, it will happen to its virtual copy."

Abby hoped it wasn't somehow her fault. "Can you move over?" she asked.

He managed, and Abby slid a robot arm into the safe and pulled out three small vials. It felt like doing surgery.

"Got them," she said.

"Fantastic," Anjum said. "Time to run our evacuation plan."

"But Malcolm's got problems," Abby said.

"Excuse *me*," he answered.

"I meant your robot," Abby corrected. "We can't leave you in here, or we'll be discovered. Lose points."

"You've got a bigger issue," Anjum said. "The zombie is back and brought a friend. They're headed your way. I think they're suspicious. You're going to have to get out of there fast, and you can't go back out into the hallway."

Abby rotated her robot around the room and looked around. She had to think fast.

"Maybe you could drill through the wall or the floor and make it down," Piper suggested.

"The floor is no good," Anjum said. "You've got zombies underneath you."

Abby used her robot arms to tip over a trash can and set it down gently so it did not make any noise. She fumbled through the trash for a moment.

"What are you doing?" Malcolm asked.

"Just a second," Abby said. She wrapped the vials in trash, then stuffed them into an open box. Shutting the box was rather difficult. She then used a plastic bag and tied it to the edges of the box. "Do you remember how I talked about the egg drop?"

"No way," Carol said, listening in. "I think we have more at stake here than seeing if you can drop an egg and have it still survive. Plus, we're like six stories up."

"This is the only engineering I can really do," Abby said. "It's going to have to work."

"No," Anjum said, his voice sharp. "Don't you dare. I'll think of something."

"We don't have time," Abby said. She moved to the outside wall, which was a window that went from floor to ceiling. She selected both her drills and got to work making a hole.

"Don't do it, Abby," Anjum said urgently. "I'll come up with another way."

"You've got like five seconds then," Abby said, a little surprised at her own decisiveness. But there really wasn't another alternative. "Time's up." She moved behind Malcolm's robot and started to push him toward the window.

"Are you going to push me right out of the—"

He didn't have time to finish his sentence. Abby sent him tumbling out the window.

"It won't hurt, right?" Abby asked. "And I don't feel bad about destroying a virtual robot."

"First one out, pick up Malcolm's pile of junk," Carol said.

"This is so embarrassing," Malcolm said.

Abby retrieved the package with her robot arms.

"Abby, don't do this. The antidote is fragile," Anjum said.

She heard footsteps outside the door. Abby extended one of her arms with the box and parachute. Then she tee-tered on the edge of the drop. She used her other robot arm to grab the glass and tilt her robot so it was completely ver-tical. She still gripped the package in her other mechanical hand. She stared at the six-story fall.

The door started to open. Abby let go.

She turned on her suction full bore. It was enough to keep her against the outside wall of the building, but not for long. She raced as fast as she could. One story down. Two. She couldn't go any faster. She felt the suction cough, and she started to drift from the wall. She threw the parachute into the air and careened toward the ground below. She could only hope that the vials would make it down okay.

CRIMINALS

To our first win," Piper said, her eyes dancing beneath her red hair. She raised her vanilla milkshake and clanked it against Abby's orange explosion smoothie. "Let's do it again in two days!"

Everyone clinked glasses. Finally something had gone as planned. The win had put them in second place overall. A decent showing on the last event and they would take the whole competition. Of course, only the best six teams were left for the final challenge, and Jacqueline's team, the Argonauts, was still in the running.

"And," Malcolm said, raising his glass again, "nobody shot a zombie, even though that sounds really fun."

Everyone clinked again.

"Why do . . ." Carol began, coming up for air from her milkshake. "Oh wait! Brain freeze!" She shook her hands and then slapped her own head. "Oh. Ug. Um. Oh. Almost." She shook her head back and forth. "There it goes. You'd think your grandpa would come up with an invention to get rid of brain freeze." She tapped Abby. "Have him put that on his list. Anyway. Why do people like the shoot-'em-up games? Instead, why don't they make a game where you shoot rainbows to form bridges so puppies can cross chocolate fountains?"

"You just don't get it," Malcolm said, setting down his vanilla-chocolate cookie blend. "Maybe if you made a game that would shoot puppies *over* rainbows *into* chocolate fountains. That could be fun."

"You can't shoot puppies out of guns," Piper said. "That's definitely *not* okay."

"But what if they like it?" Malcolm said. "What if they're a bunch of little adventure-loving puppies?"

"You can shoot *me* out of a cannon if I can land in the chocolate fountain," Carol volunteered.

"That's enough creativity," Maria said. "Don't hurt yourself."

"Back to our victory," Nia said. "Here's to Abby, and jumping virtual robots out of windows." Nia raised her glass.

Everyone clinked again.

"And to finding out a secret soon," Malcolm said, and nudged Abby.

They deserved it. They had worked hard for it. Hopefully they could handle it and they had the character to be wise with it. Abby imagined that she felt somewhat like her grandfather had when he had made the first challenges to get the keys. She liked her friends. She trusted them. But there was little that could tell her how they would react. Perhaps her grandfather thought the same about his friends. Perhaps he even thought it about her.

"All right, everyone," Anjum said in their ears. "You deserve a little celebration, but I've got some more information about the clue for the final event."

The final event. Two days away. March 29. That's when they would find out if they had stopped Muns. And if Derick stayed alive.

After they had announced that the Spartans had won the last challenge, Sarah had shown a picture of a man in a navy uniform, two rows of gold buttons down the front of his dark blue jacket, a sword at his side. He had a commanding stare, a prominent nose, and dark hair. Then she gave the clue: "A virtual Charles Wilkes."

No one knew who that was.

"I went to the Bridge and recorded some footage of Charles Wilkes. Here it is," Anjum said, showing them a video file of a man sailing.

Wow. Anjum was intense. While they had been ordering milkshakes and ice cream, he had been researching.

"Wilkes was called the sailing scientist and was the first commander of the United States Exploring Expedition. He visited the Antarctic coast, did experiments at one of the volcanoes in Hawaii, and mapped and surveyed the San Francisco Bay and the Pacific Northwest."

"Do you think those places are important for the next challenge?" Nia asked.

"Or could it have something to do with exploring in general?" Derick suggested.

"Don't be too quick to come to conclusions," Anjum said. "You'll notice that his expeditions were very experimental, and very educational. I really don't know what to expect."

Abby just hoped it wasn't a challenge for the Bridge.

• • •

His old, wrinkled eyes cracked open and then closed again.

Derick just stared, but his sister hugged him tightly. Tears of relief streamed down her face. Seeing hers somehow helped him not to cry his own.

"Hello, Grandpa," Abby said, dropping to kneel by the bed and taking her grandfather's hand. "I'm so glad you're waking up." She choked on her words. "We need you."

Derick put an arm on his sister's shoulder. It wasn't out of tenderness, though those feelings welled up inside him. The nurse was in the room. Abby had to be careful not to say too much.

They had both come as soon as they got the news, grateful to have been excused from the last minutes of class.

Derick looked over at both his parents. "Their eyes are closed now," the nurse said, "but they were opening earlier today, earlier than your grandfather's." She smiled big. "I'm thrilled, but I'm sure this is a huge relief for you." She pointed toward the next room. "The coaches spent about twenty minutes awake each." She shook her head. "Well, at least half-awake. Mr. Trinhouse appears to be coming around too."

Abby stood and squeezed Derick again. There had definitely been a time in his life when Derick would not have let her. Now he hugged her back.

Things were looking up. With last night's win, they stood a decent chance at gaining the key and protecting the secret. And now this.

Because they didn't know exactly what to expect in the final challenge, Anjum couldn't rationalize practice at *every* free moment as he had with the robot challenge. Derick and Abby had planned to join Carol and Rafa in the basement as soon as school was out. They were going to spy on Muns one more time. He was probably awake. They had to see if they could gain any clues about what was happening.

And they were going to look into the future. But that could wait just a few more minutes.

"Excuse me," a voice said behind them. Two security guards stood in the entrance of the med unit room. "We know this is terrible timing, but we need you two to come with us immediately."

"Chief Shar wants to meet with you," the other guard said.

They didn't really have a choice.

It was a somber walk to the security office. Before Derick and his sister were ushered in, they saw Malcolm, Piper, and Anjum, all being escorted by other security officers. It was Anjum who took Derick most by surprise. Derick hadn't seen him in person before. He was a few inches shorter than he had made himself in the virtual worlds they'd met in. His eyes darted everywhere as he walked, and one of his arms constantly twitched.

"Hey, Anjum," Derick said. "It's nice to meet you face to face."

"I . . . I," he stammered. "Yes. Sorry, I . . . get nervous."

Derick couldn't understand it. How could someone so smart and so confident in one situation be timid and nervous in another? Perhaps Derick was that way too, a little. He had times where he wasn't very sure of himself.

"What's the problem?" Malcolm asked as they were all escorted to a desk. Carol, Nia, Maria, and Rafa were already seated. Chief Shar and a man with short white hair stood at the head of the table. The man wore a different uniform. He wasn't from Cragbridge Hall security.

"I am going to tell you a story," Chief Shar said, leaning forward, her hands on the table. "You tell me when it sounds familiar."

Weird beginning.

"There is a company a few hours away from here called Ruminex. It is involved in very high-level scientific research and in building sophisticated devices."

Even weirder.

"Most of what they do is advanced and some of it even dangerous," Chief Shar stared into each of their eyes one by one. She was searching for something, for someone to give something away with an expression or gesture.

"It doesn't sound familiar," Rafa said. "Should it?" Everyone still looked really confused.

Anjum shifted in his seat.

"Last night, someone broke in," Chief Shar said. "Several someones."

"Is this supposed to sound familiar?" Maria asked.

"Are you accusing us?" Nia added. "Because we were busy winning first place at the Race." Her tone was a little defiant, more than Derick expected.

"Keep listening," Chief Shar demanded, her face tight. "We know the criminals were in Ruminex because they drilled holes in the walls, a hole in a safe, and a hole in a window. Plus there were drill marks on the floor above the safe. And there were signs that the security cameras had been tapped and looped, and the elevators controlled."

Mouths dropped open as the group realized what Chief Shar was saying.

"It couldn't have been us!" Carol blurted out. "Everything we did was virtual."

"Yes, for the Race it was," Chief Shar said. "But it appears that you were doing double duty."

Derick couldn't process it all. They were being accused of controlling robots that had committed an actual crime. It hadn't been just an event in the Race. "But that would mean the virtual building we broke into matched Ruminex exactly. The whole event was designed to do this."

"I did not program the challenge for that." Derick looked behind him and saw a tall student, probably three or four years older than him. Derick hadn't noticed him before. Maybe he had been escorted in early. "I made the challenge, and the building I designed was different from Ruminex."

"You're the brain behind the zombie challenge?" Malcolm said. "Awesome work, man!" Then he looked at the officer. "I mean, never mind. Potentially terrible game."

"I'm serious," the student said. "You need to look at their file because I invented a building. I didn't even use one of the preset patterns. My building and Ruminex couldn't be the same."

"We'd like to look at all your files," Chief Shar stated sharply.

It was him. Whoever had been sending strange messages in Muns's name. Whoever had been behind the thefts. It was him. He was still free and working. He had changed the files.

"Even the original idea wasn't mine," the boy said. "I got a message from someone who had seen some of my work online. He suggested it. I thought it would be fantastic and started designing."

"We'd like to see that one too," Chief Shar repeated.

"We did have to turn in our virtual designs a day early," Jess said. "If someone was really determined they could have made the robots for real."

"This is so not good," Carol said. "I didn't even know I was a criminal."

"My mama is not going to like this," Malcolm said.

"What did we steal?" Abby asked.

Chief Shar looked at the man with short white hair dressed in a different uniform. He took over. "You stole a small device, or more accurately, three copies of the same device. It controls the amount of chemicals that can be released and the speed at which they react. It has some practical uses, like being able to spread insecticide on an entire crop in minutes. The device creates a quick explosion and it can control with surprising accuracy how far the chemicals spread. It could be used to cover a farm and not the neighboring forests or highways."

"But," the man with the short white hair said, leaning over the table, "it could also be used for dangerous purposes, to spread very harmful chemicals very quickly. It has been waiting for government approval because of this potential and it has not yet received it."

Derick's head ached.

"The devices were dropped out of a window, which could have been extremely dangerous," Chief Shar said.

Abby winced. She had had no idea that she was really dropping important experiments.

"You don't think we did it on purpose, do you?" Derick asked.

"In fact, I think dropping the vials is testimony that we had no idea what we were doing," Rafa defended.

Chief Shar looked at them closely. "We aren't ruling anything out. We haven't been able to find whoever recovered the real robots you didn't know you were controlling, or the vials. The search is still on. We will have several questions for each of you."

"But the vials couldn't be here, right?" Derick asked. "I mean, there's no way anyone could get them into Cragbridge Hall." He didn't want to think about what someone loyal to Muns could do with them.

"No," Chief Shar said. "Security is too high, and nothing comes in or out without inspection. Frankly, fewer and fewer people are able to go in and out."

The door opened and the assistant security guard with the blond beard stepped in. He was flanked by several other officers wearing the same kind of uniform as the man with white hair—police from outside of Cragbridge Hall.

"We can't be interrupted now," Chief Shar said. "Unless you have new and pressing information."

"We do," the assistant with the blond beard said. "But before I get to that, I have to ask, were you involved in the committee for the Race?" He spoke directly to Chief Shar.

"No," Chief Shar answered. "And that's beside the point. I'm in the middle of an investigation."

"Wait," the assistant said. "Would you have any reason to have touched the key that unlocks the prize for the Race?"

"The key in the box? No—" Chief Shar answered, opening her mouth to continue.

"None at all?" the assistant interrupted.

"No. None at all. Now please excuse me," she said.

"The police found the three vials," the assistant announced. "They have been returned to Ruminex."

Chief Shar stood straighter in surprise. "Where did they find them?"

"In a security box, downtown," the assistant said. "One we think you have access to." Several of the officers flanked Chief Shar. One slapped handcuffs on her.

"You are under arrest," one of the uniformed officers said.

"What? This is slander and insubordination!" Chief Shar blurted out, her eyes fiery.

The blond-bearded assistant took a step forward. "I did my due diligence on Mr. Sul. He insisted that he had been set up. Part of me believed him. So I searched again for the message he claimed to have received. I didn't find anything, but something was still strange. I looked a third time, and a fourth. I didn't find a message, but I did discover a ghost file, cloaked in the most impressive way I have seen yet."

Chief Shar tilted her head, listening carefully.

"Once I opened up the file, it took me hours to decrypt it," the officer with the blond beard said. "When I could read it, I discovered details of a plot. Just pieces. But it included switching one challenge in the Race and stealing items from Ruminex."

"If this is true, the file was not from me," Chief Shar said. Her expression hadn't changed. "I want to see the evidence."

"Let me finish," the assistant said. He scratched his beard nervously. "Instead of proving Mr. Sul's innocence, finding the file further implicated him. Then I turned to Mr. Silverton's files. It took me a while to find it, but now that I knew what I was looking for, I discovered a similar ghost file. It included another message with the same digital signature as the one sent to Mr. Sul. It's certain it is from the same sender. Both Mr. Sul and Mr. Silverton were communicating with the same person. The message spoke of Mr.

Silverton putting a key in the prize box for the Race." He paused. "That was somehow part of the plan. But the person who sent the message was the one who would bring him the key."

The assistant looked at his superior. "It is possible and even likely that you are part of it all. After decrypting the ghost files and following their digital trail, you are the prime suspect who could have sent the messages. Between the three of you, you tried to steal chemicals, a robot, and now experiments from Ruminex." The assistant scratched his beard. "And it may have been you who wrote to Derick and led him to discover Mr. Sul in the robotics lab. You may have double-crossed your own team. I'm not entirely sure what you planned, but it could not have been good."

"No," Chief Shar said. "I didn't do any of—"

"The way we prove your innocence or guilt depends on the key in that box," the assistant interrupted. "When the Race is over, if there is any trace of your fingerprints or fibers from your clothing, anything we can track back to you on that key, it will corroborate my theory."

Derick wanted to pump his fist and scream in celebration. He wanted to high-five and hug the officer with the blond beard. He had caught the person who stole the vials, and she was the head of security. She could have had a terrible plan. And maybe the officer had just saved Derick's life. It felt like a huge weight had been lifted from his shoulders. Chief Shar was escorted out of the room in cuffs. She would be held on campus until they could prove her involvement or innocence.

The outside police officers asked more questions, got access to the equipment they had used during the virtual zombie race, and made the group of students stay in the room for an uncomfortably long time. Eventually the blond-bearded officer stood in front of them again. "Our searches confirm that you had nothing to do with the alterations. You didn't know you were stealing. You are innocent. But, as you can imagine, we need to be cautious. I'm still in the process of double-checking all of it." He was taking the lead of the whole process.

"Perhaps we should postpone or even cancel the last event in the Race," one of the other officers suggested.

"No," the man with the blond beard said. "Mr. Sul and Mr. Silverton and Chief Shar are detained. The only other suspects were Landon and Mrs. Flink, who I have discovered could not be involved. The vials have been recovered and returned. There is no danger. Now, we just have to prove whether or not Chief Shar is guilty."

THE FUTURE

Abby rushed down the cold metal ladders and through the thick metal doors in the basement. She wanted to feel completely relieved, but couldn't. Chief Shar had come close. And as head of security, she could have done a lot of damage. Abby didn't even want to think about what she could have had planned with the vials.

There were still loose ends. They still had to try to get the key and protect the secret. Tomorrow was the day that the saturn had prophesied Derick would die. And Muns was probably awake.

Carol, Rafa, and Derick met her just outside the Bridge room. They had been careful with so much security around.

Abby wore her heartstone and had her visor in her hand. She had run back to her room to retrieve the visor after the security team was finally done with them. "I'm not really sure what's going to happen," Abby admitted. She was hoping to learn just exactly how to see the future.

Abby stepped in front of the others, and they went into the room with the Bridge. Nothing happened. No appearance from her grandfather. She put on the visor. Through its lens, one brick in the wall stood out. She walked over to it and it shifted, opening up like a drawer. The inside of it was hollow, similar to the thick drawer the visor had come in.

"Place the object you made in my laboratory into the brick," Grandpa instructed, appearing in front of them. He looked mostly solemn, but with a tinge of excitement around his eyes.

Abby dropped the heartstone into the brick drawer and it closed. She heard some mechanical sounds and something whirring inside.

When the compartment opened again, the heartstone seemed like it shone a bit more. Apparently it had been changed somehow in the drawer. Abby remembered a similar thing happening with the sphere she had been given that authorized her to see the present.

Grandpa appeared again. "You have now discovered one of my last secrets," he said with a tired smile. "After you have inserted three keys and a sphere, hold your object near the Bridge console, and a place to insert it will appear. Inserting your object will allow you to see the future. If you want to interact with the future, you will need three keys, three spheres, and three objects that were made in my laboratory and sanctioned as yours has been." Carol and Derick still had not finished their objects. Rafa had also started, but only Abby had completed the task.

"As always," Grandpa continued, putting his virtual cane to the floor every few feet as he paced, "I give you a warning that you may not like what you see. Or you may feel great relief at your glimpse of the future. Either way, remember that I don't believe the future is unchangeable. I believe our decisions can make a difference, can change what would have been."

"You will notice," Grandpa said, his image walking toward the Bridge, "that the machine is not able to tolerate showing the future for long. Showing the future puts much more stress on it than showing the present. You only have somewhere between five and ten seconds. After that, I don't believe the Bridge can take the pressure. It will destroy itself." Abby had seen it come dangerously close when she had used the Bridge to look into the present.

"It is also nearly impossible in five to ten seconds to find any specific moment in the future," Grandpa said. "You often don't know what you're looking for, and don't have much time. If you are trying to see a certain moment, my advice would be to overshoot slightly, and then quickly backtrack to the event you want to see. Even if you don't see the actual event, the aftermath often gives more clues than the moments just before.

"Oh, and one more thing," Grandpa said, pointing with his cane. "After you look into the future, please let the Bridge rest. I believe it will need an entire day to recover, a full twenty-four hours. Anything less would do it harm."

That was a long time. This was a level above just the past or the present. And if they saw into the future tonight, they wouldn't have time again before the last event of the Race tomorrow. They would only get one shot.

Abby walked over to the invention that looked like a giant metal tree. She gazed at it a moment, taking in its grandeur. Her grandfather had really made something spectacular. It was unfortunate that others wanted to use it for terrible purposes. She thought of the future she had seen through the saturn. She thought of the Ash.

"Maybe we should plan this out a little," Derick suggested, stepping toward Abby.

"I agree," Abby said. "I think that, first, we should spy on Muns in the present. We need to know if he's awake and if he has any more plans. Then we should try to see the future, because afterward it will take so long before we can use it again."

Everyone agreed.

In a few moments, they had turned their keys and Abby had put in her sphere. They peered into Muns's mansion, another place in the present. Abby tensed. Muns's bed was empty. She had been hoping he would still be recovering.

After some searching, she found him at his desk. He was wearing a full suit, dark blue with a silver vest. His hair was slicked back, every strand in place. He was still pale, at least experiencing some aftereffects of his time unconscious. He moved his fingers, controlling his rings. His eyes moved back and forth. He was reading something. He half-smiled and then seemed to be thinking.

"You look good," a voice came in from out of view. "You wanted to see me?"

"I don't pay you to flatter me," Muns spat. The half-smile was long gone. "I pay you for your connections. Everything seems to be in order, but I want you ready just in case. Even if the plan fails, it will give me the opportunity I need."

Everything was in order? Didn't he know that Mr. Silverton and Mr. Sul had been caught? He obviously hadn't received word that Chief Shar was arrested and security was waiting to confirm her involvement. That had happened too recently. And she wouldn't have had a chance to communicate with him.

But what if he did know?

"I have a hundred and fifty soldiers from various pasts ready to make their fortunes," the voice from behind their perspective said.

One hundred and fifty? That was a small army!

Muns eyed the man carefully. "Double it!" he barked.

Abby could hear the man gasp. "I don't have the weeks or even the days to make that happen."

"And I don't have the patience for you if you do not." Muns glared back. "No more games. I'm going to end this."

The Bridge started to rattle and Abby turned the keys. They had to save the Bridge for a look into the future.

"Why does Muns need an army?" Carol blurted out. "Because I'm really not very fond of that idea."

"Me neither," Derick admitted.

"He could try to attack the school," Abby suggested, twisting her hair into a temporary ponytail.

"But we have those huge walls and more security than ever," Derick said. "Maybe it's okay that we have all those annoying security bots around."

"But that's just it," Rafa said, a few long strands of his hair dangling in front of his face. "Chief Shar was head of security. Muns was probably planning on her just letting him in. She could have done that. She supervised all the guards and the bots."

The importance of Chief Shar being arrested hit Abby. That had changed everything. Otherwise Muns would have attacked with an army. And during the Race would have been the best time.

"I'm sending a message to my mom," Rafa said. "She's doing her own research on Chief Shar. I'll have her send another message to security to beef it up."

"The only other possibility," Derick said, "is that he tries to bring the army through using the Bridge."

"He does have a Bridge," Abby said. He had stolen it from her grandfather's house at the beginning of the school year. "But I don't think he has enough keys or spheres to bring anyone in through the present."

"At least we don't think he does," Rafa said.

Abby turned back to the Bridge. It had stopped rattling and stood firm. "I guess looking into the future just became a lot more important." She took in a deep breath. "After I put in my heartstone, where do I look?" She shook her head. "Maybe I should start with when."

"I think if Muns is going to make a move, it will be during the last event of the Race," Derick said. "That's where his plan seems to be leading."

"Maybe I should set the Bridge for just after the last event tomorrow night," Abby suggested. "That way we can see what happens after and get better clues."

"Sounds good," Carol said, and gave a double thumbs-up. "And we can see my victory dance when we win the Race! Go Spartans!" She karate kicked and then broke out into a dance.

"How can you dance right now?" Derick asked. "This is serious stuff."

"Like this," Carol said, and wiggled some more.

Derick shook his head. "The final event is scheduled for seven o' clock. Knowing when it ends is trickier. They can go for a few hours, but I think most of them last just an hour. Maybe start at eight o'clock and either move forward or back in time from there."

"Where should I search?" Abby asked. "I need to plug in a place."

"If we're afraid of Muns gaining control of time," Rafa said, "maybe start right here at the Bridge." He nodded toward the large invention. "And then move to the security wall or the auditorium if you don't see anything." All of the student body would watch the final event from the auditorium.

"Sounds good," Abby said.

"I'll set my rings and count down from ten seconds so we don't break this thing," Carol volunteered. "That would be super-nasty-awful-wretched-no-good terribleness. I'll set it to count down out loud."

Abby made sure that everyone was okay with the plan, then took a deep breath. With Rafa's help, she turned the keys. She put in her sphere. Abby set her heartstone near the console and it vibrated. A small door opened above a keyhole. She slipped the heartstone inside. Rather than wasting any time scrolling, Abby changed the time code for tomorrow night. The Bridge rumbled the moment it accepted the date.

"Ten," Carol's rings called out, in the voice of an overly dramatic actor.

A faded ghost of tomorrow night filled the other side of the room, a shadow of what would be. The Bridge showed a realistic image of itself. It almost appeared to be like looking in a giant mirror, except for the people. Abby saw herself. Her future self.

"Nine."

In the future, Abby wasn't standing confidently at the Bridge's console like she was now. She was weeping on the floor, Carol beside her.

"Eight."

For a moment, Abby was stunned, taking in the scene. Something in the future would go terribly wrong.

"Seven."

There was no more time to think about it. Abby scrolled back in time. It was like rewinding through a movie. Abby in the future got up from her knees and was gazing ahead, her mouth moving and her arm gesturing at the same time.

"Six."

"You're yelling something," Rafa said.

"Five."

Abby stopped scrolling to hear what she would say in the future. "Derick, you can't possibly run that fast," her future self screamed.

"Four."

"Derick, don't! *Don't!*" Future Abby cried out.

"Three."

Where was Derick? Abby made a quick decision between the auditorium and the security walls. If her future self wasn't in the auditorium, why would Derick be there? Remembering that seeing the aftermath was often useful, Abby scrolled ahead in time slightly as she moved the perspective outside the building.

"Two."

As Abby moved out through the grounds, she caught a glimpse of Derick sprinting.

"One."

All they saw was a burst of light. All they heard was Derick's scream before Carol pulled the keys.

Derick's voice from the future echoed off the walls.

Everyone stood in silence for several seconds, their eyes acclimating back to the darkness of the basement.

"I hate that light," Derick said.

"What causes it?" Carol asked.

"I have no idea," Derick said. "But I guess we haven't stopped Muns's plan."

"We've got to try to see the future again," Abby said,

turning back toward the console and the keys. "See how we can stop it."

"We can't," Rafa said. "Unless you want to do Muns a great favor and destroy the Bridge."

Abby froze. Nothing they had done had changed the future. Even though Mr. Silverton and Mr. Sul were caught. Even though Chief Shar was arrested—it still turned out the same. Derick was going to die. Maybe they all would. Maybe this was the moment that would lead to Muns taking over and striking anyone who stood in his way with the Ash.

All their efforts meant nothing.

Nothing.

Abby wished her grandfather was awake, that he could tell her what to do. But even if he was, what could he say?

"This is crazy," Carol said. "But like Rafa suggested a long time ago, maybe we should use the Bridge to attack Muns. You could tranquilize him again."

"We can't until tomorrow night," Derick said. "The Bridge has to rest, and it wouldn't be ready until about the same time as the Race ends."

Abby twisted her hair into another temporary ponytail. "And even if we did, someone else is working for him inside Cragbridge Hall. Their plan would still happen."

"What if we go back in time and change something?" Rafa asked. "We could do something to Muns."

"We shouldn't," Abby said. "It's too dangerous. That's what we've been trying to keep Muns from doing. We might give the Ash to someone else. Maybe a lot of someones."

"Plus," Derick repeated, "we can't use the Bridge until the end of the event, unless we want to risk destroying it."

It was hopeless.

No. That wasn't right. At least not according to Grandpa.

"Wait," Abby said. "Just because we see something in the future doesn't mean that it *will* happen. We can make different choices. We can do better than we would have." Her eyes welled up with tears. "This isn't going to happen. We're going to figure something out."

• • •

Derick lay in his bed. This could be his last night alive.

He had so many questions about what Muns had planned, about what the next day would hold. But he knew Muns had someone working for him inside Cragbridge Hall. He knew Muns had an army. And he knew there were only a handful of people who knew the secret, people he knew he could trust: his sister, Carol, Rafa, and Rafa's mother. Sure, there was a chance his parents, his grandpa, and a few more teachers might wake up, but even then, how could they possibly stand up to Muns?

His thoughts churned over and over in his mind. They would have to do something different. He would have to do something better than he would have before.

Derick had an idea. There, in the dark, lying in his bed, he had an idea. It was a bit bold, unexpected. Maybe it was enough to change the future. He synced up with Abby,

Carol, Rafa, and Rafa's mother to see if they agreed. They discussed it for nearly an hour before consenting.

Derick synced up with all of the Spartans, several of them very nearly asleep. In fact, he may have woken a few of them up. He took a deep breath. "I know it's late, but we've been thinking. Tomorrow is the day of the last challenge, and we hopefully have a chance to win it."

"And that's when we'll get to learn the secret," Piper said and yawned.

Derick nodded.

"If we win, we think we'd rather have you hear the secret from us that from whomever else has offered it," Abby said.

"And if we don't win, there's a good chance we may need your help," Derick added.

Derick started at the beginning. He didn't tell it all, but he told about the Bridge and how it could really go into the past and how Muns desperately wanted that power. He mentioned that some people have keys and Muns would stop at nothing to get them. He told of all the ways Muns had threatened lives to try to gain the keys. He steered clear of the spheres that allowed those who had them to look anywhere into the present, and the heartstone Abby had that allowed her to see the future. When he finally stopped, he waited for their reaction.

"Whoa, that is crazy," Malcolm said.

"Yes, it is," Derick admitted.

"I told you this secret may be a burden," Rafa said.

"I still don't know what to say," Nia mumbled. "That

was all real, right? You didn't just give us your creative writing term paper, did you?"

"Nope. It's true," Abby said.

"Are you sure?" Malcolm asked. "'Cause that would be mean to wake us up for y'all to tell us some crazy lie. Plus, my mama doesn't approve of lies."

"It's all true," Derick promised.

"It totally, totally, *totally* is," Carol said. "And it's a really hard secret to keep."

"It brings a whole new level of importance to our last event," Anjum said. "Though I admit I will need time to think through what this means, I know I don't want just anyone knowing this information. It's potentially very dangerous."

"If things don't go as planned," Abby said, "and Muns has something more up his sleeve, we would really appreciate some help. You are some of the most talented students at this school. It's because of kids like you that my grandpa founded this school, that he took the chance on his inventions. He thought what he could help kids learn would outweigh the dangers. Perhaps we can prove him right."

MARCH 29

Abby woke up again.

She couldn't sleep. Too much to haunt her. She checked the time: 5:30 AM. She might as well get up.

March 29.

Today was the day of the final challenge. And the day the saturn said Derick would die.

While Carol snored in the background, Abby took a quick shower and then put in her contacts and put on her rings. A message was waiting—a message from Derick.

She clicked on it, and saw her brother sitting on his bed.

"Hey, Sis," he said. "I can't sleep." She heard some light snoring in the background. He had to deal with the same kind of roommate as she did. He must have filmed this sometime late last night after they spoke with the Spartans. "I'm glad we told them all about the keys and the Bridge. I think it was a good move." He paused, opened his mouth, shut it, then opened it again.

"I've had a lot of thoughts lately . . . and . . . well, maybe I won't even send this to you. Or maybe I will. I don't know." He wiped his hand over his face. His eyes were red and tired. "I guess tomorrow is the day that I might . . . die." He clenched his jaw for a moment. The moment lingered. "That is a really weird feeling. I mean, I don't want to . . ." His voice broke. He passed his hand over his face again, then shook his head. "Just in case it actually happens, I think I should let you know a few things."

Abby sniffled.

"When you think you might die, you see the whole world differently," he said. "I mean . . . some things that you thought were super important . . . just aren't. Like making a samurai game. Or impressing everyone." He took a deep breath. "And some things just seem more and more important."

Abby rubbed her eyes.

"You know," Derick continued, "it hasn't been my favorite thing to be a twin. I mean, if sometime someone had let me pick, I don't think I would have picked it."

Tears. She knew what he meant, but inside it hurt. Abby couldn't get into the school on her own. She didn't get asked to the dance. She wasn't really invited to be on a team for the Race. And now her own brother admitted that he wouldn't have chosen to be her twin.

"And it used to bug me," Derick said. "I mean, we

usually get along okay." A smile cracked his face. "Most of the time," he corrected.

Abby let out a half-laugh, half-cry.

"Some people have even asked why I got better grades than you, and did better at . . ." He didn't finish the sentence. "And I, I used to wish you were different. That you were more . . . like me."

Abby knew that Derick had been better at most everything their whole lives, but she hadn't known that others asked about it.

Derick closed his eyes for a moment. When he opened them, tears rolled out from under both eyelids. "I don't think that anymore." He wiped his cheeks. "I don't think that kids our age always see how amazing people really are. They look at all sorts of stuff on the outside—the stuff everyone can easily see. And they think that's important. A lot of the time it isn't. And I thought that way too. I even thought that way about you. But you won me over, Abs." He swallowed. "I mean, you don't stop trying and every time anyone really gives you a chance, you win them over. You don't give up. You never give up."

He blinked and used the back of his hand to wipe the corner of his eye. "Grandpa saw it in you long before I did. And you have saved everything a few times now. And hopefully you'll save the day again and this whole message will be worthless." He sniffled. "If that's the case, let's just agree to erase this thing." He laughed louder than normal. "We'll pretend it never happened."

"But if somehow tomorrow is my last day, please tell

Mom and Dad . . ." He looked away. He looked back and tried to talk, but then turned away again. "Tell them I love them." His chin quivered. "I didn't tell them that very often. But I do. Tell Grandpa that I tried and that I love him too. And I'm grateful he . . . that he trusted me. I really did try."

Abby was a complete mess. She used the towel she had hanging on her bedrail to soak up the tears.

"But you need to know that you are amazing. Sometimes the more you get to know someone, the more they disappoint you. Well, since we were wombmates, I think we know each other pretty well. And Abby, I think you just keep getting better."

He wiped his nose. "Sorry if some people don't always get it. They'll figure it out. You just keep being amazing." He didn't even try to stop the tears.

"So, tell Rafa he's been like a brother. And tell Carol that she's kind of amazing too." He smiled. "And she's pretty cute." Then his eyes went wide and he pointed at the recording. "But if I don't die, don't you dare tell her that I said that. I don't want her getting any ideas."

Abby cried harder as she laughed.

"Tell the team that I appreciated how hard they tried." He swallowed. "So . . . yeah. I guess that's about it. I love ya, sis. Remember that." He reached forward to turn off the recording. "Oh, and if I'm not around, make sure you kick Muns's trash for me."

The video ended.

• • •

Classes passed in a blur. Everyone talked about the Race, some wished Abby good luck. Jacqueline promised that the Spartans would lose. All Abby could think of was her brother and what she had seen last night.

They discussed trying to call off the Race, but they knew security needed the contest to finish so they could analyze the key and see if Chief Shar was guilty. Also, if the Race didn't end on time, an automatic message would tell everyone at Cragbridge Hall about the keys and the Bridge. They discussed not participating in the last event, but if there was any chance to get another key and protect the secret, they needed to do it. They would rush to the basement afterward just in case Muns tried anything. In fact, if they weren't needed in the final moments, those with keys could sneak off early and be ready.

But Abby had seen the future. She had seen herself in the basement. And it didn't look like it turned out very well. But she didn't know what else she could do.

She walked slowly down the hall and stepped into the medical unit. She forced herself to smile when she saw the nurse. "How are you?"

"Better every moment," the nurse answered, her voice chipper. "Several of the teachers have been in and out of consciousness all day. I think they will be back soon. But of course the better news for you is a certain three people are coming around. They may be fully awake by tomorrow. Maybe even later tonight."

Abby forced herself to look happy again. She hoped the nurse was off. She hoped they would wake up sooner. Later tonight might be too late. "The sooner they're up, the better," Abby said, moving toward their room. "Will you keep me updated?"

"Of course."

Abby walked into the room to see her grandpa's eyes open and then close. She grabbed his hand. "Grandpa, I need you. Please wake up."

He mumbled but didn't speak.

Abby looked over her shoulder to be sure that the nurse wasn't listening. "I think Muns is planning something terrible and it may happen tonight. And Derick may not survive." She whispered one more sentence. "I saw it in the future."

Grandpa stirred. Could he understand?

"Yes, the future," she whispered. "I discovered your last secret. And Derick is in trouble."

Grandpa looked again, his eyes thin slits under his many wrinkles. "Secrets?" he asked in a daze.

He spoke! He was gaining more and more consciousness. "Yeah, Grandpa. I've learned your secrets that the Bridge can interact with the past, the present, *and* the future."

He looked up at her and his lips curled. It was a lazy partial smile. "What about the last one?" he asked.

"The last what?" Abby asked.

"The last secret," Grandpa said, and smacked his lips together.

287

"Is there another one?" Abby asked.

But Grandpa closed his eyes.

"Grandpa, what do I do to help Derick?"

He didn't reply.

"Grandpa?"

He was back asleep.

• • •

Derick looked at the faces of his team. They had definitely worked hard. He didn't know what they were about to face, but he thought they had a good shot of winning. They were all gathered in a history classroom. Except for Anjum. He was with them through chat.

"Now," Anjum said, "thanks for coming. I should apologize for how I acted in the security room. It's always difficult for me when others see me in person. I should say thank you for putting up with my weaknesses. I do not like crowds. And when I say 'crowds,' I really mean any group larger than just me." He let out an uncomfortable, awkward laugh. "You have been good to allow me to use our rings to speak together."

Anjum paused. "I invited you here because before we go into the last challenge, I want to show you something. I want you to know why you are called the Spartans. Abby, I've sent you a Bridge code; please share it with the others."

Abby stepped into a booth and put in a Bridge code. She selected the option to show the event throughout the whole classroom, as a teacher would. Immediately the whole team was surrounded by two armies about to clash in a war.

On one side, soldiers with brass shields and spears and heavy armor waited. They drew close and interlocked their shields, making a human wall. The soldiers hollered out in raucous energy, building their rage. On the other side, men in hoods and robes with spears and woven shields approached silently.

Derick looked back and forth between the sides. He wasn't sure what was more intimidating: the screamers set in defense, or the silent approaching army intent to break through their lines. Both were unnerving.

Step by step they grew closer. Then the silent soldiers charged, raising their spears. The two armies clashed in battle. Spears jabbed; men screamed. The army on the defense, their shields locked together, pushed back against their attackers.

"This is one of the greatest last stands in history," Anjum explained. "Xerxes came with his Persian army and completely outnumbered the Spartans. Zoom out, Abby. You'll see better what is going on."

Abby zoomed out. As the perspective of the Bridge showed more of the battlefield, it changed Derick's perception entirely. The hooded army was massive—tens of thousands of soldiers, maybe even hundreds of thousands. The men with shields were only a small fraction of that. They really didn't stand much of a chance.

"There are 300 Spartans and 700 Thespians and perhaps a few hundred others," Anjum explained. "And for two days they held this pass against a massive army. Not only were the Spartans strong and courageous, but they were also smart. The pass to their cities was narrow. Only so many Persians could approach at a time. So even with a small army, they held off thousands."

Abby zoomed back in. She began to fast-forward. Soldiers fell on both sides, but the small army held its ground.

"They did what was nearly impossible," Anjum said. "And they would have lasted longer if Xerxes hadn't found another way around the pass." Anjum cleared his throat. "They still fought to the last man, and went down in history for their courage to fight against incredible odds."

"That's amazing," Piper said.

"Yeah, the underdogs showed the big guys a thing or two," Nia added.

"So that's why I chose the name Spartans. They never gave up, no matter how the odds were stacked against them. And now, they are legends."

"All right," Abby said, clapping her hands together and trying to sound determined. "So let's do the same."

"That's the spirit," Carol said. "But I really don't want to wear armor like them. That looks really uncomfortable. Oh, and I don't want to die."

"Don't spoil the pep talk," Derick said. "It totally worked." If he was about to die, at least he was going to go down fighting.

SANDSTORM

Remember what Landon and Sarah said," Anjum reminded. "We have to work as a team. We'll receive points for both how quickly we recognize where we are, and then for finishing the challenge in each place." That was how this stage of the Race was like the explorer. Each team had to travel through four challenges, quickly figuring out where they were and then passing a test. Once they had completed the four rounds, they would know if they had won and would get the key—or if they had lost. "Is everyone ready?"

Abby wasn't ready. She thought about the key and the secret she was supposed to protect. She thought of Chief Shar waiting, and Muns watching, and an army somewhere, probably on its way. She thought about the extra security everywhere. Rafa's mom was monitoring everything she could, on the lookout for anything strange. She agreed to watch out for Derick especially.

Derick.

All of the Spartans wore suits and visors. They stood in a lab, inside separate virtual booths that were linked together. All of them except Anjum. For the final challenge, all of the student body were gathered in the auditorium, and one member of each team would face the challenge from a booth there. The Race organizers wanted the person in the auditorium to be the team captain and Anjum had, eventually, agreed. But he insisted on being in his virtual booth, suited up and anonymous as he could be, before the crowd arrived.

Six large screens showed each team and each student could, through their rings, decide which team they wanted to follow and listen to the sound.

The rest of the team was ready to step into a virtual world.

"Let's do this!" Carol said, clapped several times, then did a few karate kicks. She still liked those.

Abby just hoped she wouldn't mess it up, that none of them would mess up. That they would do better somehow than they would have, when they didn't know how this could end. That it *would* end differently than she saw in the Bridge. She felt a bead of sweat on her temple. She wiped it away. They hadn't even gotten started yet.

"Are you ready for the final challenge?" Landon asked the full-house auditorium. They answered with a din of excitement. The auditorium scene was patched into the virtual booth so Abby and the rest of the team could see it. It wasn't a virtual experience, but they could see it all and feel the thrill of the environment. "On your mark," Landon said.

"Get set," Sarah continued. She looked over at Landon.

"Go!" they both shouted together.

"Nothing but your best," Anjum called out. "Let's win this thing."

They all logged into the same world as Anjum.

One moment Abby stood in a booth and the next she had no idea where she was. She couldn't see a thing, and some force pushed her one way, but another pushed against her in the opposite direction. She struggled to stay on her feet.

"Sandstorm!" someone yelled.

Abby put her hand in front of her face for protection and realized that she wore thick gloves and some sort of helmet. Thank heavens the virtual world prepared her with the right equipment.

"We're in the Sahara!" Nia guessed.

"Wrong," a voice responded. Abby could just make out another figure through the twisting red sand. "I'm your virtual guide and you are far, far from the Sahara. You *were* right about the sandstorm, though. Here, our sandstorms can cover far more ground and can last for days, even weeks. But, thankfully, I think this one will clear up in a few minutes. At least, that's what they've programmed me to say."

Great. A virtual guide with a sense of humor.

Abby felt a chill. A deep chill. Freezing. Not something she expected in a sandstorm in a desert somewhere.

"The Gobi," Malcolm called out. "The Arabian. The Patagonian. The Great Basin." He knew his deserts.

"No, no, no, and no. Not really even close," the guide answered. "The storm is solar-powered; the heat causes the dust to rise, and it almost always originates from a valley. Our best guess is that an asteroid hit there a long time ago."

Abby did a quick search for places where asteroids had hit the Earth's surface. "They think one hit the Yucatan Peninsula, in Arizona, in Argentina, in Chi Li Yang." She didn't know where the last place was.

"You are *really* far off," the guide said. "Your first step will give you the greatest clue. Follow me." Abby could barely see the figure move.

Abby stepped forward trying to move against the dust. When she braced herself to land again, she still hadn't. Where was the ground? Was she falling? She came down a second later than she thought she would. With the slightest movement she moved forward some more. "We're not on Earth," Abby said.

"Oh, I know my geography, but not for other planets," Malcolm said.

"Look up huge sandstorms in the galaxy," Maria said.

"Mars," Anjum answered. "The sandstorms come from the Hellas Basin and can cover the entire planet."

"For most answers in such a challenge, we would make you be more specific than just the correct planet," the guide said. "But in this one, we'll take it. One minute and thirty-seven seconds. Not bad."

The chill became more biting. Obviously deserts on

Mars did not share the same temperature as deserts on Earth.

As they moved more, the sandstorm calmed and then abated entirely. Abby caught her first look at the large red planet. The brownish-crimson sand rippled and became hardened in the distance.

"You are actually moving up Olympus Mons," the guide said, dressed in a spacesuit. Abby thought he looked familiar. Perhaps it was the face of the boy who made the challenge. "It is the second tallest mountain in the universe. It is three times the height of Everest, but because of its gradual slope, you wouldn't see that. In fact, when you're on top, you can't even really tell you're that high."

"What's our challenge?" Derick asked.

"Your challenge is . . ." the guide didn't finish his sentence.

"I'm getting a warning sign," Anjum said. "Something is wrong with my suit."

"There it is," the guide said. "And if his suit tears, the pressure is so low here that the saliva inside him will boil. He will be dead within moments. You have to get him to your rover, which is over there." The guide pointed off to his left. "And he must be alive. Have fun."

"Let's go," Anjum said, and took several floaty steps toward the rover.

The entire group followed. Each step felt clumsy; the air time was longer and they didn't get as much traction from their feet when they hit the red sand. Abby watched Anjum, carefully looking for any sign of weakness or flaw in his suit. After a few more steps, she caught a glimpse of it. "I think I see the tear in your suit," she called out. "Look there, on the knee seam."

Jess stepped beside Abby. "Could be."

"If you keep running," Abby said, "you might make it worse. And if it leaks, we lose."

"Good point," Rafa said. "Stop, Anjum."

It felt strange to have someone bossing Anjum around for a change.

Anjum gradually came to a halt. "I think you're right, Abby. I'll need to be carried to the rover, and be as careful as possible by my left knee."

Malcolm picked him up underneath his arms, Derick by the waist, and Maria and Nia at the legs. They moved awkwardly toward the rover.

"It's blinking quicker now," Anjum updated. "Hurry."

"He shouldn't be as heavy in less gravity," Abby said. "Could just two people take him?"

"Malcolm, you keep my head," Anjum said. "Nia, my feet. Now go."

They did, moving fluidly. With only two people to coordinate, they moved much quicker in skips across the red sand.

"It's beeping quicker," Anjum said, his voice louder and with more staccato.

"Faster," Carol yelled. "No blood boiling today!"

"Someone open up the rover ahead of time and be ready for me!" Anjum said.

Rafa and Derick both took off ahead.

"It's counting down," Anjum said. "10, 9, 8, 7 . . ."

ACID

Thankfully, by the time Anjum counted down to 4, Malcolm and Nia threw him into the rover and Rafa closed the door behind him.

Mars faded.

They barely had time to congratulate each other before they were in another world.

"Welcome to the second challenge of the final round," a girl's voice said. "I will be your guide."

"We're in some sort of aircraft . . . or hovercraft . . . inside a cave," Nia guessed, still a little winded from helping carry Anjum on Mars.

"Of sorts," the guide said. She was a teenager a few years older than Derick, maybe another programmer.

A calm light lit the pod. They seemed to be in some sort of cockpit with a little storage area behind it. It only had enough room for the team. Each one sat in a chair. The front and sides of the pod were large curved windows, but there wasn't much to see. As Nia had said, it looked like they were in some sort of cave, but the pod wasn't moving as far as they could tell.

"And what does this craft we're in do?" Malcolm asked. "Does it fly or something?"

"This machine is for your protection and it does fly. In a moment, you're going to need it to. Someone please take the controls."

"Jess, you're on it," Anjum said. She was used to driving all sorts of robots around. Good choice. "And everyone buckle up. We don't know what's coming."

Derick realized he was sitting in the chair with the controls and quickly switched with Jess and strapped in. Too bad. Driving a flying pod through their challenge sounded fun.

In an instant, one wall of the cave opened and light flooded in. It temporarily blinded Derick. He thought he saw a row of white rocks on the same wall that had opened. What kind of cave wall opens up? Was this an earthquake?

A flood of water crashed in, sending the pod reeling.

"Hang on!" Anjum yelled.

The water crashed both above them and below them, enough to lift them off the cave floor. The pod skirted back several feet and then plummeted down a cavern.

The team was a mix of screams and cheers. It was like a crazy amusement park ride. They dove farther and farther down the cave, which was getting darker with each moment. Then the pod splashed into a pool of water. The impact jolted Derick in his seat.

"Oh yeah!" Carol said. "Let's do it again. The Crazy Cave Fall! That landing was a little rough, though."

"Any ideas where we are?" Anjum asked. "Look up famous caves, especially ones next to waterfalls."

"Wait," Jess said. "I think I found something." She wasn't researching on her rings, but surveying all of the controls of the pod. She pulled on a lever, and headlight beams shone from the front of the pod. Everyone gazed out the windows.

"This is the weirdest place I've ever seen," Maria said. "And I've been to some weird places. Like, you should see my Aunt Magda's house when she throws a party. She makes really creepy piñatas."

The lake was yellow with white foam, and where they could see the sides and walls, it was a dark pink and folded in large rolls.

"Is this another planet?" Carol said. "Because it doesn't look familiar *at all*."

"It could also be something out of literature," Piper reminded. "*Journey to the Center of the Earth* or something."

"You are incorrect," the guide said. She had buckled up in a seat at the back of the pod.

"It wasn't officially a guess, but thanks for the update," Piper quipped back.

"You're welcome."

From above them, a stream of sludge came crashing down and into the foamy pond. The yellow liquid splashed over the windows of the pod and slowly slimed its way down.

"Gross," Nia said.

"Uh," Derick mumbled, watching the sludge. It was in a shallow end of the lake and rested on the bottom. "I think we've got a problem. Look."

Everyone watched as the sludge started to dissolve.

"That's not good," Malcolm said, pointing at the window. Small splotches showed where thin layers had worn off the pod.

"I think this is some sort of acid lake," Derick said.

"You're getting closer," the guide said. "And though you do not yet know your location, your challenge is to get out before you find out how much of this pod the acid will eat."

"There is an acid lake at the bottom of the Kawah Ijen volcano crater in Indonesia," Abby said, researching on her rings. "It can eat through metal and just touching it can burn the skin. Maybe we are somehow in a cave that flows out of that lake."

"Incorrect," the guide said.

"There are acid lakes by the Dollol volcano in Ethiopia," Maria said. "One sip and birds die. It has almost the same intensity as gastric acid."

"Incorrect again," the guide said.

They named a few more, but none were correct.

"Keep researching," Anjum commanded. "Jess, can you fly this thing and get us out of here?"

Jess nodded and began pushing buttons. "I think I've got

it," she said. The pod began to hover. "I don't have much fuel though." She tapped on a gauge.

"We only need enough to get out," Anjum said.

Their headlights showed a pinkish wall and the pod rose to where they and the sludge had dropped it. "Uh. We have a problem," Jess said. "There's no opening."

"There has to be," Malcolm said. "That's how we got in."

They hovered, waiting for a moment.

Without warning, a spot on the wall opened and a mound of sludge dropped in.

"There it is," Anjum yelled. "Now!"

Jess pushed forward on the controls and the pod shot ahead, but not in time. It bounced off the wall. The opening had closed.

They tried twice more, but the hole closed as soon as the sludge passed through.

"Is there any other way out?" Anjum asked.

Jess flew around the enclosure shining their lights everywhere. Nothing.

"I think the water level is going down," Nia said. "There has to be an opening at the bottom of the lake."

"Let me think about that," Anjum said. "I can't see how immersing ourselves in acid would help our situation. Jess, bring it down again, before we run out of fuel."

"Gross. Ew. Yucky. Nasty-not-niceness," Carol said. She bounced around like a little girl who had seen a spider. "Wait wait wait! I figured it out." She pointed at Maria.

"You said that a lake in Ethiopia has almost the same intensity as . . . ?"

"Gastric acid," Nia interrupted. "That's what digests your food in your stom—" she didn't finish the last word before breaking into a new sentence. "A stomach. We're in a stomach!"

"Correct," the guide said. "Two minutes, forty-seven seconds."

"Oh! We're super tiny," Piper said. "We were up in the mouth, the person drank, and we came down here."

"You're correct," the guide said. "This pod is proportioned to be about half the size of the average swallowable pill. You have journeyed into a virtual stomach."

"Eww," Carol said. "The sludge is food being digested. I love food. If this challenge has *any* effect on my love of eating, somebody is going to be in serious trouble."

"So if we go down through the stomach," Malcolm said, "we enter the intestines. That could take a while to digest. I think the best way is back up."

"But the opening keeps closing," Jess said, "unless it's shooting water or food back down at us."

"We need to either be able to guess when the food is about to come through," Anjum said, "and fly through it, or . . . we need to make this virtual person vomit."

"Tell me you didn't just say that," Carol said. "Grossest challenge ever."

"Anjum's right," Derick said. "And so is Carol. But how do we make that happen? It's not like we can make it stick its finger down its throat."

"Foreign objects," Malcolm said. "This pod has to be one, so the stomach is probably upset already. Can we open this pod up and throw out anything else that would rile it up?"

"I think this lever unlocks that door," Jess said, pointing to her controls, then a handle on the wall.

"Let's do it," Anjum said. They opened the door and threw out seat covers and any supplies they found. The stomach began to froth and bubble more. "Now ram the pod against the sides of the stomach. Let's use up the fuel. It's now or never."

Jess pushed the controls and the pod levitated again. It rammed into the side of the stomach. The acid began to rise.

"World's worst anatomy lesson," Carol said. "Seriously, they should have just used diagrams."

The pod rammed the stomach lining again and again. The stomach contents bubbled and riled.

"Here we go," Jess called out. "Everyone hang on."

FIRE

Derick stood at the bottom of a cliff with a large cave carved in its face. Trees, bushes, and grass filled the scene, except for a large barren patch in front of the cave. Nothing grew there. The rock from the cliff met bare dirt.

A plume of fire burst out of the cave and a deafening roar echoed out.

Derick took a step back.

"What the freaky creepy beast was that?" Carol asked.

"Was that a dragon?" Maria asked.

"I can't think of what else it would be," Nia said.

"Well, there were these bulls in Greek mythology that could breathe fire," Derick added, and touched his head, glad that all his hair was there. "But I doubt they would use the same kind of monster twice in the Race."

"I agree," Anjum said. "Let's go with the dragon idea.

And that narrows down the possibilities of where we are. We have to be inside a work of literature or mythology."

"That's correct, but not specific enough," the guide said. He wore a long dusty robe with a hood over his head. He carried a wooden staff.

Derick looked down. He was wearing armor. Gold-encrusted metal plates protected his chest, shoulders, arms, and legs. He also held a long shield in one hand and a helmet in the other. A sword in a sheath hung from his waist. He looked over and saw all of his team dressed the same, though some had a bow and arrows or a spear instead of a sword.

"To be consistent with this challenge, one of you has to face the dragon," the guide explained, pointing a covered arm toward the cave. "Alone."

"Ohhh! So awesome and so scary all at once," Carol cried out. "I mean, who hasn't imagined this before?"

"That must be part of the story," Anjum said. "Someone faces a dragon alone. Start your searches while we talk."

The beast sent tremors through the ground as it moved inside the cave.

Derick started his search. There were thousands of instances of dragons in literature. How was he going to narrow this down?

"Who's going to face it?" Piper asked, just as it roared again.

"In my imagination, I always had the guts to do it," Malcolm said. "And I know this is only virtual, but I'm not too anxious to jump in against oven-breath there.

Something that can breathe fire like that could swallow me whole."

"And you're a big bite," Carol said, then waved frantically. "Oh, I meant that in a very you're-tall-and-muscular kind of way. It wasn't a fat joke."

"Thanks," Malcolm said. "But as much as I don't want to, I'll face the dragon." He stepped forward, shifting the spear in his hand and raising his shield.

"I would too," Derick said, "but I think if we're really going to stand a chance, we'd better send in the most agile person we've got, not the strongest."

"I'm both," Carol said. "And I'll do it." There really seemed to be no situation tense enough that she wouldn't joke around.

"I think he was referring to Rafa," Anjum said. "No offense, Carol. And I believe I would be our second choice with my history in virtuality."

Rafa took a deep breath. "If you elect me to, I'll face the dragon." That was Rafa, willing and brave.

Everyone nodded. Rafa put his helmet on his head. It had a Y-shaped opening in front so that Derick could still see his eyes, nose, and most of his mouth. Rafa drew his sword and swished it back and forth through the air. Once he felt he had gauged its weight, he stepped forward. "Too bad I didn't spend more time in your samurai world, Derick. I could probably use this better." Then he lifted his shield to protect himself as he moved forward. It was long enough that if he crouched, he could get almost all of himself behind it.

It was strange to see a friend walk toward something that seemed impossible to beat. Even though it was a virtual test, Rafa would feel the heat of the fire and the pain of a talon or tooth if it got him. And Derick could do nothing.

Maybe that's how Abby had been feeling. Maybe she felt like she was watching him step into his death. Maybe he was. And maybe that was even scarier than a virtual dragon.

Smoke and fire.

"There's a story where King Arthur faced a dragon," Piper said, having found something with her rings.

"That is not this instance," the guide said.

Derick had forgotten about researching. He looked back at his screen in his contact lenses.

Rafa crept closer to the darkness of the cave.

"Saint George slays a dragon in *The Golden Legend*," Abby guessed.

"Also incorrect," the guide said.

Rafa took several more steps. Derick searched through the possible entries of literature with dragons in it. It was probably something really old. For some reason they always treat old things like they are more important, more classic, more educational. What was one of the first written stories with a dragon in it? "*Beowulf*," Derick nearly shouted out when he found it on his screen. "It's the oldest surviving epic poem in Old English."

"Correct," the guide said. "Two minutes and sixteen seconds."

"Good job, Derick," Anjum said. "Now, Derick, Abby, Carol, and Jess, focus your searches on *Beowulf*. We need to know more about the story, especially how the dragon was defeated. The rest of you, let's watch Rafa and give him counsel. The more eyes on this, the better."

"I hate that we have to just stand and watch," Piper said.

"That is how it occurred in the story," the guide said. "Beowulf insisted on fighting the dragon alone."

"Rafa," Malcolm said, "maybe you should come at the opening of the cave from along the cliff; that way the dragon won't see you coming."

Rafa sprinted to the bottom of the cliff and moved closer to the opening.

"Wow, there is no way you can understand this old thing," Carol said, reading on her rings. "It's in English, but it's just so old that it hardly makes any sense. Like, what's a 'Spear-Danes' glory'?"

"Read a summary or a more recent translation," Jess suggested.

Good idea. Derick searched through a summary. "Beowulf is the name of the main character, and he was intense. He fought monsters with his bare hands."

"But when he faced the dragon, he never went in the cave," Abby said. "Rafa, stop!"

Rafa was nearly at the entrance. He danced back to one side.

"Good point, Abby," Anjum said. "He would be on the dragon's turf and have few places to hide. How did Beowulf draw it out?"

"He screamed into the cave to let it know he was there," Abby said.

"Why would that draw out the dragon?" Anjum asked.

"I think because he liked to eat people," Abby said, squirming a little.

"So I'm the live bait," Rafa said. Walking quietly next to the cliff side, he approached the opening. "Keep researching; I can use the help. But let's see what I'm up against." Rafa stepped enough into the cave to yell, "Come on out, *dragon!*" His voice echoed several times off the walls. He backpedaled away and to the side.

Footsteps. Big ones. And a roar. The ground rumbled with each step as the dragon moved toward the cave's entrance. Derick looked around to make sure he was far enough back that the dragon wouldn't see or attack him first. They all stood at the tree line and were ready to hide at any moment. Of course, the dragon's fire could also burn down the forest.

"Stay just to the side of the opening, up against the cliff," Piper advised. "You may be able to get an attack in before he knows you're there."

"Good idea," Anjum said.

"It's not what Beowulf did," Carol said. "He met him head-on."

"I'm not Beowulf," Rafa said. "I haven't faced any monsters with my bare hands." He spoke quickly and urgently.

"Good point," Carol said. "But don't worry. With your long hair and your armor, you totally look like the good-looking hero in a movie. And the good-looking hero never dies. Sometimes the lovable sidekick does. Or maybe a less-important soldier. Or the father-figure who has to get out of the way so the hero can show his or her true potential. But not the hero."

"Somehow, I don't think movie rules apply here," Malcolm said.

Fire burst out of the opening again. Smoke followed, rising from the roof of the cave. Rafa was poised by the side of the opening, his sword raised, ready to make a surprise attack.

"How did Beowulf defeat it?" Anjum asked, his voice impatient.

"We're getting there," Derick said, still searching on his rings.

More flame shot out of the cave before a black head covered in scales emerged from the darkness. A puff of smoke trailed upward out of its nostrils. The head alone was the size of a sedan. Its yellow eyes glared, standing out in sharp contrast to the beast's dark, scaly exterior. But what was more, those eyes looked wild, maybe rabid.

Reacting, the entire group retreated farther into the trees, holding up their shields until they were far out of the range of the flames.

Rafa froze.

With each step, more of the beast's long neck emerged, the underside a dirty gray. Finally the body was close enough to the entrance to see. It filled the cave. It had to be the size of a building, a pattern of scales and thick tendrils covering its chest. Its feet dug into the ground with talons like swords. Derick exhaled, not realizing that he had been holding his breath.

Rafa did not wait for more advice. He bolted from his place and sliced where the dragon's neck met its body. His sword clashed against the scales.

The beast roared. Though the blow did little damage, the dragon wasn't invincible. A small trail of thick blue blood oozed out where Rafa had hit.

In one swift motion, the dragon swung its long neck. Its head slammed into Rafa, knocking him off his feet. Rafa grunted as he hit the hard ground. He was barely able to raise his shield in time to protect himself from the assault of flame that followed.

Derick gawked. The beast had already been intimidating before he saw how quickly it could react, let alone the charring flames. Now it seemed nearly invincible, a creature that could annihilate anything or anyone.

The dragon stomped fully out of his home as he continued to bellow out fire at his attacker. Thankfully, Rafa's shield protected him well. It must have been made to withstand such an attack, made for a dragon slayer.

A trail of spikes jutted out from the dragon's spine and tail. Its wings bore sharp spikes as well and unfolded to a length of over half a basketball court.

For a brief moment, the flames ended. The dragon had to breathe in between attacks.

"Move, Rafa," Anjum yelled. "Try to stay behind it, where it can't see you—or move as quickly against you."

Rafa immediately raced toward the back of the dragon.

The beast's huge jaws clamped down where Rafa had been only a fraction of a second before. Rafa weaved behind it and barely dodged a strike from its large tail. He thought quickly enough to jab with his sword as he went and caused a few more gashes. He was doing amazingly well under the circumstances.

All that aside, it didn't seem like Rafa was coming close to being able to slay the dragon. It was more of a desperate attempt to stay alive.

"What do I do?" Rafa yelled, trying to double back so he wasn't face to face with the beast.

Derick looked back at his summary through his rings. "Uh," he mumbled, then he scanned words he didn't want to believe. "He dies."

"*What?*" Rafa yelled.

"Beowulf dies." Derick broke the terrible news. "I haven't read the end yet, but it's already telling me that this is Beowulf's final battle and he won't escape with his life. He might still beat the dragon, but I don't think it ends well for him." If the beast took down a legendary hero, how was Rafa supposed to succeed?

The dragon lunged, spinning toward Rafa. The Brazilian leaped backwards, but one of the dragon's razor teeth slit across his arm. Rafa screamed and fell, clutching his wound. He raised his shield in time to again avoid being cooked alive.

Derick read as fast as he could. There had to be something, some sort of clue. They wouldn't have made a challenge that couldn't be won.

Out of the corner of his eye, he saw the dragon beat his mighty wings. The gust of wind flipped Rafa onto his side. The beast lunged again, and Rafa rolled out of the way.

Derick found it. At first he didn't realize what it meant, but then it dawned on him. He grabbed his sword and screamed, running right at the dragon, the magnificent beast of terror. His legs pushed him forward, his mind wanting to turn and race back the other way. With every step he came closer to the talons and spikes and teeth and flame. The dragon turned in time for Derick to catch its lowered head with his sword. The steel rang and bounced off the scales more than Derick expected, but it also left another gash.

The dragon raised up on its back legs and roared, its wings outstretched. Derick bolted. "Beowulf only defeated the dragon because his friend came to help," Derick yelled. "Even after Beowulf told him not to."

Derick looked back as he sprinted. It was as though he stared at death; a flood of fire swept toward him. Derick raised his shield just in time to keep the flames from engulfing him. His hands burned as the shield got hotter and hotter. He could feel his skin searing, even under his gloves. He clenched his teeth and bellowed out in pain and determination.

When the fire paused, Derick's shield was a melted mess of what it had been. Apparently, his was not as strong as the one Rafa had. His was not meant for facing dragons.

Rafa attacked from the other side, jabbing his sword

between the scales in the dragon's side. Derick had distracted it long enough.

But the dragon didn't fall. It roared and turned on Rafa, who raced to get out of the way.

Derick slashed again.

An arrow flew through the air and bore into the back of the dragon's head.

Malcolm lumbered in from the side, booming out a battle cry. It was like he came barreling in for a tackle, but instead used all his force to spear the dragon in the leg. The beast thundered. Malcolm yelled back, caught up in the competition.

Anjum rushed up the dragon's leg and drove his sword in under its arm. Derick could hardly believe his quickness and agility. Anjum leaped to safety before the dragon could turn. He really was impressive.

More arrows flew.

"We figured if you could come help, so could we," Nia said, launching another arrow. Abby and Carol were doing the same, though Abby still hadn't improved her marksmanship from the labyrinth.

The beast whirled its mighty head and breathed fire in every direction. The Spartans ducked and dove, trying to find cover.

"Maria, to the top of the cliff," Anjum commanded. "Nia, attack the tail. And I'll distract it."

Anjum screamed at the beast, waving his hands. Then he barreled right at it. Derick had charged the beast, but this was different. Anjum had its attention. He was squaring off against it, knowing it was focused and ready to attack back with all its strength. Intense.

The beast flew only a few feet, then slammed down next to Anjum. The wind knocked the student from India backward, and with a swipe of its talons, Anjum cried out and fell.

Everyone attacked at once, coming to their leader's aid. Maria had enough time to get several feet up the cliff and then she leaped onto the dragon's back. She moved with all the grace of a dancer, but a deadly one. She drove her swords in between the dragon's scales.

Derick swung against it again and again. Rafa tried to stab it with the sharp edge of his shield. Nia, Carol, and Abby moved in closer and rifled arrows at the dragon's head. Malcolm pushed again on his spear, driving it deeper into its leg, while Piper came in with another stab.

Finally, the great dragon reared back and fell to the earth.

ME? OR ME?

All of the Spartans erupted in cheers—in exhausted, but victorious cheers—as the world faded. They had just done what had felt impossible; they had defeated a dragon.

One more round left.

But nothing happened. No other world came into view.

"Isn't there supposed to be one more challenge?" Derick asked.

"Yes," Anjum said, still winded from the battle with the dragon. "This is strange."

"I guess they're having technical difficulties," Nia said.

"Or not," Abby said. "This may be the last challenge. We're in the virtual booths in Cragbridge Hall."

"That is correct," a voice said. "Now for the final challenge, join your leader in the large virtual booth on the auditorium stage."

"Go! Go! Go!" Anjum screamed.

Derick shot out of his booth, seeing the others do the same. It was a bit more cumbersome to run in the suit he had to use for the virtual booths, but he tore down the hallway as fast as he could. Security guards and bots lined the halls—a reminder that they were being watched very carefully, that there was more than a simple competition at stake.

Abby was several yards ahead, her runner's legs carrying her faster. Derick glanced back to see Malcolm lumbering in the rear. He was big and the slowest of the bunch, but still rather fast. Rafa was also behind Derick. Normally, he would be close to the lead. He was probably worn out from fighting the dragon.

They burst through the open doors to a packed auditorium of students. The crowd erupted in screams and applause. Whoever designed this ending knew how to create excitement. It seemed that the whole school was on their feet stomping and cheering.

It only fed their energy. Derick rushed up the aisle and leaped onto the stage. Several small booths lined the outside, but one large booth stood in the center, big enough to fit the entire team. One by one they filed into the large virtual booth in the center. Anjum was already there, cowering against the back corner. The whole team had come to him.

They closed the door, the sound of the crowd dimming outside of their box.

That meant they were in the lead, right? They were the first team in. Or was this it? Was just getting here the end?

Everything went quiet. The team waited in the dark.

The inside of the booth lit up with a minotaur, and then Derick with a sword. At first Derick thought he was under attack again, but realized he was seeing highlight footage from the labyrinth challenge. The next image showed the team rushing Anjum back to their rover on Mars. Abby ran across campus for the last square in the first challenge. Highlight after highlight appeared all around them. Though muffled, they could hear the crowd returning to their screams. The same images must have been portrayed in the auditorium as well.

"Congratulations!" Landon's voice came in strong, "to the winning team of the 2075 Race—the *Spartans*!"

They had done it.

Derick high-fived Rafa, who was smiling bigger than he had ever seen. Malcolm hugged them both and Derick thought his lungs would burst. He looked over at Abby, who had tears in her eyes. They had worked hard, had given their all, and they had done it. As soon as Malcolm let go, Derick hugged his sister.

"We wanted them to experience their win as a team, in virtual reality," Sarah explained. She showed on a screen inside the booth. "We also wanted a way to congratulate them one by one. We'll have each of them step out, take a bow, and you can applaud their great work. Then they can open the box to gain the key . . ." Her voice faded, as did the team's view inside the booth. After a few moments, the crowd began to murmur.

"I believe," a voice said, and then a virtual version of Mr. Silverton appeared in the booth, bald and pudgy, "you were told that at the end of this challenge, the winners would learn a secret. I promised you that." What was happening? How was Mr. Silverton's image coming across the virtual booth? Had he escaped?

But the image changed to Mrs. Flink, with her bushy red hair and standing shorter than Mr. Silverton. "Or was it me? Did I promise a secret?" It changed to Mr. Sul. "Or me?" Then Chief Shar. "Or me?" Whoever was doing this had recreated all of the prime suspects virtually. What did it mean?

"At any rate," the virtual Mr. Silverton said, smiling through his dark beard, "you have tried hard, worked together, and not given up." Derick didn't believe this was a compliment. Virtual Chief Shar returned. "As promised, I will tell you more. I have sent you the message, but I might as well tell it while I'm here."

Derick watched as the changing virtual narrators told the greatest and most dangerous secret he had ever heard and that he had risked his life to protect. He double-checked to make sure that those outside couldn't also hear it. It seemed to be a conversation just for the winners, but his heart still raced. Derick surveyed the faces of the team. Thankfully, they knew this already.

"Some in this very virtual room have keys to control time," the virtual people inside the booth said. "And to those who don't, I'm at least partially sorry that you are caught in this dangerous game." There it was. That sounded like something Muns would say. "You should have chosen your teammates better. I'm afraid you'll suffer for it."

Derick looked at his team, their faces filled with questions and fear.

"You see." It was back to Mr. Silverton. "Those with keys had to pass through challenges to earn the secret, and I made them pass challenges to try to protect it. In the past, they used avatars to take back what I had stolen. So I had them use robots, which are also avatars, to steal something for me. And in the past, Abby and her friends rescued the hostages I took. So now you are the hostages. This booth is locked tight. You cannot get out."

Immediately, Malcolm tried the steel door to the booth. It wouldn't budge. Rafa joined him and they slammed into it together. Nothing.

"I have another secret I need to share with you." Now it was virtual Landon. "And I think it's time to let everyone in on this conversation."

"Everyone in the auditorium can see him now," Nia reported, checking her rings.

The image switched. It now showed a device, small, like a vial. "This is an interesting contraption," a voice said. There were no longer changing images. "I know, I know. You think Chief Shar stole them and the police got them back. Well, I took the liberty of switching out at least one with a very believable copy. I'm good at switching things out with fakes. I did the same thing with Mrs. Flink's key."

Derick's heart beat faster. The vial was here, and whoever was behind all this was definitely free and still in charge.

"So that leads us here." The screens still showed the vial. "When it explodes, a cloud of tranquilizer will cover this school. I took the liberty of using chemicals from the school. I stole them the same way I did to frame Mr. Silverton. I couldn't have him double-checking my messages. I used a robot, similar to the kind I framed Mr. Sul for trying to steal. I couldn't have any more of his nosy questions. And this device will explode with such force that if anyone is nearby, they likely won't survive."

The voice paused a moment, letting the gravity of the situation sink in. "So, I thought I'd do you the favor of not telling you where it is. If it is outside, it will seep into every building. Or if it is inside, it will create such pressure that it will explode windows and doors and creep outside. But it does not blow away or fade for weeks. Unless you evacuate, everyone in the school will be comatose for months."

Derick shook his head. How could they have ever seen this coming?

"Right now," the voice continued, the vial still displayed on the screen and in the virtual booth, "as you can see, it is timed to explode in thirty minutes." A screen on the vial counted down the time. "It is somewhere here on the Cragbridge Hall campus." The last image faded and a different voice remained in blackness. "I believe it's time for everyone to go."

Derick heard the chaos of screaming and shouting. Whatever Muns's plan was, it involved evacuating
everyone.

"Except, of course, for you," virtual Mr. Sul said to those
inside the booth. This part was obviously meant for only
them. "Now it's your turn to be the hostages. No one can
get you out. When the bomb goes off, the gas will seep into
this container through any creases and hinges and when you
wake, Charles Muns will have your keys and all power over
time." The image of Mr. Sul laughed. "I also locked in the
teachers and the Cragbridges in the medical unit. I thought
it fitting that they should join you."

POUNDING

The Spartans pounded on the doors several times, but they didn't budge.

Outside of the booth, a security officer spoke into the microphone on her rings, which amplified her voice. "Stay calm, but evacuate quickly. Do not return to dorms or rooms. Leave the premises immediately. I repeat: Do not return to your dorms or rooms. Leave the premises immediately." Other security guards tried the door to the booth from the outside. They needed to get everyone outside the school.

"We've got to get out of here," Maria said. She kicked at the sturdy door and winced.

"I really don't like this Muns guy," Malcolm said, panting from all his effort against the door. "And if my mama knew about him, he would get such an earful he wouldn't be able to see straight."

"He has us trapped," Abby said, her stomach sinking.

"And if it wasn't for you guys getting us into this," Maria said, pointing at Derick and Rafa, "we'd be safely walking out of here like everybody else."

"We didn't know this would happen," Rafa defended. "We were trying to . . ."

"But you knew this was dangerous," Maria snipped back.

"Your lives were probably already on the line," Piper said. "But now ours are too."

"Did you want us just to sit back and do nothing?" Derick yelled. Perhaps it came out more powerful than he had intended. "Should I have stopped and decided someone else would take care of it? That I'm just a kid and I should let the adults deal with it?"

They didn't have a response. Abby looked at her brother, his eyes still glaring intensely.

"We had to try," Derick said. "We had to."

"But we failed," Nia added.

"It's not over," Abby said, "but it doesn't look good. Everyone else with a key will be escorted out of the school grounds. Out there they aren't as protected. Muns's men can attack them and take their keys. They will be wide-open targets." She thought of all the men Muns had at his command. It would be easy. Then again, why so many? It seemed like they would only need a few who knew which teachers to attack.

"And then they can come in and get our keys," Rafa said. "Because we'll be tranquilized and dreaming."

"Also," Derick said, "Muns's men can take the keys straight to Muns. They won't have to pass through any more security checkpoints. They won't have anything to stall them."

"Muns comes up with some terrible plans," Carol said, pressing against the door once more. "If only he could use his talents to plan something else. Like weddings. With this kind of thought, they could be killer."

"*Killer* is probably the right word," Maria said.

Nia slid down the side of the virtual room until she sat on the floor. "So, we're trapped and the evil guy wins."

"No," Abby said, her mind working fast. She didn't know how to get out, but quitting wasn't an option. "We find a way out of here, and then we find the bomb and use the Bridge to send it somewhere it won't hurt anyone."

Everyone looked at her.

"That's *if* we can get out of here," Malcolm said. Anjum had crouched on the ground next to him. He said nothing.

"And *if* we can find the tranquilizer bomb," Piper said.

"Give this a chance," Abby said. "We can think of something."

"She's right," Derick said. "We can stop this."

Abby's insides reeled. Could they? At least if Derick was trapped in the virtual booth, he wouldn't die, right? Then again, if the girl from the future was right and Muns would run everything and people would fear the Ash, that wasn't any better. They couldn't give up. Muns couldn't win.

"I'm in," Carol said. "But that's no big surprise. I'm always in." She clapped her hands together and started looking at the walls for a weakness. Abby did the same.

"How did they make the tranquilizer bombs and get them inside the school?" Piper asked.

"Good question," Derick said, moving to take his turn slamming against the locked door. "After we stole the vials from Ruminex, one of Muns's men must have gotten them and brought them into the school somehow."

"If we can get to the Bridge maybe we can search everyone who has come in over the last few days," Abby suggested. "We should be able to find who brought them in."

"But we won't have a lot of time," Derick reminded. "The Bridge can't handle it."

"We have to try," Abby said.

"The police came in to question us," Rafa said. "Do you think one of them brought them in? They probably wouldn't have been scrutinized as well as anyone else coming to the school."

"Good theory," Abby said. "Especially when they were here to investigate Chief Shar. We'll start there."

"But they left," Piper pointed out. "At least I think they did. So there would have to be someone on the inside in Cragbridge Hall to take the vials, put the chemicals in, and set them up."

"We have to get to the Bridge," Abby said. "We can use our keys and look into the recent past and see who brought it in and who they handed it off to."

New cries and screams rent the air outside the booth.

Thunt. Thunt. Thunt. The sound of security guard stun guns going off sounded outside the booth.

"What's going on out there?" Maria asked.

The entire virtual booth shook, jolted to one side. Most of the Spartans fell over. "What was that?" Nia yelled.

Anjum crumpled closer to the ground, covering his ears.

Again the booth shook. And again. Each time, everyone inside was jolted. Finally, the booth cracked a couple of inches between the door and its frame.

Abby saw something brown with a horn.

"Some monster is trying to kill us!" Piper yelled, peering out of the crack.

"It's not trying to kill us. It's saving us," Derick said, his voice rising.

"What?" Nia said.

"And it's not a monster," Rafa said. "It's my mom." A huge smile crossed his face as he synced up his rings.

There were more shouts and they heard the bull grunt. It hit again. Just a few more times and there would be enough of a space for them to get out.

"Thanks, Mom," Rafa said over his rings. He must have synced with Abby and Derick too, because they heard her response.

"You're welcome," she said in her Brazilian accent. "But I don't have long. I'm sure they're coming after me in the avatar lab." She grunted as she hit the booth again. "We all need to try to find and stop the bomb." Again a grunt. "I almost have you out."

Abby turned to the group inside the jolting booth. "I know this is all crazy, and dangerous, and sudden, but once we are out of here, we could really use your help. We've made a great team. We won a challenge against the best students at the best secondary school in the world. We came together. But this is more than a game. Everything is riding on this."

Another slam against the booth.

"Once we're out," Derick jumped in, "security will try to evacuate us. If you want to help us, get away and then meet us at the dead-end hall outside of the language classrooms—the one with the janitor closet at the end. That's where we get to the Bridge."

"My mama would tell me to help," Malcolm said. "She wouldn't like evil people taking over stuff. Let's do it."

Another slam against the wall.

"I'm in," Nia said.

"I'm not sure," Maria said. "But I can help for twenty minutes and if things aren't going well, I'll still have time to get out."

The way the others looked back at her, it seemed that they might agree with that strategy.

"I'll help," Piper said.

Jess nodded.

But Anjum shook his head. "No. No. I can't." It seemed strange to see their commanding leader so weak, so undetermined.

"We need you, Anjum," Carol said. "You're our leader."

He shook his head faster, over and over. "I can't. I can't."

With the next hit, the metal bent more—bent enough.

Rafa signaled to the bull his mother controlled to stand down, and he slid out, followed by Piper and then Abby.

Security guards surrounded them. They had been charged to get everyone out of the school. But they seemed confused. They didn't know whether to shoot at the bull or not now that it had opened the booth. Behind them the auditorium still had hundreds of students trying to get out with other security guards doing their best to keep them calm.

With the booth open, Rafa's mom charged at the security guards, causing them to scatter and dive off the stage.

"I guess Muns didn't plan on having a giant robotic bull on our side," Carol said. "I'll need to give her a high five later."

Then the bull fell limp, crashing against the stage floor with a thump. Security must have gotten to Rafa's mom in the avatar lab. They were on their own.

"Scatter!" Abby yelled.

TRACKED

Derick leaped off the stage, raced up the aisle, and got lost in the crowd of exiting students. He found spaces between people and pushed his way through. The process was slower than he liked, but finally he got out into the busy hall.

He snuck in the opposite direction of the crowds. In the hall he had chosen, he'd have to take the long way to the dead-end hallway, but he would get there. He walked into the giant commons area and saw a security guard walking the other direction in front of him, probably doing a sweep to make sure everyone was on their way out. Derick ducked under a table, just in case he turned around.

"Anyone within the sound of my voice, you need to exit the building," the security guard called out using his microphone. "All human guards, make one more sweep, then exit with the students. The security bots will finalize the evacuation. They are built and programmed for this type of scenario." It made sense. Get the humans out and leave the robots.

The guard hadn't seen Derick. Derick waited for him to continue down the hall.

Derick was just about to get up when he heard a wheel across the floor behind him. A security bot. It was several yards behind him and hadn't necessarily spotted him. Maybe he could make his way underneath the tables to another hallway.

More wheels, this time from another direction.

One of the two arriving robots bent down and looked right at him. Busted.

"Please exit as quickly as possible," the bot said, its voice clear and professional.

"No thanks," Derick replied. He raced over the top of one table and jumped to the next, the security bots rolling after him.

"That is the wrong direction," the bot protested. "Please exit as quickly as possible."

Derick didn't stop.

"I've got three security bots on me," Malcolm said, his voice coming through Derick's earpiece. "And I hid backstage for a few minutes. I don't know how they found me."

Derick moved faster, zigzagging just in case they tried their stun guns.

"I've got a few on me too," Nia said, "and I ran outside the building. I'm trying to double back in."

"One is following me," Rafa said, "and they are faster than I thought."

"They got me," Piper said. "I'm being hauled out of the school." In the background Derick could hear a bot telling her to quit resisting. "And they're a lot stronger than you'd think." As Derick moved between tables, ducking down, he heard Piper struggle some more. "I don't know how they got me. It's like they knew where I was going to be."

It was. It was like a group of them knew exactly where Derick was hiding. There were security cameras in most of the halls, but the humans had all evacuated. Could the robots be hooked up to them somehow? No. That didn't make any sense. How would a robot know the difference between a human moving on-screen and another robot? Maybe they had another way of tracking them.

●　●　●

Abby rushed out from behind a set of stairs backstage. She had weaved between the storage items from old plays, trying to make her way to an exit. A security bot appeared out of nowhere and grabbed Abby's arm. Its metal fingers were cold and hard against her wrist. "You have to leave. There has been a threat," it said. It must have been hot on her trail before.

"No," Abby said. "I have to take care of something." She writhed, trying to break free, but it held fast and grabbed her with its other arm.

"You need to evacuate," the security bot repeated.

"No. Please," she said. "I can't explain it all to you, but

I have to stop this bomb." She didn't know if she could actually reason with a security bot, but she had to try. She couldn't do anything if she was escorted out by security. In fact, she was sure she would walk right into Muns's hands.

• • •

Derick leaped onto another table. He was grateful for all the avatar practice. Leaping from one thing to another was normal for him.

"One has me," Abby called out.

"I'm fine," Carol said. "Oh, grumpy gorilla, they're here! Gotta move!"

Why were they losing? They could face a dragon, destroy a minotaur, steal a zombie cure, and save one of their own on Mars. Why couldn't they do this? Derick realized something was missing. "Anjum," he said. "I know it's hard, but we need you."

"I . . . I," he began, but didn't finish. If only Anjum would get his head in the game. He knew where all of them were; he could guide them to where they needed to be.

He knew where they all were. The thought rang in Derick's mind.

Anjum had set up another sync before this event, so they could all speak to one another even if they had to go into different virtual worlds. That sync was still live. But Anjum was just a kid. He wouldn't be on Muns's side, would he? Derick couldn't risk it. "Everyone," he said over the rings, "all I can think of is that maybe we're being tracked through Anjum's sync. We have to log out and start a different sync without him."

"What?" Carol said, panting. She was probably still running away from bots like Derick. "Are you saying Anjum is leading the robots to us? Because he's probably still in the booth. He was having a breakdown."

"Think about it," Derick said. "We're all being tracked and Anjum is the only one who can know where we all are. He had us all sync up together. I don't want to assume too much, but we have to be safe."

"It's not me," Anjum said. "I'm sorry I lost my cool back there. I can help you all get out. Now Malcolm, you're going to need to run down the language hall, then take a right."

"Should I listen to him?" Malcolm asked.

"Yes," Anjum said.

"I'm not sure," Maria said.

"No, I don't think so," Abby said. "Listen to Derick."

"Listen to me," Anjum said. "You've got bots on your trail. I can get you out of there."

"Where are you, Anjum?" Rafa asked.

"I'm still in the booth," Anjum responded.

"How are you still safe in the booth?" Rafa asked. "Shouldn't bots be coming after you too?"

Anjum didn't answer.

"I'm logging off," Rafa said. "I'll send out a sync without Anjum that only lets us talk. No one can track us."

Derick leaped off another table and climbed over a railing to the stairs. He raced to the next floor, managing to log out of their team sync as he went. He ran down a hall, turned a corner, and ducked into a classroom. The security bots passed him by.

• • •

Abby pulled at the security bot's arm, but couldn't get out of its grip. It dragged her toward an exit from the stage.

She thought about how little she really knew about Anjum. Other than when they were interrogated by the police and in the booth just now, all her interaction with him had been virtual. What did she know? He had led them through challenge after challenge, helping them get the victory. And he guided them to steal the vials that now threatened the school. And if he was on Muns's side, wouldn't he want to make sure they really got the job done right? It was all part of the plan.

She struggled against the bot some more. There had to be a way out of this.

But Anjum couldn't have done everything. He was with them when the lights went out. Well, he was with them virtually. Was it possible that he was guiding them virtually while being somewhere else physically himself? No. He would have to be in a booth and give them his full attention to do what he did. There had to be someone else.

The security bot stopped. Abby turned to see Anjum smash a small barrel—a stage prop, over the bot's head. When it still stood, he picked up the remnants of the barrel, whacked the bot again, and then kicked it over. The robot released its grip as it fell.

"I'm so sorry," Anjum apologized. "Not for knocking out

that bot." He looked down at the robot that was trying to get up. He hit it again. "But for everything else. I didn't know what was at stake. I've been so afraid," he apologized. "And I'm scared easily. I'm even afraid of people."

"What are you talking about?" Abby said.

"Someone threatened me that if I didn't let them take over my virtual persona, they'd hurt my family." That sounded like Muns. Abby thought of having to rescue hostages in Brazil because of Muns's threats. He was ruthless and apparently had forced his hand on Anjum.

"It wasn't me the whole time you've been competing," Anjum continued. "It was someone with software to sound like me who used my virtual person to impersonate me. I watched the whole thing. I'm so sorry."

Did that make sense? Could it really have been someone else? It did sound like something Muns would plan. And if one of Muns's followers wanted to enter the Race to make sure they succeeded and stole the vials, they would have to impersonate a student. School administration didn't let adults in. What better student to impersonate than a virtuality genius? In a way it was logical. But could she trust him now? Or was this just an act? He *had* just bashed a security bot to save her.

"Who threatened you?" Abby asked, her mind still racing.

"I don't know," Anjum responded. "They gained access to hack into the school's virtual booths easily enough, so I'd guess someone in the school has to be involved. But once they were in, it could have been a teacher or someone on the other side of the country—or the other side of the world, for all I know."

It could be someone on Muns's own estate, playing with them this whole time. But there had to be someone else on campus to give them access to the booths and to physically accept the vials.

Abby had to act fast. "Apology accepted," she said. He couldn't have made all of that up. Plus, she could really use one more person on her side. And if he was lying and tried to cross them, Malcolm could beat him into the ground. "Now let's get out of here."

The two rushed out of the backstage and down the hall.

Anjum let out a small laugh. Whoever had been impersonating him in the virtual world had used some great software. It had been very good, but not perfect. His laugh sounded slightly different. "I've never done something so exciting before," he said. "Not in real life, anyway. This is better than virtuality."

The two sprinted through the school. Anjum was slower; he probably wasn't as physically active as Abby. "Come on, you've got to be faster," Abby called back. "No offense." She couldn't resist.

"I probably deserve that," Anjum said.

They had to duck into two separate rooms to avoid security bots. Abby peeked around the next corner, then had to quickly turn back. Guarding the dead-end hallway was a small army of at least twenty security bots.

Abby and Anjum backtracked to a classroom. "They are guarding the entrance to the basement with a bunch of security bots, and they aren't going to move." She spoke over the sync so the rest of her friends could hear.

It hit Abby all at once—*security*. Whoever was pretending to be Anjum had sent security bots after all the Spartans, and a corps of security bots guarded the way to the basement. There had to be an undercover traitor in security.

The officer with the blond beard.

He was an expert in tracking messages; he would probably also be an expert in hacking in and leaving untraceable ones. With that expertise, he could also hack into a virtual booth and give another of Muns's men access to impersonate Anjum. The person who would have been most likely to discover him was Mr. Silverton, so he framed him first. And then he framed both Mr. Sul and his own supervisor to make sure he wasn't detected. Now he headed all of security—and he was the problem.

Abby explained her theory and the fact that the real Anjum was next to her over her sync.

"You may be right," Rafa said. "Let's use the avatars. We can use them to break through their line of security bots."

"The avatars are blocked," Rafa's mother said. She had joined the sync. "They caught me once. Thankfully, I managed to escape. But when I got back to the lab there was a large group of security bots guarding it."

"Great," Carol said. "So we just have to find a way into the basement, and into the avatar lab, and find a tranquilizer bomb in like the next twenty minutes or we are all unconscious for months and Muns wins. No problem."

"We won the Race," Abby said. "We came together. We beat a minotaur and a dragon and zombies. We can do this."

"But those were games," Malcolm said.

"They were practice," Abby answered, her voice bold and sure. "Now it's the real thing."

ATTACK

I t's a pleasure to be leading you for real," Anjum said over their new sync. "I have watched all of your challenges with envy. I must admit that I personally would never have chosen to join your team from the beginning. No offense. But having witnessed what you are capable of now, it is a grand pleasure to lead you, especially since it really counts."

"The real Anjum is a little nicer than the imposter one," Carol said.

"Not really," Anjum answered. "That's all you get. We'll need your best. Your *very* best. I'm sorry we don't have more time to plan, but we can do this. Now let's trash some robots."

Abby tensed, knowing that the dead-end hallway was coming up. Carol was right behind her. This had to work—and work quickly.

"Watch out! Security bot," Anjum warned. "Derick,

Piper, Maria, and Malcolm, get back!" He waited for them to comply, then continued, "Remember that as soon as they see us, we're in trouble. Not only will they know where we are, but they may also send reinforcements." He let out a short laugh. "It is quite similar to the zombie challenge. Let's do it again."

After a few minutes and a few more instructions, Abby saw the dead-end hallway. It was time to pick a fight with security bots.

"All right," Anjum said through Abby's earpiece. "On the count of three I want the first wave to attack. And I want to lead this one personally."

Abby was in the first wave. She took a deep breath.

"One, two," Anjum counted, "three! Go! Go! Go!"

Abby turned the corner. As the security bots reacted, pulling their stun guns up, Abby was very glad she wasn't there in the flesh. She and the rest of the team had decided to fight robots with robots. From the robotics lab, Abby drove her robot car, one of the four prototypes Jess had made, around the corner and began to shoot nuts and bolts wildly.

Anjum drove another bot back and forth, shooting with impressive accuracy. The only one better was Malcolm.

"It's about time I got to shoot stuff!" Malcolm yelled. "*Oh, yeah!*" His bot hit security bot after security bot in the face with its metal pellets. "I think mama would be okay with me shooting in this situation."

The security bots jumped into action, reeling on their wheels toward them, their stun guns firing. Of course, the stuns didn't have the same effect on other robots. It would take several direct hits—at least—to make any kind of difference.

"They're pretty good at attacking back," Malcolm said, veering to the side to dodge a stun shot.

"Pull back!" Anjum said. All of the Spartans' bots pulled back around their corners. The security bots split up and came out to attack. Some had minor dents in their faces and bodies from the metal pellets.

"Release the mowers!" Anjum screamed. "Second wave of attack!"

A mower bot shot by Abby's car. Its protective shield had been removed, leaving its churning blades exposed. It crashed into a security bot's legs, rattling and chomping at the metal. The security bot toppled over, knocking down another. One by one, several bots fell. The others were quick enough to get out of the way.

"Now the welders!" Anjum cried out.

Derick and Rafa flew in with the choppers, the welders strapped beneath them. Flames spurted out of small welder bots, thin machines designed to attach metal to metal. Jess controlled the arms, pointing the fire at different bots as they drove through. More bots toppled over. Anjum drove with his drills on and out in front of him. He took the legs off of several bots.

"Would you mind if I joined the excitement?" a polite voice asked.

Anjum let out a loud and obnoxious laugh. "I think now would be perfect."

"Thank you," Jenkins answered. "I would like that very much."

A quad lurched forward; the robot bench with legs carried a load. On its table was Jenkins's large shell, the torso of a humanoid bot. Jenkins sat in the cockpit in its face. His torso swung a large baseball bat, smashing it into the security bots. "Thank you so much for lending me your equipment, Malcolm," Jenkins said, swinging at a bot and knocking its arm straight off its body.

"I told you that you'd like baseball!" Malcolm called back.

"It isn't Ping-Pong, but for what we are trying to accomplish, I think it is working rather well." Jenkins knocked two more bots out with another swing.

"Boys," Carol sighed, now shooting forward with her drills out. Abby had also joined the fray.

In less than another minute, the security bots were out of commission.

"Abby, Derick, and Carol, surrender control of your robots to Jess and run from the lab to the basement," Anjum commanded. "Jenkins, stay there and make sure the entryway stays open. We don't want more bots coming back before the three of them can get there." His voice rose. "The rest of you, let's go open the avatar lab. We'll need the avatars to defend our real bodies at the robotics lab. My guess is that security is coming after us here as we speak and these robots will only defend us for so long."

"And when you have the Crash with you," Nia said, "you might as well let them do their stuff."

• • •

Derick opened the door from the inside of the robotics lab, then promptly closed it. "They were faster than we thought," he said. "We've got security bots outside the lab." He was so sick of them.

"We can bring our robots back to the lab and fight our way through," Anjum said.

"We don't have time," Derick said. He started to pace the room.

"What if we send out something before you?" Jess suggested, leaving her robots for a moment. "Would that work?" She brushed aside her blonde hair as she waited for a response.

"What do you mean?" Derick asked.

Jess moved her fingers and several more walking benches emerged from lab storage. "Let's send two quads out to pave the way, and have the rest of you ride on the other two."

"Like we bowl them over?" he asked.

"Oh yeah," Carol said. "Bowling robots!"

"It's worth a shot," Abby said.

Four quads approached the door in a line. Derick got on the third and Abby and Carol shared the fourth. The quads' surfaces were ridged, no doubt to help grip whatever they carried. But it didn't make them comfortable.

"Hold this sheet metal up, in case they try to stun you," Jess said, handing them each a sheet. It was wobbly and they could bend it around themselves.

"All right," Derick said, hoping this was going to work.

They only had sixteen minutes left until the bomb covered all of campus in tranquilizer.

"Are you ready?" Jess asked.

"We're wrapped up like metal burritos and we're ready to plow over some robots!" Carol squealed.

"Let's do it," Derick added.

They opened the door and the two quads barreled out against the security bots, knocking many of them over. Jess had programmed them to turn as they rode, so their wide side could take out more bots. One of the quads tripped up enough on the fallen security bots that it toppled entirely, but it crushed another bot on the way down. The other quad continued on in the opposite direction of the dead-end hallway. Several security bots followed the distraction.

"Let's go," Derick said, and pulled the sheet of metal tighter around him. He felt the lurch of the quad beneath him. It felt more like riding a horse than a robot. Each limb moved up and down in succession, but Derick didn't have a saddle. He tried to better balance himself as it picked up speed. He was out the door, rushing through the middle of the remaining robots and on his way to the dead-end hallway in no time. He slipped his leg out from under the sheet metal to kick over one of the bots. He quickly pulled it back in and felt the sheet metal being hit with stun blasts from the bots.

He looked behind him, risking a peek through the sheet metal, to see Abby and Carol only a few paces back.

The quads could move faster than Derick had expected. Great. They needed all the time they could get.

Without warning, Derick's quad tipped and tumbled

over. He crashed onto the floor, the sheet metal fumbling and rolling out of his grip with a thunderous clap. His quad had been tripped. A security bot grabbed his wrist. Derick pulled against it, but it was like wearing a pair of living handcuffs. "You need to evacuate," it said, and started to pull him down the hallway. Another pair of bots waited for Abby and Carol.

"No!" Derick cried out. He kicked again, toppling the security bot before it could knock into the other quad. Abby and Carol moved past.

Derick tried to wrench free, but the bot held strong. Abby and Carol had to make it even if he couldn't. But without him they would only have two keys and two spheres. That wouldn't be enough to do anything. With his free hand, he reached inside the secret compartment in his pocket and pulled out his key and sphere. "Abby!" he yelled, and threw them. It was an awkward throw, but the two precious items arced toward the moving quad.

Abby caught the sphere, but the key had veered too far to the left and out of reach. She had to jump off the quad to retrieve it.

A security bot raised its gun to fire at Abby. Derick lunged to get in the way.

His world went black.

• • •

"No!" Abby yelled. She tried to race back to Derick, but Carol had come back for her.

Carol grabbed Abby and with a grunt and a yank pulled her back onto the quad. "I'm being the meanie friend right now, but look at all those security bots." She pointed to a small crowd of bots that had gathered and started to fire on them. "Aaah!" Carol pulled the sheet of metal over them just in time. "So rude." She shook her head.

Abby squirmed again. She had caught a glimpse of one robot towing a limp Derick down the hall. It was taking him away, out of the building, toward the gates—toward Muns.

"He's not dead," Carol said. "He's just unconscious. In fact, this will probably make it so he's safer than he would have been."

It was nothing like the scene from the little saturn. There was no explosion of light. Maybe Carol was right. Maybe they had already changed everything and Derick would be safe.

"They caught Derick," Abby said over the sync to the others. "A security bot is taking him out of the school."

"We'll get on that," Anjum said. "I'm glad the two of you made it. We're probably almost to you on our way to the avatar lab."

"Just save him," Abby said.

"You take care of the bomb," Anjum said. "I'll make sure we get Derick back."

The quad raced down the hall much faster than Abby could have. It turned the corner and they passed by the array of robots controlled by Anjum and the others. Several of them raised their robot arms, cheering for them. They traveled farther down to see Jenkins swing and hit two more security bots. He waved with his free hand. "I thought I should keep the way open for you, madams." He did a small robot bow inside his cockpit.

"Thank you, Jenkins," Carol said. "Just saying that makes me feel like a rich lady at a manor." She giggled.

"You're very welcome," Jenkins responded.

Carol giggled again. "Of course, the fact that you're knocking down robots for me doesn't make me feel much like a lady in a manor."

"I don't understand," Jenkins admitted.

"Never mind," Carol said.

Abby jumped off the quad and hit the secret point on the wall that opened the doorway into the basement. It was a specific spot on the crown molding against the ceiling. The two friends hurried down the corridors and ladders until they used a key to open up the entrance to the Bridge.

"We've got eight minutes," Carol said. "Nothing like cutting it close."

"Quick. The keys," Abby said, motioning for Carol to join her.

Carol followed suit and they put their three keys in the Bridge. Abby also put in a sphere. It only required one sphere to see the present, but three to enter it. One would put less stress on the Bridge for now.

Thankfully, the Bridge seemed to be working fine. There were no initial side effects or consequences from looking into the future a little over twenty-four hours ago. Abby moved the controls on the Bridge and found two days before. She thought back. What time had the officers spoken with her? It had been late afternoon. She plugged in her best guess for a time and moved the perspective of the great invention to show the security gates. They were tall concrete walls, with a booth beside them for security guards and bots. Someone coming out or in had to pass through two large sets of doors, and be approved both times.

Abby had to scroll back and forth through time before she found the police officers entering campus. They walked beside the blond-bearded assistant from the gates to the doors to the Hall. He opened the door for them.

"Wait," Carol said. "Right there."

"Where?" Abby asked, rewinding.

"Right when the blond-bearded terrible dude opens the door. Watch his pockets."

Abby gritted her teeth when she saw a police officer pass by the blond-bearded officer and drop a package into his pocket. "There it is," Abby said.

"Now fast-forward," Carol said. "Follow him."

Abby knew she didn't have much time. The Bridge couldn't handle it. She sped through their hours of interrogation. She saw him speaking with other security officers, filing reports on Chief Shar, and finally going back to his quarters, where he pulled out the device. He'd had it on him the whole time he had been accusing his superior officer.

The security officer pulled out the chemicals he had stashed in a supply closet. Abby didn't have time to find out when he stole them, but it really didn't matter. The message at the end of the Race had said he used one of the robots in the lab. With his hacking skills, he could have stolen a bot out of the robotics room and slipped into the chemistry lab.

He probably would have taken the time to make it look like another teacher, or Landon, was using the robot too—just in case anyone discovered him. He could have even programmed the security bot on duty to simply be in the wrong place. He could take care of any security footage. He could have even done it while he was assigned to watch over that hall.

He pulled out the package the police officer had smuggled in for him and unwrapped a vial. Carefully he assembled the tranquilizer bomb. And then he reached for more supplies. Abby's heart sank.

"He made two bombs?" Carol blurted out, and palmed her forehead. "We stole three from Ruminex. He made two fakes and only returned one."

"Now we have to find and stop two," Abby said, her heart pounding.

"Double the work. Double the pressure." Carol synced up with the rest of the team. "The freakshow made two bombs. This is going to go down to the wire."

Anjum responded, "How can we help? We should be into the avatar lab in a few minutes. We can use the avatars to retrieve whatever bombs there are. Or we can retreat and try to retrieve them with these bots."

"We should be able to get them with the Bridge," Carol said. "But we'll let you know if we need you."

Abby used the Bridge to follow the blond-bearded security guard through the next day, but at night, he returned, grabbed one of the bombs and walked through the halls of the school. He said hello to all the security guards, and checked on all the bots. He did a thorough inspection of the auditorium. Bots lined the walls, making sure there was no foul play. But of course, he had probably programmed them. Underneath one of the seats about ten rows from the front, he strapped down a tranquilizer bomb.

Muns always had to make his revenge fitting. Derick and Rafa had first saved Abby's grandfather in an auditorium. He had been held hostage there. And now the Spartans were supposed to be locked inside a virtual booth in this auditorium. Abby and all of her team would have been the first to be tranquilized.

"It's time to get that bomb," Abby said. She moved the setting on the Bridge to the present. There were a few security bots still on duty, rolling through the aisles. It looked like they were simply looking for any stray students, but the blond-bearded security officer had probably set them to guard the tranquilizer bomb.

Carol called out over the sync where they had found it.

The Bridge started to shake.

Abby moved the perspective of the Bridge close to the bomb and added two spheres. The Bridge tremored again. "Grab it," Abby told Carol.

Carol moved to the other side of the room, and crawled from the basement of Cragbridge Hall into the auditorium. She stayed low to avoid being seen by the security bots. She spent several moments trying to pull at the thick tape used to strap the bomb down. She was trying to do it quietly so she wouldn't draw any attention.

A security bot paused, then turned to roll toward the aisle. Perhaps it had heard her.

"Hurry, Carol," Abby whispered. "A bot is coming."

Carol moved her lips, obviously mouthing words she wanted to say but couldn't. She had to be quiet.

The bot approached her aisle.

The Bridge shuddered.

"Oh, it's impossible to do this quietly," Carol whispered in frustration, then pulled on the tape with all her might. It ripped clean of the seat with a loud GRRRRAAAATT.

All the bots in the room turned their heads toward the sound. The bot who had been investigating reached the right row and raised his stun gun.

"Oh dearie," Carol said, getting up and running toward it. That was the direction she had come into the auditorium from, and the direction she had to go to get back into the basement.

The Bridge shook again, rattling the metal branches that crept up into the ceiling. Abby shifted the perspective of the Bridge closer to Carol.

All the security bots raised their guns, but the closest bot fired.

The instant Carol crossed in, Abby turned one of the keys. A fraction of a second longer, and Carol would have been out cold.

"Whew!" Carol sighed. "That was crazy close." She looked down at her hands and the tranquilizer bomb. "Where do we put this thing?" she asked.

Abby hadn't thought about that. "I don't care as long

as it's somewhere else away from people and far away from here."

Carol nodded several times. "Yeah, I don't want this thing to blow up in my face. My face is way too stunning for that."

"Help me turn the keys back," Abby said. They had to be turned in unison to gain access to the past or present. As soon as they twisted the keys together, the Bridge rumbled and rattled. It hadn't been given enough time to calm.

"That really doesn't sound good," Carol said. "We'd better hurry."

Abby nodded as she began to change the Bridge settings.

"Remember the part about this bomb killing anyone who is right next to it when it explodes?" Carol said. "I really don't want to die right now." She shook her head, her hands still firmly holding the tranquilizer bomb. "I bet you're not super fond of the idea either."

Abby shook her head. "Let's get rid of it."

The Bridge shook again, loud and deep.

The Sahara Desert filled the other side of the room. Where there had been the dim cold floor of the basement, miles of sand dunes rose and fell under a scorching sun. A wave of suffocating heat overtook the room, making it feel like an arid wasteland. "We don't have much time," Abby said. "Hurry, throw it in."

Carol hurled the tranquilizer bomb into the sand. "Sorry if there are any cacti and lizards out there! You might take a long nap."

The Bridge rumbled hard, its branches creaking and

shaking, but Abby couldn't shut it down. She pulled two spheres to relieve some of the pressure, but went back to searching for the blond-bearded security officer in the recent past. She found the spot when he set the bomb in the auditorium, then fast-forwarded.

"I was kind of hoping we could see the big explosion in the desert," Carol complained.

"No time for that," Abby said, checking the time. "We still have another bomb, and only three minutes."

The Bridge rattled, shaking the entire room. It was a small earthquake in the basement. A piece of metal fell to the floor.

"It's falling apart," Carol said.

Abby didn't answer. She watched as the security guard took the next bomb out of his quarters and looked up at the security tower. It was a perfect place for the tranquilizer bomb to go off. It would explode over the entire campus and the tranquilizing cloud would settle over it all. Plus, the second place Muns had kept Grandpa captive was in the *Hindenburg*, high in the air. The top of the tower was the highest place on school grounds.

"It's on the tower," Carol announced through her rings to the rest of the team.

The Bridge quaked and more metal fell off its branches.

"One more," Abby said.

The entire Bridge shifted an inch along the floor and several entire branches fell from their places. One nearly crashed onto Abby.

Carol pulled the keys. The scene of the tower faded.

355

"We need to get the other tranquilizer bomb!" Abby yelled, reaching for the keys.

"No," Carol said. "Then there wouldn't be a Bridge left here and Muns would win. There has to be another way."

"Like what?" Abby asked.

"I have no idea."

EXPLOSIONS

Derick opened his eyes. It felt like someone had clubbed him on the head. He closed them again, trying to block out the pain.

He felt his body moving. Was he just motion-sick, or was he actually going somewhere?

He forced himself to open his eyes again. Three security bots were carrying him toward the gates to leave Cragbridge Hall. The memory of minutes before came rushing back.

Derick struggled against the metal grip of the bots, but they held firm. After all he had done, after all his work, he was going to be pulled away from the school by programmed machines. Embarrassing. At least he had passed off his key and sphere. Muns might get him, but he wouldn't get those.

The last of the student crowd ballooned at the gates. It would be a few minutes before he was out.

Student after student crossed through the open gates and left the school. Guards were escorting Mr. Silverton and Mr. Sul. They both had keys. Maybe they had spheres. If security hadn't confiscated them before, they were both about to hand them over to Muns whether they liked it or not. If Muns's men had already taken just one more key from anyone else in the other council, then Muns would have power over the past. If they had spheres, one more would allow him to interact with the present. Then, if they didn't get rid of the tranquilizer bomb, no one would be able to stop him.

Derick thought of the future. He thought of the Ash.

He heard Carol relay that they had found the other bomb on the tower. He looked over at it and wanted to spit. Just under the top, he saw something strapped to a pole. The tower that was supposed to keep the school protected held its greatest danger. Several security bots stood at their posts in front of the tower. Many more than on a usual day.

Carol announced that they had to pull the keys out of the Bridge. They only had a few minutes.

Derick wriggled madly. He had to get free. He was the closest to the bomb. He had to stop this.

One of the robots carrying Derick fell to the ground, followed by another. Derick tumbled with them. He twisted his body in time to see a car robot taking out his third robot with its drill.

"Thanks," he said.

"You're welcome," Jess answered through her rings.

"Anjum sent me. The rest of the team is fighting the robots at the avatar lab."

Derick looked up at the tower and took off running. It was up to him. It was like the first challenge in the Race. He was the closest. His team was depending on him to get this done. He'd have to find a way past the robots, climb the tower, and race the bomb down to the Bridge in time. Surely they could start it up for the split second it would take to throw a bomb through. He would have to be the fastest he'd even been.

He remembered the flash from the saturn's footage, the flash from the future. It had to be the tranquilizer bomb exploding. If that was right, if it was showing him this future, he would reach the bomb, but not get rid of it in time. And the explosion would be the last thing he'd ever feel.

He'd have to run faster, do better. He had to change the future.

Or . . .

•   •   •

"Derick, are you okay?" Abby asked over her rings.

"Yeah," he panted as he spoke. "Jess came and saved me."

"Where are you?" Abby asked.

"I'm going after the second bomb," Derick said.

"We have just over a minute left," Carol said.

"Just get ready to crank up the Bridge so we can throw the tranquilizer bomb out of here," Derick said. "You won't have time to change any settings. We'll only need half a second."

"Have you got the bomb already?" Abby asked.

"No, but," he said, painting some more, "I'm on my way."

"You can't bring it here in time." Abby was panicking. It would take a minute to even climb the tower. "Derick, don't get close to that bomb." She pictured the scene from the saturn over and over. She could hear Derick's scream in her head.

"I need someone at every door between the tower and the basement room," Derick said, his voice calming. Was he not running anymore? "I'll be coming fast. Rafa, take the first. Use an avatar if you need to. I'll need someone else at the door in the dead-end hall."

"I'll take it," Rafa's mom said.

"Abby and Carol, stay there to turn the keys," Derick commanded.

"Derick, no!" Abby protested. "I know you want to save the day, but this is impossible!"

"I can do this," Derick insisted.

"No. You can't," Abby said. "No one can. Don't get close to that bomb. Come down to the basement." Her voice was filled with emotion. "Down here we're safe. It's like a bomb shelter. After the Bridge rests we can use it to get out."

"Then what?" Derick asked. "We let Muns destroy this whole school? We let him terrify everyone else? Then school won't be in session again for how long? I've got this, Abby. Trust me."

"I want to." She was weeping now. "I . . . I can't lose you. I can't! You're my brother. You're who I look up to. You have to be here. You . . ." Her words choked in her throat.

"I can—" Derick started.

"There's no way!" Abby interrupted, frantic now. "No way anyone could possibly run fast enough from the tower to here. You've only got thirty-five seconds. No one can—"

"Abby," Derick cut her off, "who said anything about running?"

"What?"

"Did you know that some animals can go up to 200 miles per hour?"

"Derick, you're not making any sense."

"Have you ever heard of a stoop?"

• • •

Derick sliced the straps with his talons and ripped the bomb away from the tower. The robots had fought their way to the avatar lab and Derick had been the first person inside.

He flapped his wings hard twice and then he dove. He needed all the speed he could get.

Again, he felt the rush.

He tucked in his feet and cut through the air with his beak, his small body falling story after story.

Faster, more.

He tried to tilt his body to gain more speed.

361

The ground was getting bigger, closer.

He had to do this just right.

Not yet.

"Stoop. Stoop. Stoop," he could hear Rafa chanting. He must be watching from his place at the door. Members of the Crash joined in.

He couldn't pull up yet.

Not yet.

He waited after the moment he had pulled up before.

A little more.

"Stoop. Stoop."

He waited longer than he had seen Rafa or the other members of the Crash wait. He needed all his momentum.

Now! Derick tilted his wings and swooped forward. He glided right over the ground, the bomb only inches away from it. Now that he had his speed, he lifted a little and shot straight at the door to the main building on campus. Rafa held it open.

"Keep up the speed!" Rafa yelled.

"Oh, I'm not slowing down." Derick rocketed through the hall, past the commons, and down to the secret hallway. It did take some adjusting, flying where there were no conflicting air currents. He found himself flapping more to compensate.

"How much time?" he asked, rocketing through the hall.

"Nineteen seconds," Carol answered. "Wow, this tension is crazy. You can do this!" she cheered. "Because if you don't, you'll just bring it closer to all of us and explode the Bridge and all of us with it."

She was right. Derick flapped harder as he passed Rafa's mother—and Jenkins and his shell—holding the secret door.

"Thirteen, twelve," Carol counted down.

Derick dove down where the ladder was and through the dark corridor. It was harder to see in the dark underbelly of the school. And going as fast as he was, he barely had time to react to twists and turns.

"Eight. Seven. Six. Five."

Derick flew through the large metal doors as Carol held them open.

"Four. Three."

He was in the same room. He caught a glimpse of his sister at the Bridge. The keys were turned, the Bridge rocking in its place.

He threw open his wings, and flung the tranquilizer bomb with his talons. It passed into the desert and exploded. The other bomb Carol had thrown in before exploded simultaneously. A burst of tranquilizer cloud rocketed toward them at amazing speed, but faded to only a ghost of itself a fraction of a second before it could fill the room and destroy them all.

Abby had twisted the keys.

The Bridge began to settle.

Derick panted. "I told you I could do it."

"Show-off," Abby retorted. Then she hit her knees. "You changed it. You changed the future."

"Yeah. I guess I did."

DON'T YOU DARE
APOLOGIZE

The Spartans' sync exploded with cheers.

"That was crazy," Maria said. She had obviously stayed and not bailed out early like she had threatened.

"*Yeah, Spartans!*" Malcolm called out.

"I'm sorry that I couldn't help," Piper said from outside the gates of the school. "Dumb security robots."

"Congratulations, everyone," Anjum said, his voice lighter than usual. "We just won something so much bigger than a contest."

"Oh, yeah, we did!" Carol said, jumping up and down. She turned to Derick's falcon that had just dropped a bomb into the desert. It was perched on the console of the Bridge. "High five!" Derick reached up one of the falcon's feet, but Carol slowed when she saw the talons. "Eep. Lots of pokeys on that one." She gingerly touched her hand to the robot bird's foot.

For several minutes, Abby stood there, basking in her relief. Her brother was safe. They had saved the school and her friends and all those locked up in the medical unit. She hugged Carol. She just breathed in and relaxed.

The giant metal door behind them opened.

Abby whirled around to see Coach Adonavich, the dark-haired gym teacher. She had been unconscious for weeks. "Abby," the coach said, out of breath, in her thick Russian accent. She had obviously run there from the medical unit. "What is going on?"

"We're okay," Abby answered. "We're okay."

"We just kicked Muns's plan all over the place," Carol corrected.

Mr. Trinhouse, a large black man, stepped in behind Coach Adonavich. Abby's heart started to beat faster. More of them were awake.

When one more figure passed through the large metal doorway, Abby rushed across the room.

Her mother.

Abby buried her head in her mother's shoulder. She wanted to laugh and cry and dance, all at the same time. She just hugged.

"Where's Derick?" Abby's mother asked.

Abby looked over at the falcon avatar. It had gone limp. "I think he's on his way," Abby said.

"Sorry, it took us a while," Abby's mother said, pressing

her hand against the back of Abby's head, then smoothing her hair. "We had to break out of the medical unit."

"Coach Horne and Mr. Trinhouse ruined four beds slamming them into the door before it gave," Coach Adonavich explained. Coach Horne was a gym teacher and had been a professional weightlifter.

"You did more than your share taking down that door," Mr. Trinhouse said back to Coach Adonavich. She had been a gymnast and was capable of amazing physical feats.

Coach Adonavich nodded.

"Then we had a problem with a few security bots," Abby's mother continued the story.

Mr. Trinhouse raised a stun gun, still attached to a robot arm. "I had to borrow a couple of these to get us through." He glanced over at Abby's mother, who looked at the floor. She had dropped her stun gun to hug her daughter.

"Then," Abby's mother continued, "we had to persuade an extremely polite robot at the entrance that we were okay to come down, and he shouldn't hit us with a baseball bat." Her last words were half-spoken, half-laughed. "I have to admit I wasn't expecting that. He insisted that a girl named Jess approve us."

Abby smiled, but tears still streamed down her cheeks. "Where's Dad?" she asked.

"He's still waking up," mom said. "So are a few more. The tranquilizers affected each of us differently, but I think we should all be back to normal before too long."

Another figure stepped into the room. He was

large—and carrying someone. It was Coach Horne, with Abby's grandfather in his large arms.

"I said, 'Set me down,'" her grandfather commanded. "Just because I'm old doesn't mean I can't walk."

"It has nothing to do with being old," Coach Horne said in his deep voice. "You've only been fully awake for a few minutes." He obediently set down Oscar Cragbridge.

Abby ran to her grandfather, but paused at the last moment to be gentle as she hugged him. He embraced her in return, his arms weaker than usual. "I'm so glad you're here," Abby said.

"By the look of things," Grandpa answered, "I think it is I that should be glad that you are here. I believe you have quite a story to tell us."

Abby nodded. "I think we just barely escaped." She began to tell them the essential points of what had just happened. Derick came in panting when she was nearly done. Rafa had used an avatar to make a way through the security bots so Derick could join them. Derick exchanged hugs with his grandpa and mom, holding them longer than usual. Carol also stood up and spread her arms wide. Derick reluctantly gave her a hug as well. He let go, but Carol didn't. It took him three tries to free himself from the blonde seventh-grader. When Abby mentioned that everyone else had been evacuated, Grandpa's face grew solemn.

"So," Grandpa said in a grave tone, "we must assume that Muns will shortly have a collection of keys, and perhaps spheres. It will only take as long as it takes someone to travel from here to Muns's estate." He took several short steps, leaning heavily on his cane.

Abby nodded.

"How long has it been since the bombs should have gone off?" Grandpa asked.

Derick glanced at the time on his rings. "Almost fifteen minutes." Time had passed quickly as they hugged and spoke to one another.

"We may still have some time," Grandpa said, and winced as he tried to take a few steps toward the Bridge. "With any luck, even in Muns's fastest private plane, it may take another few minutes to travel to his estate."

"We're sorry," Derick apologized. "We tried to—"

"Derick Cragbridge!" Grandpa interrupted, and slammed his cane against the hard floor of the basement. It looked like his strength was returning. "Don't you dare apologize! You have done great feats of bravery and intellect. You too, Abby! In every way, you too." He looked at both of them, his eyes intense. "And all your friends." He leaned forward on his cane, perhaps having become too excited for his condition. "The world owes you a great debt. And as for Muns, we will face whatever comes together, and we will win." His voice grew louder with the last three words.

He spoke with such conviction that Abby believed him. She had always believed him, except for what he said about her. She hadn't always believed that she had the great potential he claimed she did, but maybe he was a genius in more ways than she thought. Maybe he had seen things in her she hadn't dared to believe of herself.

"Um, guys," Piper said through their sync, "I think we've got a problem. Let me show you what's going on outside the gates." An invitation for a live feed popped up and Abby clicked on it. Jumbled footage sprang into view. It showed the crowded scene outside the gates, where Piper had been dragged by a security bot.

"Down! Get down!" someone yelled. As the crowd obeyed, a security guard pointed his stun gun, but someone else fired on him. He fell to the ground.

"What's going on?" someone asked.

"Stay down," a security officer barked, then was shot and fell limp.

A woman moved through the crowd, expertly weaving between students and shooting down security officers. Two more soldiers joined her. Then several more. Her numbers were increasing. They shot security guards, policemen, and the bomb squad that had arrived on the scene. Security bots joined them, taking down all the officers who were there to protect the students and the school. The bots were obviously still under the control of the officer with the blond beard. The attackers made their way toward the campus gates, stunning anyone who opposed them. One of the men even stunned several students who were simply in his way, and walked over their unconscious bodies.

"This is a full-on war out here!" Piper yelled over the shots.

"Grandpa," Abby said, "you need to see this." She included everyone in the basement on the link.

"Muns's men," Derick said. "It's been too long and there are no signs that the bomb went off. They're coming in."

Abby looked at her grandpa. "He's sent all his men in now that security is down."

Immediately Grandpa called on his rings, "Security, this is Oscar Cragbridge. Secure the main doors. Do not let the attackers in! I repeat, do not let the attackers in!" He took a deep breath, still recovering from his time unconscious.

"This is insane," Carol blurted out.

Abby looked back at the footage. Several security guards rallied to protect the gates.

"Muns likely has his keys," Grandpa said solemnly. "And now he wants to destroy the Bridge." He began to explain why he thought the attack was happening, as all in the basement watched it unfold. "If he has enough keys and perhaps even spheres from the teachers who evacuated, he can use the copy of the Bridge he stole months ago. The Bridge here is the only thing that may be able to counteract anything he would do, anything he would change in time. If he can destroy it, he controls all of time."

"Uh," Piper interrupted, "are you still watching this?"

The security guards and soldiers shot at each other, a crowd of students and teachers ducking in the crossfire. Several on both sides cried out and fell to the ground, but the security guards were outnumbered and outgunned. One of the security guards flicked his fingers, initiating the close of both sets of the large metal doors. The doors lurched toward each other, surprisingly fast for their size and weight. Muns's soldiers raced into action. Two ran to each set of doors and unpacked two cases. They quickly assembled hydraulic metal braces that clanked against the doors and pressed against them, keeping them from closing. During the process, the last of the security guards was stunned unconscious. The few remaining police officers and members of the bomb squad outside the gates fired away at Muns's soldiers and the security bots, but they were hopelessly outmanned.

The soldier in the lead simply stepped through the braces and onto the grounds of Cragbridge Hall. He surveyed the area, his gun pointed in one direction and then another. He eventually waved another soldier through behind him. They came one by one.

But it didn't end. A steady stream of soldiers came onto the grounds.

"How many of them are there?" Carol asked. "This is a freaking army."

The soldiers at the head of the group pushed forward toward the building, as more poured through the opening.

"There are hundreds of them," Piper said. Abby remembered that Muns had asked for hundreds. He got what he wanted.

"What do we do?" Abby's mother asked.

"We need to stop the army and use the Bridge to travel through the present, find Muns, and take back our keys," Grandpa said, as matter-of-factly as if it was a simple to-do list.

"They'll be on us in minutes," Coach Adonavich said.

"I think I have a few friends who can help," Derick

suggested. He didn't wait for approval. He commanded through his rings: "Crash, I need you. Let's keep those soldiers away from our building. It's time to do what you do best."

"I'm on it," Rafa said through the group sync. "*Vamos!*"

"I'm right behind you, son," Rafa's mother said.

"Now we're talking!" Malcolm joined in. "I'm gonna pick out something big and mean."

"I'm going to pick out something bigger and meaner than yours," Nia added.

"I have some stress I'd really like to work out," Maria said. "And maybe some payback for having that stress in the first place."

"I really wish I was inside and could help," Piper said.

"You've done a ton, Piper, just keeping us informed," Abby said. "Thank you."

"Anjum and Jess," Derick said. "Get whatever robots you can out there. We need all the help we can get. I'll grab an avatar and join you." He began to run toward the door that led out of the basement.

"No, you won't," Grandpa corrected. "I need you here. We'll need to cross through time to get Muns's keys. Find something you can both attack and defend yourself with." Grandpa shuffled over to the Bridge, had Coach Adonavich help him turn the keys, inserted a sphere, and began searching the present.

Mr. Trinhouse raised his stun gun. Abby's mother picked up hers. Coach Horne grabbed a branch that had fallen from the Bridge and broke it. He kept the largest club-like piece, and gave the next biggest piece to Coach Adonavich. Derick, Abby, and Carol snatched the leftovers. They weren't large, but were the size of short baseball bats and could do some damage.

"Clever," Grandpa grumbled, working the console. "Muns has moved his Bridge." Grandpa searched from one room in Muns's estate to the next. "It may take me a few more moments to find him. It is not easy to move and likely not out of his estate."

"I should be able to get us a better view of what's going on outside," Mr. Trinhouse said, moving his fingers, controlling his rings. He was an engineering teacher and very good with machines. Since Piper was outside the gates, they had only been able to see what was going on from her perspective. When the gates had partially closed, they had lost most of their view. "I helped design and install most of our security system; I should still have access or be able to override the protocols." Abby couldn't help but realize that had he been conscious during all that had happened, Mr. Trinhouse definitely would have been a suspect.

Soon a glimpse of the outside appeared in Abby's contacts. First she saw a falcon stoop. It let out a cry as it opened its talons and grabbed the barrel of a soldier's gun. In a flash, it ripped the weapon from its place and used its momentum to slam the barrel against the helmet of the next soldier and two after that. It was enough to knock two of the three unconscious. The bird flung the barrel in the direction of a fourth soldier, and attacked a fifth. It grabbed the soldier's shoulders with its talons, shifted its momentum, and flapped hard to one side. The man fell.

The robot bird launched back up into the sky, only to be greeted by hundreds of bullets. Their guns were not set to stun anymore. Several pierced through the robot falcon body. Abby cringed, knowing that whoever was controlling the bird could feel all of the pain of the attack. They had just picked a fight with hundreds of armed men, and were paying the price.

A rhino barreled out of the school and at the army. Two gorillas and a lion were only a pace behind. Another falcon stooped down from above. Anjum was barking orders over their sync, coordinating the attack.

A few moments later, a series of robots joined the battle. Quads ran through the ranks. Mower bots were set loose. Small helicopters took to the sky. Even Jenkins came rushing out in his shell with his baseball bat.

Abby glanced at her grandfather as he worked the Bridge. He still had not found Muns.

"I can't stand just watching as my friends do all the work," Derick said, pacing the basement floor.

Coach Horne put a large hand on Derick's shoulder. "Just get ready to help here. We may have the more difficult assignment. We have to get the keys from Muns and he will have guards. All we have is a couple of stun guns and some broken pieces of metal."

Abby swallowed hard. Coach Horne was right. She looked back to the outside. A falcon fell. A lion jumped on several soldiers, pummeling them to the ground. Then the beast took so many bullets it could only knock out a couple more soldiers before crashing limp against the lawn. The rhino and the two gorillas did the most damage, rampaging through the attackers. Abby guessed that the rhino was Malcolm and the gorillas were Rafa and his mom. The rhino was so huge and powerful, and the gorillas moved quickly and, strangely, gracefully. But they too took on a barrage of bullets. Though they had stopped sixty to eighty soldiers, there were still a couple of hundred more.

The robots did their part, causing chaos and knocking soldiers to the ground, but bullets could stop them too. The defense couldn't hold out forever.

"We can't stop all of them," Malcolm called out, breathing heavily. "There are too many." He cried out; another bullet must have hit him.

"Fall back," Anjum said.

"No," Rafa rebutted. "We keep going. We never quit."

"Not to give up, but to be smarter," Anjum explained. "Get inside the building and wait for them to enter the doors. No matter how many of them there are, they can only enter a few at a time. Then their numbers do not mean as much."

"Like the Spartans," Maria said.

"Yes," Anjum agreed. "Just like the Spartans!" His voice grew. "We will make our own last stand!"

Grandpa didn't look over his shoulder, but called out, "Abby and Derick, I really like your friends." The perspective of the Bridge moved to just outside a room. "This is the last place large enough," Grandpa explained. "I believe

Muns is inside with the Bridge." He moved forward, but suddenly stopped. "Umph," he gasped, and faltered. Then he stumbled to the ground.

"You are trying to do too much too soon," Abby's mother said, running to his side. "You need to relax."

"No," Grandpa said. He rolled over and tried to cough, but nothing came out. "This . . ." He stopped and struggled for breath. "This . . . is . . . something else. Something more."

"What do you mean?" Abby asked. She had followed right behind her mother. Derick hit his knees beside her.

"I don't know," Grandpa admitted, rolling onto his back. He took short breaths, gasping them in like he couldn't get enough. "Extreme . . . pain." He gritted his teeth. "It's running all through me." He choked for more air.

Abby stared at her grandfather and then the perspective just outside of Muns's Bridge. It hit Abby hard. "The Ash," she mumbled.

"Oh, no," Derick whispered.

"What?" Abby's mother asked.

"I didn't explain it," Abby said. "Muns has . . ." Tears came. "He . . ." Her words caught in her throat.

"He's gone back in time," Derick took over. "And he changed something. Maybe he killed Grandpa—he did something so he won't exist anymore." Derick took a deep breath. "And now, he'll be gone within an hour."

"But if he dies sometime in the past, then the Bridge will have never existed," Coach Adonavich pointed out.

"Muns is too smart for that," Derick said. "He must have attacked Grandpa after he had already invented the Bridge."

"We have to hurry and—" Abby's mother started, but groaned. She opened her mouth to speak again, but gasped for air and fell to the ground.

Abby screamed.

Derick yelled.

Abby knew what Muns had done as soon as he had gotten his keys. His first move had been to eliminate those who had tried to stop him. He had gotten Grandpa and Abby's mom. Her father had probably already been struck also. It was just a matter of time before Abby and Derick also felt the Ash. It was very possible that Abby's entire family had only an hour to live.

LIGHT

Abby took over the controls of the Bridge. Grandpa wasn't in a position to lead anymore. Now it was up to them. She didn't know what she would see when she moved the perspective beyond the door and into Muns's room. And she didn't know what the others in the room would do as soon as they could see it. Would they want to rush in and try to take on Muns's armed guards? Was that suicide?

Out of the corner of her eye she saw movement. A man. A soldier, with a giant barrel mounted on his arm, came into the basement room out of nowhere. He aimed at the Bridge. Abby turned to look down the barrel of a loaded cannon.

"Soldier!" Derick yelled, and pointed at the intruder.

The soldier flicked his finger, but before the barrel launched its small missile, Coach Adonavich lunged at him, knocking him to the side and causing the shot to fire off course. It slammed into the corner of the room and exploded, sending a thunderous boom echoing through the room. Several branches of the Bridge caught on fire, while others were blown clean off.

Muns must have used the keys and the spheres from his Bridge to send the soldier right into the basement. Muns wasn't holding anything back.

Another soldier entered, and Mr. Trinhouse and Coach Horne immediately jumped into the fray. Derick and Carol both raised their shards of metal from the Bridge and waited for any others to surprise them. There was no telling where they would come in. With Muns using his Bridge for the invasion he could use any angle. They had to be ready for anything.

Abby moved the perspective from her Bridge to see Muns's room. It was completely surreal. A small squad of soldiers was running in through Muns's Bridge there and Abby could see them arriving where she was in the basement of Cragbridge Hall. It was like watching herself in a movie—a movie that was about to end in tragedy.

Abby had no idea what to do. She could cross over into Muns's room, but most of those on her side were already in a life-and-death battle with armed soldiers. She could try to take on Muns's armed guards herself and fight for the keys. Derick and Carol would follow her. But would that do any good? Would those attacking her Bridge take over first?

"Abby," Grandpa choked out. He lifted up his cane. "The final . . . secret," he whispered. "Put my cane . . ."

His words failed, but he extended his cane and pressed his finger to the metal band. The outside covering of the cane sloughed off and Abby saw a wonder of mechanical pieces integrated and woven together. Grandpa pointed to the Bridge.

Abby heard another large shot crash into a wall.

"Keys, spheres, . . . your object, . . . and this," he whispered.

What would happen? Abby already knew how to go into the past, the present, and the future. What else could possibly be left? Abby obeyed though, putting her heartstone in the Bridge. Immediately it rumbled. Then she brought the cane close to the console. A small circular hole twisted open, just enough room for Abby to slide in her grandfather's cane all the way up to the handle. Apparently there was more to this cane than Abby thought.

The other side of the room did not fill with another scene. There were no great wars or figures from the past, no school or mansion from the present, no girl in trouble in the future. Everything was completely white. More than white. It was as if the other side of the basement of Cragbridge Hall were filled with light.

The sound of fighting once again demanded Abby's attention. Coach Adonavich leaped high, kicking a soldier in the face and knocking him unconscious, but another fired his weapon. The athletic coach stumbled. She was shot again before Mr. Trinhouse stunned the soldier with the gun he had taken from a security bot. The coach fell to the ground.

"No!" Coach Horne thundered. The giant coach punched a soldier so hard he flew back several feet and slammed into another man with a gun. But two more attacked.

Carol had picked up Abby's mother's stun gun and was doing damage of her own. Derick was swinging his piece of metal, barely dodging soldier fire.

This was impossible. The Ash. Soldiers. They were outnumbered and outgunned. They couldn't hope to last long. Plus an army of men was attacking above them to get inside the school. Muns had them trapped.

She only had one choice. "Derick, Carol," Abby screamed, "into the light!" She grabbed Carol and pushed her in. She pulled Derick into the white just as another soldier fired.

THE LAST SECRET

For a moment it was as though Abby had stepped into light itself. She had to hold her eyes closed for several seconds at a time, then blink over and over. She kept trying to focus on anything, to figure out where she was, and especially how it might help.

"This is crazy," Carol said. "You pushed me into some light world. I can't see a thing."

"Where are we?" Derick asked.

Abby felt relieved to hear their voices. She couldn't see them through the light. "I don't know," Abby admitted, shading her eyes from the light with her hands. "Grandpa said this was the last secret."

She blinked a few more times and saw a couple of darker spots in the white. Then Abby heard a voice, a voice that brought comfort all at once. "Hello." It was her grandpa.

"And welcome to a place you probably never thought existed." He cleared his throat. "I'm not sure that's the best way of putting it."

Abby squinted as she looked around. Her eyes were getting used to the light and she could see some varying shades of color against the white background, but she still couldn't focus. She saw an image of her grandfather, wearing his usual blazer and slacks, his cane by his side.

"If you have made it here," he continued, "you already know my secrets of being able to pass into the past, and the present, and the future, but this is a space between. It is outside of time." He spoke the last words slowly and deliberately. "That may take a moment to think about. But when you step back into the basement of Cragbridge Hall, it will be the exact moment when you left. No time will have passed, for you are not *in* time now. Everything that happens here is independent of any time."

"I think he just hurt my brain," Carol said.

Abby thought she understood, but wasn't sure. Thankfully, her grandfather had more to say. "If you think of time like a street, normally we travel forward through the present toward the future. With the Bridge you can change directions and drive the other way—through the past. Or for the future, you can speed up down the road. You can also pull into a side street and explore another neighborhood in the present. But this . . . this is as if you simply park the car. You are not traveling anywhere."

On a certain level it made some sense. If it was possible to travel into the past, and to different parts of the present, or even into the future, there could be a time or space between.

"I didn't see this one coming," Derick admitted. Abby could see him fairly clearly now. He still held the piece of the Bridge he had brought from the basement.

Abby took a deep breath. It felt wonderful. She was out of the stress, out of the barrage of bullets, away from the Ash, out of the last moments before Muns triumphed.

She sat down, safe for the moment.

"As you can see," Grandpa said, his image gesturing toward the out-of-focus shapes behind him, "I've spent quite a bit of time here." He grimaced and then laughed. "I guess *time* isn't the best word to use to explain it, but . . . that doesn't matter." He slouched a moment. "It began when I had something I didn't want to face. It could have been a presentation, or a heated debate, or," he said, his voice dropping, "just feeling lonely after my wife passed." He cleared his throat. "It has been a place where I could escape." He pointed behind him. Now Abby recognized that the other splotches of color were inventions. There was a simulator, a metal shop machine for making lockets and keys, a Chair, parts of avatars, and more. A few chairs and tables surrounding the machines were covered with various parts and charts. It was like Grandpa had another lab entirely.

"You can bring anything here," Grandpa explained, "and as long as it doesn't need a connection to the outside world, it will work. I have brought many things, though I also had to bring a generator to power them." His image paced back and forth. "This is how I was able to invent so much in one lifetime. I could come here. As long as I had the patience, I could work on inventions like the Chair, or the brain sync for the avatars. I had all the time I wanted. It was also how I was able to make all the lockets, the box, the cube, everything I've used to share secrets." He coughed. "I could get more done than was humanly possible because I wasn't tied to human time."

Abby had always been amazed at how much her grandfather could do. Knowing about the space outside of time made her feel better. He'd still had to earn it, to work it all out, but he could do it without pressure or hurry. And he had more time than the average person, which allowed him to achieve more.

"This would be so awesome for homework," Carol said, gesturing with her hands as usual. She carried something that Abby couldn't quite make out. "Or to study before a test you have in five minutes. You could even take a nap and go in all refreshed and everything."

Abby's eyes became completely acclimated just in time to see that Carol still held a stun gun she had picked up in the basement, and it was pointed right at Abby.

"Carol," Abby said calmly, "please don't point that at me."

"Oh," Carol said, surprised. "Sorry about that. It would be terrible to accidentally shoot you now, but the bright side would be that we would have enough time to wait for you to wake up."

"It's still not something you want to go through," Derick said, who had obviously experienced it.

The white wasn't as brilliant anymore, but was just as clean and vivid. Abby began to pace, pushing experimentally against the white ground. It didn't feel hard or soft; it was just there, just existing. There were no walls or ceiling or sky. It was simply more white—a place without anything.

"I think we have a lot more than homework or a test waiting for us when we go back," Derick said.

"Yeah," Abby agreed, taking a few more steps, "but at least we can take as long as we want to decide what we're going to do."

"True," Carol said, setting down the stun gun to be extra careful. "Maybe we should do some yoga. You know, relax a little. Then we can figure out how to fix up that mess with clear minds." Carol stretched her legs out, bent forward, and twisted her body.

Derick tilted his head, trying to make sense of Carol's stretch. "That doesn't look relaxing at all."

Abby walked around the inventions. She tried to breathe deeply, tried to think it through. "Okay," she said. "The first problem we have to face is that the basement is filled with soldiers who are trying to destroy the Bridge."

"Second," Derick said, "we have an army of soldiers attacking who will fight their way through Cragbridge Hall down to the Bridge to join the others. I don't know if they'll take prisoners or just shoot people. They were doing a number on the avatars."

"Third," Carol said, "I don't think I can get up." Her legs and arms were twisted together and her body was off-balance on the white ground.

"Please, Carol," Abby said, looking down at her friend, "it's not time to joke around."

"Oh, I'm not joking," Carol responded. "I'm totally stuck." Abby walked over and lent her a hand.

"Third," Derick picked up where they had left off, "Grandpa and Mom, and probably Dad, have the Ash." There was a slight tremor in his voice. "They'll die soon."

"Fourth," Abby said, continuing on, her voice determined, "I think Coach Adonavich may be dying too. She was shot several times."

"Oh, I hate Muns," Carol said. "I hate him more than pollution, bad movies, playground bullies, terrorists, people who leave a bunch of really insensitive comments on the web, thieves, raisin cookies when you really thought they were going to be chocolate chip, and people who kick puppies!" She shook her head. "No, that doesn't even get it started. I hate him more than—"

"Just stop," Derick cut her off. "Let's think about this."

"We also have the huge problem that Muns now has keys *and* spheres," Abby said. "He can change anything in the past or invade the present. And with our Bridge under attack we can't really stop him."

Derick paced for a few moments. "So, to sum it up: the good news is we have all the time—or moments outside of time—we need to think about what we should do. The bad news is that our situation might be impossible."

They all stared at each other.

"Wait a minute," Carol said. "There has to be a way. I mean, we have a time machine."

"Yeah," Abby said, "but it's being attacked."

"No, wait," Derick said. "She has a point. What if we could somehow get past the soldiers and use the Bridge to go back in time. Couldn't we stop this?"

Abby thought for a moment. "Grandpa taught us over and over again that we shouldn't go back in time to change tragedies, but I don't see any other way."

"I'm pretty sure," Carol said, "that when an evil mad-man is changing time and is going to conquer the world and ruin the future and destroy everything that's good and pretty and fun and awesome that it's an exception."

Abby nodded. "But even if we could get back in the basement and stall the soldiers long enough to use the Bridge, where in time would we go?"

"It would be intense, but we could go back in time and kill Muns before he caused all this trouble," Derick suggested.

"That's gross," Carol said. "Though part of me wouldn't mind going back in time and kicking Muns super hard, right in the shins . . . with metal boots." She paused. "That shoot fire."

"Metal boots that shoot fire?" Derick asked.

"I bet I would look good in those," Carol said.

"We could go back and stop the Race," Derick suggested. "Maybe visit Silverton or leave a message for Chief Shar tipping them off that the blond beard guy is totally working for someone else."

"That sounds like a good idea to me," Carol said.

"But then Muns will still wake up and try something

else crazy," Abby pointed out. "If we go back in time, there has to be a way we can really stop him, keep him from ever coming after us again."

"Why don't we go back to the beginning of the year," Carol said, pacing around with her finger tapping her temple, "before Muns first attacked, and send in the police or something?"

"I don't know," Abby said. She was sitting on the white ground. "First off, I'm not sure the police would believe us. Plus—this is going to sound a little silly—what if we do that and we don't remember what we've been through?" She pulled back her hair. "I mean, wouldn't it eventually be like none of this ever happened?"

"Yeah," Carol said. "I think that's the point."

"But," Abby said, "although this year has been crazy and dangerous, it's also the year I made friends with you. What if it changes that? And it's when I finally figured out that I just might be . . ." Her words trailed off, as she got lost in thought.

"Might be what?" Derick asked.

Abby looked up. "Might be worth something. Might be something kind of like what Grandpa says I am."

Derick nodded. "I know it sounds cheesy, but you are."

"Oh, yeah, you are!" Carol said, and pumped her fist. She took a couple of slow steps. "And to tell the complete, don't-hold-back-anything truth, this year has been really important to me too." For once, Carol paused and slowed down as she spoke. "I know I act all crazy and excited, and I talk fast and flirt a lot with cute boys." She winked at Derick. "And I really like that, especially the boy part." She winked again. "And a lot of the time I do feel that excited, but sometimes I don't. Sometimes it's a bit of an act."

Abby had never thought of that before. She thought Carol was always naturally excited.

"And I know," Carol continued, still speaking slower than normal, "some people think I'm just silly. Some people even think I'm annoying." She raised her hands. "Can you imagine that?"

Abby shook her head, though she'd heard others claim Carol was annoying. She glanced at Derick; she could tell he was trying hard not to respond.

"Well, I've always been around a lot of people; but sometimes I'm lonely. There's a difference." Carol paused again. "But this year, I made the best friends I've ever had in my whole life." She wiped a tear from her eye. "See, I even cried. And that wasn't even a fake I'm-just-acting tear. That was the real deal." She looked at it a moment on the tip of her finger, then turned to Derick. "Do you want to keep it?"

"No thanks," Derick refused.

Carol shrugged and flung the tear to the side. "And with my best friends, I helped save the world. Not bad for an annoying girl."

"Not bad at all," Abby said. "And you're not annoying."

"I know, right?" Carol said. She took in a deep breath. "Your turn." She pointed at Derick.

"My turn to what?" Derick asked.

"To reflect on the year and tell us what you learned and how good of friends you made and how you really think I'm cute," Carol said.

Derick flashed a worried look at Abby, a look that asked if Abby had told Carol about the message he had sent when he thought he was going to die.

Abby shook her head.

"You *do* think I'm cute," Carol said, watching the brother and sister interact. "I knew it. I *knew* it."

"Why would you say that?" Derick asked, forcing the question out.

"Because of the look you just gave Abby. You were all like, 'Did you tell her? Because I know I've told you how I think Carol is absurdly attractive and fun and funny.' But Abby was like, 'No, I didn't tell her, but you totally did tell me that.' See? You think I'm cute!"

"That's *not* what happened!" Derick defended, his face reddening.

"Then why are you blushing?" Carol asked.

"I'm not."

"Your cheeks are red."

"No, they're not," Derick denied. "They just look that way against all this white."

"What*ever*," Carol said. Then she added in a whisper, "You totally think I'm cute."

Abby smiled wide. It felt good. She knew she had more than her share of troubles to deal with, but it was nice to take a break, to remember her brother and her friend. In fact, it helped her remember why it was so important to try to save everything: to help people like them.

"We've got big problems to deal with," Derick said. "I'm not reflecting on the year, and we're not talking about how cute anyone is." He blushed a little more, but not as badly as he had before. "Let's stay on topic."

"My point was," Abby said, "that I'd like to keep all I've learned this year. Maybe there's a better way than changing it all. Plus, I kind of think Grandpa wouldn't want us to change it. He taught us that it's during the most difficult times that normal people become heroes. And maybe . . ." Abby paused for a moment. "Maybe that's us."

"Okay," Derick said. "What if we only go back in time far enough to stop Muns, but not too far back? When would we go?"

For several moments, the group of friends all stood, lost in thought. Abby got up and walked around the inventions, thinking hard. A possible plan came into focus. *Would that work? But that would only solve half of the problem.* She paced some more. *But what if she . . . ? That might do it.* It may be the only way to keep Muns from destroying everything.

She thought through the scenarios a few more times. Finally she spoke. "I think we only need to go back about fifteen minutes," she said. "I think if we go back to the time right after you stopped the bombs, I know how to stop Muns. It will take two parts of a plan and we'll have to work fast."

Carol rubbed her hands together. "Am I going to love it?"

Abby smiled. "You just might. But first, we have to figure out how we can get back into the Bridge and have enough of a chance to go back in time about fifteen minutes."

Derick glanced around the room. "I've got an idea for that. It's not much, but it might work."

FIFTEEN
MINUTES AGO

Derick had his hands full. He looked down at the weird array of objects he carried. He hoped it would work.

For several moments, he stared at what he thought was the way back to the basement of Cragbridge Hall. He wasn't sure where the exact step was that would get him back into the room with the Bridge and the fight. It was easy traveling from the Bridge to wherever or whenever they wanted to go; but once they were there, they couldn't see their way back. He looked over at his sister. "Are you ready?"

She took a deep breath. "No, but let's do it anyway."

"Yeah," Carol said, and tried to make her voice low. "Let's do this!"

Derick stepped forward.

Nothing. He was still in the white space.

Another step.

Still nothing.

"Enough of this," he said, and ran several steps forward. In a flash, the white disappeared and he was back in the chaos of the basement. Though Abby and Carol had been several steps behind him, they appeared at the same time. Because they were all coming from a space outside of time, no matter when they crossed back in, it would be the same moment. It was a crazy deep thought. But Derick didn't have time to think about that. He had soldiers with guns to worry about.

Derick threw object after object at the soldiers in front of him. He had found Grandpa's plans and, with the machine that could make lockets and boxes, had made more of the stars that could shock you. Thankfully, Grandpa had gloves with this machine as well.

He heard some yelps. One soldier fell to the ground.

Carol hurled an avatar monkey head with all her might at one of the men with a large gun barrel. It didn't hit him directly, but it was distracting. Perhaps he'd never been attacked with a robot monkey head before. Carol had already started shooting her stun gun. Between her and Mr. Trinhouse, the soldier was stunned and fell to the ground. They just had to buy themselves a few more seconds.

Derick threw more and more objects as Abby ran to the Bridge. Carol and Mr. Trinhouse shot at anything they could. Coach Adonavich swung her makeshift metal club.

"I'm there," Abby yelled.

"I thought of a problem with our plan," Carol shouted, shooting again. "I know, bad timing."

Derick couldn't listen now. Out of the corner of his eye, he saw the other side of the basement change. It was another Bridge with Abby and Carol there and a falcon. It was fifteen minutes ago.

Derick turned to cross into the past, but saw a soldier break free from his fight and take aim with his huge barrel. Derick threw a few objects at him, but missed the target. Thankfully, they distracted the soldier for a moment.

"Get in the past!" Derick yelled.

He and Abby ran toward the other side of the room, but Carol didn't. She rushed toward the console of the Bridge.

"But we need to turn the keys, or they'll come after us," Carol shouted. "I'm on it."

As Derick dove toward the basement fifteen minutes ago, Abby doing the same, he realized that Carol was right. Midair, he caught a glimpse of Carol ready to turn the keys.

Thaboom!

Deafening screams.

A blinding flash of light and a wave of heat.

And Derick hit the floor of the basement fifteen minutes before.

Once he hit the ground, he scrambled around to try to see what had happened on Carol's side. Of course he couldn't. From this side of the Bridge, no one could see back. If he had to guess, the soldier had shot and destroyed the Bridge. He probably killed Carol in the process, maybe even a few more of those fighting against Muns. He blinked hard. If Carol hadn't stayed back to turn the keys, perhaps the explosion would have followed them, burning them to nothing. Or perhaps the Bridge would have been destroyed and their connection severed on its own. Either way she was extremely brave. And either way they only had fifteen minutes to stop Muns.

• • •

"Where did you come from?" Carol asked. It was not the Carol that had just sacrificed her life to save Abby's and Derick's. It was Carol fifteen minutes ago. "I thought you were right over there." Carol looked over at another Abby, Abby fifteen minutes ago. She was still looking at a scene in the desert where two bombs had just exploded. "You *are* over there!" Carol realized.

Knowing what Carol had just done in the future, Abby hugged her. "This isn't going to make sense, but we're from fifteen minutes in the future, and you just saved our lives."

"That doesn't make sense," Carol said, still looking back and forth between both Abbys. "But it's awesome. And you're welcome."

"This is so weird," the Abby from the past said, looking at her future self.

"We don't have time for celebrations or explanations," Derick said. He jumped on his sync with his rings. "Guys, if we don't act quickly, Muns completely wins in about fifteen minutes. Crash, I need your help. Call the police and security and tell them there are armed soldiers outside the gates that are planning to force their way into the school. Hopefully Abby and I will stop Muns from giving the order to attack, but just in case, I need you to grab some avatars and be ready at the gates. Lock them up, hold them tight, and whatever you do, don't let them in."

"But we don't know about any armed soldiers," Malcolm said.

"Malcolm, I just came from the future," Derick said. "Trust me." The falcon that was in the basement cocked its head. It was controlled by Derick of the past. He was obviously trying to comprehend what was going on. "And, Derick?" Derick added. "I mean, Derick in the past that is still in the falcon? Go help. I really wanted to last time and didn't get the chance."

"I'm not sure my mama is going to believe this," Malcolm said.

Abby had joined the sync as well. "Let's just hope this works," she said. "And then you'll get to talk to your mama about everything." She cleared her throat. "Jess, we need your robots in the basement, but you have to be quick." She turned to herself from the past and Carol. "Do you think you two could run to the lab and help her control them?"

"Yeah," Abby from the past said. "I guess I should trust myself." She put her hair in a temporary ponytail and ran with Carol out of the room.

"Watch out for the security bots!" Derick yelled behind them.

"Okay," Jess said. "We're on it."

Abby began to explain over the sync. "The guard with the blond beard is either traveling or about to travel to Muns's estate to give him the keys and the spheres. We can transfer the robots through the Bridge and bring them back as well, but the rest is up to you." She filled in more of the details of the plan.

"And, Anjum," Derick said, "we need you down in the basement as well. We need you to put together the best virtual world you've ever made."

"Is there a virtuality machine down there to make one?" Anjum asked.

"Sort of," Derick said.

"But you said Muns is going to win in the next fifteen minutes," Anjum said. "I can't make it that fast."

"Oh," Derick said, "once my grandfather gets down here, I've got a way that you can have all the time in the world."

RETURNING
THE FAVOR

Good work," the man with the blond beard said, and shook a lady's hand. As she exited the plane, he put one more key with the others he had recently collected inside a steel briefcase. The lady had stolen the key from Mr. Silverton, the oaf he had framed for his own theft of chemicals from the lab. Over the last few minutes Muns's loyals had brought him the keys they had taken from those who had been evacuated from Cragbridge Hall.

"Put it up in the air, but hover for a few moments," the man with the blond beard said to the pilot. "I want to see the explosion." He had worked too hard for this not to see it finished. He was capable of amazing strategy and accomplishment. Muns had seen it. He had seen it years ago when the officer was only a student coming out of Cragbridge Hall. The school had claimed he would go on to do great things, but he hadn't. None of his opportunities had panned out, none of his interviews had brought the job he'd so desperately wanted. Especially not Ruminex. They had called him back several times, but at the last minute had denied him. His dream of developing complex programs for experimental machines had slipped right out of his reach. And Muns had been there every step of the way to console him and tell him that he deserved better. Once this was all over, Muns would change the past. He would have the opportunities he should have had. He would get the life that should have been his.

The fastest private jet in the world fired up and lifted several feet off the top of a hotel near Cragbridge Hall, ready to rocket forward whenever the security officer gave the word. It would travel the four hundred and sixty-three miles to Muns's mansion in just under twelve minutes.

The officer checked the time. The tranquilizer bombs should have gone off by now.

He looked at the keys one more time, then locked the suitcase. All the dials were set to his prints. Unless someone melted the case or cut through it with some pretty heavy-duty equipment, the only one that could open it was him.

The plane hovered for another several minutes while he waited for the giant chemical cloud that would leave anyone in Cragbridge Hall unconscious for weeks. Perhaps he hadn't timed them right. No. He was sure he had. Why hadn't they gone off?

Vvvvvvvch.

What was that? He stood. Had he heard something, or

was it some part of the plane just doing what it was supposed to do?

Vvvvvch. Vvvvvch.

It was definitely something. It almost sounded like someone was doing maintenance work on the plane. He followed the sound.

Vvvvvch. Vvvvvch.

It led him farther into the plane. The ceiling of the bathroom. He tilted his head and listened well. It sounded like drilling. The sound moved. He moved with it. At first it went farther into the bathroom, and then it came back the other way. He stepped back into the main cabin to see that a door to the plane was open. The wind was blowing into the hovering plane.

Something moved across the floor.

A robot car. It had the suitcase with the keys inside it gripped in its robotic arms.

"*No!*" he shouted, diving for the car.

The robot car shot away easily. It drove out of the open door.

The man scrambled to the open hatch. Both the case and the robot car fell for several stories and then simply disappeared.

Then Derick Cragbridge stepped into the plane out of thin air, holding a stun gun. "This is for Carol," he said, and pulled the trigger, stunning the guard. His world started to go black. "If you ever try to explode tranquilizer bombs on innocent people again," Derick said, "you can fully expect someone to appear out of nowhere and shoot your evil backside." Derick shot again and stepped backward, mysteriously disappearing.

• • •

Charles Muns stood at the Bridge he had stolen months ago. He was ready to use its power, its endless possibilities. He was flanked by armed guards.

Any minute now his inside man would arrive in his private plane and deliver his keys and his spheres. Muns had worked for years to prepare him. When he'd discovered Oscar Cragbridge's secret, he had known he would need someone like the boy to infiltrate Cragbridge Hall. Muns had told the boy of his talent, told him he could have a great future. He had lied and told the boy that he had no opening in his own companies, but that he would help him get interviews with other successful businesses. He had blackmailed or threatened the companies to keep them from hiring him. He had needed the boy wanting. He had suggested applying for a security job at Cragbridge Hall to build his experience for a few years. Muns had needed him there. And he'd needed him to be desperate for more.

As soon as the young man arrived today, Muns would send in his army. They were at the ready. He couldn't allow others to have access to the only other Bridge in existence. He would be in control. He could change it all. The man who had, years ago, conned Charles Muns out of much of his college savings would be destitute for his entire life. The woman who had fired him when he didn't call in late for work, because he was weeping on his mother's grave on the anniversary of her death, would lose every job she ever got. All those who had mocked him as a child would feel the sting of harsh words about them being broadcast to the whole world. Those who had refused to adopt him would lose their own children. And his father would drink alone. Always alone. He would drive alone. Muns would never let his father near his mother after Charles was born. And he would never let his mother ride in the car with him. Never. Especially when his father was drinking. And she would never trust him. He wouldn't be around. The greatest tragedy would never happen. Everything would be different. Finally.

But first, the Cragbridges would need to be out of the way. He would use Oscar's own invention to travel to the recent past and then kill them. It would simply catch up to them. He would take Oscar first, then the parents. He would leave Abby and Derick utterly alone and terrified for a few moments before he took them too. They had to feel it. They had been too much trouble to die easily.

He pressed his fingers against the console of the Bridge, thinking through his plans again, waiting for the keys.

A person appeared out of nowhere.

Two people.

Flashes from guns.

Muns's guards fell.

It all happened in under a second.

But in that time Muns recognized the two people, the two kids who had invaded his estate: Abby and Derick Cragbridge.

"You imbecilic cretins!" Muns screamed, his insides

boiling with hatred. He reached out for the twins. He would give up all his plans to strangle them now.

Abby fired.

As Muns's world went dark, he heard more guards rushing down the hall toward him.

A few minutes later, Muns awoke, slightly disoriented, and looked around. He was in his own study.

"Are you okay?" one large guard asked him.

"Mostly," he spat. "Why did it take you so long?"

"We came as fast as we could," another guard explained.

"We're sorry they stunned you," the first guard said, "but we got them." The guard pointed toward the floor.

Muns looked down. There on the ground were the bodies of Abby and Derick Cragbridge, completely still. The two pests. The two surprises that had done so much to ruin his plans.

"They won't wake up for several minutes," the guard said.

"Sorry to interrupt, but I believe you want something I have," a man with a blond beard said. He smiled and opened a locked steel case. Inside it was a collection of keys and spheres. "This cost me more trouble than I thought it would."

Muns let out a breathy growl. He wanted this so badly. He grabbed the keys and the spheres, feeling them between his fingers. They were control, power.

Muns activated a sync with his rings. "Send in the army," he commanded. "I want that Bridge destroyed. And don't let anyone stop you."

Now was his time. All of time was his.

Muns looked at the guards. "I want several soldiers in this room in one minute!" One quickly began to communicate on his rings. "First we get rid of the Cragbridge family, then we send soldiers directly into the basement of Cragbridge Hall. They won't be able to stop us."

Muns looked again at the motionless bodies of Abby and Derick. He grabbed a guard's gun and stunned both children several more times. Then he changed his mind. He didn't want to kill them quickly. He would devise something special for them. Perhaps the *Titanic*—or the *Hindenburg* again. Perhaps he would put them in a concentration camp and let Hitler's men torture them. Perhaps he would simply drop them in the desert and let the life gradually choke out of them.

He would decide later.

He watched in sheer delight as his plan unfolded. In a matter of minutes, Oscar Cragbridge and his son and daughter-in-law had been taken care of. The soldiers crossing the grounds of Cragbridge Hall had to fight off avatars and robots, but eventually made their way to the basement. When they got there, the soldiers Muns had sent in through his Bridge had already done their job. They had met some resistance, but eventually destroyed the Bridge and those who were trying to use it.

Finally.

And now he got to decide what he would do with Abby and Derick. And what he would do with all of time.

THE END OF
THE YEAR

Grandpa laughed. He laughed a hearty, full-belly, can't-stop laugh. "Abby and Derick, though I always admired your heart and your determination, I think you may be complete geniuses."

A large group stood outside of a virtual booth: It was Grandpa, Coach Horne, Coach Adonavich, Mr. Trinhouse, Abby's mother, Abby, Derick, Carol, and the rest of the Spartans. And Abby's and Derick's father had just joined them.

"Sorry, I'm a little late," Abby's father said. "Apparently I slept through most of the action. Why are we all looking at a virtual booth?"

"Because," Grandpa said, "we have a most distinguished guest inside." He pointed at the booth with his cane.

"Who?" Abby's father asked.

"Charles Muns," Grandpa chuckled.

Abby's father's mouth dropped open. "I don't understand."

"He doesn't either," Grandpa said, still giggling. "You see, your daughter and your son used the Bridge to sneak into Muns's home and stun him. Then they brought him here, where a bright student with quite a talent for making virtual worlds had prepared everything. When Muns woke up, he thought he had won. In his own virtual world, he is still going forward with his plan. That kept him from sending in more of his men, or trying anything else desperate. And we will let him stay in the booth until the authorities arrive." Grandpa tossed his cane in the air and caught it. "Then he'll have to answer a lot of questions, about why someone he hired stole dangerous bombs and why he hired an army to try to attack my school."

They couldn't tell the entire truth about either of these facts. The authorities wouldn't find two of the stolen vials because they had exploded in the Sahara, and they wouldn't be able to tell them how the bombs had gotten there. But they would have the footage of the vials from the Race, and the blond-bearded officer's involvement in stealing them in the first place and setting up Chief Shar. Thanks to Malcolm's alerts, the police and security had already discovered and detained most of the soldiers Muns had ready to attack. Thankfully, because Muns was in a virtual world, his order to attack had only gone to virtual soldiers. The real soldiers had not yet made their move.

"I have a feeling he won't be walking free for a very long time," Grandpa said, still grinning.

"Attack the school?" Abby's father said.

"Yes, honey," his wife said. "You've slept through quite a bit."

"Is the school okay?"

"We'll have some issues, I'm sure," Grandpa said. "After what has happened this year, I'm sure parents will be concerned for their students' safety. Thankfully, we haven't lost one. In time, our good reputation will return."

"I'm sure I have a lot to catch up on," Abby's father said.

"Yes," Grandpa said. "And the best people to tell it would be your son and your daughter."

Abby and Derick both smiled.

$$\bullet \quad \bullet \quad \bullet$$

The electric guitar faded, and a woman in a glittering dress approached the edge of a large stage. The piano came in light and slow.

Oh, no. Another slow song.

Every Race ended with a dance.

"Oh, yeah!" Carol yelled. Abby watched as her best friend sprinted through the crowd to get to Derick first. He didn't see her coming until she was only a few feet away. He didn't have a chance. Apparently Carol didn't care that the DJ had just finished announcing that this was a boy's choice dance.

Abby laughed out loud. She couldn't help it. At least

Derick was there, alive and breathing. And he *had* admitted that Carol was cute.

And there was only one Derick and one of her. When they had traveled back in time fifteen minutes, there had been two of both of them. After those fifteen minutes were over, both Abbys and both Dericks melded into one. Abby wasn't completely sure how it had happened, but it had. And she was grateful it had.

Abby was just glad the Race was over and everything was okay.

She took a deep breath as a boy passed her and asked a girl in a purple dress to dance. She watched as another boy asked a girl close to her. It was all happening again. She thought of what her brother had said in the message he'd sent when he thought he was going to die: sometimes people her age didn't always see what made someone else so amazing. Maybe sometimes the very best girls aren't invited to dance.

But it still hurt a little. She knew it didn't make her any less pretty or fun to be around, but it bothered her.

She walked toward the door.

Then she stopped. If she could win the Race and destroy a tranquilizer bomb, she could face a slow song.

Abby began to walk around the gym. Boys too shy to ask girls leaned their chairs up against the walls or joked loudly with their also-too-shy friends. At first, Abby thought she'd find one that looked the shyest, the easiest to ask, but then she remembered all the ways she had been brave before. Might as well do it right. She searched until she found someone she wanted to dance with. A boy from her English class. He was speaking with several of his friends.

Abby's pulse quickened as she walked up to the group. In some ways she would rather face a tranquilizer bomb.

"Hey, Greydon," she said, hoping her voice wasn't trembling. "Do you want to dance?"

Her heart beat loudly.

"Um, I think it's boys' choice," one of Greydon's friends said.

"Okay then," Abby said. "Do you want to ask *me* to dance?" She couldn't believe how brave she was being.

Greydon smiled. "Um. Sure. Would you like to dance?" He took her arm and they walked into the crowd and started to dance. It had worked. It had actually worked. And Greydon didn't even seem disappointed.

The dance was both fantastic and awkward at the same time. They tried to talk a little, but they practically had to scream to hear each other over the music. It's really hard to get to know someone that way. She was pretty sure he complimented her on how well she'd done in the Race. And thought she was pretty cool. Before she knew it, the dance was over.

"Thanks," Abby said.

"Yeah, thanks," Greydon answered, and turned and moved back to his friends.

That went all right. It took a little courage, but it went all right.

But Abby hoped the next slow dance wasn't for a little while longer.

411

The woman in a glittering dress faded and the next song began.

"Well, congratulations on your win." The words came from a girl. They were a compliment, but they sure sounded like an insult.

Jacqueline.

Abby hadn't seen her approach, her boyfriend in tow. "And you even talked a poor boy into dancing with you."

"Hey, Jackie, calm down," the boyfriend said.

She sneered back, for once being rude when a boy could see.

"Thanks for the compliment," Abby said, ignoring that it wasn't meant as one. "And Greydon seems nice."

Jacqueline smiled like a beast about to eat. "Sooner or later he'll figure out that you don't deserve to be here, that you—"

"I'm sorry," a deep voice said. "You saying something?" Abby turned. It was Malcolm. He stood tall and broad-shouldered, his large arms folded over his chest. He glared down at Jacqueline through his dreadlocks.

But it wasn't just Malcolm.

It was everybody. Anjum, Maria, Piper, Rafa, Derick, Nia, and Jess.

Nia folded her arms too and stood on her tiptoes. "Yeah," she said.

"I . . . I," Jacqueline stammered.

"Because if you've got a problem with Abby," Maria said, "you've got a problem with all of us."

"I don't have a problem," Jacqueline said, backing away

from the group. She smiled big, showing off her gleaming teeth. "You must have misunderstood what I was saying."

"Leave my sister alone," Derick said firmly. "Don't misunderstand that."

Jacqueline and her boyfriend walked away.

"Yeah," Carol added, "or I'll give you some of this." She did a karate kick. "Or this." She did another. "Or maybe some of this." She chopped in succession as fast as she could.

"Carol, give it up," Malcolm said.

"Are you sure I can't just kick her once?" Carol asked, pantomiming a kick. "Because I really, *really* want to."

"I can fight my own battles," Abby said.

Carol nodded. "All right. You've definitely proved that. So *you* kick her."

Abby laughed. "No. That's not my style." She would let it go. She'd prove every day that she belonged at Cragbridge Hall, that she was good enough. Maybe Jacqueline would figure it out; maybe she wouldn't. That was her choice.

"It doesn't look like her boyfriend appreciated what she was saying," Piper said, and pointed across the gym. Jacqueline tried to grab his hand, but he pulled away. He said something they couldn't hear, and pointed in Abby's direction. Maybe over time people figure out how we are. They see the good or the bad—whichever we try harder at.

Mr. Sul stood on the stage at the front of the gym. He brushed back his dark hair. "Thanks to everyone for coming to this dance," he said, his voice amplified. He didn't have the charisma of Landon or Sarah. "I have a few announcements that should probably be shared with the whole school. Thankfully, the bomb threat was an empty one," Mr. Sul lied. Of course, telling everyone that there *had* been bombs—and that they had been discovered using a time machine, grabbed by a student and a falcon, and thrown in the Sahara Desert, where they had exploded safely away from everyone—probably would have been too complicated.

Abby glanced over at Derick. She was incredibly grateful to have him around. He had done better than he was supposed to. He had changed his future. And she was very optimistic that his future from here on out looked very bright.

"As I'm sure you've heard," Mr. Sul continued, "sadly, we did have a member of our security involved in several thefts. He is awaiting trial now." Abby and the Spartans would have to testify in the case. "We are sorry for all of the trouble, but we must be cautious in these situations." He gazed over the entire student body. "We are also grateful for those security and police officers who discovered armed people in the crowd outside the school. We aren't sure what their intentions were, but our security had it well under control."

Abby remembered all too well how it would have gone if she hadn't changed it. She remembered the battle, the soldiers invading the school. Thankfully, with Muns stunned and in the virtual booth, he never had the chance to give the final order. The soldiers were detained before they could do much harm.

"And now, I'll turn it over to our student body officers."

Mr. Sul stood awkwardly on the stage while Landon and Sarah walked out.

"Thank you, Mr. Sul," Landon said, wearing a big smile, a black suit, and his hair in its usual spikes. "And thanks again for coming to the dance that ends . . . the . . . Race!" The crowd cheered. Sarah, wearing a black dress with a silver jacket, moved her hands up and down, signaling for more noise. The crowd answered. The student body officers both held the audience's attention much better than Mr. Sul had.

"We never got a chance to fully recognize our winners," Sarah said. "Please welcome to the stage . . . the Spartans!" After the first cheer, Sarah cupped her hand to her ear and got more noise from the crowd. "Come on up, guys!" Both Landon and Sarah waved the team to the front.

A slow dance, and then having to go in front of everyone from school. Not Abby's favorite night.

Abby made her way to the stage. Most of the team beat her there. She hoped her light-blue dress looked okay.

"One more round of applause for Anjum, Jess, Malcolm, Nia, Maria, Piper, Rafa, Carol, Derick, and Abby!" Landon cheered, working the crowd.

Abby tried to smile big and wave, but she was pretty sure it was clear that she was completely uncomfortable.

Sarah reached into a black velvet case and pulled out a trophy. "Each of you gets one of these!" she said, holding the trophy high.

"You have proved you are some of the best and brightest at this school," Landon said. One by one, Landon and Sarah gave each of them a trophy.

"And of course," Landon said, "there is still the box." A security officer, flanked by two more, brought out the black box. "Because of the recent controversies, security is going to have to check out the key inside the box." The students in the crowd didn't know how to react. Each member of the Spartans pressed their fingers to the box. Abby could feel herself being scanned, and then the box fell open. The security officers took the box away. Grandpa would make sure that Mrs. Flink got her key back.

"Here is a replacement key," Sarah said. "It unlocks a safe in the Cragbridge Hall main office, a safe that contains scholarships for all the members of the team for the rest of their years at Cragbridge Hall."

The crowd went crazy. It was an expensive school to attend, and the team members had all just received free passes. "And unlimited milkshakes for the rest of the year?" Carol asked hopefully.

"Don't push it," Abby said, elbowing her friend. But she knew very well her grandfather would give them to Carol if she asked. He had upped the scholarship prize to the team's entire stay at the school. The real prize had only been for a month's tuition, but a group of students *had* saved the world, so Grandpa felt he could reward them a bit more.

"Now let's get back to dancing!" Sarah said.

The crowd responded with yells and jumping up and down.

Before they left the stage, Anjum called all of the team together. They huddled in a circle. "You deserve these," he said, pointing to the trophies. He still looked a little nervous with all the people around. "You deserve them more than most people here know." He smiled. "The person impersonating me told you he wanted you happy on this day, the day you won. Are you?"

Abby smiled and nodded.

"Did we ever figure out who was impersonating you?" Piper asked.

"No," Anjum said. "And he could have been anywhere. Mr. Silverton is still trying to track it."

"Well, if we find him, let's use the robots again and I'll shoot him for y'all," Malcolm said.

"One more thing," Abby said. "I know my grandpa told you how much he appreciates all you've done and how grateful he is that you've promised to keep his secret." Abby paused. "I am too. And I was hoping that if we ever have any sort of emergency again, that we could call on you."

"Definitely," Nia said.

"The Spartans will make another stand—whenever you need," Anjum said.

"I'm just glad it wasn't a last stand," Maria said.

"So am I," Malcolm said. "And so is my mama."

Abby was grateful too. It had been so close.

They had done it. Abby stood next to Derick in the circle and just squeezed his shoulder. She didn't want to embarrass him. He squeezed back. She'd had quite an experience her first year at Cragbridge Hall. She wondered what the future would bring. She had felt tempted to use the Bridge to see, but she'd decided against it. Even if it wasn't good, she would just have to do something to make it better. Might as well just work for the better future without seeing it.

ACKNOWLEDGMENTS

I used to teach. Those were good days. Once a year I, along with some other teachers, would invite students to be as creative as possible and do a project related to a theme we had studied. The students astounded us. They painted pictures, wrote and recorded songs, took amazing photos, engineered model buildings, and filmed and edited impressive movies. I remember one of them even made a giant rubberband ball bigger than your head. (I don't remember how the ball fit the theme, but I definitely remember that ball.) I learned that if you give students a little room and a little time, they will create something awesome. Though they never designed virtual samurai worlds or relay races using crazy inventions, I think the seed for the Race was in there somewhere. Thanks to all the creative kids out there!

ACKNOWLEDGMENTS

As always, I have a lot of other people to thank:

Shelly, my amazing wife, my first reader, the one who picks up the slack in the family while I'm trying to hit a deadline and runs our home while I'm touring the nation: I love you. Thanks for letting me chase this dream.

My kids, aka the five most important reasons I write: Thanks for loving books, and thanks for loving mine. Oh, and I'm definitely grateful you were excited and not embarrassed when your dad came to do an assembly at your school.

My parents, brothers, and sisters: You couldn't be more supportive. Thanks for spreading the word, and driving for hours to surprise me at signings. You rock!

The schools I visited: Whether you were in Las Vegas, LA, Utah, Kentucky, Indiana, or any of the other great spots, thanks for letting me visit. I kind of love speaking to kids about books and dreams.

Brandon Mull: I loved touring with you. Plus, it was a great excuse for old friends to hang out. Thanks for leading me on adventures to find unique places to eat. And thanks for calling my hotel room to wake me up when I totally would have snored right through our signing. (We were both running on only a couple of hours of sleep.) I owe you.

Chris Schoebinger and Heidi Taylor: Thanks for continuing to believe in Cragbridge Hall! And thanks for the feedback to make it better.

Karen Zelnick and Mary Beth Allen: Thanks for setting up my book tours. You put in a ton of work and do a great job.

Brandon Dorman: Awesome cover and inside

illustrations. You've got a gift! Thanks for helping my story come alive.

Richard Erickson: Thanks for the design and great use of your talents.

Derk Koldewyn: Thanks for all the editing help. I really need it. You make me look better and improve my crazy stories.

My agent, Rubin Pfeffer: Thanks for your thoughts, guidance, support, and work.

My beta readers: Kirtlan Morris, Matt Crawford, Dan Reed, Jessica Moon, and Matthew and Owen Hatch: Thanks for shooting through my manuscript and giving me feedback. Thank you. Thank you.

And you: Thanks for reading! Thanks for giving me a shot. I hope you loved the ride.

DISCUSSION QUESTIONS

1. Through the device that looked like Saturn, Derick learned about his future. Would you like to receive a message about your future? Why or why not?

2. Derick made a virtual samurai world as a possible event in the Race. If you went to Cragbridge Hall and could design any event or challenge using any of the inventions that exist there, what would it be?

3. Abby wasn't invited to be part of a team for the Race. She also wasn't invited to dance. How would you feel if you were in her place? Have you ever felt left out or lonely? How does Abby change by the end of the book? What do you think helped her change?

4. Throughout this book, the students of Cragbridge Hall participated in the Race. What competitions do you participate in? If you were able to participate in any of

the challenges in the Race in this book, which would it be? Why?

5. When Derick practiced how to fly as a falcon, the Crash pressured him to stoop. Do you think it was okay that he gave in to the pressure? When is it okay to do what your friends want you to, and when isn't it?

6. Each member of the Crash had different talents in addition to being great with the avatars. For example, Maria was a good dancer and Malcolm was smart at geography. What are your talents? What subjects in school are you good at?

7. What did you learn in this book about Joan of Arc or Nathan Hale? Do you think you could do something you believed was right, even if you knew it would end in your death?

8. Anjum was an intense leader. He demanded the best from those on his team. What did you think of his leadership style? What were some of the advantages? What might be some of the disadvantages?

9. During the labyrinth challenge, Carol was able to guide and give advice to Abby, while Piper helped Derick. If you had to face a difficult challenge and could choose anyone to be your guide, who would you pick? Why?

10. Grandpa Cragbridge taught that the future is never certain; we can always make choices to make it better. Do you believe your choices can change the future? Why or why not? What is one thing you can do that might improve the future?

11. In one of the virtual challenges, Derick discovered that Rafa did not have to face the dragon alone. Derick could help. All of his team could help. How do your friends help you? How can you help your friends?

12. If you could design a Race in your school using the equipment and technology of today, what kinds of challenges would you invent? Who in your school would you choose to be on your team?

RECOMMENDED READING

For more information about Nikola Tesla:

McPherson, Stephanie Sammartino. *War of the Currents: Thomas Edison vs. Nikola Tesla*. Minneapolis, MN: 21st Century Books, 2012.

Rusch, Elizabeth. Oliver Dominguez, illustrator. *Electrical Wizard: How Nikola Tesla Lit Up the World*. Somerville, MA: Candlewick Press, 2013.

For more information about falcons:

George, Jean Craighead. *My Side of the Mountain Trilogy*. New York: Dutton Juvenile, 2000.

Laubach, Christyna M., René Laubach, and Charles W. G. Smith. *Raptor! A Kid's Guide to Birds of Prey*. North Adams, MA: Storey Publishing, 2002.

RECOMMENDED READING

For more information about dinosaurs:

Lessem, Don. Franco Tempesta, illustrator. *National Geographic Kids Ultimate Dinopedia: The Most Complete Dinosaur Reference Ever*. Washington, DC: National Geographic Children's Books, 2010.

Signore, Marco. Matteo Bacchin, illustrator. *Giant vs. Giant: Argentinosaurus and Giganotosaurus*. New York: Abbeville Kids, 2010.

For more information about Mount Everest:

Blanc, Katherine, and Jordan Romero. *The Boy Who Conquered Everest: The Jordan Romero Story*. Carlsbad, CA: Hay House, 2010.

Venables, Stephen. *To the Top: The Story of Mount Everest*. Somerville, MA: Candlewick Press, 2003.

For more information about Benjamin Franklin:

Frandin, Dennis Brindell. John O'Brien, illustrator. *Who Was Ben Franklin?* New York: Grosset and Dunlop, 2002.

Krensky, Stephen. *DK Biographies: Benjamin Franklin*. New York: DK Publishing, 2008.

For more information about Joan of Arc:

Wilkinson, Philip. *Joan of Arc: The Teenager Who Saved Her Nation*. Washington, DC: National Geographic Society, 2007.

Yeatts, Tabatha. *Sterling Biographies: Joan of Arc, Heavenly Warrior*. New York: Sterling Publishing, 2009.

RECOMMENDED READING

For more information about Nathan Hale, the first American spy:

Hale, Nathan. *Nathan Hale's Hazardous Tales: One Dead Spy*. New York: Amulet Books, 2012.

Olson, Nathan. Cynthia Martin and Brent Schoonover, illustrators. *Nathan Hale: Revolutionary Spy*. New York: Capstone Press, 2006.

For more information about Greek myths and the minotaur:

Jennings, Ken. *Greek Mythology*. New York: Little Simon, 2014.

Limke, Jeff. John McCrea, illustrator. *Theseus: Battling the Minotaur*. Minneapolis, MN: Graphic Universe, 2008.

For more information about robots:

Davis, Barbara J. *The Kids' Guide to Robots*. North Mankato, MN: Capstone Press, 2009.

Jones, David. *Mighty Robots: Mechanical Marvels That Fascinate and Frighten*. New York: Annick Press, 2005.

For more information about Beowulf:

Marshall, Henrietta Elizabeth. *The Story of Beowulf*. New York: Dover Publications, 2007.

Morpurgo, Michael. Michael Foreman, illustrator. *Beowulf*. New York: Candlewick Press, 2006.